D0831849

Updrift

ERRIN STEVENS

For my husband, Michael. Everything good comes from you.

PRAISE FOR UPDRIFT

"Best mermaid book I have EVER read? Updrift by Errin Stevens."
- Ben Alderson, Top Vlogger according to *The Guardian* and *Teen Vogue*.

"I DEVOURED it."
- Casey Ann Books

"Updrift gives sirens a sexy makeover in this gorgeously evocative read. Compelling and romantic, you'll be thinking about this book long after the last page has turned." – Mia from @cosyreads on Instagram

"I highly recommend you chick this out if you like a little something different, and a good romance." – Katelyn, The Fearless Reader

"This book will blow away any other mermaid/siren book you've read." - @bibliophagist_omniligent on #bookstagram

Dear Reader,

Updrift likely began in my girlhood – I'm thinking 1976 – when the mythology of Hans Christian Andersen's "The Little Mermaid" sank its teeth into me and ate me whole. I honestly wonder at our decision to shelve fairy tales in the children's section when so many of them are these brutal, brutal tragedies… and "The Little Mermaid" is no different. Seriously, read "The Little Match Girl or "The Red Shoes" at your local library and just try to walk away undevastated!

I remained captivated with TLM's mythology throughout my twenties, when the story simmered beneath my struggles to finish college, establish myself in a career, run the modern dating gauntlet and try to look breezy and confident during it all, which I did NOT accomplish. A husband and child and three jobs later, I finally sat down to try and make sense of modern life and modern womanhood; and Andersen's fable helped me write it out. In this sense, Updrift was a way for me to knit up my own coming of age via a kind of corollary post-mortem.

But Updrift is not an autobiography, and neither is it TLM retold, although I'd love for you to see a reflection of the original in my book. Can you guess who best mimics Andersen's heroine? When you've finished the novel, think back on who was most compelled to abandon friends and family for love, who in the end preferred his own destruction to that of his beloved. It's twisted, I know, but hopefully in the right way.

Happy reading, everyone.

E.S.

ACKNOWLEDGMENTS

Thank you to my parents for their support and encouragement as I worked on this often ridiculous plan to write novels. I know you've felt my triumphs and failures as your own, and I'm sorry about that. I'm especially grateful to my mother, who listened to every passage, traveled to conferences with me, cried with me, laughed with me, and believed in my stories even more than I did. I love you, Mom! My high school English teacher, Liz Schroeder, is and will always be a goddess for all the beautiful care and attention she showed her students—Mrs. Schroeder, I still use that rush-write trick you taught us in College-Bound English.

I have too many other family members and friends who have helped (tolerated?) me on this journey. Please know I love you all. Without you there to write for, I wouldn't have the heart to do this!

"The cure for anything is salt water — sweat, tears, or the sea."
Isak Dinesen

PART ONE

CHAPTER ONE

The pleasure cruiser floated on billowing waves a mile off the Atlantic shore, its small group of passengers reclined in various stages of stupor on the modest deck. The sun, white-hot and high in the June sky, pummeled the seafarers with its heat, penetrating and dulling the attention of even the most preoccupied until all were calm, quiet, and drunk on their own leisure.

To her disappointment, Kate was the only child in the party, but she was used to solitude and entertained herself as she often did with a game of imaginary play. For this interlude, she lay on her stomach, her chin resting on crossed arms as she peered over the boat's edge into the sapphire water. Her lips moved as she whispered, hoping to conjure a sea turtle or dolphin to play with, although nothing swam her way.

She became hopeful when a long, silvery blue fish appeared. It paused just past the depth where she could determine what, exactly, it was, and it swayed to catch her attention.

It's teasing me.

At which point, it vanished. Kate strained closer to the ocean.

Too soon a brilliant, turquoise-colored fluke startled her from just below the water's surface, the body attached to it out of sight under the boat. The tail rippled out and back again, gossamer and fantastic. *Come*, it beckoned. Kate reached down to touch it and slid noiselessly into the water.

Her mother told her later she heard her laughing then, and how panicked she was when she realized Kate had fallen overboard. Kate herself was unconcerned, already racing off with her new friend, a boy named Gabe, caring only for his invitation to play and the adventure he promised if she could escape from her mom. The passengers on the boat appeared impossibly far off, although she heard their shouts to let go of the dolphin, which confused her, since she was holding on to a boy. Her life vest floated, detached, useless, and well out of her reach. She yelled to everyone she would be all right, that she was swimming to shore.

"But she can't swim!" her mother cried. Kate disappeared as the boating party scrambled to follow and to call for help.

On the shore, two shockingly pretty women waited for her as she and Gabe exited the water. Kate walked ahead of her new friend, who was now escorted by a dark-haired lady whispering admonishments in his ear.

"We were just playing, Mom," Gabe complained.

Kate smiled at the red-haired woman who approached her and took her hand. *I'm Anna,* she heard her say, or imagined she heard her say, since the only actual sounds she recognized were those of the surf and the wind. Anna stopped by a blanket littered with the remains of a picnic.

Would you like some lemonade? You must be thirsty.

Kate accepted a cup and checked on Gabe, who now wore swim trunks rather than... whatever he had worn in the water. She couldn't recall. She waited for him to catch up. He asked if she wanted to build a sandcastle, and she said okay.

When her mother, Cara, reached the shore, Kate could see she was frantic, running awkwardly in the sand to get to her. Anna, the other woman, and Gabe's mother oriented themselves in a semi-circle around her and Gabe, all of them frowning at her mom's progress. Kate scowled at the hovering adults and whispered to Gabe, "Can you make them go away?"

Gabe sneaked a peek at his mother. "We should go in the water again." They stood to act on their intention but the adults stepped in their path.

"Absolutely not," Gabe's mother scolded them. They slumped back down by their would-be sand castle.

"Catherine!" Her mother gasped when she reached her. And for all Cara's petting and kisses Kate felt as if she'd never been in bigger trouble. "Did you fall in? I was... I was beside myself... and where

3

did that dolphin come from? I can't believe you weren't hurt!"

"It's okay, Mama," Kate replied, confused by the repeat reference to a dolphin. But as her mother could see, nothing bad happened. "I was with Gabe…" Kate began.

"That was quite something, wasn't it?" Gabe's mom interjected, catching Cara's gaze. "We have a friendly dolphin in this bay." She ruffled Kate's hair. "I guess it liked *you*. I'm Carmen Blake, Gabe's mother." She gestured to the other two women. "And these are my sisters, Lydia and Anna." She offered Cara her life vest. "Here. This is your daughter's."

Given Cara's agitation she decided not to say she'd taken the vest off when she shouldn't have. The nylon belts were cut and frayed, the clasps still secure, and Cara studied the straps – which Gabe had cut with his knife – with a frown.

"What on earth… ?" her mother murmured, examining the belts. She must have had more urgent questions however because she dropped the vest to her side and started asking them. Why had she left the safety of the deck? Where had she gone, and why didn't she stay put as asked? How had she ended up on the beach so quickly? Kate noted the glowers Anna, Lydia and Carmen gave her and decided she wasn't supposed to answer. To her relief, the trio's strange intensity distracted her mother. Her scrutiny shifted.

Her mom's voice became strained and her next words sounded like an apology. "I was watching her, I swear."

"The kids were just playing," Carmen said kindly. "I got to them right away and no harm was done. Kate's fine, although I'm sure you had quite a scare."

Her mom's brow creased "You got to them? I looked everywhere in the water for her. *Everywhere*. I didn't see anything; not you, not the boy, and certainly not Kate. And I feel just awful. I was dozing and oblivious while Kate pitched herself overboard." She lowered her gaze to her hands. "Thank you for saving her." She emitted a small, frustrated laugh. "And I'm grateful you haven't called Child Protective Services on me."

Carmen placed a hand on her mom's shoulder, at which point Kate literally felt the tension leave her mother's body, saw her frown soften into something less worrisome. Good. Her mom's torment was disturbing all of them and she wanted it gone. She tugged her mother's shirt. Could she go play with her friend?

Cara tracked the fast-advancing contingent of friends from the boat, led, Kate saw, by her Aunt Dana and escorted by a bunch of people in uniforms. "The Coast Guard needs to talk with us, hon. So, unfortunately, we need to go." Gabe added his protests to Kate's, but no one listened to them.

Carmen offered her mother a small envelope. "We're having a birthday party for Gabe next week at the house." She indicated a large Cape Cod up the hill from the water. "You came just as I was filling these out. I hope you and Kate can come."

"Perhaps we'll take you up on that. We just moved here and I'd love for Kate to make a few friends before school." She glanced anxiously at the clutch of humanity marching their way.

"I'm sorry but you'll have to excuse us. Thank you for keeping my daughter. I'd like to say I'll return the favor, but I hope I never have to. I'm so sorry this happened . . ."

Carmen dismissed Cara's statement with a wave of her hand. "It was nothing. I hope you can come to the party."

Her mother promised she'd call to RSVP and offered a quick smile to Lydia and Anna before leaving. Kate followed, waving forlornly to Gabe as she went.

After assuring themselves Kate was unharmed, conversation among the adults centered on how much time had passed between her fall off the boat and the present. Cara maintained it couldn't have been more than a few minutes, and the others agreed although they couldn't, considering the hour, reconcile how quickly the afternoon had passed. "We sailed at ten this morning," Aunt Dana stated, "which means we were on the water six hours. It seemed like so much less." Everyone appeared confused.

Her mom spoke with the coast guard, signed a form, and then steered her toward the parking lot. "Let's go home."

"Can we come back tomorrow?" Her mother kissed the top of her head. "We'll see," she hedged. This meant, Kate knew, a visit the next day was unlikely.

They did not return to the beach the next day but Kate heard her mom on the phone saying they would attend Gabe's birthday party. "Can we bring anything?" Which was followed by, "No, my husband – Kate's dad – is no longer living... No need to apologize, really, I'm used to it, and please don't worry, although I will have my sister here... Great! We'll bring her...Yes, I'll let Kate know."

Her mother smiled at her after she hung up. "Gabe is thrilled you're coming," she reported. Her smile faded. "Although I'm not sure I'm thrilled to be going."

"We're going," Kate told her adamantly. She hurried away to avoid any possibility of argument on the subject.

Her claim staked, she resumed her typical approach to her mother's distress, which was to ignore it since her mom worried about everything as far as she could tell, always had. Especially after her dad's death, when they'd felt alone and stuck, her mom had been perpetually anxious, both for the lonely future facing them and because she'd needed to find a job. Thanks to a government education program and grandparents able to babysit, Cara obtained a library sciences degree. But she'd never, in Kate's memory, been anything but a worry-wart.

Kate didn't have any clear memories of her dad. From what her mother had told her and from pictures, she knew he was popular and athletic in high school, understood he'd made a go of the family's farm implement business, and she knew he and her mom were very much in love. The machinery accident that killed George Sweeting stole all but her mother's physical presence from Kate as well, until they relocated for Cara's job. After the funeral Kate only noticed their brokenness when she was over at other houses with intact, un-grieving parents and lives that did not revolve around sadness. When Kate did not spend time apart from her family, she did not notice the emptiness as much. Consequently, she came to prefer being at home or at her grandparents', where the oppressive grief hovering over her was normal.

Her Aunt Dana sent them the ad for the librarian job that would take them out of their joyless world. The ad was too modest to suggest the impact it would have on them, just a short, bold headline stating, *Librarian Wanted*, followed by a contact name and phone number for interested applicants. The job was in some unheard-of town in North Carolina.

Her mom told her she wasn't sure what compelled her to call but she maintained the call saved them. "All we have here is connected to your dad, Kate. I can't escape the grief in this place, and I can't live with this grief anymore.

"I have to try. We need something new." Kate had nodded solemnly and laid her head against her mom's leg, not really understanding but wanting to comfort her.

She went along to Griffins Bay for the interview, sitting quietly with her books and doll on a bench outside an office while her mother learned the specifics of her new job on the other side of the door. It was March there and warmer than back home. The air was different too, not the hard, dry force of nature that swept across the fields surrounding their little town in Kansas, but fresher and definitely wet. This place smelled new to Kate, exciting. She felt hopeful for the first time she could remember.

Her grandparents cried when Cara told them they were moving, but they supported her decision to leave. Grandma Mary held her mom's face in her hands when she told her, "There's nothing for you here, Cara. We know that. You take this chance to be happy. Just bring Kate back from time to time so she can remember her old grandma and grandpa in Kansas."

Her mother sniffled the first three hours of the two-day drive, but as they left the flat, plowed plains of home, her sadness faded. By the end of the first day of travel she smiled at Kate and made light conversation. They stayed at a hotel that let them make their own waffles for breakfast, which Kate thought was the best. "My little trooper." Her mom brushed her cheek with her palm. "We're starting a wonderful new adventure together, aren't we?" Kate returned her mother's smile. "I think so, Mama."

CHAPTER TWO

The first few weeks after their move passed at an easy enough pace which persuaded Cara she could make it as a single parent with no one she knew close by. They'd come in May and she didn't have to start work until June meaning they spent unhurried, constant hours together at the beach or café or movie theater, all unprecedented freedoms she wouldn't have enjoyed even a month earlier. She was revitalized and interested in what she was doing for the first time in years, but distrusted her reprieve from despair, that it would last. She had been too profoundly lost since her husband's accident, her emotions too buried for them to feel anything but strange and unstable outside the context of sadness. Here though, she woke each day with tentative optimism, willing to contemplate new engagements with anticipation. She nursed a small hope she might finally be recovered.

Her daughter's resilience bolstered this hope because she so quickly demonstrated signs of thriving in their new place. After their first week – during which Kate enjoyed too many treats, too little structure, and more time with her mother than Cara had ever been able to give her – she remarked, "North Carolina is a *way* better place to live than Kansas."

With the cash she had from the sale of George's business, she purchased a house in Childress, a town with more affordable real estate ten miles inland from Griffins Bay. Both she and Kate would have to commute to work and school but the house was worth it – small and picturesque, butter yellow with black shutters, dormers over the upper windows, and a spacious yard with a garden outside the back door. Someone, a long time ago, had put a tire swing on what was now an immense hickory tree in the front. To Cara, the place was a storybook idyll.

The burden of grief she had carried the previous two years continued to lighten as the days passed. Dana helped her scrub every surface in the house and paint the walls with warm, vibrant colors. She found discounted vegetable plants at the local nursery, which she promised Kate she would coax into a bounty harvest in the garden area out back. She indulged her daughter in a garishly bright yellow and pink color scheme for her bedroom, adding cheerful pillows and fabric accents of every pattern imaginable. The result was an exquisitely pretty, charmingly jumbled little girl's room. Cara knew what she was doing and was proud of herself. Kate, too, was impressed.

And Kate *was* impressed, with their new home, her new room, and all her mother's fresh demonstrations of competence since leaving Kansas. She felt as if her mother had freed her from something awful, like she'd been bound in baling wire from her grandfather's old shed, and Cara had snipped her out of it using bolt cutters. Her mother was finally someone she remembered, someone she'd badly missed. She drank in their contentment until she was full from it, and then reached for another glass.

Their final, and to her mind, most profound transformation occurred in the kitchen. In her depression, which comprised the whole of Kate's conscious memory, Cara had relied on a small cadre of prepackaged dinner options to sustain them. She had no appetite and no will to cook during the time following her father's death, so she didn't. Kate became an unenthusiastic eater when presented with the mushy, overly salted or tasteless options she was consistently served, so both of them came to regard mealtime as an unpleasant chore. Following a few days of scrubbing out cupboards and organizing pans and utensils, however, her mother made a dinner that changed Kate's outlook on mealtime forever.

It was roast chicken. Kate came downstairs, drowsy from an afternoon nap, to investigate the irresistible smells coming from the kitchen. Cara seemed again like she had *not* been crying, which was becoming the new norm since they'd come to Childress. The bread maker was out on the counter, perfuming the air with its toasty aroma. The sharper smells of onion, garlic and lemon provided their own compelling undertone, and the whole package of scents put Kate in a happy trance.

"Hi, honey," her mom said. "Wanna help me make supper?"

"Sure!" She slid a chair over to the sink.

Kate watched dubiously while her mom seasoned a chicken and put it in a roaster, adding lemon and onion to the cavity. She held out a sprig of something green for Kate to sniff.

She wrinkled her nose. "It smells like a Christmas tree."

"It's rosemary," Cara laughed placing the sprig inside the bird.

While the chicken roasted she helped her mother set the table, something they never did. Cara put on some music, and they played cards, her mom smiling diabolically when she told her, "Go fish," before laying down her hand. Kate had never seen her mother so lighthearted.

The chicken, which made such a dubious impression raw, eventually smelled too good to be true. After filling their plates they ate silently, savoring every bite, contentment settling over them like one of her grandfather's evening prayers. Cara had glazed the carrots with brown sugar, and Kate demanded seconds. She used the buttermilk bread from the bread machine to sop up every last morsel and finally, after she could eat no more, rested against the back of her chair and sighed. She couldn't remember a better dinner at home, nor could she recall a happier time with her mother.

Kate knew she was responsible for making them late to Gabe's party, but she needed to review *all* the options at the store to be sure she brought the perfect gift. Her mother had tried to hurry her by picking out part of their present – a pail and shovel for the beach. Kate selected plastic sea creatures to bury in a nest of shredded paper, refusing to rush. She was determined to delight her new and only friend.

They were the last to arrive, which was no big deal in her opinion, certainly not worth the irritation her mother and aunt had expressed since leaving the store.

"Thank God for all these adults," Dana murmured and then sped toward a group of grown-ups standing by the table.

Gabe tore around the corner wielding an inflatable shark as big as he was. "Hi, Kate! I was waiting for you. We can play in the sand but Mom says we can't swim today." Carmen was right behind him.

"That's right," Carmen said sternly. "There's too much going on today to watch you kids in the water." Gabe regarded his mother as if she was nuts while Cara cast her grateful smile.

"You let me go out on my own all the time!" Gabe protested. Then to Kate, "She's not making any sense."

Carmen's glare at her son should have blistered him. "Gabriel Jonathon Blake, I do no such thing." She leaned down to whisper something in his ear. Gabe was subdued but still irritated when she'd finished. "Fine. But can Kate and I go play now?"

"Let's introduce them to people first honey; did you have trouble finding us, Cara?"

"Not a bit," her mother replied. "Here. I know you didn't need us to bring anything but I've been baking." She handed Carmen a plate of cookies.

Carmen peeked under the wrapper and grinned. "Thank you. I love my treats and I'm sure these are yummy. Let's drop them off where they'll be safe, and then I'll show you around."

They went into the kitchen and Cara's mouth fell open as she saw three children between the ages of two and four sitting at the table. "Um, are they eating *sushi?*"

Carmen avoided Cara's eyes. "Why, yes! Kids will eat anything if they're encouraged."

The children really were eating raw fish and seaweed, as if these were their favorite things in the world to munch on. Carmen hurried to usher the two of them away but her mother continued to stare over her shoulder. "I couldn't get my daughter to eat fish sticks," she murmured.

"So, you mentioned Kate's birthday is coming up. When's the big day?" She winked at Kate.

"June thirteenth," Kate answered. "Mom says I can make the

cake."

"Hey!" Gabe exclaimed. "That's my real birthday too!" And they jumped up and down singing, "We have the same birthday! We have the same birthday!" Carmen regarded them with bright intensity for several seconds before leading the group to the living room. They approached a threesome of adults and two teenagers.

"This is my husband, Michael, and my brother-in-law, Samuel, and his wife, Anna, who you met on the beach. And these are their sons, Simon and Aiden." Carmen linked her arms lightly around her husband's waist. "This is Cara and little Kate. Cara's sister, Dana, is over talking to the Mattegins." Everyone shook hands and a couple of the adults rumpled Kate's hair. "Cara and Kate just moved here," Carmen offered. The adults talked about where Cara and Kate had lived in Kansas and what brought them to Griffins Bay.

Kate stared at the group with open curiosity – which, had Cara noticed, would have earned her a scolding her for being rude. With his fine features and dark hair, Gabe most resembled his father but he had his mother's eyes. Simon and Aiden could have been twins; both were blond and tanned and wore wild expressions. All of them, including Carmen, had a vague glow about them – hair, skin, and eyes – Kate noticed. Nothing overt but they shared a physical vitality she found distinctive and beautiful.

She surveyed the room and noticed other guests with these features, which caused her to conclude they were all related. Not that anyone would have noticed this similarity; the most apparent quality was every adult male wore, as far as she could tell, the same glasses. Dark, rectangular frames with heavy lenses distorting their eyes. Lenses that reminded her of her grandfather and his friends except none of these people were as old as her grandfather.

She heard her aunt's voice, tinged with exasperation on the other side of the room. "Is *everyone* here a marine biologist, then?" As if on cue her mother inquired what the adults in their little group did when not attending birthday parties.

"I'm a marine biologist," Michael responded.

"And I'm a marine biologist too," Samuel added. "I teach at the university in Sommerset." He nudged the boys on either side of him. "These two are still in high school. Carmen's the only career rebel in the group." He smiled at her.

"So, you're *not* a marine biologist?" her mother commented wryly.

"Geneticist," Carmen replied. "I freelance from home, writing and reviewing scientific articles mostly. And I'm not technically even a rebel. I studied marine biology as an undergrad. How did you come to be our town librarian, Cara?"

When they were finally allowed to wander off and play with the other children, they didn't, choosing instead to keep to themselves and hide under a big table covered by a tablecloth. They were quiet so no one would disturb them as they pretended they swam again, recreating their race through the seaweed forest as if they were the fastest, most agile creatures in the ocean.

CHAPTER THREE

Kate and Cara's home life settled into a pleasing and comfortable rhythm revolving around the garden, cooking, and Cara's job at the library. They made substantial dinners on the weekends and twisted the leftovers into simple but satisfying meals during the week with very little fuss, a pattern Kate soon adopted and followed without help. The roast chicken she'd enjoyed became chicken sandwiches the day after, and chicken soup the day after that. She loved cooking with her mother, which led to gardening with her as she was sent out for herbs or a leek or carrot. She initially asked what something was or if it was ready to eat, but she soon became a proficient helper.

Their gardening habit attracted conversation and local growing advice – and ultimately friendship – from neighbors out for a stroll. One afternoon when her mother was reading to her on the front steps, a frazzled, buxom woman with three daughters stopped at the sidewalk leading to their house. They were carrying a basket and a tray of plants.

"Hello, there!" the woman called cheerily. "Are you the new owners? We live down the street, and we've come to introduce ourselves. I'm Alicia Wilkes."

Her mother rose from the steps to greet them, wiping her hands on her shirttails. Kate hid behind her legs as the quartet approached. "I'm Cara Sweeting, and this is my daughter, Kate. I'm afraid I've been in the garden this morning and my hands aren't clean enough to shake."

"Neither are mine!" Alicia laughed and showed her hands, which sported the same green-stained fingertips her mom had.

"Oh well, in that case," Cara grinned, extending her hand. Kate gawked at their pretty visitors, keenly interested in their freckles, curly hair, and matching sundresses.

Alicia placed her arms around her girls. "These are my daughters, Maya, Sylvia, and Solange. I think Maya and Kate may be the same age. Is she in first grade this year?"

"As a matter of fact, she is. She's six as of this month," Cara replied. Kate regarded Maya shyly.

"Maya will be six in July. I've been meaning to get down here to meet you but haven't been able to break away," Alicia apologized. "We brought you a roast and a cake too, since it's such a pain to cook and unpack at the same time. Oh, and we noticed you working in your garden, and so we brought over extra plants from our batch of seedlings. Just toss what you don't want."

Her mother thanked her. "Do you have time to come in? I could put a pot of coffee on, and we could all have cake. Kate and I will never be able to eat all of that on our own."

Alicia hesitated, but Maya whispered, "Please?" She smiled down at her daughter. "That actually sounds nice. I don't suppose anyone will die if I don't get to the bank today." The group drifted in the front door and into the kitchen, the two women talking about the plants Alicia had brought, and Kate lagging behind to better evaluate Maya. She liked her, and muscled her sisters out of the way at the table to be by her.

Cara closed her eyes after taking her first bite of cake. "This is fantastic. I take back what I said about Kate and me not being able to eat something like this on our own. I could eat the whole thing myself."

Alicia eyed her mother's thin frame. "It wouldn't hurt you if you did. Sylvia's the baker in the family. She deserves the credit for this one." Sylvia beamed.

"My mom's thin because she doesn't eat enough," Kate blurted out. "Grandma says it's because my dad died."

Maya stared at her in alarm. "You don't have a daddy?"

Her mom and Alicia hissed simultaneously. "Catherine!" and "Maya!" they barked. They flashed each other quick smiles of apology.

Cara explained, "George died three years ago in a farm accident." She shifted her attention to Sylvia. "You've got quite a talent, Sylvia. Honestly, this cake melts in your mouth. What's in the glaze?"

When everyone had finished, Kate asked if she could show Maya her room. Her mom agreed but Alicia's assent came with a stern warning. "Fifteen minutes, Maya. And I don't want you making a fuss when it's time to leave."

Maya barely waited until they were away to pull on Kate's arm. "What happened to your daddy?" she demanded.

"He fell on a farm and got killed. It was an accident. My mom was really, really sad."

Maya was thoughtful. "Did you see him when he was dead?"

Kate shook her head. "My mom wouldn't let me." She squirmed, wishing she'd never have to think about that time of her life again. "Your dad's a dentist?" she ventured.

"The best one ever," Maya bragged. "And he's very safe so he won't die." She studied the contents of Kate's room. "What toys do you have?" Kate brought them out, which absorbed their attention until Alicia called for Maya to go home.

The Wilkes, Cara discovered, lived two blocks from them in Childress. Like her, Alicia's husband, Jeremy, commuted to Griffins Bay where he worked at his own dental practice. Alicia stayed home with Maya and her two older sisters and she complained about not having playmates around for Maya to stay active and busy. When Cara started her job at the library, Alicia offered to keep Kate at her house.

Cara initially told her no. "I don't want to impose."

"Look at it this way, Cara," Alicia argued. "It gives Maya someone to play with and frees me up. And I don't want to put my nose in your business but you're a single mother with a household to support. You can avoid a couple of months of childcare costs this way."

"I don't know… It's a short step between asking for favors and taking advantage of someone, maybe losing their friendship."

"You aren't the one asking. I'm offering," Alicia insisted. "And I wouldn't offer if it didn't benefit my family, which it does. I'm giving it to you straight, Cara: It would help if Kate were here to play with Maya."

She considered agreeing, on the condition if Kate became a burden in any way, Alicia was to say so immediately. Alicia cast a sly glance at Maya. "How about we let the girls decide?" Kate and Maya cheered for the option of being together, of course. Their pleas drowned out her arguments until she gave in, laughing.

By the middle of summer, Dana and her husband, Will, didn't visit as often; although Dana still came down twice a month. Cara put her to work in the garden or had her help with bigger tasks too hard for her to do alone, like washing windows, painting the porch, or replacing the cement on the front walkway with pavers. Dana chattered steadily about her business responsibilities or client antics or upcoming trip with her sales group, while Cara worked alongside her, half-listening or daydreaming.

Cara was long used to these conversations, which she believed were an excuse for Dana to underscore the contrasts between them. The take-away was unflattering – was meant to be, in Cara's opinion – and referential to what Dana saw as her sister's *unfortunate choices* following high school. Substantively, this meant a lot of talking on Dana's part – about her job, the influential people she knew, and the extravagances she enjoyed – and not much at all about Cara. Even now, when Cara had completed a degree, transferred five states away, and everything was in flux, Dana did not delve.

As she pretended to listen to her sister blather on, Cara wondered if Dana would ever stop thinking of her as a disappointment. The characterization had become unfair – not to mention galling – because when Cara had married young and dropped out of college to have Kate… well that had been when she was twenty. Writing anyone's epitaph at that age was ludicrous.

And unfortunately, Dana was the emissary on this front for their entire family, which was only the two of them and their parents. But still. Following George's death, Dana had ended up leading the effort to save her after their father's campaign had failed. "A library sciences degree? It's just not likely to lead to prosperity, Cara," her dad had counseled. "Not that I have any expectation you'll listen to me, but why don't you try something in the health care field, or business, like your sister?"

"This is a good fit for my skills and interests, Dad. Besides, most of the jobs in my field are with government, and the government isn't likely to go out of business anytime soon. Think of the job security angle."

Her dad didn't argue with her. Dana did, however.

"Cara, don't you want more for yourself?" Which Cara took to mean, *don't you want what I have?*

Dana had graduated from college with a degree in business and landed a job with a promising information technology company right out of school. The company experienced moderate success until it stumbled into the lucrative field of healthcare records management, which catapulted the firm to national prominence and significantly advanced the careers of its employees. Like many in her situation, Dana dug in, completing her MBA via online courses and night school; and then committed herself enthusiastically to longer hours as her responsibilities and salary grew. She worked hard, and when she analyzed her station in life – which Cara thought she did too often and too publicly – she had a little too much to say about her own accomplishments.

"All it takes is a strong work ethic, Cara. If you apply yourself you could get somewhere in this world too."

More than anyone Cara had ever known, Dana saw her life through the filter of professionalism, a quality she believed epitomized the very best of human intercourse no matter the context. According to Dana, process improvement schematics worked just as effectively in romantic relationships as they did in sales project management, and no activity was too inconsequential to benefit from applied business principles. Dana definitely had the coffee maker that ground the beans and brewed the coffee according to a timer specifying when the coffee would be perfectly fresh for her morning routine. Following her marriage to a man who was equally career-driven, Will Fletcher, Dana behaved even more as if she had cemented herself in success and happiness.

So Cara was not surprised after she announced her intent to

become a librarian, Dana seized on the chance to advise her. "You'll never make any real money doing that. Let me have you talk with a few of my colleagues about successful choices they made in your situation."

Cara stared hard at her sister and swallowed back about ten snarky comments she'd wanted to make. Instead, she settled on, "No. Thank you."

Dana's irritation flared. "Why wouldn't you?"

"Because I don't think you really understand *my situation*," Cara intoned. She'd thought but did not say she didn't believe Dana understood *her* either but decided not to put too fine a point on things. "If you want to help me, talk about something interesting, like a good book you've read or your opinion on the national healthcare debacle." Dana tsk-ed and shook her head but held her tongue.

The exchange was familiar to both of them, Cara knew. She found Dana way too eager to give advice and she bristled at the implication she couldn't make her own way. Dana, Cara was sure, felt she was trying to help and didn't get why Cara wouldn't let her. Regardless, Cara always left these interactions upset – as did Dana, she suspected. Which did not lessen her frustration.

In fairness, Cara had never told Dana how repetitive and strident she found her sermons, so Dana likely didn't know. Heck, since she did not specifically name her salary and list all her accolades for vendor of the month, she probably thought she was holding back. And actually, Cara understood her sister's perspective on this front since she saw the practice so widely executed by others. She also remembered how hard Dana had worked to achieve their father's love when they were both girls, and how violently she'd cried when she fell short of the mark. Dana deserved better, and Cara felt protective of her. She knew why Dana acted as she did.

She tried to shield Kate from the worst of their acrimony, although she saw her daughter take notice anyway. Later, when Dana had changed her ways and Cara felt she could be more open with Kate on the topic of her relationship with her sister, she described Dana as she'd seen her. "Dana was trying to show the best of herself according to a set of rules that rewarded her. A lot of people act that way. But if you examine not what she had, but what she *didn't* have – a rich home life, long-time friends, interests outside of her profession. She wasn't working to convince others she was happy, she was trying to convince herself. That's why she beat us all over the head with her pretty stories." Cara's face fell. "What bothered me most was how she didn't realize her heart and mind were bigger than all that. She deserved more."

Growing up, Kate thought her aunt had quite a bit – cars, vacations, all the freedoms of easy finances – and she couldn't imagine what *more* Dana might deserve. And while she and her mother never truly lacked, their existence felt precarious by comparison, the fun they enjoyed a ton less... well, fun. Consequently, she was a little jealous of what Dana had and did. She concluded her mother must be too.

She also assumed jealousy motivated her mother's criticisms, which made her disregard them. She understood her mom's frustrations – Dana's condescensions were obvious – but she couldn't blame her aunt for valuing self-indulgence over boredom and drudgery. Why wouldn't she?

During high school especially, Dana served as an exciting counterpoint to Cara's practical persona. Her mother's worries were familiar because she lived with her, and she sometimes found them tedious. Dana didn't appear to have any worries, or at least, didn't have her mom's, and against the backdrop of laundry to do, bills to pay, and no real care over one's wardrobe or makeup, her aunt's stories about her travels, as well as her lovely clothing and expensive perfume enveloped her like a cool breeze on a hot summer day. Her teenage self decided quickly she wanted to be like Dana, not her mother.

Later on, she cringed to think of her shallow comparisons of the two women, and the value she placed on Dana's appearance over her mom's demonstrations of love and duty. For years though, her mother couldn't compete, and not just on the fashion and jewelry front. While she knew her mother was proud of her performance at school, Dana's praise, not her mom's, rang in her ears as she strived for academic excellence. "Work hard at your studies, Kate, and you can enjoy the same rewards I did."

Her friendship with Maya, she found, further defined her prejudices and ideals concerning the most important women in her life; and at first her loyalties shifted further toward Dana. She broached the subject one afternoon at Maya's house. Throughout the dozens of family get-togethers with the Wilkes', she noticed how no one in Maya's family could tolerate Dana. Well, they tolerated her, but they didn't seem to like her much.

"What have you guys got against Dana?"

Maya's reply was circumspect. "Mom doesn't like it when she asks her about going back to work." Kate had seen how Alicia's choice to leave the work-a-day world completely fascinated Dana, and while her aunt was always careful to introduce the subject, her curiosity provided a spark to the dry tinder of Alicia's beliefs regarding work and family.

Kate thought Alicia overreacted. "Hmm. I think she's pretty and has cool stories." Maya shrugged.

Kate loved the image her aunt put forth of the good life and the path to self-fulfillment, and she continued to listen devotedly to Dana throughout her childhood. Her reward for all her admiration was endearment; Kate found herself cast in the roll of protégé worthy of Dana's sponsorship, a role she very much came to value as she mused over her own career options and life's choices.

Eventually, her mother stopped trying to school her beliefs against Dana, which was when she began to notice the difference between her aunt's vision of happiness and the unhappiness it seemed, in fact, to create. She would not be convinced the benefits weren't worth the cost, however. Not yet.

CHAPTER FOUR

Gabe, Maya, and Kate attended grade school together that first autumn, and their families formed a loose sub-community filling their free time throughout the year. In warmer weather, they were often as not at the beach in front of the Blake home, although interestingly, they never seemed to do much swimming. Or rather, the Blakes didn't. Cooler weather drew everyone inland, either inside one of their houses for dinner or around a fire in someone's back yard. Regardless of where the families were, the conversation was always lively, the company interesting, and the meals thoughtfully prepared.

In school, the trio formed their own discrete social club, which remained intact throughout their elementary grades. Kate saw Maya excel all around as an exemplary student who also made good in almost every sport she tried. Kate herself was an unadulterated bookworm with her cooking and gardening hobbies playing sidekick.

Gabe was harder for Kate to categorize because he was unlike anyone else she knew. Lanky, skinny, and eventually wearing the trademark Blake eyeglasses, he dominated academically and was quickly pegged by their peers as a brainy geek, which did not tell the whole story, as he was also athletically capable. But despite his abilities, Gabe didn't gravitate toward any extracurricular activities, and particularly when it came to sports, this struck Kate as odd. He was so quick and agile; he was a natural in virtually every P.E. activity at school. He was often the first person picked when it came to team sports, with good reason. Not only was he fast and strong, but he kept his head when the competition was heated, and more than once, this meant his team won.

But when it came to formal sports endeavors, Gabe did not participate. He was courted by classmates to join Little League and play organized soccer and football, but he always declined. In what was to Kate the most interesting of these refusals, she saw Gabe say 'no' to the school swim team.

"Gabe, you love to swim," Kate admonished, "and I know it's been a while but we swam for hours when we were five – you were super-fast and could hold your breath forever. You'd probably start winning titles left and right."

Gabe guffawed. "Well, yeah. That's where I'd *really* be a freak, Kate." He shuffled his feet. "The chlorine irritates my skin and I spend enough time in the water as it is. I don't need any more swimming practice." And that was pretty much the end of it. Despite gentle encouragement from the coach and a few teachers, Gabe remained steadfastly unaffiliated – with the swim team or any other team the school offered.

Sometimes Kate thought about how, other than that first time they'd been together, none of the Blakes actually swam when she was at their house, even when they were in their swimsuits on the beach. Her curiosity drove her to bring this up one afternoon when the families were together. They picnicked by the water with Michael, Carmen, Gabe, Anna, and all of the Wilkes family. Kate put her sandwich down at one point. "Why don't we ever swim when we're here?"

The Blakes all stopped chewing and there was a pregnant pause as Carmen and Michael exchanged speaking glances. Gabe studied the blanket they sat on. Michael cleared his throat. "Well, you know, I've never really thought about it. It seems to me we've been swimming with you often enough. Weren't you just in earlier today with your mother?"

"Yeah, but you and Carmen and Gabe don't ever go in with us."

Carmen tsk-ed her. "Of course we do, Kate!" Anna rose suddenly, saying it was late and she had to get home for dinner. Michael stood behind Kate, resting his hands on her shoulders and her conviction the families never swam together faded. In fact, she developed the vague impression Michael was completely right, they had, of course, been swimming together often with the Blakes, although she couldn't recall specific occasions.

"You know, we swam so much in the early days, and then it can be kind of a pain to dry off all the time," Carmen said. "Maybe we don't go out as much as we used to." She winked at Kate and asked her mother about her lettuces, which were wilting no matter how often she watered. Cara stated they were probably bolting but she'd be happy to take a peek. The families began packing up.

And that was the end of Kate's ability to inquire after the Blake family's swimming habits. If Gabe was in the water all the time, she'd have to take his word for it, because she never saw it.

Kate recalled one other swim with Gabe when they were younger, but unlike the vivid memories she had of their first adventure, she discounted their second one as soon as it was over.

She couldn't even accurately place the event in time but it was during her second or third summer in Childress. She went with her mother, as she often did, to the beach by the Blakes' home, with the Wilkes and the Blakes – Including cousins – all present as usual. They'd spent several hours lounging in the sun and wading in the water, and all exhibited the fuzzy behavior of extreme relaxation. From the corner of her eye Kate saw something leap out on the water. The others did as well, registering the flash of turquoise and yellow breaching and submerging too quickly for identification. Everyone's heads swiveled to the same point on the water. Carmen and her cousins seemed to materialize – one second they were several yards away, and the next they were not – beside them all, touching everyone on their backs or arms.

For Kate, time stilled as she and everyone else drooped into the same, semi-awake condition. But Carmen's hand lost touch when she pleaded with Michael, "Go! Get them!" During this brief moment of freedom Kate bolted toward Gabe. Gabe encouraged her, gleefully, to run and hurry into the surf with him.

Carmen stayed with the others but Kate could tell she worried most for her and Gabe. Michael answered his wife's panicked expression with the promise, "It's okay. I'll fix it." He dove into the ocean and disappeared.

With Gabe holding her hand, Kate relaxed into the same dreamlike state she'd felt with Carmen a few moments before. Gabe lost no time executing their get-away; he told Kate to take a breath and pulled her into the nearest wave.

When Kate next thought to check, they were far enough out for the people on the beach to appear miniaturized. She thought she and Gabe were near the spot the strange fish had breached. "I'll be right back," Gabe promised before diving beneath them. She felt his hand on her foot. She was not the least bit afraid.

In fact, she felt blissful and calm, as if she couldn't wait to wake up to tell Gabe and Maya about this wonderful dream she was having. The ocean was an intense, cobalt blue and she floated on the big, gentle swells like a baby being lulled. When she peered down she could see three long fish below her, one of which idly reminded her of Michael. Eventually, the two smaller fish and the Michael fish swam toward the shore. Gabe surfaced.

His expression was savage and bright. "Isn't it fun?"

Kate nodded. She couldn't remember ever feeling so content. In her dream, the subtle sheen of Gabe's skin was more pronounced, his eyes silvery and piercing. She thought of him as a freer, wilder version of the boy she knew, one who was less reserved, more buoyant, uninhibited, and also more himself.

"We'll take the long way back," he told her, and his excitement was infectious. "Take a big breath, Kate." She did, and they slid under the waves again.

They swam at a leisurely pace this time, meandering without urgency around whatever interested them. Although they couldn't literally talk under the water, they could communicate just as well.

Let's go to the cave by the reef, Gabe suggested.

Will we see a shark? I'm afraid of sharks, Kate replied.

No, they only hunt here at night, and they won't bother us, anyway.

Schools of colorful fish swam through shifting rays of sunlight penetrating the water around them. When they skimmed the surface of the reef, Gabe pointed out objects he found noteworthy or pretty. Every once in a while, they went to the surface so Kate could breathe.

You could hold your breath longer if we practiced this, he advised at one point.

Kate's reverie changed when a blue-tinged Carmen swam up alongside them, smiling and wagging her finger at her son. Gabe's grin was unapologetic.

My mom came to get us, so I guess we're done.

The next thing Kate knew, she awoke on the beach. She and her mother sat up and yawned. At the same time, the Wilkes family also roused from an impromptu nap, blinking and disoriented.

Cara stretched. "My goodness! I didn't realize I was tired."

Alicia and Jeremy also apologized for falling asleep. "Wow." Jeremy studied the sun's position on the horizon. "The afternoon's already gone. We'd better get home."

Kate went to sit by Gabe and Michael as Carmen and Cara gathered their things. She rushed to tell her story before she had to leave. "I dreamt you were a fish," she told Michael. She addressed Gabe. "And you and I had the best time by the reef. But your skin was different. You were different." She became thoughtful.

Michael's smile was enigmatic as he placed his hand at the back of Kate's neck, his eyes focused on some point behind her. As Kate recounted the whole of her experience, the story became more and more firmly unrealistic, any hint of actuality dissipating as soon as the words left her mouth. "The dream felt so real," she finished, feeling as though she'd lost something important and like she might cry.

As Kate and Cara made their way to their car, Kate noticed Gabe's cousins, Simon and Aiden, playing Frisbee. She tried to remember when they had joined them and realized they must have arrived during everyone's nap.

CHAPTER FIVE

Cara dug into running the library, apparently with an enthusiasm the community hadn't seen in decades. "You're a wonder," and, "My family loves coming here, now – the place used to put us to sleep," she heard again and again from her new patrons.

By all reports, the retired librarian she replaced was a straight-laced practitioner who kept everything in impeccable order but didn't venture outside old-school, traditional library protocols. Cara hurried to add drama and reading programs for little children and teenagers, organize new book clubs and book drives, and refashion the library into something of a meeting hub for the town's social and professional clubs.

The clubs responded with a cash infusion, raising funds allowing her to completely remake the building's interior. She transformed what was once a dark and austere space into a light-filled place of comfort and energy with colorful chairs, area rugs, and murals replacing the dark, uniform arrangement of the prior administration. She reorganized the shelves to create semi-enclosed reading areas containing soft, cozy seating options. Outside, she enlisted the local gardening society to replace the lawn completely with flowers. She even tilled the wide boulevard running alongside the building to accommodate a community vegetable garden, an act that cemented her place in the hearts of the townspeople forever.

"It's like Eve's garden out there," a woman commented to Cara one afternoon. "My sister and I come here every single morning with our boys to pick that berry patch clean. You've given us a treasure, I kid you not." Volunteers flocked to help.

Socially, Cara still felt like a loner, mostly owing to the fact she was single and relatively young with everyone else in town her age coupled in long-term relationships. She suffered through several awkward attempts to set her up with a brother or uncle or cousin but nothing ever came of it.

When Kate was in the fourth grade, she questioned why this was. "Do you not like any of these guys, Mom? Don't you want a boyfriend?"

"Despite how I've been acting, I *would* like to meet someone. It's just not as easy as it was before. I mean, I've always been shy, and then when I'm with these guys, all I can think about is what things would be like long-term. And then I come up with a thousand ways I or you or he can be disappointed and stuck and miserable. I can't even get to the short-term part.

"End of the day, it's too complicated and I'm too difficult," she concluded. "But, ugh. I know I'll never get anywhere thinking like this." At that point, she began wearing her wedding ring again when she went out, which did nothing to deter the people who knew her but did fool acquaintances who didn't. The charitable dating set-ups came to a halt.

She found the Blakes a curious exception to the *let's introduce Cara Sweeting to someone* campaign. Despite the presence of any number of male relatives continuously cycling in and out of their house – and her own company – Carmen and Michael never once tried to orchestrate a romantic encounter. Cara mentioned how she was actually relieved to go somewhere without the nerve-wracking prospect of a potential date showing up, with everyone in town watching on the sidelines.

Part of the challenge with the Blakes, Cara believed, was none of their male company stayed for long. She found all of the Blake men attractive but they were also strangely unforthcoming emotionally, and they were always on their way to somewhere else. At any rate, even Kate acknowledged nothing was going to happen during the three and four days the Blakes had these visitors.

But the summer Kate turned fifteen, Cara surprised them both by responding to someone. She'd brought Kate to the beach by the Blake house in the early evening for one of their typical Sweeting-Wilkes-Blake gatherings around a bonfire. Carmen and Michael also played host that evening to several men who appeared to be relatives.

The air cooled after the sun set, driving her and her daughter to their car for an extra blanket. As they walked back, a crab scuttled at Kate's feet, startling first her and then Cara, who jumped backward, stumbled, and laughed.

Before she could catch herself, she backed into a man facing the fire. He spun around, bracing them both reflexively before stepping away and placing his hands in his pockets. Cara blushed and laughed out an apology.

His face broke into a lopsided grin. "No problem." He was obviously a Blake of some sort, evidenced by the wave in his hair, and more obviously, his thick, rectangular glasses. "I'm John Blake, one of Michael's cousins," he confirmed.

"Cara Sweeting," she responded. "I'm the town librarian." She felt her cheeks flush as she smiled at him. She shook his hand and glanced at Kate. "This is my daughter, Kate."

John's attention never left her, and he kept her hand. Cara felt a growing sense of astonishment as he lifted it to his chest, wrapping his other hand around her wrist. His expression become pained. He studied her face with absolute concentration. Then he sagged with what seemed like relief, released her, and put his hands in his pockets again. She couldn't manage to breathe properly, and her smile felt frozen.

John smiled warmly at her then, and Cara was grateful he'd gotten over his discomfort. She wondered what she had done to cause it.

"It's nice to meet you, Kate," he said to her daughter.

"My mom's not married," Kate blurted out. "She just wears her wedding ring so she doesn't have to get set up on dates."

"Catherine!" Cara groaned. "For crying out loud!" She pinched the bridge of her nose and squeezed her eyes shut.

John nodded sagely. "Good to know. I promise not to set her up with anyone. Although," he peered at her, "pretending to be married seems a little extreme?"

"No, no." Cara waved her hands. "It's my old wedding ring... my husband died when Kate was three. I just wear it sometimes when I go out. I know it's probably silly."

John inclined his head to one side. "I know how that is. I lost my wife too." The look they shared thickened the air around them with intimacy.

Carmen and Michael joined them then. "Hi, guys. We saw you, um, shaking hands with Cara, John," Carmen said, her eyes glinting with amusement. "Yes, Cara, we thought we'd better come fill you in on this guy." Michael's grin was devilish. John stared hard at him. Cara thought she heard him say, "Leave. Now."

She would have preferred privacy as well but Michael and Carmen seemed disinclined to leave them alone. Which didn't need to deter her from making conversation, she decided. "So," she addressed John, "at which university do you currently teach marine biology?"

He frowned. "Marine biology? Who told you I taught marine biology?"

Her eyes widened. "I have met approximately four thousand of your relatives, and with the exception of Carmen here, every blasted one of them is a marine biologist. So, I figure you're either a marine biologist or you're not really related to these people."

John lifted his chin coolly. "I'm an ophthalmologist."

She was dubious as she considered him. "You're not a marine ophthalmologist? You're just a regular, garden-variety ophthalmologist?"

"Well, there was that one whale that needed cataract surgery of course but I can treat non-marine life too," he replied, his voice even.

"Ooo!" Kate interjected. "You can help all of these people here wearing those kooky thick glasses . . ." She trailed off as she realized he was one of the people wearing the weird glasses. "Sorry," she mumbled.

"No worries," John responded with a laugh. "I actually *am* helping all these people with the kooky glasses." He flashed Carmen and Michael a grin. "It's a sort of genetic quirk we share in this family. We don't need to wear them all the time, we just see better in certain situations if we do." Then he removed his glasses and smiled, and Cara was smitten. "Kate, why don't you go find Maya and Gabe. I'll come get you after a bit."

She saw Kate convene with Gabe and Maya a little ways away but paid her little attention the rest of the night. She chose instead to pursue a conversation with John, who she thought might be the most handsome, charming man she'd ever met.

During the next week, Kate gathered from Carmen that John Blake had found her mother attractive and interesting but his professional commitments were to keep him away from Griffins Bay for the foreseeable future.

Her mother took the news well. "That's perfectly understandable. We all have busy lives."

Carmen persisted, however. "He really took to you, Cara. His life is a little complicated though, and I wonder if he isn't thinking it's better not to start anything."

Cara's smile was sad. "Well, it might be that my life is complicated. I kind of went on and on about my job and Kate and our gardens. We might just seem like too much work to an outsider."

Carmen sighed, and Kate thought she was even more disappointed than her mother over the lack of potential romance with John. "No. I don't think so." She brightened. "Cara, have I ever told you about my astrology hobby? Have you ever had your chart done?"

Her mom's smile was thin, her mistrust evident as she replied, "No. I don't believe in that kind of thing."

Kate knew this wasn't strictly true. On a lark once, when they were in New Orleans for a library sciences convention, they had ducked into a booth advertising psychic readings with openings that day. The lady read tarot cards for Cara, and the analysis had left mother skeptical. "You will have a long and happy marriage, and you will have two children," she predicted.

"Well. *That* was a waste of time," Cara whispered on the way out.

Carmen began gathering her supplies. "Let's do your chart, just for fun." She glanced her way. "I've actually already started one for you, Kate." Her mother slumped onto a stool while Kate stared eagerly at the rolls of paper Carmen laid out. Her mom was reluctant but she began answering Carmen's questions, which stretched well into the afternoon.

That same summer, Gabe informed Kate and Maya he would not be coming back to school next year because Carmen planned to home-school him.

"What?" Kate shrieked. "Why on earth would she do that?" Other than Maya, Gabe was her best friend and she thought they should all stick together through their debut into the scary world of high school. The way Kate saw it, their mutual bookishness and high combined geek factor protected her from the onslaught of personal doubt she would suffer outside of their company. Everything embarrassed her when she was alone – her growth spurt, her feet, and her braces – pretty much all of her physical attributes. With Gabe and Maya, she didn't dwell on these things so much.

Maya was almost mad. "That sucks. Who are we going to hang out with? And who are you going to hang out with?"

"Hopefully you two still, if you don't mind taking time away from your *new* friends." Gabe was bitter, and Kate could see he was not leaving them by choice. He was so despondent; she and Maya went to him to console him. "You can't get rid of us, Gabe," she promised. He seemed a little cheered by their support but they all remained glum.

"It's gonna suck without you," Maya reiterated. Kate had to agree.

In August, Kate went to Dana and Will's in Philadelphia for two weeks, a tradition she would continue through high school thanks to steady petitioning from her aunt. "There are a couple of day programs at the art institute, and a drama camp run by the university here I think Kate would get a lot out of," Dana proposed during one of her visits. Cara put the offer to Kate.

"It's only two weeks," Kate reasoned. "It kind of sounds like fun. What I'll miss is the time in the garden and reading at the library but I can still do those things when I get back."

Dana hugged her. "It's settled then! I'll make the arrangements. Kate, honey, I'm so excited for you to get a taste of city life!" She left the room with her cell phone engaged.

Her mother's smile was sad as she stroked her hair. "I'm coming back, you know," Kate told her.

Her mom continued to sift through the longer locks resting on Kate's shoulder. "I know. And I think this is a good idea. It just makes me realize someday, and it will get here too quickly for me, you'll be venturing off on your own."

"Should I tell Dana I don't want to go?" She felt conflicted; she wanted the experience Dana offered but was anxious to relieve the ache this desire caused her mother.

"No, honey. I think you should do it. You'll get some new experiences I'm sure you'll enjoy. I'll just miss you, that's all."

Her flight to Philadelphia was short, and Dana and Will both waited for her when she arrived, waving when she exited the plane. They chatted steadily with her during the drive home, which seemed to take only minutes.

Kate had been to visit her aunt and uncle one other time with her mother but she'd been too small to remember anything. Now, she found their home intimidating.

The house was gorgeous, of course; a stately colonial Dana and Will had meticulously renovated. It was about three times the size of the two-story Kate shared with her mom in North Carolina – Kate's own bedroom had a fireplace, a window seat, a bed with a canopy, and was almost as big as their main floor back home. She thought her room – and everything else, for that matter – was like a picture in a design magazine, and while its beauty captivated her, it also made her vaguely homesick.

She worked to hide her awe of her surroundings, as well as the lifestyle that went with it, hoping she didn't appear as unsophisticated as she felt. Despite Dana's intimations concerning the comforts she and Will enjoyed, seeing their life first-hand was not the same as hearing about it. They had a cleaning service come once a week, and as they had no children or pets, their home was always spotless and composed. As far as Kate could tell, everything was perfect. The colors, the lighting, the scents, the fabrics, even the towels. And the fact they didn't physically have to keep up with the place made their situation seem effortless as well. After the first day, Kate admitted she felt enchanted… and a little envious.

But both of her day camps were a tremendous, engrossing pleasure. She vowed to take the techniques she learned in theater class back to her school in Childress and put them to good use in drama club. The classes at the art institute opened her eyes too, for the first time, to the beauty of pieces she'd previously taken for granted. The teacher spent ample time considering the perspective of a particular painting and the subtle use of color or shading to suggest a mood or create a dynamic.

On a more practical level, she learned to write descriptively about her new experiences. She was assigned to keep a journal in her art class, and she so enjoyed the endeavor, she began a private journal as well. After her classes each day, she came back to Dana and Will's stimulated and restless, which drove her to try cooking in her aunt's magnificent, chef's-grade kitchen. She then wrote about what she made in her diary, finding the analysis she employed at the art institute worked just as well for meal descriptions.

Dana and Will were impressed by her culinary efforts and made every night into a celebratory affair with wine, linens, candles and fresh flowers on the table. And the more Kate complimented their home and lifestyle, the more satisfied they seemed.

Half way through her stay, her aunt queried her. "Are you having a good time here, Kate? Would you rather be helping your mother back at the library?" Will refilled their drinks and smiled at his wife over her glass.

"No way! I mean, I love helping my mom out at the library but this is so great. It's so beautiful here, like a story."

Dana and Will appeared gratified. "Maybe we can make this an annual event?" Will offered.

"And I get to cook as much as I want?" Kate countered.

Dana pretended exasperation. "I *suppose* we can endure a couple of weeks of home-cooked meals from you each year." She smiled quickly. "But we might have to make an extra run to the health club each day if we eat like this every night." Everyone laughed and tucked into the cobbler Kate had prepared for dessert.

As much as Kate enjoyed Philadelphia, she was relieved to come home. She'd missed Maya, Gabe, and her mother, she realized; the familiarity of her life washed over her like a warm, soothing bath when Cara hugged her. Kate hadn't thought she was lonely at Dana and Will's until she felt the easy intimacy of her life in Childress again.

"Did you have fun?" her mother asked.

"Oh, Mom, it was so *interesting*. Dana and Will's place is

completely stunning, of course, and they have this unbelievable kitchen I cooked in every night – I have to show you the journal I kept – and the classes were just the best. I feel like I learned so much . . ."

Belatedly, she checked her mother's expression to see if her enthusiasm was hurtful. Cara didn't seem jealous but just in case Kate told her, "Of course, I missed you like crazy. Can we go to the library first thing tomorrow so I can check out the garden?" Her mother squeezed her. "Of course, honey."

Maya reported via texts she was up to her eyeballs in sporting activities that summer, attending multiple camps in succession; and Gabe was curiously busy as well, although he wouldn't specify with what. Kate found herself with more time on her hands than usual but she focused on writing and her hobbies rather than seek out other friends. Aside from Gabe and Maya, she decided she didn't particularly want other friends.

One afternoon when she did feel lonesome, she went over to the Blakes' to see if she could catch Gabe. "Kate! You should have called ahead," Carmen chided. "Gabe's not here."

"Drat. Where is he?"

"Swimming, I think." She made a vague gesture toward the water.

"I've got my suit on. Could I catch him?"

"He and his dad are quite a ways out. They're on the boat. Come in, though. I have something to show you."

In her office, Carmen reached for a scroll from her bureau, which she spread on her drafting table. "I've been working on your astrological chart," she announced, beaming.

The sheet before them covered the entire table and contained a plethora of planetary maps, dates, and lunar schedules. Carmen employed a complicated color-coding system Kate couldn't decipher, although the effect, despite the dizzying amount of information depicted, was organized and beautiful.

"I could put this into a digital format but I think it's kind of pretty in ink, don't you?"

"I would frame this and hang it on my wall," Kate told her solemnly.

"No you wouldn't!" Carmen laughed. "This contains a lot of personal information you might not want on display."

Kate cocked her head. "None of it makes sense to me. What does it mean?"

Carmen scanned the chart with a practiced eye. "Here is the alignment of the planets relative to where and when you were born," she pointed to a place on the sheet. "This was the phase of the moon, and here are astrological activities relative to your parents' charts that affect your life."

"This must have been a lot of work, Carmen. How long have you been doing it?"

"These things take a long time to put together," Carmen hedged. "I jotted down initial information way back when we met. Do you remember when you first came to the house, for Gabe's birthday party?" Kate nodded. "When Cara told me you and Gabe had the same birthday, I began your chart. It wasn't difficult, since I had one going for Gabe too. I just mapped information that was similar."

Kate breathed out a low whistle. "This is really impressive. But I still don't understand what it means."

Carmen paused, seeming to deliberate where to focus next. "Here." She placed her index finger near the middle of the sheet. "This shows the stronger influences on your nature that manifest themselves as physical characteristics. And this area suggests personality traits. In general, you're physically attractive." She hip checked Kate and grinned at her. "You also have excellent concentration, you're loyal, and you're slightly introverted." She moved her finger to another planetary grouping. "Which is unusual for a Gemini. Gabe's chart shows the same thing for him, actually."

"Does it tell me how many children I'll have, or if I'll die young?"

"Not exactly. This isn't a tool for predicting the future so much as for helping determine a best course of action given the circumstances. And the future can change, depending on who you interact with and what their astrological influences are."

Carmen retrieved two additional scrolls from her desk. "I shouldn't do this but I have to show you something." Her smile was conspiratorial as she laid another map over Kate's. "This chart is mine." Kate noticed how it showed the same prolific array of graphs, lines, and colors but it differed from the one Carmen had drawn for her — different color scheme, different arrangement of graphics. Carmen then unrolled another scroll and placed it over her own. It was too familiar. Kate picked up the top two charts to glance again at hers.

"Hey! This one is just like mine!"

"It's Gabe's. I've never seen such similar charts."

"So, what does *that* mean?"

Carmen's expression shuttered. "It means you and Gabe share a similar astrological alignment." She rerolled her charts brusquely. "Anyway, it's just something I thought you'd find interesting."

"I do find it interesting," Kate told her as Carmen put the scrolls away. "I just don't quite understand it."

"That's because we haven't quite discussed it yet," Carmen replied. When Kate waited for her to say more, she offered, "I promise to go over it with you again when you're older, okay?"

Kate shrugged. "Sure." She glanced at the clock on the wall. "Carmen, I have to get back to the library. Tell Gabe I stopped in, will you? And thank you for showing me your charts. They're really something."

"You're welcome, Kate. Tell your mom hello for me." Kate left reconsidering her distrust of astrology and wishing she'd been able to catch Gabe.

Maya and Kate stuck together as best they could at school, even though their interests led them in different directions. Maya's athletic abilities grew with every challenge she assumed, eventually gaining her inclusion in practices and training for a bigger and bigger portion of each day. Although she was too young to play varsity, she attended summer camps and scrimmaged relentlessly in the off-season with the older players who were starters. She was dressing for varsity by sophomore year.

She was also a strong student, although studying was her parents' stick to the carrot of athletic involvement. "Your studies come first," Jeremy had insisted when they discussed expectations going into Maya's freshman year. "We're very proud of your accomplishments in volleyball but if your grades suffer, we're taking you out." Maya's grades never slipped, and she continued to improve on the court.

Under Alicia's orders, neither Maya nor Kate were allowed to date, something Kate was surprised Cara complied with, as she thought this issue should be solely under her mother's authority. In front of Cara, Alicia informed the girls, "We'll talk about it when you two are juniors, and not before. I care too much about you both to let you get all caught up in things you're better off waiting to experience." Her mother didn't even consider her outrage over receiving social restrictions from a neighbor, even a close one. "She's right on this, Kate. I want you to listen to her." Kate huffed and marched away.

Not that she had any specific prospects. She maintained her bookworm social status and prided herself in getting good grades. She had to really work for them in math but she did the work and received the resulting As. She also participated in speech and drama, which she enjoyed because they tied together her interests in written and oral communications. Outside of school, she still loved to garden, cook, and read. Every moment she wasn't engaged in those activities, she helped out at the library, which remained her favorite haunt whenever she could steal away.

As threatened, Carmen and Michael home-schooled Gabe for all of senior high, meaning Kate and Maya no longer saw him during the week, although their families still got together on weekends. Kate sorely missed Gabe's quick, incisive wit at school. Neither she nor Maya came up with the same sarcastic asides Gabe did, which had so often made difficult social situations palatable. She felt as if she and Maya lost half of their personality when he transferred.

She continued to spend two weeks each summer with her aunt and uncle in Philadelphia, where she reveled in the luxury of their impeccable home, signed up for an interesting class or two, and cooked like a maniac in their fabulous kitchen. As she got older though, she started to see through the story they told her about their life, the fervency with which they represented themselves eventually fostering skepticism over the perfect image they worked to project.

On the subject of children, for example, Dana had something to prove. "I see what it does to women I've worked with, Kate. It's a rare person who doesn't falter on the job after having kids. I mean, they're always sick, or have kept their parents up at night, or mom and dad need time off to be at some school event. I know this sounds harsh but I just think it makes you exhausted and unable to perform." Her philosophy on this subject was typically followed by her philosophy in general. "It's an unpleasant truth, maybe but a truth nonetheless: you can't give it all to your career and raise a family. And everyone needs to work."

Kate couldn't help but think of her mother on these occasions. Granted, her mom was no tycoon but she made a living and enjoyed community support for the job she did. During the times Kate had been sick, or her mother needed help at the library, board members or volunteers pitched in. Kate questioned if work and family needed to be classified in the black-and-white terms Dana ascribed to them; although she conceded the ongoing lifestyle Dana and Will had might require stricter rules of engagement. And while she loved and admired her mom, Kate still wondered if her aunt's lifestyle wasn't worth the price.

Her mother was always sad when she hinted at these ideas. "Oh, honey. The desire to have children, or be part of something bigger than yourself in this life is healthy." She took her hand. "You're too smart and too kind-hearted to be happy with Dana's situation for very long. You'd figure out in pretty short order just making money isn't a big enough box to live in. Plus," she chucked Kate's chin, "I want grandchildren." She seemed to consider her next words carefully. "And I wouldn't necessarily accept Dana's assertion her life is perfect, Kate."

By the time Kate was in senior high, she saw more of what her mother meant. She noticed, for instance, Uncle Will drank a lot. So much, she couldn't tell how much, and so often, she couldn't discern between when he'd been drinking and when he hadn't. She saw too how her aunt and uncle's endearments for each other were easily given but casual, even empty. Their glances darted away from each other when they spoke, and while they were never unkind to one another, neither were they genuinely warm. It was as if they were each too preoccupied with a private dilemma to register the other's true state of mind.

She caught all of these nuances, which did not alter her overall perception of the Fletchers but did make her doubt the details of the pretty picture she saw when she was with them. She no longer accepted her aunt's advice and opinions at face value.

CHAPTER SIX

The summer Kate turned seventeen, she often went to Griffins Bay with her mother to spend the day at the library reading or working in the gardens. One such Friday in late June, Cara handed her a packet.

"Would you mind delivering this to the Blakes'? Carmen is researching the first settlers in the area, and I came across some information for her."

"Sure." She'd love an excuse to see Carmen, although she'd heard Gabe was in Maine for the week and regretted she'd miss him.

"I get done at three, honey," Cara reminded her. "Don't forget and make me wait."

The day was made for landscape artists and casual strolls, the sky a brilliant blue, the sun a crystalline yellow, and all around were the sounds of people enjoying themselves. With nothing to distract her but the buzz of outdoor activities and a pleasant breeze, her half-mile walk went quickly. She approached the Blake house in high spirits.

The Blakes had made interesting modifications to their traditional beach home over the years, effectively blending modern architectural elements with classic styling to give the structure a freshness that somehow went with its original charm. And despite its expansive setting and prominence, the house gave the impression of privacy. Kate noted how discreet side-mounted box awnings hugged many of the windows from the inland side, presumably directing the view from the interior toward the water but also restricting visibility into the home. Seaside, a series of sculptural, wave-like walls hid an ascending walkway between the ocean and a platform Gabe mentioned had once served as a deck for entertaining. The Blakes had built the deck out as a small guest cottage, offering visitors coming from the water a private path much of the way to the main house.

But she approached from the inland side this time, skipping up the steps of the deep, gray porch to knock at the door. She heard a burst of masculine laughter inside, which was unusual, and she tensed. A few seconds later, an absolutely stunning man opened it, smiling to welcome her in.

The normally tranquil Blake household had transformed into an upscale frat house of sorts with the presence of more than a dozen truly beautiful young men. They were everywhere, milling around and lounging, looking as if a modeling agency had sent them over for a retro, Ivy League fashion shoot. Every single one of them oozed charm, vitality, and – Kate could think of no better word for it – virility. Several stood around a flat screen television to watch qualifying races for the U.S. Olympic men's swim team. They seemed amused.

She stood wide-eyed inside the front door, not sure she wanted to navigate this group to find Carmen. Maybe she could just hand off the envelope and apologize later to her for being in a hurry. Her greeter closed the door behind her, however. The sound startled her. What happened next unnerved her.

"Hi, I'm Luke Hokeman." The door opener extended his hand. "Catherine Sweeting," she replied. She had no idea why she gave her formal name, which was used almost exclusively by her mother when she was in trouble. In fact, she felt like she was in trouble. She mustered up enough bravado to extend her hand.

Instead of shaking it as she expected, Luke turned it so he held it almost to his chest, and she panicked as she thought he might raise her hand to his lips. Did guys still *do* that? He placed his other hand gently around her wrist, she could swear to God, to check her pulse.

41

"Are you home for summer break from college, Catherine?" He smiled. Distracted and more than a little terrified, she dropped her envelope, which attracted a different man to her side, bending to retrieve it. Yet another of the party came to stand behind her, placing his hand proprietarily at the small of her back. "Come in and sit down." She broke out into a sweat.

"Hoke, Libby, Gins – back off and give the poor girl some air." Kate felt weak with relief as she saw Gabe bounding lightly down the stairs. "Hi, Kate."

He took her hand from Luke and tucked it through his arm, a gesture that would have been remarkable and strange in any other situation. He grabbed her envelope and led them firmly away from the front door and its trio of male sirens. "And no, she's not home from college, Hoke," Gabe threw over his shoulder. "She's seventeen, which is I think what you were getting at. Too young for yo-oo-oo-ou," he sang, grinning down at Kate.

"Not too young for you though, looks like," someone teased. "You're not supposed to be in the running yet. Why don't you give this one up and wait your turn?" Bass laughter rippled across the room.

Gabe paused to stare at the group with mock admiration. "You guys are so smooth. Desperation gets the girl – is that right?" Guffaws all around. One member of the group high-fived Gabe as he and Kate left the room. Kate's legs shook.

"Um, Gabe, who *are* those guys?" she squeaked.

"Cousins." He laughed out a cough in which Kate may have heard the word, *horny*.

"Wow. They're all so . . ." Kate trailed off, at a loss to identify what she'd just seen.

"Yeah, and don't think they don't know it. Mom!" he called. "Kate stopped by."

Carmen was alarmed when she poked her head out of her office. "Hi, Kate. I wasn't expecting you today. Is everything all right?"

"Oh, yeah… no, I should have called," she stammered. "My mom mentioned you were reviewing information on the Griffin and Hutchins families. She said you're doing some research on the first settlers here? She photocopied some old letters and articles for you and gave them to me to drop off." Kate gave her the envelope.

"How thoughtful!" Carmen gushed but she still wore a worried frown. "I'm afraid I have a houseful and won't be able to chat for very long. Did you meet any of our guests?" She sounded like she hoped not.

"Unfortunately, yes she did," Gabe cut in. "I got to her before they ate her, but only just."

"Hmm. Yes, well maybe you could take her back to the library, Gabe? Is your mother still there, or did you drive over from Childress?"

"I came from the library," Kate replied. "I told Mom I'd be back by three. And I thought you were at your aunt's in Maine, Gabe."

"I'm leaving today," he informed her. "I've got time, though. We could even grab lunch at the Bait Shop."

Kate checked her watch. It was one thirty, and she was hungry. "Let's."

"Gabe? Why don't you take her out the back door," Carmen advised.

"Good idea."

Carmen hugged Kate. She and Gabe then went the long way to reach the rear of the house, neither of them anxious for a repeat encounter with the group holding court in the front rooms.

At the restaurant, Kate quizzed Gabe over their sandwiches. "You have a lot of male cousins. Why are they in town? I can't believe I've never met them."

Gabe was slow to answer her. "My mom's throwing a party tonight. It's kind of a family reunion."

Kate remembered a comment she'd overheard at Maya's house from her older sister, Solange. "Oh yeah, I think I heard something about that from Solange Wilkes." Then, remembering the Wilkes were not related to the Blakes and the party wasn't entirely a family reunion, she felt horrible. She and her mother hadn't been invited. "Oh," and she dropped her gaze so Gabe wouldn't see how hurt she was.

Gabe's expression became pained. "You're wondering why you and your mother weren't invited, aren't you."

"Well, no," she mumbled to her lap. "You're free to invite whoever you like. It's your party."

"It is most definitely not my party," Gabe snapped. "And we're *not* free to invite everyone we like, and… and I really can't think of a good excuse to give you as to why you were not." He blew out a sigh and stared up at the ceiling as if for inspiration. Kate watched him, curious. "See, it's really not going to be your mother's kind of party, and as for you, well, you saw how my cousins were this afternoon. It's just not a good idea. God only knows where you'd end up."

"What's that supposed to mean? I mean, they're not… doing anything criminal, are they?"

"No-no. They're all decent guys, actually. It has to do with timing more than anything." He chewed his thumbnail, examining Kate with a worried frown. "They've just got out of school and several of them are probably going to be kind of… drunk… and they can get a little rowdy. And we're a little too young for that, according to my mother. That's why she's shipping me off to Maine."

"Oh. Well, that makes me feel better then. Sorry. It was rude of me to bring it up."

"No, I brought it up. You guys are close family friends. *I'd* wonder if it were the other way around." He let out a short laugh at this idea.

Kate examined Gabe more closely, realizing he'd grown since she'd last seen him. In fact, if it hadn't been for the company they'd just left, she would have been surprised by his appearance. He looked great. His dark hair was thick and wavy, his face had become more angular and masculine, and he was filling out. She realized he would soon fit in very well with all of his cousins, and this bothered her. She didn't want to think about how other girls, probably all of her classmates, would flirt with him if they saw him now. She also noticed he wasn't wearing glasses for once. "Gabe, you look really good, by the way. Did you get rid of your specs?"

"Forgot to put them back on, I guess." He slid his glasses out of his shirt pocket and started to place them over his nose but stopped. He smiled at her. She felt a thrill go through her, and she was utterly unable to stop the smile that came to her face in response. She felt the ground of their friendship shift underneath them.

"Do you realize this is our first unchaperoned outing together, ever?"

"Lunch at the Bait Shop," Kate teased, reaching across the table to tap his hand with her straw. "We're such troublemakers."

He laughed and put his glasses on. "I can see getting into a little trouble with you."

Kate pretended surprise. "What could be riskier than this?"

"One day, if you're lucky, we'll figure that out. Or maybe it's if I'm lucky. You're so pretty, Kate." His expression was guileless and warm.

Kate flushed with pleasure and felt the last vestige of their easy childhood companionship float away. In its place was something more guarded and exciting. She felt a new twinge in her heart and slight nausea in her stomach. She also felt compelled to bolt out of there at a dead run. She looked at the clock, and the time decided for her.

"Yikes! My mother will be waiting. I've got about two minutes before she calls Carmen."

"Now that's a real risk." Gabe laughed. "At least, it is if we want more unchaperoned lunches. Off we go." They threw a wad of bills on the table and sped out the door.

"So, when are you back in town?" she asked when they reached the sidewalk. Usually, the families had plans to get together but Cara hadn't mentioned anything coming up.

"I'll be back in a few days, and then I'm around until the middle of August."

Kate frowned. "What's in the middle of August?" Her school didn't start until early September.

"Well, in the reclusive and nutty style of education my family adheres to, I'm going away for school this year. For the next two years, in fact."

Kate felt a crushing disappointment, which she suspected leaked through her voice when she responded, "Why? When did you decide to do that, and where are you going?"

He blushed and dug at a crack in the cement with his toe. "It's certainly not my decision, and it's kind of, well, a boarding school. All the kids in my family go. I mean, all the guys go," he amended.

She felt numb. "Out of state, I assume?"

He glanced toward water. "East of here."

Kate wracked her brain to think of a land mass between here and Europe. "So, is your school located on the rocky outcropping at the far side of the bay, or are you off to England?"

Gabe worried another crack with his shoe. "I'd really rather not talk about it, Kate. Look, I'd better run. I'll catch up with you next week sometime." He gave her a quick hug and loped toward the beach.

Kate stared after him for several seconds, trying to understand her anxiousness and wondering what she was going to do about it. She sprinted to the library to avoid being late.

Kate drove home with her mother from Griffins Bay, her curiosity about the Blake party grossly impeding her ability to concentrate and make conversation. She bolted to the phone to call Maya as soon as they entered the house, attracting a suspicious stare from her mother.

"Maya, how'd you like to crash the Blake party with me?" Kate whispered into the receiver.

"Oooo, girl, I like how you think. I'll be right over."

When Maya knocked, Kate yelled to her mother they were going into town and would be back in an hour or so. She grabbed Maya's arm, hurrying her away from the house so they could talk.

"I had lunch with Gabe today, and there's something fishy going on at the Blakes' tonight. I want to spy on them." Maya furrowed her brow, perhaps, Kate thought, because she disapproved. "Do you think we shouldn't go?"

"No, it's not that. Yes, I want to go, I'm just trying to think of how we can both get away from our parents." After a moment she looked cautiously hopeful and proffered a solution. "How about if you tell your mother you're staying at my house, I tell mine I'm staying at your house, and then we meet at neither of our houses to drive to the Blakes'?"

It sounded like a workable plan. They stopped at the store for a juice before heading home. When it came time to part, they agreed to handle their parents individually and then meet at the drug store at seven. "I'll switch the porch light on if I can't swing it," she told Maya.

"And I'll give you a call if I can't. Just call me, for crying out loud. This isn't a James Bond movie."

"Right. Okay. I'll call if I can't come."

The ruse worked, and Maya was at the rendezvous just as Kate arrived. Maya had use of a car and had told her folks she wanted it to drive down to see a new litter of puppies at a classmate's house outside of town. She and Maya killed a couple of hours at the municipal park, loaded into Maya's car, and then the game was on.

Kate's initial worries about sneaking up unnoticed on the Blake house were unfounded. Scads of people and their cars – easily three dozen – gave them cover as they approached. It was dark out too, so she and Maya blended seamlessly with the incoming crowd. When they got near enough, they ducked back toward the beach and hid in the bushes surrounding the fence by the pool. Kate was gratified they would have a perfect view of the action.

What she saw was fascinating. Just breathing gave her an adrenaline rush. She and Maya giggled with the intoxication they felt, as well as at avid manner in which the party guests checked each other out. Excitement crackled in the air like electricity.

Gabe's cousins milled around the grounds, pausing to flirt with the women they came across – or more aptly, hunted down. All of them executed a comical sequence of activities once they'd engaged a girl in conversation, which they all did without difficulty. The progression was almost identical to what she'd experienced with Hoke earlier that day.

She watched several misfires take place where a woman would start to talk with whichever man cornered her; he would remove his glasses, look into her eyes, and smile. Then he took her hand exactly as Hoke had Kate's, holding it near his chest while placing his other hand around her wrist. Often, the girl became unnerved and backed away toward her friends. The guy would grin sheepishly, and his cousins would murmur, "Loser," or, "Denied!" or, "Man down."

As the evening wore on, these interactions became more purposeful. Around ten o'clock, Maya's sister, Solange, entered the fray. She was stunning; a vital presence as she crossed the yard to check in with Michael and Carmen. All of the men noticed her, and her eyes narrowed in quick acknowledgement of their romantic intentions. She ignored them until she'd greeted her hosts.

Luke Hokeman got to her first after Carmen and Michael moved away, and his approach was much less playful than it had been with the women before her. He did not reach for her hand right away, keeping an intimate but respectful distance as they talked. His formerly flirtatious manner was now focused and serious.

They spoke for about a half hour, Solange never once looking away, even when she was approached by two other hopefuls. "Get lost," she told them without shifting her attention from Luke. "We're talking."

Maya and Kate acknowledged something significant was taking place but they could not completely hear Luke and Solange's conversation. "This is a thousand times more interesting than anything you and I could have dreamed up doing," Maya whispered. Kate agreed.

After another ten minutes, Solange flattened her hand against Luke's chest, their gazes on each other intense and unwavering. And, as he had before with Kate, Luke clasped Solange's hand in one of his and circled her wrist with his other hand. His eyelids drifted to a close and he started to bend toward her, as if to kiss her. Solange withdrew a couple of inches and discreetly shook her head. Then, twining his fingers with hers, she led him away.

At this point, Kate and Maya were startled by someone behind them. "Gotch-ya!" Gabe smirked as he wound an arm around each of the girls' waists. They both stifled screams.

"What the hell are you doing here?" Kate snapped, scowling to hide her embarrassment at being discovered.

"I had the feeling you'd show up, and I didn't want you getting sucked into this gig. You'll thank me someday."

"Yeah, well, my sister Solange was definitely just *sucked into this gig* and disappeared with some guy," Maya commented. "Should I be worried?"

Gabe grinned. "Is she heterosexual and of age?"

Maya's eyes widened. "She's twenty-one and as far as I know, likes guys. She sure seemed to like the one she left with."

"Then don't worry about it. And you two really need to get out of here. Let's go." He started to pull them away. "Uh-oh." All three of them ducked into the bushes when they saw his mother coming out of the house with a phone to her ear.

Carmen ambled to the end of the yard near their hiding spot, a concerned look on her face as she talked into her cell. "No, Cara, *please* don't come over. I really haven't seen them . . ." She looked blankly at the phone, swore, and then looked up. "Maya? Kate?" she called in the darkness. The kids froze. Carmen paced away from them, dialing another number.

"John? Ugh! I hate to bother you but we think Cara's daughter and a friend snuck over tonight. I mean, we're not sure the kids are here but they're not where they said they'd be either, and I think Cara and Alicia are on their way over." She paused to listen to a response. "I know, I know. I just thought I should give you a call and tell you. I mean, tonight of all nights!" Another pause. "Okay, then. We'll see you in a bit."

Kate stiffened with fear. Her mother was coming? Maya's parents too? She didn't know whether to run or hide or give herself up. Maya let out a low moan. "I'm in so much trouble. I should just go and throw myself into the ocean right now." They all stayed crouched where they were, frozen with indecision.

Michael Blake surprised them from their contemplations. "All right. Inside, you three." He stood behind them, glaring. Gabe swore under his breath, rose, tucked his hands in his pockets and hung his head. He passed his dad while carefully avoiding eye contact. Maya and Kate were slower but they also kept their heads down.

Michael didn't wait to get in the house to start upbraiding them. "I'd better not hear you all planned this little stunt together. You of all people should know better, Gabe."

Gabe sputtered. "Of course not, Dad. I had lunch with Kate today, and when she mentioned she'd heard about our party from Solange Wilkes, I had a hunch she might sneak over. I turned around when I was halfway to Anna's."

Michael seemed slightly mollified. "Well, that's better than it could be, I guess. But you know the risks of having uninvited guests to this kind of thing, Gabe. It wasn't your place to intervene. You should have told your mother or me."

"I wasn't sure she'd be here!"

Kate shot Gabe a dirty look. The traitor. He glared back at her. "What?" he grated. "I told you this afternoon it wasn't safe for you to come."

On this, Michael took Gabe's side, something Kate did not much appreciate. "You girls have no idea how much trouble you could have caused. You had *no business* coming here tonight."

By the time they entered the house, Kate heard Carmen letting Cara and Alicia in the front door. Michael excused himself saying he needed to get back to his guests. Maya groaned when she heard her mother. "I'll be grounded 'til I'm thirty."

"You got that right." Alicia came in, her eyes blazing, with Cara two steps behind her. "You violated a trust you will not enjoy again anytime soon, young lady. Let's go." Alicia gripped Maya's arm and ushered her away.

Kate's mouth fell open when John Blake entered the room from the back of the house. She hadn't seen him since that night on the beach almost two years ago. Cara also stood rooted to the floor.

"Um . . ." He stalled as he saw her. He ran his hand through his hair, which, strangely, was dripping wet. "Carmen called to warn me you were coming by, and I was in the area . . ."

Cara stood unmoving from her position by the entryway. Carmen looked from her to John and back as if making a vital decision. "Cara, I'll talk to Kate and Gabe, if you don't mind." To Kate's complete astonishment, Cara didn't even spare her a glance as she and John considered each other.

"Sure."

John started to cross the room.

Carmen propelled Gabe and Kate down the hall. "Into my office, boys and girls." Gabe watched Kate with a worried expression, which she noted only briefly in order to see what was going on with her mother. John closed the distance between them and reached for Cara's hand, his other hand circling her wrist in a way that was now familiar to Kate. Almost immediately, he dropped Cara's hand, wrapped one arm around her waist, and bent to kiss her. Her mother tilted her face, closed her eyes, and raised herself on her toes to meet him. This was the last thing Kate saw before Carmen shut her office door.

Carmen closed the door behind them and leaned against it with a sigh. "Kate, I know I should be mad at you but I'm so glad you're okay, I'm not. And if everything goes well out there tonight with your mother, I'll actually be grateful to you." She turned to her son. "I'm proud of you for checking on your friends, honey. You did the right thing by coming back, so I'm not mad at you either.

She went to the closet. "We're going to be in here for a while, so I'm breaking out the Scrabble board. After we're done with that, I'm setting Kate up in one of the guest rooms to stay the night."

"But . . ." Kate started to protest before Carmen cut her off.

"No buts, no excuses, no questions, and no other options. Pick out your tiles," she ordered.

CHAPTER SEVEN

They were all were grounded, of course. Kate learned Jeremy had driven by her house late in the evening and noticed Maya's car missing. When he called to see if the girls had made it back, her ruse with Maya fell right apart. Cara had apparently become so worried she threatened to call for a police search, until Jeremy remembered Solange's comment about the Blake party. He had a hunch they'd sneaked out, and he convinced Cara to call Carmen before calling nine-one-one.

Maya's parents were the most upset over the evasion, so she received the harshest punishment. Technically, all three were under house arrest for two weeks; although Gabe and Kate were pretty much free after three days. Maya was truly grounded during that time – no calls, no privileges, no going out. In addition, she lost use of the car for one whole month.

Gabe regretted the incident but Maya and Kate did not. "What I regret is I didn't have a better plan to avoid my parents finding out," Maya lamented. "I wouldn't have missed that for the world. Plus, it helped me understand what's going on with Solange."

Kate agreed. "That whole thing was fascinating, Gabe. I didn't know your relatives could be so fun."

Maya and Kate began calling the party *the Blake orgy*. Gabe winced at the moniker but did not challenge it. And while Kate didn't witness anything that actually spelled out what happened with the couples they watched that night, the proof was definitely *in the pudding*, as Maya put it. According to her, Solange left a message with her parents the following morning on how she'd decided to take a trip with a friend. She said she'd be out of touch all week and then disappeared. Alicia and Jeremy hadn't been able to reach her.

Kate was at Maya's house when Solange came home a week later. She arrived with Luke Hokeman in tow and no explanation for her sudden departure or for her change in plans to finish college, news she announced too casually at the dinner table that night. "I'm staying with Luke, and I'm not going back to school." She continued to cut primly into her steak, ignoring her parents shocked gasps.

Kate felt she shouldn't be party to this exchange, although, for all the attention she received in the wake of the bomb Solange just dropped, she might as well have been invisible. Still, she attempted a discreet rise from her chair with the intention of departing. Maya clasped her hand under the table and tugged her back into her seat. "Stay with me," she pleaded in a low voice. Kate sat down quietly and tried to make herself unobtrusive.

After a few seconds of recovery, Alicia and Jeremy's shock became anger. "That is not up for negotiation, Solange," her father told her. "A degree is one of the only things you can get to ensure you'll have any earning potential, some stability, down the road. You've already studied ahead. You could take summer classes and finish early."

Luke appeared to endear himself greatly to Solange's family when he supported them. "They're right, Solange. I'll find a job in Boston by your school. I think you should finish, get your degree." After a long pause, she said she'd consider it.

Alicia still squirmed, however, and given her artless efforts to capture Solange's attention during dinner, Kate surmised she wanted a private conversation, one Solange was unwilling to provide.

By dessert, Alicia was done with diplomacy. She came back from the kitchen carrying plates of cake, one of which she placed in front of Solange before gripping her shoulder. "Since you won't speak with me alone, I guess we'll do this here. I think I have a pretty good idea as to what's going on but I'd like to hear it from you. Am I right in understanding you met this young man eight days ago?"

Solange smiled kindly but with condescension. "I know how this must seem to you, Mom, but this is not just a fling, I promise. Luke's waiting to bring it up because it has been such a short time but we're getting married. I love him, he loves me, we're sure we want to be together. That's what's going on."

"Solange!" Alicia exclaimed. "What's your hurry? You're twenty-one years old and you've never been on your own. Why not wait a couple of years?"

"Mother, what for?" Solange replied gently, but with steel in her voice. "If you're worried I'm not my own person yet, that I need more independence, you haven't been paying attention." Alicia didn't say anything, although her expression spoke volumes.

Solange softened. "Listen, I know this because you taught it to me: I am a strong, smart, capable woman. Just like you. I know what I'm doing, and I know this is right."

After several tense moments, Alicia relaxed her shoulders and her mouth stretched in a sad smile. "I don't suppose I'll overcome your romantic ideals *and* inborn tenacity," she allowed. "Tenacity I probably passed on." She smoothed Solange's bangs from her forehead, the gesture tentative and bittersweet. "I guess we should shop for wedding dresses." Solange squealed with delight as she stood from her seat and wrapped her mother in an embrace. "Thank you," she whispered. "I couldn't do this without you."

When they released each other, Alicia faced Luke, who stood awkwardly from his chair. Alicia went to him and put her arms around his waist. "Welcome to the family, son. You do right by our girl, you hear?"

Luke hugged her back. "I'll do my best," he promised humbly.

Whatever John Blake's business commitments had been prior to the party, Kate noticed they no longer kept him away after it. His presence was now all but constant at the Sweeting home; he left during the day to tend to his business, returned for dinner, and stayed into the evening each night. By the end of the month, he had purchased a small building in Griffins Bay, which he began to renovate into an eye clinic.

Kate had never seen her mother so happy. Over the next several weeks, Cara blossomed while she watched, her features becoming more vibrant, her figure softer, her eyes more lively. Kate loved how her mother's face literally shone with pleasure these days.

And she felt livelier too, somewhat to her surprise. She had no memories of her father living with them, and she thought they'd been perfectly happy since moving to Childress. Consequently, John's presence filled a hole she hadn't known was there, with an energy that made their previous existence seem too quiet and dull by contrast. She felt as if they had gone from living in black-and-white to living in color.

She realized she could have felt more conflicted about the changes taking place at home, but when she tried to consider the loss of time with her mother and John's abrupt entry into their family life, her attempts at pessimism seemed hollow and kind of silly. Mostly, this was due to John's caring attention to her as well as her mother. His affection never came off as contrived or obligatory. He was easy to talk with, fun to be around, and so intelligent and thoughtful she couldn't *not* like him.

Another reason for her quick acceptance of the situation was the extent to which Cara and John made long-term plans. John demonstrated via words and deeds he meant to stay by them, no question. He and her mother talked openly about getting married as soon as possible but did not want to detract attention from Luke and Solange's wedding in August, selecting a date in late September instead for a much smaller affair. And it wasn't a conversation about just the two of them, but about Kate too. Somehow, she was an integral part of the happy life they were creating. Kate didn't doubt her place in the new order of her world.

Of the twenty or so couples Kate had watched milling around the night of the Blake party, including Cara and John and Luke and Solange, all were engaged or already married by the time of Solange's wedding. This, of course, led to speculation as to whether or not any of the women were pregnant.

Gabe appeared uncomfortable and as if he knew more than he was letting on. "Probably."

"Wow. It really was an orgy," Maya teased. Kate giggled.

"No, it wasn't," Gabe insisted. "An orgy means everyone had

indiscriminate sex. These couples are monogamous and... it's not the same thing at all." But while he continued to defend the event, he didn't appear comfortable with his family's role in it either. Curious about what he wasn't admitting, Kate made a few additional inquiries but he did not explain.

The rest of the summer revolved around social events surrounding Solange and Luke's upcoming wedding. John, Cara, and Kate also started functioning as a family, running errands together and for each other, going to movies, playing board games, and taking strolls around the neighborhood. They also spent time working on John's clinic to get it ready to open in August, an activity that gave Kate an unexpected sense of belonging.

On the wedding front, Cara held a shower for Solange for which Kate cooked, and they attended two others. Maya and Kate were both recruited to be bridesmaids, which meant dress shopping, fittings, and a couple of trips to the salon to try out hairstyles. All the girls were required to take dance lessons, which Maya and Kate did scornfully and with purely comic intent. Sylvia studied cake decorating – like someone possessed – In order to produce a perfect representation of the cake Solange wanted at her reception.

"I know roses are traditional but I want marigolds. The color is so rich, and they match the time of year better, I think."

"I'm on it." Sylvia acted as if she'd been entrusted with a mission to save the planet.

Kate saw Gabe frequently that summer, but they were always surrounded by friends and family now. Following their conversation at the Bait Shop, she was never quite at ease around him again, always a little nervous when she talked with him and overly anxious to know what he thought of her. Thankful her flightiness was diluted by the presence of others, part of her still yearned for a chance to be alone with him, so she could further explore the new feelings that had emerged during their lunch.

She was surprised and happy to learn Gabe would be in the wedding as well. Surprised because she'd never heard him mention Luke Hokeman in all the years prior to the day Kate had met him, so she didn't think they could be close. But she didn't really care; she secretly relished the idea of being with Gabe at the reception, her in a formal dress with her hair done up. She wondered if he would think she looked pretty. She had no doubt he would be handsome in a tuxedo.

One week before the wedding and two weeks before the opening of the clinic, John planned a long weekend for all of them in New York. "Things have been hectic this summer, and they're going to get worse when the clinic opens, so I think we should sneak away."

They had a wonderful time. Times Square exploded with energy and activity, really not something one could understand without seeing; and Central Park was its own oasis in what was an inconceivably huge city to Kate's mind. They ate out lavishly every night, got tickets to a Broadway show, and ordered decadent breakfasts from room service each morning. John had reserved a room for Cara and Kate and one for himself but they usually ended up all together, talking and eventually falling asleep on top of the covers or on the couch, dressed in whatever clothes they'd worn to dinner.

On the last night, John treated them to dinner at a restaurant within walking distance from the hotel. She and her mother both wore new outfits they'd purchased at a ridiculously expensive boutique earlier that day; Kate wasn't able to consider the cost of what she wore without remorse but delighted in the results the clothes gave both her and her mother. John was dashing in a suit and tie. She and her mom held hands on the way, giggling at Kate's assessment, "I feel like we're living someone else's charmed life."

The meal itself was incomparable, each bite pure bliss. After four exquisite courses, the three of them rested before dessert, and John ordered a bottle of champagne for the table. When it was served, they snuck a little into an empty water glass for Kate so they could all toast.

John raised his glass first. "To the two most beautiful women I know."

"To good health and good fortune for my loved ones." Cara raised her own glass.

Kate hesitated to find the right words. "To being a family." Her mother's eyes teared as they all sipped their champagne.

John rose from his chair and reached into his jacket pockets, drawing out two small boxes. He came around the side of the table, knelt between her and her mother, and cleared his throat ceremoniously. "I have something for each of you." He handed Kate one of the boxes. "Kate, you should go first."

She opened it carefully. Inside was an engraved locket with the initials *CLB*. She guessed at the meaning of the first two initials. "Catherine Lucille... ?"

"This is a bit of a risk, I know, but I very much want us to be a family in every way, Kate. The *B* stands for Blake." John swallowed. "I'd like to formally adopt you. It's a symbolic effort, of course, where we would all have the same last name, but there are some practical considerations too, concerning benefits and estate planning and things like that. It will be easier for me if you're legally my daughter.

"But if you are at all uncomfortable or feel it would be disrespectful to George, I'll understand." His voice softened. "I'll always think of you as a daughter, though. There's not much you can do about that."

Her mother clasped John's hand to her cheek, closing her eyes. Kate was too moved to speak at first. She eventually realized Cara and John both waited for her to say something and she hurried to keep them from further suspense. Her voice was strained with emotion when she answered.

"I feel so special. This is such a wonderful thing for you to do, John. It would never have occurred to me, an adoption, but now that you've asked, I can't think of anything better. I'd love for us to be a family in all ways."

"Whew!" John laughed. "I'm so glad! Thank you for accepting this. Me, my offer, for making everything good even better." John knelt by her mom. "This one's for you, Cara."

Her mother stared tearfully in his eyes for several seconds before opening her box, which held an anniversary ring set in platinum, along with a platinum band. "We've been talking about it for weeks now but I should have had a ring right away . . ." John's voice was low, his expression intense and kind as he watched her.

Cara wrapped her arms around his neck to kiss him, and offered a brilliant smile when she drew back. "You did this perfectly, John. Thank you. Thank you, so much."

CHAPTER EIGHT

According to the RSVP count, the Wilkes house would be bursting at the seams with relatives for Luke and Solange's wedding. Oddly, but in keeping with what Kate saw as covert-as-usual, Blake-like behavior, she watched Carmen decline hospitality to any guests from Solange's side despite Alicia's respectful inquiry. Kate, Alicia, and Carmen were working in the library garden when Alicia first approached the subject. She was as surprised as Alicia was by Carmen's refusal.

"I'm sorry, Alicia. We'd love to help, really, but we're getting a whole entourage, about twenty people coming, and they're basically taking over the house. I'm honestly trying to figure out where my little family is going to sleep." Carmen closed her eyes as if she regretted either the situation or that she'd revealed any details surrounding it. Kate tried to imagine what kind of guests would come into someone's home and displace the family. And she wondered why Carmen and Michael would ever agree to such an arrangement but she didn't have the courage to pry.

Alicia responded graciously. "Not to worry. We'll figure it out." Carmen and Michael continued to apologize thereafter but neither

58

explained why a group of strangers had the ability to occupy their very large house to the exclusion of close, long-time friends.

When Cara drove her to the Blakes' two days before the wedding, Kate's confusion became complete. Black-suited men and women, wearing security gear and headsets, toured the property and inspected the house for unknown reasons, eying everyone who approached with suspicion.

One of them stepped in front of her and her mother before they reached the steps to the porch. "Are you friends of the Blakes?"

"We are," Cara replied irritably. "Who are you?"

"Security, ma'am. I'll escort you in."

"Um, Carmen? Why do you have security guards crawling all over your house?" Kate asked as Carmen led them inside.

"Don't be silly. They're exterminators. We're having a problem with termites." She addressed her mother. "And you didn't need to make a special trip *with Kate* today. I could have sent John's tux over."

Cara sniffed. "We were in the area. Let this be a lesson to you, Kate. Never put off yard work or you'll get termites nesting under your house. And then you'll get rodents after that, of course."

Carmen squeezed her eyes shut and shook her head. "Such good advice. I could come up with some advice of my own for your mother." She handed Cara a garment bag and propelled them toward the front door. "See you Saturday," she said sourly.

As they left with John's tux, Kate remarked none of the vehicles – luxury, black, mostly sedans – parked around the house sported exterminator signage, or any other kind of signage, for that matter. "They're very high-end exterminators," Cara explained, quickly changing the subject to what she called the *daily dinner dilemma*.

The wedding day began in a frenzy because the female half of the wedding party overslept. The families also had relatives in town from hither and yon who needed to be shuttled about or entertained; several from the Wilkes side stayed at Kate's house, meaning Kate had spent the night at Maya's to free up her bedroom. She'd stayed up late talking with the Wilkes girls too, so they all awoke groggy.

"We don't need to be awake to be groomed, do we?" Kate inquired hopefully. Maya shoved her away and told her to hop to.

To add to Kate's nerves and excitement over the event, she learned the night of the rehearsal dinner she and Gabe were paired for the processional. They flashed each other huge grins when they heard this news. Gabe leaned down to whisper in her ear, "I'm so relieved! I thought they were going to send me down with Kathleen and a barf bag."

Kate knew Kathleen as one of the women from the now-infamous Blake party and an early participant in the marriage mania that ensued. She'd married one of the Blake cousins in a civil ceremony in July, was admittedly pregnant, and struggled with violent fits of nausea. Solange had already told her to sit out if she didn't feel up for the whole bridesmaid thing, practically begging her not to vomit during her wedding. But Kathleen insisted she could make it through. Kate doubted it.

Breakfast alleviated the last of Kate's sleepiness, with eye-popping portions too big to fit on the large plate Jeremy handed her through the door. Kate ogled the pie-size blueberry muffin, precariously balanced on too many scrambled eggs before complaining. "Holy cats. This is more than I can eat in one whole day. Are they expecting us to fell timber before the ceremony?"

Maya broke off part of the muffin before shuffling into her closet. "It's a tradition at weddings among the guys in our family, which is actually kinda helpful with this many people to feed." She inclined her head toward the stairs. "They have a great time trying to outdo each other. Listen." Kate heard the men's loud, raucous voices and booming laughs coming from the kitchen.

"Good for them. As long as they don't expect me to actually eat all this."

She spent the rest of the morning and early afternoon at the salon getting herself and everyone into their dresses and then at the church for photographs. The bride and groom had opted to wait for joint photos after the ceremony but photos with just Solange and her bridesmaids were taken early. One picture, which Kate came to treasure, was of just her and Maya, cheek to cheek with their arms around each other, both smiling hugely.

When the bridesmaids and groomsmen gathered at the back of the church, Kate stood beside Gabe at their spot in the line-up. "You look really handsome," she told him shyly. And he really did, his tuxedo accentuating his lean, athletic form, his wavy hair shining and perfect. He started to comment but just then, several of Carmen's *exterminators* appeared, quietly demanding they step aside for a few final guests to be seated. Without waiting for a response, they presented their backs to the wedding party, providing the newcomers with a guarded aisle into the church.

Kate was astonished. Who would dare come in this fashion, seconds before the wedding march began and comfortable making the bridal party wait while they found their pew? Gabe placed his hands on her shoulders and guided her from the doorway. At Gabe's touch, Kate felt a familiar contentment overtake her and instead of considering the etiquette of the situation, thought instead on the pleasure of Gabe's nearness.

Her enjoyment stalled when a regal couple and their entourage appeared inside the church doors. They were very nearly a wedding party themselves, complete with a gown, tuxedo, and attendants of their own. Kate's gaze darted to Solange, expecting her to take offense but her expression reflected nothing but welcome. She could almost hear a gracious greeting as Solange nodded toward the latecomers.

She let out a small, bewildered huff, which brought the head of the male half of the couple around sharply in her direction. She was momentarily stunned by the man's sudden, intense focus on her, a sensation that deepened as his attention persisted. She didn't think to worry or turn away, and her regard back at him was open, curious. She was dimly aware of a harsh intake of breath from Gabe behind her. She ignored it and allowed herself to be absorbed in the stare of the man facing her.

Within seconds, the periphery of her vision softened, darkened, and then imploded until she saw only the eyes of the gentleman drinking her in. She was aware of his clinical, meticulous perusal of her and very briefly felt his intense curiosity, but unlike any other interaction she'd ever had, she intuited nothing from him. Not warmth, anger, happiness, or feeling of any kind. Odd.

Almost as quickly as it had begun, the episode was over and the man pivoted toward the sanctuary, the gowned woman on his arm. His face was blandly serene, betraying nothing of the scorching evaluation to which he had just subjected her.

Kate felt like she was coming out of a trance, her first conscious sensation that of Gabe standing by her, watchful. He grasped her forearms and searched her eyes. *Are you all right?* His expression was wary.

Did he say that out loud? He must have. "I'm fine. I think." She summoned enough energy to hide her confusion. "Who are they?"

"Sort of… well, diplomats. Peter and Kenna Loughlin."

"Royalty?" she guessed.

Gabe was astonished. "Yes. Yes, in fact."

"That was his wife?" she pressed.

"His mother," he clarified. He focused on her intensely then, the effect calming, although, since she did not lose herself this time, it was a weak reflection of the experience she'd just had. And of course, instead of the nothingness she'd felt from Peter Loughlin, she was flooded with a sense of Gabe. Then, as he held both of her hands in his, her curiosity evaporated as she felt the righting of her reality. Here was Gabe, boyish and charming and warm, just as he'd always been; and they were there to stand up for Luke and Solange at their wedding. She smiled at him.

He smiled back. "We're on." He tucked Kate's hand in the crook of his arm, holding it there with his other hand. "Keep breathing," he reminded her, "and don't lock your knees, okay?"

"I'm all over it," she promised. They started down the aisle.

When they were stationed at the altar, everyone's attention returned fully to the wedding at hand. Solange appeared at the back of the church with Jeremy, her hair an intricate masterpiece of braids, her dress perfectly hugging her graceful figure, her face radiant with joy. Luke's eyes blazed with emotion as she proceeded. Once at the front, bride and groom seemed to forget about the crowd gathered around them, their eyes only on each other, small smiles playing at the corners of their mouths.

As Kate watched them, she felt their shared feelings of insulation; how they weren't listening to the words the pastor spoke over them. How sweet she found them, and how surprising they could make such a public moment private. Once, during the vows, she scanned the pews to find the two who had made their disturbing, last-minute entrance. Peter's gaze burned at her for a fraction of a second before fading into inexpressiveness, so quickly she wasn't sure he'd been watching her. She shifted her attention back to Luke and Solange, resolved to keep her focus where it should be from then on.

When the ceremony was finished, everyone transitioned to the reception hall for the dinner and dance. After the first dance featuring the wedding couple, and the second dance featuring the parents, the wedding party took the floor.

Other than the two occasions Kate had now walked with her arm in Gabe's, this dance was the only traditional couple-like activity she'd done with him. She noticed the strength in his hands and shoulders, and how the air between them radiated with warmth. He'd grown so tall, she had to tilt her head up to see his face. He smiled down at her, and she felt dizzy.

"You're delicious. I could eat you."

"You'd have to like hairspray, then." Kate wanted to make light of his comment, although it gave her a thrill. "I think we were each required to use two gallons . . ."

Gabe laughed. "That is one of the better things about being a guy. I got ready in twenty minutes. How long were you girls tied up?"

She shook her head sadly. "We had to be at the salon at nine, and they didn't set us free until after one. You should have seen all the equipment and goo required to pretty us up. The army should consult with Ruby's Hair Salon on how to whip our forces into shape." He chuckled.

"So, when do you leave for boarding school?"

He sighed. "You had to bring it up, didn't you?"

She rushed to reassure him. "No-no. We don't have to talk about it."

"Well, it's probably a good idea if we do. I leave on Monday, and they're pretty strict about getting calls and e-mails."

She was instantly upset. "Monday? As in, two-days-from-now Monday? And why can't you call or e-mail? I thought you called it a school, not a prison."

"Two-days-from-now Monday is when I leave, and I'm of the opinion the term *school* is promotional in nature. It sounds more like a prison to me too." His mouth drooped. "We can call and e-mail on Sundays."

They danced without speaking for a minute while Kate tried to accept what he was saying – in less than forty-eight hours, he would disappear so completely from her life; they wouldn't even be able to text. The music changed to something quicker paced, but they stayed in their waltz. "When do you come back?" she managed, her heart in her throat.

"The usual. Thanksgiving, Christmas, Easter, spring break."

She hesitated, feeling she risked revealing too much by asking, "Any chance I could come visit you?"

"Virtually none. It's all boys, and even if I could get you there somehow, which is unlikely, you'd have to pretend you're a guy. I don't think you could pull it off." His thumb stroked the small of her back.

She blushed with pleasure at his words, but the thought of his departure again made her desolate. "So this is it then, until Thanksgiving." She hoped she didn't sound as hysterical as she felt.

Gabe located his parents, who glanced their way from time to time; and then searched out Cara and John, who were doing the same. "I've got an idea. Do you see the clock on the wall to my right?" She pretended to casually scan around her until she saw the clock he'd indicated.

"Yes."

"We'll finish this dance," he continued quietly. "Then, I'll talk with my parents for a few minutes. You should find Maya or get yourself some punch. I'll tell my folks I'm leaving early so I can pack, and then I'm going to disappear. You hang around for another ten minutes; make sure they see you here without me. When it's safe, try and sneak out to the lower garden in back, okay?" She nodded.

"I'll be waiting for you."

His plan worked. She saw him excuse himself from his parents' company while she chatted with a couple of the Wilkes cousins. She waved to the Blakes and her parents. Providentially, the band played the beginning bars to a fast song, drawing a large, enthusiastic group onto the dance floor. Kate pretended excitement to blend in with them. Then, with the flashing lights and thick crowd, she escaped without notice.

She found Gabe by the pergola. "You made it!" he whispered and without pause, drew her into him. She wound her arms around his waist and rested her head against his chest while he reached down to guide her face up to his. Their gaze met briefly, a tenderness between them tapping a wellspring of happiness in Kate that flooded from her heart through her extremities. His kiss was sweet and gentle but evoked a powerful wave of emotion unhinging her from everything she'd previously thought important. Tears sprang to her eyes from the force of her feelings. Gabe leaned away to frown at them. "What's wrong?"

She smiled. "Absolutely nothing. That was just amazing, that's all." He brushed her tears away and placed his forehead against hers, closing his eyes.

"This is probably not the best idea in the world but I don't care."

"Why is this not a good idea?" She thought this might be the best thing she'd ever done in her entire life.

"There's a bunch of stuff you don't know about me and my family, stuff I can't really tell you. And it affects you if we're together." His expression became brooding. "It's kind of a catch twenty-two. You should know more about me before you become involved with me but the things you should know are things I'm not allowed to tell you unless we're involved."

Kate considered this information before answering him. "Why don't you just tell me, Gabe? This should be obvious, but say whatever you need to say, I promise to keep it to myself, and then we can decide what to do from there."

Rather than answer, he bent to kiss her again. She felt intoxicated.

When their kiss ended, he pulled back. "Tempting, but I can't. It's not that simple."

Kate had forgotten what they were discussing and had to think before it came back to her. "It's as simple or as complicated as we decide to make it, Gabe." She put her hand tentatively up to his face.

He seemed to deliberate hard before responding. "Well, I'm going to tell you something. This," and he gestured between them, "is going to get more difficult for me as time goes on. That's one thing. If I come back to visit you next year and grab your wrist and start mooning over you, run away or be prepared to be stuck with me for the rest of your life."

"Next *year*?" Kate's heart sank. "I don't know what you're saying. And I actually would like an explanation of the wrist-holding thing. Why do you do it?"

Gabe held her hand to his chest, wrapped the fingers of his other hand around her wrist, and then bent to kiss her once more. He stopped when his lips were almost to hers and whispered, "I'm checking your pulse. Please don't ask me to explain." Then he closed the remaining distance between them, and Kate once again forgot their conversation

"This is going to sound weird but I'm hoping to put the rest of this conversation off for another two years. Can we do that?"

Her heart seized at the torture in his eyes and at the idea of putting this, whatever it was, off for two years, which seemed like an eternity. She told him the truth. "I want to be with you, and I don't want to wait two years." She felt pathetic and knew her laugh sounded weak. "Is that selfish?"

He sighed in frustration. "No, but it's not really possible, either. I actually am leaving for school, and I really won't be around."

Kate's shoulders sagged. "How about if we think of it in smaller chunks. You'll be home for Thanksgiving, right? And then a month later, for Christmas? Easter's a couple of months later... if we consider it that way, we're not talking about two years, which sounds like forever. We're just talking a month or two between visits, right?"

Gabe laughed softly. "Yes! We'll be like drug addicts kicking our habits! One day at a time!"

At that moment, she heard several people calling them. "Gabe? Kate?" Both sets of parents were searching for them. She and Gabe became perfectly still. Carmen scanned the garden from ten yards away and then drifted toward the front of the building.

Kate resigned herself to all of it – Gabe leaving, their more imminent separation because of their parents, and how she didn't and wouldn't know why she couldn't see him. "I guess you'd better get going, and I'd better get back." She attempted a smile... "One more kiss, please," and she perched on the balls of her feet.

"Yes." Gabe leaned down to meet her. The intensity of their kiss drowned out every other sight, sound, and thought as they pressed themselves to each other. The moment was airless, timeless, and as profound as anything Kate had ever experienced.

John's voice brought them up short. "Kate? Gabe?" he called from too close. They stilled and waited until they heard him leave.

Gabe was more still and silent than any human being she'd ever encountered. "*Sshhhh.*" And after a pause to let John get well away, said, "I'd better get out of here. Try to scoot back to the reception, and I'll call you tomorrow." He kissed her briefly once more, saying, "Ha! I snuck in another one." Then he was gone.

Even though she'd let him go, Kate felt bereft. Tears filled her eyes and her throat closed in an effort to stave them off. She was irrationally hopeful and profoundly disappointed at the same time. On one hand, she was thrilled she would see Gabe again and to know he cared for her. But she was devastated to think of the next two years without his companionship or any answers to the riddles he'd just posed. And what if he met someone at boarding school? She consoled herself with the reminder it was an all-boys' facility. As she wound her way around the building to the entrance, John and Cara found her.

"Kate! Where did you run to?" Her mother seemed far too concerned.

She knew she sounded defensive when she answered her. "I just came out for air."

John became suspicious, scrutinizing her face. "Did you run into Gabe on your way out?"

She didn't have the guile to lie well, so she told the truth. "I did see him as he was leaving. And I've been up since forever, and I just got a little hot and tired. It felt good to get away from all the noise and the crowd. We should get back to the reception, though." She hurried past them through the door.

John and Cara followed silently, and in Kate's opinion, flung silent accusations. She raced into the reception hall to avoid a full-on inquisition.

CHAPTER NINE

True to his word, Gabe called the day after the wedding but seemed to be under the watchful eye of one or both of his parents because they didn't talk long and Gabe's conversation seemed guarded. He promised to call or text *from time to time*. She told him to try and have fun and to hurry back. "I'll miss you," she settled on after a brief silence where she struggled to say something that didn't make her sound as needy as she felt.

His response was too light. "I'll miss you too, Kate. We'll get together at Thanksgiving, okay?" And that was the end of their talk.

She left later in the week for Philadelphia to stay with Will and Dana, grateful for the change in scenery and the distraction her camps and cooking obsession afforded her. She sent Gabe an e-mail about her classes and experiments in the kitchen. He responded they ran like slaves at his new school. He couldn't wait to try some of her concoctions personally.

I'm not supposed to write to you too much, Kate. If you don't hear from me, please know you are always in my thoughts.

XXXXXX!

Gabe

Kate was happy to be in his thoughts, because goodness, he was certainly in hers. And she was confused as to why he wasn't allowed to communicate with her. By whom? His parents loved her like a daughter, and Cara and John thought just as highly of Gabe. Why all the secrecy?

When she returned home from Philadelphia, she touched on the topic with her mother. Without revealing any details about her exchange with Gabe at the wedding, Kate told her about Gabe's e-mail. "Do you have any idea what he meant?"

"A little bit," Cara hedged. "I'm sure everyone would be very happy if you and Gabe end up together, Kate. We just want to make sure you both get through school first."

Kate was incredulous. "Am I the only one to notice tons of people date and do other things in life at the same time? Don't you and John date *and* each hold down jobs, for example?"

Her mother avoided her gaze. "Well, of course you're right." When she faced her again, her expression was apologetic but her tone was firm. "Honestly, you need to try and put it out of your mind for a while. There are very, very good reasons not to get involved right now."

More half-answers and mysteries. Kate threw up her hands and stomped out of the room.

As it turned out, she wasn't given any other option than to wait. Carmen called a few weeks later to report Gabe was spending Thanksgiving with a classmate, and they were going to Europe for Christmas as a family.

In addition, Cara and John had some very big news to share with her.

As discussed, they held a small wedding ceremony in September with the local justice of the peace at the courthouse. Kate had never seen her mother so radiant, and she'd been pretty radiant since John came into their lives. Immediately following the ceremony, they signed adoption papers, making the three legally, officially a family, and then Kate stayed at Maya's house while John and Cara took a short honeymoon. Afterward, Kate, Cara, and John resumed their habits of the previous three months, except John was there late nights and early mornings too. They'd somehow found time together outside of what Kate saw however, which she learned when they called her to the living room for a family meeting.

Cara began the conversation, and she was worried about something. "Here's the thing," she announced. "You're going to have a little brother or sister running around soon."

Kate clutched her excitedly. "Really?" Then she realized her mother and John had only been married a month. "When you say *pretty soon*, when do you mean, exactly? Don't people typically wait to announce these things until after the first trimester?"

"Yes, that's right. They do. And we are through the first trimester . . ." Her mother glanced at John.

"Cara is due in March, Kate," he stated. "We've known about this for a while but we waited to tell you because we wanted to involve ourselves, you in particular, so this transition wouldn't be a shock for you."

She counted the months in her head and thought back to the party at Carmen and Michael's house, wondering if that was the start of all of this and thinking it probably was. "That night at the Blake party . . ." she began, but then closed her eyes and extended her palms. "Wait. Forget I said that. It's none of my business, and I don't really want to know."

John stifled a laugh. Her mother settled her arm on Kate's shoulders. "This really is the last way I would want to announce this to you. But the night of the Blake party did set everything in motion. And I'm breaking all the parenting rules here by saying, *do as I say not as I do*, but this is exactly what we both are telling you now."

John took over, and while Kate avoided eye contact with him, she listened to what he had to say. "Unlike the rules of society at large, which many people seem to take or leave as they find convenient, my family's rules concerning love and marriage are iron clad. We can't explain that completely right now but perhaps you've already discussed this a little with Gabe?"

Kate blushed and held her tongue, unwilling to share anything she'd discussed with Gabe. But she remembered his comment about grabbing her wrist and being glued to her side for the rest of her life, and she felt she might burst with all the questions she couldn't voice.

John nodded, as if she had answered him. "With any luck, you'll understand completely in a few years." Kate grit her teeth, angry that everyone, including Gabe, had some timeline for informing her which spanned years. All the evasions had become annoying.

Cara noticed. "I'm sure this is frustrating for you, honey, but it's all being done to protect you. Our point, other than to let you know I'm pregnant, is to tell you not to assume by what you've seen this summer it's okay to become physically involved with someone you're not committed to."

Kate stared at her, unable to withhold her skepticism. "Do as you say, not as you — and every couple present apparently — did that night of the Blake party? Is this what you're saying?"

John answered again. "I just told you we do things a little differently in my family, and I'd like to point out every couple who was there that night is now married. No one, and I mean no one, was… what do you kids call it? Hooking up."

Kate didn't give in to the urge to laugh but neither did she argue.

"How to put this the right way?" John mused. "You are simply not allowed to share yourself with anyone unless you are in a committed relationship. I'm pulling out all my newly minted parental credentials to lay down this law, but for your mother and me, this is important." Kate was mortified but appreciated his sincerity.

"Please remember too my dating behavior from the time your father died to the time John and I met," her mom reminded her. She'd lived like a nun, as Kate well knew.

But she felt she was behaving like a petulant child, which she didn't care for. "Listen, I'm excited we're going to have a baby in the house. And all of your words ring true. I'm more irritated by the secrecy surrounding your family's romantic habits, John. No one, including Gabe, will explain anything to me, and I don't like it." She dropped her gaze then, disappointed she'd referenced her discussion with Gabe on the subject.

John softened. "Can you understand this is about what we have to do, not what we want to do?"

"No. I don't understand." Then she sighed. "But I guess I'll go along with it. Because I don't seem to have a choice."

Her mother stroked her hair. "Not this time, honey."

CHAPTER TEN

Kate was unsurprised to discover all of the women in the couples who counted the Blake party as their beginning – including Solange – were expecting. True to his word, Luke followed Solange to Boston College where he hired on as a teaching assistant. In order to finish her degree before she had her baby, Solange carried extra credits that would allow her to graduate in December. From all reports by her family, she was exhausted but getting through school.

Meanwhile, Kate helped John and her mother prepare for their own addition to the family. Her mom found out she was having a boy, although their plans for decorating the nursery were set before the ultrasound. She and John wanted to make the room into a fish bowl, as far as Kate could tell, which meant undersea-themed wallpaper depicting schools of colorful fish and equally brilliant corals and anemones. She and her mother papered the walls and ceiling, even painted the floor blue. Despite her initial ambivalence, Kate found the effect magical, as if she started floating whenever she entered the room. John assembled a crib, matching dresser, and bookshelf. They added a rocking chair, and deemed themselves ready.

Dana and Will came for Thanksgiving, ostensibly to share the holiday with them but more obviously, Kate thought, so Dana could counsel Cara on how to run her life after the baby came. Her mother did her best to defuse Dana's more strident efforts, and to protect the lazy, chill vibe everyone else enjoyed. But eventually she was blunt and stated, yes, she planned to take three months off, and, yes, she was keeping her job, and could Dana maybe accept, for once, her life was her own business? Her pointed look Kate's way was a dismissal Kate chose to ignore. She'd never seen her aunt and mother argue in front of her and the performance was too interesting.

Awkward silence ensued, until a big play in the day's football game drew everyone toward the television. As the tension deflated in the kitchen, Cara moved her cutting board by Dana's.
Her aunt stopped chopping briefly to acknowledge her mother's arrival before resuming her task. "I don't mean to be difficult," Dana lamented quietly. Cara put her arms around her.

"You're just concerned for me, and I know that. But you don't need to worry about me so much, okay? I can take care of myself, Dana."

The sisters let silence accomplish the last of their reconciliation, which Kate had seen before. She knew the fight was over when she saw them laughing together over some private joke. Afterward, the day went on as if the outburst never happened.

Later that night, unable to sleep, Kate crept down to the kitchen for a drink of water. Dana sat at the table doing a crossword puzzle. "You can't sleep either?" she asked her aunt.

Dana leaned back in her chair. "Have a seat and talk a minute," she invited. Kate seated herself and grabbed a section of the paper. "That was quite a conversation we had today before dinner. What did you think of it?"

"I think you and my mother have strong opinions about your work and home lives."

Dana snorted. "You got *that* right. But how do you feel about all of this, your mom getting married and having another baby?"

"Truthfully, I'm happy, Dana. I really like John. And perhaps more importantly, I trust him. He's just this salt-of-the-earth, solid person. And my mom's so happy — it's great to see her fulfilled for once. I was worried about leaving her alone after graduation, and now she has someone. I'm relieved."

"Hmm. Maybe. Have you thought about where you want to go to college? And not that you need to know yet, but have you thought about what you'd like to study?"

"I've applied to a couple of schools and won't hear back until later in the year. Why?"

"Because if you're generally in the area — as in East Coast-ish, I could maybe help. You know, nose around for an internship, or summer job, if you want. What are you interested in?"

Kate studied her hands, not sure she wanted to talk about her post-high school dreams yet. "I haven't discussed this with anyone. I'm thinking about a degree in Journalism. I know it's hard to break into but I'd love to be a food writer."

Dana nodded approvingly. "I think you'd be good at it. I happen to have contacts at a couple of magazines too. I could try and get you in the door with one of them if you like?"

Kate was instantly excited. "Would you? That would be so great, Dana! I'd really appreciate it."

"I won't make any promises but I'll see what I can do. Let me hunt around." Her expression became cautionary. "Your first job will probably be slave-like in nature. You know that, don't you?"

"Of course! It doesn't matter!" Kate gushed. "I'll file papers, sweep the floors, whatever it takes!"

"Okay. I'll see what I can figure out."

Although Kate wasn't hearing much from Gabe, she did hear from his mother. As the time for the baby to arrive drew near, she had the impression Carmen and Cara had discussed ways to keep her occupied during those first few months, maybe protect her from feeling neglected.

"Your mother and I have hatched a plan I want to talk with you about," Carmen announced during a phone conversation one day.

Her suspicions were confirmed. "Mm-hmm. Let's hear it."

"Great. You've been accepted at Sommerset University, right?" Kate told her yes, that's where she was planning to go. "Well, how about if Michael and I help you take care of a few of your general credits before you get there?"

Kate was interested. She was already enrolled in advanced placement courses for college credit through the high school, which Carmen knew, so she was curious as to what she was thinking. "How would that work?"

"Basically, we can augment the credits you're taking through the school with a couple of extras." She seemed to be reading from a list of requirements as she paused. "Michael could cover your core science requirement with a biology study. And between the two of us, we can take care of your fine arts, phys-ed, and possibly your history, too . . ."

For no clear reason she could articulate, Kate was interested in having as many credits under her belt as she could before entering college formally. But she was also worried about being able to complete the coursework Carmen described in addition to the academic load she already had, and she shared her concern with Carmen. "Do you think it's feasible? Will the college even let me?"

"I do think it's feasible. Not easy, and I think you'll have to drop all – and I do mean *all* – of your extra-curricular activities, not just the ones at school. But you've done really well, and Sommerset's a small, private school willing to make unique study programs for its students."

Kate hesitated. She could be talked into giving up drama club but gardening, reading, and cooking? Those, she would miss.

"Let's make up a schedule," Carmen proposed. "We'll map out the courses Michael and I would teach you and see the actual time everything will take."

"That makes sense."

The next day after classes, Kate brought a new notebook and three-ring binder over to Carmen and Michael's. They ushered her to the kitchen table and sat down to tackle her scheduling assignment.

"It's helpful you already know what you want to study, Kate," Michael told her. "I called the university for a list of the course and credit requirements to complete a Journalism major. I also contacted an academic advisor for you and discussed our plans with her." He slid a piece of paper across the table. "This is her contact information, as well as a list of professors you'll be working with."

"The college will charge for this but John and your mother will

75

cover tuition," Carmen added. "So, the only issue will be if you want to undertake these studies now."

Kate experienced a burgeoning sense of pride in herself – this kind of offer from Carmen and Michael felt like recognition – but she also felt overwhelmed. "You guys have put a lot of thought and effort into this already. I'm just not sure I can do it."

Carmen and Michael looked at one another as they always did when she was around, as if they had a secret they were keeping from her. "We're wondering if you won't appreciate the flexibility this advancement will give you," Michael eventually offered. "You could finish college early and... and end up with more choices."

Carmen placed a hand on her arm in encouragement. "Cara and I spoke with your high school teachers, and everyone's sure you're capable. But you will be busy." She showed Kate the schedule she'd outlined. It was very, very full but as they went through it, Kate saw it was viable. She really wouldn't have any free time, especially if she planned to help at all when the baby came. Carmen seemed to read her mind. "You'll still see that baby, honey. But you won't be responsible for him, which is probably for the best." Kate decided to take her at her word. And she agreed to the new, insanely busy program they'd proposed for her.

She wasn't as confident in herself as everyone around her seemed to be, but given the encouragement and financial support she received from her parents – and the very generous commitment of time and help from Carmen and Michael – she put forth her best effort. She was beyond busy, and her previously sparse social life became nonexistent. Maya was almost equally tied up with her studies and sports obligations, so Kate didn't feel responsible for them not getting together as much. Their primary interactions consisted of late-night and early morning texts, and they scarfed down lunch together every day in about ten minutes, but they almost never had any real time in each other's company.

In some ways, she was relieved. Her crazy schedule meant she had less time to brood and think about Gabe, and because she didn't see Maya like she used to, she didn't have to reveal her romantic interactions with him, which she was inexplicably unwilling to share.

Perhaps because they hadn't actually started a dating relationship, Kate didn't want to feel awkward if nothing came of it.

She also found comfort in the frenzied overtones of the few e-mails she received from Gabe. Wherever he was and whatever he was doing, he sounded exactly as swamped as she was. Moreover, he knew about her undertaking and his parents' role in it, and he understood perfectly when she complained about having no time for herself.

In terms of physically seeing Gabe again, Kate had pretty much given up hope of knowing when that would be. Carmen and Michael went away with him for every holiday that year, and when she expressed curiosity over when he was coming back, they would smile obliquely and tell her to be patient. In order not to feel vulnerable or appear desperate, she pretended she didn't care.

She had the distinct impression her parents and the Blakes colluded with one another to interfere in any potential relationship between her and Gabe. The thought caused her to question her judgment; surely they had better things to worry about than a teenage romance, and wasn't she, perhaps, being paranoid? Nonetheless, the impression persisted. In fact, she wondered if the race to prepare her for early graduation from college was also related to their efforts to get between them although she didn't see how. Something was definitely off, though.

In February, Dana called about her efforts to secure her a job at a food magazine. "I have what I hope is good news. One of my editor friends agreed to have her assistant call you. She liked your writing samples and is impressed with your grades. If they like what they hear, they'll let you hang around the office this summer to file papers and sweep the floor. You will not be paid but you'll get a taste of professional life and maybe make a couple of contacts for later." The news was bittersweet to Kate. She wanted to be closer to home to be by her new baby brother, and she really wanted to be around when Gabe was back. His comment last August about seeing each other *next year* no longer seemed far-fetched. But an opportunity to volunteer in a bona fide food journalism environment was too good to pass up.

Kate's interview went well; she was offered the job, and she accepted it. Dana warned her again she was unlikely to get any actual writing experience that summer; she counseled her to work to understand the publishing process and all that went into putting a monthly magazine together. Kate was to stay with her and Will for the summer, and via correspondence, she would continue chipping away at the courses Carmen and Michael were teaching her.

In March, after fifteen hours of labor, Cara gave birth to a healthy, eight pound, four ounce boy. They named him Everett, and with his first mewling cries, their family life was permanently transformed.

Kate was with her mother and John for the delivery, an experience that forever changed her understanding of what it meant to be a woman and of what it meant to be married to someone and have a baby with him. The theoretical consideration of birthing a child was obliterated by its physical occurrence, a bloody, painful, remarkable event that played out thousands of unremarkable times each day across the world.

Seeing her mom come through the experience as she knew most women did and watching her parents hold their little boy for the first time revealed a fundamental facet of human nature to her in the clearest of terms. The infant's utter dependence on his parents, and the tangible emotional commitment reflected in their expressions appeared as the biological mandate it was. Kate remembered her mother's comment to Dana about leaving her baby to go file books at the library, and she suddenly understood no job would outrank caring for Everett now, be it working as a librarian or leading a small country.

Kate also recognized the tenderness and exhaustion in her mother's eyes, since she had seen these sentiments directed at her so often during her own childhood. She had a new appreciation for what her mom felt and did for her, for what it meant to her to be her mother. Kate was humbled as she slipped her little finger into the tiny hand of her new brother, and she knew the love and responsibility she felt for him was only a shadow of what her mom and John felt at this moment. But her big-sister heart still overflowed with love for her new family and the place she had in it; and with gratitude for the glimpse she'd been given of how much her mother loved her.

Admittedly, she was a little jealous during the next months, because Cara and John really did not have time for her. She knew this was not a rejection of her, just a function of trying to have a house, a job, and a family all at the same time, with one member of that family crying, eating and sleeping in two-hour time chunks. Kate didn't need anyone to make her breakfast, and so no one did. She had to remind herself this didn't mean anything more than everyone was busy and she could make her own breakfast. She hid her petty feelings by cooking each morning, hoping to appear generous and helpful.

Although she helped care for Everett a little, her mother and John shouldered the bulk of the work involved in keeping him fed, clean, and dry. John tried to get up with the baby one night a week so Cara could get some sleep but she complained she woke up anyway and he shouldn't bother.

"Someone has to be awake and function in the outside world for the next three months, and I'm not going to be able to cut it, no matter how much sleep I get on Tuesdays." She smiled tenderly at her husband. "It's only for a little while, John. I'll be fine. You do plenty."

The small amount of help Kate provided by making the occasional meal actually did help her feel better. She never made anything complicated but it was always nutritious and filling, and it met both the need for sustenance and her need to be relied on in some fashion during this period of their lives.

"You're a lifesaver," her mother told her, staring with reverence at the poached eggs over spinach Kate had made for her. Her eyes closed after her first forkful. "You put nutmeg in the greens, and I want to live again." She sighed and ate more.

Fortified she'd helped substantively, Kate could better focus on her course load and contingent assignments, which nearly crushed her. She tackled each and every task each and every day, which made the school year pass by quickly indeed.

CHAPTER ELEVEN

Of course she missed Gabe at the end of the year. Again, she couldn't help feeling their parents orchestrated their segregation although she lacked evidence to confirm her suspicion. She left for her aunt and uncle's the first week of June so she could begin her job at *Culinaria* magazine. Gabe, she heard, was staying at school an extra week to complete some unspecified independent study course.

She stocked the freezer at home with all manner of quick dishes and sauces, accompanied by notes on how to prepare them. She cried letting go of little Everett. "It figures," she sobbed. "He's just starting to sleep during the night and stay awake during the day. I'm going to miss so much this summer."

John was the first to hug her goodbye. "We'll send pictures every day," he promised. He lightly punched her arm. "It's gonna seem empty around here without you. Try not to get too fond of Philadelphia, okay?"

Her mother hugged her hard and kissed her forehead. "I love you so much, honey. Be careful in that big city for me, won't you?" She told them she wasn't likely to get out of the office long enough to get in any real trouble, so not to worry. And she was off.

Once installed at Dana and Will's, she organized her things and leafed through the math book Michael had sent along for the course she was to finish that summer. She couldn't wait to get that credit behind her, and she started the first assignment before going to bed that night.

The enormity of her endeavors hit her as she switched off her light. In the dark and without the sounds of her parents and baby brother around her, she felt an overwhelming loneliness. Why was she doing this? If she was successful, this effort would only take her more quickly away from the nurturing comfort of home, a home she wouldn't have for much longer anyway if she followed the normal life's path of people her age. She became plagued with self-doubt. From what Dana had told her, her new boss was a taskmaster with an eagle eye for errors and no tolerance for imperfection. Who did she think she was, she wondered? And what was she thinking, tackling a job like this on top of college coursework? She cried herself into a fitful sleep, missing her mother horribly, confident she would fail at her volunteer job. At least if she did fall flat on her face, she could go home.

She didn't feel significantly better the next morning but she decided to wait and see if the worst would happen rather than expect it. Dana and Will were all business as they prepared to leave for work, each draining two cups of coffee and reading three newspapers while Kate made herself an egg and toast.

"Keep your head down and your nose to the grindstone," Dana advised before breezing out the door. Something in Kate's expression must have given her pause, although Kate wasn't sure if she intended to comfort or scold her. Dana patted Kate's arm awkwardly. "Buck up, now." And then she and Will left.

Kate's first day passed at light speed, became her first week, and then her first month before she could take a breath. She followed Dana's advice and kept focused on her work, which proved to be the only path to survival as an employee – even an unpaid one – at *Culinaria*. Her supervisor, Vicki Simons, deserved her reputation as a fear-mongering workaholic. Kate stayed on top of her assignments and out of Vicki's way.

Still, work was pretty much her whole life that summer. Aside from happy hour interactions with her coworkers, which made her job almost enjoyable, her only other social activity that summer consisted of texts and e-mails with Gabe and Maya. Gabe didn't seem to have the same restrictions during the summer as he'd had during the school year but neither was he as warm and intimate as he'd been with Kate in person. She considered the possibility he was policed, which felt ridiculous, or that he no longer hoped they would become involved, which seemed more likely.

She decided not to think about it anymore. From her current vantage point as a young woman working for a college degree and basic career skills, she wasn't going to be available, especially with Gabe at his school and her at hers. She stopped herself from remembering their exchange in the garden last August, and with the insulating factors of time and distance, decided she didn't feel so sure she would one day be with him.

But she reveled in her bantering exchanges with Gabe and Maya, which made her cry with loneliness even as she laughed at what they wrote. Dana and Will travelled for business two to three days each week, and their beautiful home felt especially cold and empty when she was alone. When she traded missives with Gabe and Maya, she felt her friends' camaraderie wrap around her like a security blanket, helping her retain a sense of herself she would otherwise have lost. At work, she had to be careful not to presume or make mistakes; she felt drained of her personality, as if she was merely a picture of herself. Writing back and forth with her friends reminded her who she was and delivered a measure of comfort she desperately craved.

By the end of the August, she had completed another college course and managed to survive her pseudo job at *Culinaria*. And while Vicki Simons didn't send her off warmly, she handed Kate her business card and told her to call next spring. "You were more a help than a hindrance this summer, and that's refreshing in a new person. The staff liked you too. Call me next March, and I'll see if I can find a place for you." Kate thanked her nervously and all but ran out of there.

Her aunt was delighted with Vicki's parting comments. "Good work. That bodes well for you for next summer." Having barely made it through this summer, Kate couldn't bring herself to feel excited about doing it all over again next year. She smiled wanly at Dana and excused herself to pack.

She was ecstatic to get home. Everett was an entirely different baby by this time, smiling, grabbing everything and trying to hold himself up on all fours. He'd started sleeping through the night sometime in the middle of the summer so Cara and John seemed a little less exhausted than they had when she'd left. They both hugged her tightly when she arrived, telling her again and again how much she'd been missed.

"You've matured," her mom commented approvingly.

"I sure feel like I've been gone a lot longer than three months."

Maya was away at a volleyball clinic when Kate returned, and she wasn't able to see her until a few days before school began. The two jumped up and down at their reunion, giddy to be in each other's company again. Maya was taller and leaner and... something else Kate struggled to define. She settled on self-possessed. Maya reminded her very much of Solange now, her bearing and confidence stronger than she remembered.

Gabe, predictably, had been sent to his boarding school two weeks earlier. The only hint Kate received he still thought about the two of them came in August in the form of an e-mail on Luke and Solange's anniversary. "Happy anniversary, Kate," was all it said. She quelled the butterflies she felt in her stomach, unwilling to think about his touch, kiss, and the emotions she'd experienced that night. When they next saw each other, would she still feel the same way? Would Gabe's companionship seem as magical to her? She tried very hard not to think about it.

Her senior year was an almost identical copy of her junior year, although she had no interest – and little participation – in the normal social dramas of teenage society. With the exception of Maya, her classmates were at best tolerant of her and at worst dismissive because she was such a flaming all-work-and-no-play achiever. She nursed some level of resentment related to this situation, although her loneliness was less profound than it had been in Philadelphia. With everyone's encouragement, she stayed the aggressive academic course she was on and generally felt superior to her classmates with active social lives. She told herself she would leave for college in a few short months, and she didn't care if she wasn't a part of anything here.

Maya protected Kate somewhat from her self-imposed isolation, because Maya *was* popular and integrated into various cliques, and with her sponsorship, Kate was included, without any particular enthusiasm on her part or that of her peers, in group activities from time to time. And while she disliked the constant worry she had over whether these activities were worth the social awkwardness and the time away from her studies, she enjoyed giving the appearance of normalcy, to her family and perhaps most of all to herself.

She graduated at the top of her class but declined to give the valedictory speech. Who honestly wanted to hear what she had to say about a collective high school career where she wasn't really part of the collective? She felt proud of her small rebellion, deferring to the class salutatorian to speak instead, arguing he had a better-rounded experience and a stronger rapport with the student body. Dana disapproved of her decision.

"You shouldn't shy away from an opportunity like that, Kate. It's a nice thing to mention to people you want to impress." Kate silently but vehemently disagreed. She couldn't imagine a conversation where her telling someone she'd given a speech in high school would make them want to spend any time with her whatsoever.

Her mother backed her up, both in private and with the school. "These last two years have been too hard on you. I can't stand how sad and lonesome you seem. I don't want you to give a speech you don't want to give. In fact, I don't want you to do anything more you don't want to do."

"Does that include going to college?" Kate teased, expecting her mother to revert back to her *you're almost done* encouragements. She instantly regretted her comment when her mom's eyes filled with tears. "I honestly don't care if you wait to go. We need help at the library; you're already two years into your degree. Please take a break if you want."

Kate had already agreed to another summer internship at *Culinaria*, an opportunity Dana assured her many aspirants would give up a kidney for. Kate avoided her mother's gaze to escape her concern. She just couldn't consider what Cara offered, although she appreciated the sentiment behind it.

Graduation marked the end of everyone's big push to help her get ahead of the game in college. She couldn't understand the reason for the switch. Instead of one-dimensional conversations about her current or upcoming schoolwork, her parents, Michael, and Carmen talked with her as they used to, about cooking, gardening, fiction, and politics. She felt as if they suggested she ignore her goals of the past two years.

But she could no longer accept her choices were about what her parents and the Blakes thought were best for her. She now knew what she had done and what she would do moving forward were most important to *her*. And if she was no longer a super-student, get-ahead kind of gal, who was she? She wasn't an athlete, she wasn't popular and surrounded by friends. If she relaxed her focus in the area she excelled, wouldn't she be even more sad and lost?

Her confusion worsened at lunch the day she headed to Philadelphia. She left the house at noon, driving in the opposite direction first to pick up school documents from John in Griffins Bay. John smiled when she entered the clinic. "Hey, Kate." He shrugged out of his lab coat. "Do you have time for lunch before you go?"

"Sure! I'm reluctant to face the music in Philadelphia, so anything I can do to procrastinate is a good thing." She made a face. John laughed.

At the restaurant, someone swooped her up and whirled her in a circle. After a second of terror, she realized Gabe was the perpetrator. "I caught you at last!" he exclaimed.

"Gabe!" she squealed, unbearably happy to see him. "Where did you come from? I thought you didn't get back until next week!" Her insides tingled with warmth. She couldn't believe the instantaneous transformation she felt, as if she'd been sleeping for the past year and awoken to the most beautiful, exciting world possible.

Gabe let her go, keeping one of his hands on her arm, shaking John's hand with his other. "I thought I had a shot at actually seeing you, and I worked like a dog to make it happen. Can I join you?" He ushered Kate onto the bench before him and sat down before John could respond. "That's a rhetorical question, John. Have a seat, won't you?" He gestured to the other side of the booth.

John disapproved of something but he couldn't contain his smile as he slid onto the bench. "How did you find us?"

"I was on my way to see if I could catch Kate before she left, and I saw her car."

"I didn't think you knew my car," Kate grumbled. "Have we even seen each other since I got my license?" Gabe snorted and shot John a dirty look.

"Seriously," Kate groused, "does anyone else know you're here? I feel like we need permission to be together." She tried to gauge John's reaction. He put his forehead in his hands.

"Carmen and Michael are in on my plan. John now knows. Your mom may be in the dark." Gabe's grin was wicked.

"Fabulous." Kate was so unbelievably glad to see him. She yearned to touch him, hold his hand, or loop her arm around his but she didn't have the nerve. She continued to smile, feeling like an idiot. "So, what are you doing this summer?"

"I'm staying home, for once. Taking an independent study course with my dad. Wanna stay?"

For an instant, Kate envisioned not going to Philadelphia, instead helping her mother at the library, digging in the garden, and spending time with Gabe. Her heartbeat accelerated as she realized how badly she wanted this. Gabe in the abstract, as he'd become over the past two years, was a very different proposition from the real, breathing, beautiful Gabe smiling at her now.

But she didn't see how she could stay with everything already set up at her aunt's. "I can't imagine our parents would approve. And I've been given this golden opportunity to prove myself as the ultimate slave at *Culinaria* this summer. Dana might actually kill me if I back out on her." She again checked John for his response.

Gabe's stare at John was flinty. "I can protect you from Dana. Just don't answer your phone for a while. She'll figure it out."

Although she felt she and Gabe were both addressing John to an extent, she spoke specifically to her dad this time. "What do you think?" She was pretty sure he didn't approve of the idea. Not that he could stop her... but she couldn't seriously entertain the idea of staying home, could she?

"I think reasoning with eighteen-year-olds is a fool's mission." He grimaced. He regarded Kate kindly. "I understand your desire to take a break but my advice is to stay the course, go to your internship, get through college. Get it behind you."

Gabe's smile hardened as he deliberately scooted toward Kate so the side of his body was tight against hers. Kate felt he had just issued some sort of challenge... but their contact distracted her from thinking too much about what sort of challenge he meant. She relaxed against him, more calm and centered than she'd been in months. She felt John's kick to Gabe under the table. Gabe did not budge.

"You're further along in your studies than she is. She's worked really hard to get to this point. You would undermine her?"

A feeling of lassitude pervaded Kate, and she gave herself to it. She knew she should participate in the conversation taking place but she felt too wonderful sitting there, being held by Gabe. Maybe she should stay this summer, she mused. Becoming progressively more relaxed, she wondered idly if this was what hypnosis felt like. She really didn't care what anyone else thought was good for her right now, she was not moving, not if John told her to, not if someone bombed the restaurant and the walls around them crumbled.

"I don't see it as an all-or-nothing proposition," Gabe shot back.

John closed his eyes. "Gabe. You're eighteen."

"Nineteen, actually."

"Fine. Nineteen. Whatever." John muttered under his breath before continuing. "In two years' time, two short years, you and Kate will be degreed and employable, capable of undertaking whatever you want. You've already demonstrated the self-discipline and patience to do this. Keep it up a little while longer. Finish what you started."

Gabe leaned his head on the back of the bench. "I know you're right. I have an easier time with that line of thinking when I'm toiling away on my own, of course."

John raised his eyebrows as if Gabe was missing something obvious. "And so?"

Gabe reluctantly shifted away from her, and she almost cried from her sense of loss. With what felt like superhuman effort on her part, she kept herself still and did not beg Gabe to come back to her. John's glance her way came to her like an apology. Gabe seemed as tense as she was.

"I know, I know," Gabe said to no one in particular. "That was cheating." He offered Kate an apologetic smile. "I suppose we should let you get on your way."

Without Gabe touching her — and given the decision they'd just made to forego each other's company yet again — Kate felt overexposed and vulnerable. And tired. And then annoyed. "Will the stupidness never end?" She patted Gabe on the leg to get him to let her out. "All-righty, then. You two ladies stay here and spin your evil webs. I'm going back to my all-work-and-no-play reality, I guess." John grimaced while Gabe laughed.

"Good one, Blake."

He folded Kate into a hug once she stood, and she again felt a hypnotic, blissful paralysis. John pulled her away gently to hug her himself, which somehow made the transition away from Gabe less painful. She knew if she intended to actually leave she'd have to do it soon or risk public embarrassment by falling to her knees right there and pleading with them to let her stay.

She peeked at Gabe, which was a bad idea. He was as miserable as she was, an observation she couldn't dwell on if she hoped to make it out of there. John put his arm around her shoulders and guided her to the door. "Hang in there, kiddo," he encouraged. He pressed a kiss to her hair and propelled her lightly toward the front of the restaurant. "Call us when you get to Philly."

She trudged to her car.

She had too much time to think during her drive but she let her musings take a gentle, circuitous route to the issue of her non-starting romance with Gabriel Blake. For a while, she turned up the radio and let the loud music blast her into a brooding stupor. Then, as the sun started to set, she mused over what was going on, and what she could or should do about it. She laughed when she remembered how horrified she'd been when Gabe had asked her to wait for two years, wondering what she would have said if he'd told her the truth, how any relationship they might have wouldn't start for another four. She was glad he hadn't known, or hadn't told her.

She believed both of their parents supported a relationship between them. But then why would they work to delay it? She thought back on the dozens of romantic dramas she'd watched play out among her peers in high school, regretting her utter lack of participation. Perhaps she would feel more confident if she were more socially practiced. As it was, she just felt lost and stupid and kind of stuck, unable to see her way through this situation to some more comfortable outcome.

And what outcome did she want? What outcome did Gabe want? Was he really waiting for her as he seemed to be? She thought this seemed like a foolish hope on her part. And, if he was waiting for her, and if they did become free to explore a romance in two more years, what did *that* mean? They were both through high school and attending different colleges. What if one of them got a job in Texas or Oregon? Would she move to be by him, or he by her?

She chided herself for considering this possibility. "One meeting with Gabe in two years, and I'm plotting cross-country transfers." She vaguely remembered this feeling from her junior year, when she figured out she wouldn't see him at all, and her mother had told her to put him out of her mind. This situation was no different. As she had then, she forced herself to think about being away from Gabe instead of being with him. Being away from him left her with a college career and job skills to chase after. Wanting to be near him just left her wanting, with no option for fulfilling that want, possibly not ever.

She turned the music back up and committed her thoughts to her job in Philadelphia. She could not afford to brood over Gabe right now, she decided. By the time she got to Dana and Will's, she resolved herself against trying to figure it out. She would simply discipline herself not to consider Gabriel Blake.

She felt more competent at *Culinaria* than she had the previous summer. She saw a few new faces but many she still knew, and this familiarity helped her feel as if she fit in. She was given a few small writing assignments this time around, help coming from many of her coworkers to ready these pieces for publication. She learned a great deal about editing and developing a flexible writing style; and she saw in retrospect how green she'd really been the previous summer. She felt doubly grateful to everyone who had shepherded her through her first professional experience.

Dana and Will remained unchanged in their living habits; their home was as lovely and inviting as ever; they both still worked like indentured servants; and they traveled every week for business, leaving her with huge chunks of time alone at their house. The crushing loneliness she'd felt the previous summer revisited her, although she was better at distracting herself from it this year. Just as she had learned to do when she thought of Gabe, she shifted her attention to something else when she felt isolated and anxious. Usually, she chose to read a novel or peruse cookbooks or go for a walk. As she had last year, she started to feel like a buried version of herself, her personality firmly in check as she executed all her responsibilities and duties, and – when those had been fulfilled – diversions she had at her disposal.

In an effort to avoid all her debilitating fantasies about Gabe, she didn't allow herself to think about him, and she stopped responding to some of his texts and e-mails, whereas before this summer, she opened and answered each communication promptly. Now, she made herself wait, and she didn't answer every message. If Gabe noticed her new electronic behavior, he didn't mention it but he wrote to her less frequently. She told herself this was for the best.

Her summer passed quickly. After returning to Childress for a few days, her mother and John loaded Everett into the car and drove her to Sommerset University. As she watched the other freshmen parting from their parents, Kate realized she was past her first separation from home and childhood, and although she was sad to be leaving again, she was grateful to not experience the raw, fresh emotions of that first goodbye. Still, her mother cried as she hugged her, making Kate promise to write every day and come back as often as she could. Kate hugged her back tightly but she did not cry.

Her roommate reminded her of several of her high school classmates. Sarah was pretty and perky and had been, according to her own report, popular before coming to college. Kate immediately disliked her, knowing this was unfair. Sarah tried diligently to engage her in conversation about old boyfriends and hilarious high school escapades, her heavily made-up eyes intentionally wide and her smile overly sincere as she talked. Kate was polite but blunt, eventually telling her she didn't have a romantic history to pore over, and high school was something she'd survived.

"I'm an unrecoverable bookworm. Really, I can't be saved." She scrounged through her welcome packet to retrieve a device for offloading her would-be friend. "Did you see this flier from the alums about the ice cream social? You should go." She resumed her unpacking to discourage further attempts at camaraderie.

Sarah's answering smile was uncertain. "Okay... I guess I will." Kate heard the door close, pleased to have so easily put Sarah off her scent and on the hunt for easier social prey. She wondered if she'd see a request from student housing for a new roommate.

Over the next few months, she did make small attempts to integrate socially by approaching a few similarly reserved girls on her floor and forming study groups with them. One girl was a performance pianist who introduced her to the performing arts library, where they spent the occasional hour listening to musical recordings, the pastime preferable to shopping or watching sitcoms in Kate's opinion. Another girl was into yoga, which she also enjoyed from time to time.

Beyond those interactions however, she quickly fell into the same pattern she'd established as a junior in high school, which consisted of a heavy course load, intense studying, and little socializing. She exchanged daily texts with Maya, who was playing volleyball on scholarship at Penn State, and she e-mailed or called home each day as well. As always, she felt as though she lived two lives: one as a reserved, severe, and dedicated student bulldozing her way through college; the other as a less confident young woman, one who was afraid of her future, and who nursed a secret desire to hide herself away. She only saw this side of herself when she messaged back and forth with Maya or talked to her mother.

She did not allow herself to think of Gabe.

In an attempt to keep her professional train rolling, she established a correspondence contract with *Culinaria* that year as well. It paid almost nothing but she was happy to respond within the absurd deadline constraints in exchange for experience she could include on her resume. She also volunteered at the school newspaper, which quickly promoted her to managing editor thanks to her real-world experience.

In the spring, Kate interviewed for and landed a job at a lifestyle magazine in Sommerset. It was not intended to be a summer position although the editor agreed to work with her class schedule in the fall should things go well through August. She had no illusions about this being a result of her impressive credentials; she was adequately qualified, a little desperate, and she came cheap, which made her roughly as alluring as she could be to a publication like *Sommerset Journal*. She called home to tell her parents the good news.

"Oh, honey, good for you!" her mom gushed. "Will we get to have you here at all this summer, then?"

"Truthfully, I don't know, Mom. I'm sure I can figure out a long weekend somewhere, but I'll mostly have to hang out here." Her mother caught her up on Everett's antics and happenings at the library. She asked if she'd heard from Maya, and Kate gave her what news she had. Cara reported Solange and Luke were expecting their second child, and Sylvia was staying with them in Boston while she completed culinary training. She mentioned Carmen and Michael's plans to spend the summer in Ireland with family there.

Kate didn't bring him up but Cara informed her Gabe had been accepted into an eighteen-month academic program in Dublin. The disappointment of knowing she wouldn't see him this summer crept over her anyway, although she'd never assumed she would see him. "He'll graduate with his master's at the end of it." Kate could hear the pride in her voice. And she couldn't stop herself from trying to find out more.

"Will he come home afterward? I mean to Griffins Bay?"

"I don't know what his plans are. I heard he was considering medical school. He's been talking with John about ophthalmology. But you should call him yourself." Her mother's suggestion sounded too tentative to Kate. "Unless, that is… are you seeing anyone at school?"

She was definitely fishing. "No, I'm not." Kate sighed, wondering if it was wise to share this information. "I'm afraid I've kind of forgotten how to interact with people outside the context of studying or work."

"Ease up on yourself, Kate. You should get in touch with Gabe. I'm sure he'd love to hear from you." She paused before saying carefully, "You know, the Blakes all seem to find someone to marry after college."

Kate felt sick to her stomach. "Mom, are you trying to tell me Gabe is seeing someone?"

"No! Honey! No, not at all. I just . . ." She sounded sad as she trailed off. Then she said in a rush, "I just feel like you've crammed about eight years of adult life into the last three, and the hope from this end is an early graduation will give you more flexibility in terms of marrying and having children. But now, I worry we pushed you too hard, and you're investing everything in a career and not hoping for anything else. I want you to have a better life than that."

Kate was so relieved Gabe wasn't dating someone, she felt high. She blew out a breath she hadn't realized she held. "I'll be done in one year, Mom. I promise to start thinking about my romantic future then." She laughed to put her mother at ease.

But to her surprise, her mother was satisfied with her response. "I think that's a terrific plan. I just wish there was some way to make you happy in the meantime."

"I don't know that I'm unhappy, Mom. In a way, getting through school this way, which is to say very quickly, has its advantages."

"Yes, well, I know you're missing out on a lot, and I can't help but regret that for you. I think it will all be worth it in the end, though." Kate didn't think she sounded too confident.

After hanging up, Kate checked messages on her computer. Gabe had left one for her and Maya about his Dublin plans. She replied to them both, congratulating Gabe, and she shared news of her *Sommerset Journal* job with them. As usual, she felt happier and less constricted communicating with her old friends, which showed her, by contrast, how introverted she was otherwise. She viewed herself as she might a stranger, as if she was waiting for her real life to start, but she didn't know when that would be, or what she should do to prepare. Unwilling to wallow in this familiar pool of doubt and worry, she signed off and dove into studying for final exams.

CHAPTER TWELVE

The week of her twenty-first birthday, Kate graduated from Sommerset University. She'd finished a year earlier than her peers, with honors, prepared for a job in the field of her choice. In trade, she'd foregone forming close friendships in college, the kind most people she knew kept throughout their lives; and she had declined to participate in a whole host of social activities defining the typical American collegiate experience.

As she marched across the stage to accept her diploma from the university president, her small entourage of fans hooting their support, she felt equal parts relief and terror; relief for the fact she would never again have to sprint but sprint through a life that centered only on school and work and more school. She was truly free for the first time in four years.

Her terror was for the great unknown she now faced, how she wasn't sure what to do with herself from here on out. With the experience she'd amassed at *Culinaria* and *Sommerset Journal*, she landed a job with *Conde Nast Publications* starting in mid-June, a coup her aunt assured her. Even a demanding new job, however, would not compete with the schedule she'd kept since she was seventeen.

Her terror was for the hole in her abysmal social life work would in no way fill, and for the choice she now faced on what she was going to do about that.

Before starting her new job, she spent two weeks at home in Childress. The Blakes had invited her to stay with them in Italy for all or part of that time, but as she knew Gabe would not be with them – and had not mentioned Italy to her himself – she sent her regrets. "Maybe next summer, dear," Carmen wrote back.

Kate was delighted to play in the garden at home and help out at the library again, with no urgent assignments hanging over her. She planted a new border of flowers at the house, tamed the raspberry patch at the library, and played in the kitchen, experimenting with whatever was ready to pick out back. She brought Everett to the park and read him his favorite books. They all relaxed as a family in the evenings, watching a movie or playing croquet on the lawn. Kate's old sense of self came back to her.

She had a harder time with her next parting from home. Unlike when she'd gone to college, this departure felt more final. She was leaving under no one's guidance but her own, to her own apartment, and a regulation, grown-up job. Her mother tried to reassure her. "Don't think of it like that, Kate. Be careful of how much of yourself you give away. No job is worth all your time and energy, no matter what it is. If you get overwhelmed, call me, and we'll figure something out."

Dana's advice was the exact opposite. "Keep going. Dig in, work hard – harder than anyone else – and watch how you get promoted and recognized. You'll be happy you did."

She smiled politely at her aunt, disbelieving this advice for the first time in her life. Dana's professional efforts had yielded her a nice house, expensive cars, and pretty clothes but they had not made her happy. She was willing to concede Dana's choices may have made another person fulfilled and content, although she doubted it. But she could see killing yourself at work did not result in a happy life based on Dana's example.

She didn't know where that left her, but she only knew of one way to approach the job she was going to, and that was with the best effort she had. The paces she'd been put through at her school paper and internships gave her, on day one, experiential knowledge few first-timers shared. Too, her appreciation for the harried pace of publishing – and for the pressured contributions of everyone on a publications team – resulted in the respect and inclusion she would need to advance. By the end of July, Kate managed her job smoothly and had made herself useful to another editor in the office whose sponsorship she sought. She was so stimulated and gratified by her competence – and the opportunities it brought – her comparatively bleak social life didn't chafe so much, although she could never quite obliterate the desolation hounding her in quiet hours. The outcome of her all-career focus, professional recognition aside, would not hold her forever, she feared.

She socialized more than she ever had – ate lunch with colleagues, attended happy hours and evening excursions with others her age, ones she'd met through work or in her neighborhood – and the interactions were fun. But they weren't gripping or deep enough to replace the intensely scheduled existence she'd maintained, and they did not erase her worries about how lonely her life might be in another ten years if she didn't figure out a better plan.

Hoping to take some small control over her destiny, she started a blog. She did it discreetly, so as not to alarm managers and coworkers who needed to believe they had harnessed all her creative talent; and she developed it purely for her own enjoyment, which did, in fact, help with her desire to steer herself rather than feel driven.

She'd forgotten the reasons behind her chosen career, the trance she got into when she wrote; or how absorbed she could become in a recipe, its structure or style, or a compelling photograph of an interesting dish. She operated under the username *Mavenly*, and used her Twitter account to front announcements and links to essays on her site. Her articles were quirky, irreverent expositions on cooking and whatever aspect of private life she deemed worthy, be it what she ate for breakfast, where she found the coolest local gardens, or what homemade solution was best for washing sheets so they felt like heaven. Her subject matter was old-school but her perspective wasn't, and she knew from the responses she received she shared something meaningful with people like her, young professionals who valued a little sanctity after work hours without slaving to have it. She built a small, devoted following, and she loved it.

On a Tuesday in mid-August, she came home to a message from Gabe. "I'm in Griffins Bay. Come see me. I need to talk to you."

Her lungs deflated and her stomach became a block of cold, iron ore that weighted her onto her chair. She felt the same way as she had when Gabe had surprised her at lunch with John, like she'd been sleep-dreaming this entire past year, or maybe viewing her life through a soft-focus lens, and now here she was in an over-bright, amped up world she didn't recognize. She put her head between her knees, holding the phone in her hand, and struggled to decide on her response. She dialed half of the phone number to her parents' house in Childress but hung up. She didn't want to talk to her mother. She started over and redialed the number Gabe had used to leave his message.

He answered on the first ring. "Hello?"

She couldn't catch her breath. "Gabe! I just got your message." Awkward silence. She wasn't sure what to say next.

"How soon can you come home?" It was not a request.

"I'm supposed to be in a meeting late Friday. Are you home already?"

"Yes. I got back this afternoon."

"I can't leave until after my meeting." This suddenly seemed like an eternity away to her. "Can you come here, instead?" She did not know what gave her the courage to be so forward but she felt inexplicably courageous.

He sighed. "No. It's better if you come here. I'll explain why when I see you. Can you be here Saturday?"

"I'll leave Friday after work," Kate promised. "Is everything okay?"

"Everyone's fine, if that's what you mean. I want to talk, that's all."

"And it can't wait?"

"Ha. You sound like my mother." His voice softened then. "There's no emergency. I just want to see you." She heard equal parts humor and frustration in his tone. "Do you want to wait?"

Kate steeled herself against the desire to shout her response. "No. I'll be there."

"I'll be at the beach."

She was now on fire to get out of her Friday meeting. She actually felt like resigning so she could leave sooner. She even mentally composed an e-mail to her boss as she hurried back to the office. *Thank you so much for giving me the opportunity to work here these past three months. I have to check in on a romantic prospect back home, so I quit. Best wishes.* Lunacy. She laughed at how quickly she was willing to throw over her carefully built career plans to spend time with Gabe.

So good Dana can't see me now.

She powered up her computer with the intention of churning through as much work as she could, freeing herself for the weekend. After an hour, she was startled to hear the elevator ring and the door open. Her supervisor, Janice, exited the elevator car.

"Working late again, Kate? Did we overload you this week?"

"Not at all. I got a message from an old friend asking if we could get together this weekend, and I want to get ahead of things so I can scoot back to North Carolina after Friday's meeting."

Janice studied Kate briefly, went to her office for a file, and then meandered back to perch on the edge of Kate's desk. "I just came back to get through some copy before tomorrow," she said absently. "How long is your friend in town?"

Kate examined the surface of her desk. "I'm not sure." Shouldn't she know the answer to this question?

"Well. You've been working pretty hard, I hear, and not just since you've come to us," Janice continued.

Kate laughed nervously. "Who told you that?"

"I went to school with a friend of your family's I believe, Carmen Blake? She's had such nice things to say about you. And, also, I try to pay attention around here." She smiled wryly. "I've got a proposition for you. We have to trim costs in the department, and I could offer you a month off, unpaid, if you'd like. I don't want to lose you, however, so don't feel obligated to accept."

A temporary resignation. Kate couldn't believe her good fortune. She eyed Janice tentatively, hoping she didn't appear as eager as she was to say *yes.* "You're sure I wouldn't compromise my opportunities afterward?"

"You would not. We like for people to take editorial leave from time to time. It results in better writing. You haven't been here long but we have Alan available to cover for you until he goes back to New York, and it could actually work well. Is this something you'd like to consider? We could start it this coming Monday, if you want."

"I . . ." Kate struggled to think through her options, although she was already sure of what she wanted. And she was taking this leave no matter the career risk, although she didn't want Janice to know what a fair-weather employee she'd become. "Yes. I would love to take you up on your offer. If you're sure it's no inconvenience, that is."

Janice stood. "Perfect. It's decided, then." She grabbed her folder. "We'll see you tomorrow morning."

Kate worked at an insane pace the rest of the week to have her projects in good shape for Alan. With Janice's sponsorship, her coworkers accepted news of her leave graciously, any envy tempered by the fact the leave was unpaid. And for once, she felt no shame over her lack of social participation the past few years; having had nothing compelling her to spend her earnings – like spring breaks or shopping excursions with girlfriends – she'd saved enough to take this time off without worry.

Friday morning, she packed her car, deposited her monthly bills in the mailbox, and left for the office. At the end of the day, she thanked Janice again and told everyone she would see them in a month. She somehow kept from running out the door.

She had not warned her mother and John she was coming, and though she had time to call them on the road, she didn't. Her unconfirmed suspicions regarding their efforts to preclude her relationship with Gabe left her wary. If this was her chance to find out why everyone had been so evasive these past four years, she would do absolutely nothing to jeopardize it. She ignored her phone and daydreamed her way through the five-hour drive home.

She parked in the lot by the beach and removed her car keys. The night sky was thick with blackness, and she saw no one else – no other cars, no people, no signs of campers or hikers on the sand. Despite past warnings ringing in her head from parents, teachers, and officials not to wander the beach alone at night, she did not hesitate to leave her vehicle for the water.

No one was there.

She felt a crushing disappointment, even as she realized she and Gabe had not discussed a time to meet, just a place. And the night was so dark. She couldn't see more than a few yards in front of her. She toed the very edge of the surf.

The weight of anticipation she'd been carrying all week caught up with her, sapping her strength so much her legs failed. She sank to her knees in the soft sand and closed her eyes to feel the wind on her face. She tried to determine what to do. Around her, the roar of the waves drowned out all other sounds, and the ebony sky stretched out limitlessly, its very size a powerful reminder of her own powerlessness.

She did not know how to find Gabe here.

All of the emotions she'd denied feeling the past four years enveloped her now, overwhelming her with their poignancy. She wondered if she should have tried harder to be with Gabe, if she should have fought against the wishes of their parents, acknowledging even as she had these thoughts, she would not have made herself oppose them. But she also realized nothing she'd been working toward would bring her lasting happiness, not recognition at work, not her aunt's approval, not a portfolio of published articles. She saw with new clarity how the path she was on would not bring her more security or happiness, not to any real extent; how achievement would be no more the holy grail of fulfillment for her than it had been for Dana. As of this moment, the difference between her and her aunt was she knew this.

What she really wanted was to talk with Gabe. She needed to understand their separation through high school and college, to know why they were driven so hard, to look into his eyes and see again what she had first seen when they were seventeen. She felt she would be forever stuck if she could not know these things and know them now.

She stood up then, resolved. With a certainty she hadn't felt since she was five, she recognized what mattered to her. She felt her own humanity as it had been given to her when she was born, not as a theoretical set of activities she'd developed along the way. She saw her approach to adult life up until now as a contrivance, one taking all her energy to maintain, her boulder to force uphill again and again, her disappointment in her progress predictable and repetitive as the boulder inevitably rolled back down. She was done carrying that boulder.

She stared out at the sea and yelled at the top of her lungs for Gabe. Some part of her knew she should be calling toward the beach but she could not shake her desire to stand where she stood and cry as she did. She saw a splash far out on the inky water, and she stopped shouting.

Time slowed to a standstill. She felt each second distinctly now, each beat of her heart an echoing, singular throb; each breath a slow-motion ordeal as she waited without an ounce of patience left in her. Her closed eyes welled with tears of sheer frustration. She felt the droplets grow during each microsecond of their formation, felt each small emission of hope and longing that filled them, until they burst forth in a slow rush of salt and heat, so heavy with import they crashed to the sand at her feet like breaking granite.

And then, at last, she was in his arms, his wet clothes saturating hers, his salty lips crushing her own, his breath tickling her face as he whispered her name between kisses. Any doubt she'd had about their feelings for each other evaporated. She felt the same sense of hypnotic bliss she always did when they touched and she thrilled to the knowledge, at last, they had enough time and freedom to be together, to fully commit themselves to whatever course they would travel. She touched Gabe's face with longing and wonder.

"Are you really here? Is this really happening?"

Gabe held both of her hands in his and laughed softly. "Hold that thought. I have the feeling you'll be asking that a lot over the next few hours."

Kate scanned his face for anxiety or worry, feeling nothing but contentment herself. "You have something to tell me." She vaguely wondered why he'd been swimming fully clothed and so late at night... but she didn't care, not really.

"Finally. Yes. Are your parents waiting for you?" She could see the thought pained him.

She dropped her gaze, unwilling to see his response to her answer. "They don't know I'm home." She hesitated to confess the next part. "I have a month's leave from my job." She knew she might be giving too much away by saying this, but then, this was Gabe, the reason she'd taken time off in the first place. She peeked at him to check his reaction.

He was stunned. "A *month?*" His expression was so severe, she shut her eyes again. But she took courage from her own conviction and straightened to regard him levelly, her confidence restored when she saw he was pleased. He wrapped one of his hands around her wrist. "We have time," he murmured, the intensity of his gaze draining every thought and feeling out of her not centered on him. "I thought I was going to have to figure out a way to be by you after this weekend."

"You still might."

Gabe tilted his head to one side, his eyes and skin silvery in the moonlight, reminding her of his appearance during their swim as children. His whole demeanor, in fact, was more as she remembered those many years ago, too sweet to be antagonistic, but more challenging and wild than he was otherwise. She could feel the conflict between objectivity and defiance balancing within him.

His smile brimmed with secrets. "I've got to get you in the water. Will you come for a swim?" He let go of Kate's waist to take her hand. His gaze was steady, intent. She knew in that moment she would go anywhere with him.

"Let's go."

He didn't hesitate. Without realizing, she'd waded with him into the shallows. He wrapped his arms around her and twisted them into the waves.

"She was especially looking for the young prince, and as the ship fell apart, she saw him sink down into the deep sea."

– Hans Christian Andersen
The Little Mermaid

PART TWO

CHAPTER THIRTEEN

Gabe had studied all the myths as a child. In the old stories about mermaids, irresistible sirens sang to hapless sailors and called them to their watery deaths. Traditional lore suggested the mermaids acted from a vain desire to prove their appeal – or from a capricious desire to demonstrate their predatory skills – and the attraction was supposedly all on the part of humans. But as Gabe well knew, the longing was intense on both sides. Their voices, promising love and adventure, and their exquisite beauty gave mermaids their magnetism. Humans drew their ocean counterparts to them with their perceived soulfulness. This soulfulness, expressed as a rich array of emotions humans unwittingly radiated, caused mermaids to sing in their best voices, to use their most fervent pleas to join them in the water.

Men and women were equally vulnerable to these calls, although in the early seafaring days, men succumbed because men traveled the seas. The widely accepted reports on how monstrous and unappealing male mermaids were—made, the community believed, by human men who wished to discredit their fishier romantic rivals –

were nonsense. The stories were pure conjecture anyway, since few people had actually seen males of his species. Had everyone been knowledgeable and honest, they would have reported mermaids, as a race and individually, were lovely.

Gabe preferred the term siren, given how non-gender-inclusive the *maid* part of the word mermaid was. He certainly didn't feel like a maid now, with a beautiful, bewitched and bewitching girl in his arms as he swam to Shaddox Island with her. He was elated and struggled to restrain his speed, which he had to, because Kate's system wouldn't withstand it. So he went slower than he preferred, kept her head against his chest, and maintained her slow heart rate and oxygen absorption. He brought her to the surface to breathe every ten minutes.

Even for him, though he'd played in the night water a thousand times before, the swim was magical. He delighted in the visual silence the darkness added, making the world around them all gentle grays and soft shadows. What he could see, Kate pressed close to him, was all the more singular and moving because there was little else to see.

And he reveled in the hundred quiet sensations he intuited from her, immersing himself in the vibrant abundance of feelings she emitted, experiencing her euphoria as his own. His longing intensified as he did this, and he hurried to tell her everything, and get them to their island.

I've brought you here so you can see what I am and know me here. I want to be with you, want us to be together always. When we give ourselves to each other, our bond will be life-long. This is how we marry. It is what I want more than I can say.

Her response to him was painfully sweet. *I have always wanted you, wanted this.*

He kissed her when he brought her to the surface for air. Moonlight reflected off the bubbles they released, silvery, graceful, and buoyant, spreading like a profusion of flowers strewn on a vertical path above them.

"I've waited so long for us," he murmured when they broke the surface. "I've wanted to tell you things, to have you here with me. Do you see what I am? What's happening?"

"You're a fish. A mermaid." He winced. "You've just, sort of, proposed to me, and it makes perfect, wonderful sense. My life, with you and your mermaid ways, finally makes sense to me. I can't believe I get to be with you." Her joy suffused him.

"*Mermaid* only applies to women, Kate."

She tilted her head thoughtfully. "What do I call you?"

He let the terms *lover* and *husband* echo around them despite his silence. Aloud, he said, "I'm just Gabe for the time being. But technically, I'm a siren."

"Okay, Gabe. My Gabe. Siren it is." Contentment and love flowed from her like heat from the sun, which compounded their mutual longing into a cyclical, intensifying hunger. He leaned into her.

His voice was thick when he next spoke. "Kate. If we stop here, we may not make it to Shaddox Island."

"You know, that's completely fine with me." She pressed herself against him.

He shuddered when he reached under her shirt to rest his hand at the curve of her waist, but then he stilled, his regret palpable. "We should wait until we get to the island. You're less likely to drown, and it's better if we hold off just a little longer anyway . . ." As he scanned her feelings, his conviction wavered.

"Wait for what?" she asked skeptically. "And, don't forget the last time we had this conversation, mister. It was *four years* ago."

He found her chagrin comical, which gave him the emotional distance he needed to break her spell, at least break it enough so he could abandon his almost-seduction of her here. "That wasn't my fault! And I'm only talking about a few hours, maybe a day."

"But I get to stay right by you? Is that a promise?"

"Yes. I can't tolerate any other option."

"Fine," she conceded unhappily. "Let's get to this island."

CHAPTER FOURTEEN

Love was a prison. No, that wasn't right. Love was the trap that led to the prison. But maybe he placed blame where it didn't belong. How Will wished his issues were due to some simple, off-center emotion he'd experienced fifteen years earlier. And if he was being honest, which, at this point, he really tried to be, falling for Dana had been a calculated endeavor. He'd approached the relationship in the same way he believed she had, where emotions were at best a secondary consideration.

He swirled the ice in his highball, drank it down, and was for the millionth time grateful for the effect of the alcohol, which allowed him to think about his life without the accompanying despair he felt when he was sober, which was almost never. He'd tried at first to simply avoid his troubled feelings, but that hadn't worked. Eventually, his restlessness won out, resulting in multiple trips to the men's room during the day, where he hid in the stalls for minutes at a time wrestling with his anxiety.

He found relief one evening when he'd stopped at an old watering hole on his way home from work, a place he and other up-and-comers went for happy hour before everyone married and started their families.

"What'll it be?" the bartender inquired.

"I don't know." The gin and tonic the bartender proposed proved just the ticket, cooling his throat and sending caressing rivulets of calm through his veins. Ah. The relief was so sweet.

He'd gone home that evening feeling more hopeful than he had in ages. *Everyone gets stuck in a rut*, he reasoned. *Nobody's life is perfect, everyone suffers. Especially people with smaller bank accounts*, he thought with a dark smile. His choices would surely be worth something in the end. He and Dana made love that night for the first time in months.

He made his stop at the bar a nightly habit. He wasn't after oblivion, just numbness, which differentiated him from actual alcoholics, he believed. He just needed to consider his situation objectively, something he could not do while his heart raced and ridiculous tears threatened behind his eyes.

For a while, a very short while, the two or three drinks he threw back on his way home from the office carried him through. Then he found he could cope with an additional cocktail at lunch, and then later again, with a nip of something at breakfast.

Eventually, he blamed Dana for his malaise. She was just so one-dimensional and serious all the time. He'd found her attractive, of course, back when they first met; although he'd known better than to rely solely on physical appearances. At that time, he shopped for the whole package, the pretty, smart, accomplished, ambitious woman who wanted what he did, which was success in the business world and the life of affluent couples he admired. He'd been smitten with Dana's appetite for advancement and impressed by her seemingly tireless dedication to her goals. He proposed when she graduated with her MBA.

But she was just so… inhumanly steady. She never wondered, as he did, if they were like gerbils on a wheel, running and running to no purpose. He decided she was the reason he felt unfulfilled. He tested this theory by having a couple of affairs when he was out of town, but like the alcohol, his pain was still with him when the buzz wore off.

And he was ashamed of himself. Not for his sexual indiscretions, of which he was not proud, but for his cowardly willingness to blame his wife for his own inability to tame his feelings. Dana, after all, had not been the one to renege in their marriage; he had. With this understanding, he realized he loved and admired his wife. He saw her as beautiful, diligent, and misguided, and he genuinely loved her. But he could not ask her for what he needed. Instead, he drank more in order to feel less.

When he got it right, the balance between consciousness and numbness, he considered his role in society as a man, as a husband. He'd been a gifted athlete growing up, which initially defined his masculinity for him and he was happy for it. His romances throughout school were also loosely predicated on his physical strength and speed. But business school had changed the game for him, when prowess at his desk became the key to his power and identity. In order to gain back that feeling of strength and competence, he'd swallowed the sales-driven notion money was power was success was happiness, swallowed it whole. By the time he questioned this premise, he was too far down the road to disengage, too old to play the athlete but too young to endure the pointless cycle of work and empty achievement any longer.

If only Dana would talk to him, maybe he would feel better, get better. If only his life were not quite so small despite its expansive trappings. He could not see a way out that made sense.

He remembered a conversation with a former college classmate at a reunion several years back. His friend lamented how his wife had changed from being willing to take on the world with him, to insisting she work part time when they had kids. "Man, if you'd told me she'd switch like this back when we were dating, I wouldn't have believed you."

Will's problem was the opposite; Dana had remained steadfast – in her commitment to build an admirable life outside the house, of foregoing having children. He was the one who wanted something different. His fantasies – not his wife's – for a more personal home life, with a child or two and all the interrupted sleep and mess they seemed to bring with them, drove him into the men's room stalls.

What he was living for was not worth it. Moreover, he could not hope she would change for him, and he could not tolerate his own depression any longer. He pondered his condition for what he hoped was the last time. In lieu of a letter, he wrote his wife a list.

Suicide is a cowardly act.

I drink because I'm suffering.

I can't figure out how not to suffer without compromising you.

I truly love you, although you may not believe me.
I'm sorry.
I'm a coward.

More than his drinking or his affairs, this decision gave him the relief he sought. Peace was finally, definitively close at hand. He researched his options on the internet. He was not surprised to read white men were three times more likely to commit suicide than anyone else. *Superman, indeed*, he thought grimly.

In the end, he went with the method that felt right, not what was quickest or most efficient. He decided to jump. Maybe he would feel exhilarated and alive one last time. Maybe he would feel as sorry as he should for what he was about to do. Whichever, he wanted a conscious, physical death, not simply to fall asleep and never wake up.

He flew to Maine on a morning Dana traveled for work. They'd stayed at a bed and breakfast there near a magnificent cliff early on in their marriage, and he'd never forgotten a particular view. The house sat on an out-jutting high above the ocean, the water below free of the boulders punctuating the shoreline elsewhere. He could not be sure, but the inky blue color of the sea in that place suggested deep water. He smiled as he imagined the icy liquid closing around him, a powerful tide carrying him deeper still. He was not a strong swimmer.

On the cliff, the flask he'd brought in case he needed courage lay unopened at his feet. For the first time in five years, he'd gone almost an entire day without a drink. He could barely suppress the craving in his body and the shake in his hands, which, had he not been about to do what he was, would have driven him to consume even more than he usually did. He wanted to die sober.

The sun started to descend along the western horizon but was still casting light when he stepped to the very edge of the cliff. The wind seemed to whistle the most inviting, uplifting tune. He closed his eyes and listened, the sound lulling him as he contemplated the ocean below. He inhaled deeply, proud to finally be taking action against his misery. He jumped soundlessly from the edge and plummeted into the crashing waves.

CHAPTER FIFTEEN

Gabe pointed to a large shape looming in the distance. That's the base of the island, he told her. We'll swim to the south side, where there's an inland access.

Her apprehension grew the closer they swam, which he understood as he considered the structure from her perspective. The underwater reef surrounding Shaddox imposed like a military threat, with sharp, treacherous rocks resembling giant skewers jutting outward in every direction. In fact, his people had fashioned it as a fortress, and to evoke the fearful response Kate had to it.

This is the island? Our sanctuary?

Yes.

She tugged at him. *It's terrifying. I don't like it.*

Wait, he advised.

They swam to a sheer rock face and followed it up, Gabe having to almost drag her through the water at this point. When they broke the surface, a huge expanse of craggy, barren rock greeted them. Here too, Gabe knew the effect of what she saw, which was a grayscape of misery – nothing but hardness and sharpness without a hint of plant life. She became nearly paralyzed with dread, which he intuited but could not alleviate.

"Just wait," he encouraged. "It's not what you think."

They reached a ledge, and he placed one of Kate's hands on it. "I'm going to let go of you for exactly ten seconds while I grab supplies." He kept his voice even in the hopes she would stabilize. She didn't. "You're going to feel cold and afraid so just know I'm coming *right* back. Will you promise to wait here and count to ten?" Kate gritted her teeth and nodded. "Whatever you do, do *not* swim underwater, okay?" He placed her other hand on the ledge and inched away. "Count to ten," he reminded her, and then he dove.

Her feelings weren't as easy to read as they'd been when he touched her but he could still sense her terror. All traces of her happiness evaporated the second he released her and he knew he didn't have much time before she gave in to despair. At twenty feet, he located one of the ubiquitous supply caches located in siren-made concavities in the rock face, Kate's panic following him the entire way. He delivered a menacing warning to the wild, silvery blue shapes flitting far beneath them, who stared up hopefully at Kate's floating figure. They flinched deeper but continued to watch Kate with a creepy kind of anticipation. Gabe retrieved a water-pack containing clothes, a flashlight, and a cell phone. He shot to the surface.

Kate counted breathlessly when he breached behind her, and he saw her straining away from the ledge. "Swim down! Swim away!" the shapes below screeched to her. He allowed the familiar flush of transformation to overtake his body until he was swimming toward Kate again, this time using his legs.

He caught her just as she loosened her hold on the ledge, bringing the arm she had extended away back into her body. She calmed down slowly, her breathing ragged and her heart thundering despite his concentrated effort to help. "You're okay; you're going to be all right." She clutched his shoulder until he bruised and kept her eyes shut. Eventually, she opened her eyes to glare at him.

"Yes. I am going to be okay. But please don't ever, ever do that again."

"I promise. Next time I'll take you with me. I thought I could get what we need faster this way." Her glare did not soften.

"Really, Kate, I'm sorry. Was it so bad?"

"Indescribable. Complete hopelessness."

Gabe felt abashed. "I've only heard stories. I'm sorry."

They exited the water via a flight of steps that began in the shallows and extended onto a plateau, flattening to a narrow path inland. With every step, Kate's uneasiness increased, and she eyed ever more reluctantly the harrowing landscape so at odds with Gabe's enthusiasm to reach it. Nothing she saw made sense – not the awful scenery in front of her Gabe had promised she'd love, not his excitement, or his urgency. She stopped and tugged at his hand.

"I don't think this is a good idea."

"It's not what it appears, Kate. Trust me." She somehow ignored her misgivings to continue forward. Even so, his hand on hers was the only force keeping her from pivoting on her heel and diving back into the ocean in a panic.

They came to a chasm in the rocks no more than three feet wide spanning an indeterminably deep, possibly life-threatening rift. Gabe jumped lightly over it, keeping Kate's hand so she would follow. Before she could protest, she was on the other side, and when she landed, the island's appearance transformed.

Instead of a forbidding, inhospitable expanse of rock, she saw an abundant Eden, with palm trees, lush grasses, and flowers perfuming the air. Lights twinkled from the surrounding trees and bushes, bathing them in a fairy-like glow.

"It's magic," she breathed. "Where did all of this come from?"

"This is what's really here. What you saw under water and on the shore is a fortified illusion, so people won't come."

"A fortified illusion?"

Gabe led her along a path up a hill during his explanation. "We can suggest images to the human mind, false images disguising what people actually see. Usually, this means appearing as a dolphin or sea lion or something to humans who see one of us in the water. But in this case, we have layers of illusion in place, built by many of us over hundreds of years. This type of effort and complexity results in a fortified illusion. It's very difficult to dispel."

"So, am I imagining all of this too? You, here? You're a mermaid? That swim we were just on?" Kate was no longer sure she could trust her perceptions at all.

Gabe grimaced. "Use the term *siren*, please," he begged. "I always picture myself in drag when I hear *mermaid*, and I'm not very pretty." He shuddered. "And unfortunately for you, this is all real, all happening, and I am what you saw me to be in the water."

Kate nudged him with her shoulder. "You know, I always wanted to date a siren."

Gabe offered her a brief, sad smile. "I'm afraid you're not going to get much out of this in terms of traditional dating," and she remembered Gabe's statements when they first entered the water about how sirens married, how their commitment to each other is permanent. *Fine by me*, Kate thought, more relieved than anything else. Their courtship had dragged on long enough in her opinion, and she didn't need movie dates and dinners out to convince her of their relationship at this point. Gabe squeezed her hand.

"There's my family's cottage." He pointed to a small house partially hidden behind a grove of trees at the top of the hill they'd just climbed. Kate could hear the close, dull roar of the ocean, the sound predictable and rhythmic, and as soothing as a lullaby. She realized how tired she was, which made sense when she figured out how long it had been since she'd last slept. Not since before her last day at work, before meeting Gabe in Griffins Bay, before swimming several hours to reach the place they were now. An entire lifetime had passed since she had climbed out of the covers of her bed in her apartment two mornings ago. Gabe yawned and leaned down to whisper in her ear, "Yes. I'm tired too."

The cottage was set back on a jagged high cliff and offered expansive views of the ocean to the north and east sides of the island. Upon reaching the house, Gabe led them across a patio winding around to a back lawn, where they paused to admire the ocean and stars from the home's exquisite elevation.

"The view is stunning. Is this your parents' place?"

"Along with a few other Blakes. My family owns it."

"It's heaven."

Gabe gave her hand another squeeze and led her into the house. "I want to show you what I was talking about on our way here, see if I can make us both feel something related to your pulse and blood pressure." Anticipation mixed with panic froze its way down her spine.

She found the cottage more traditionally appointed than the house in Griffins Bay, as well as smaller. A cornerstone had a date from two centuries earlier chiseled on it, and she guessed the place had never been significantly reconfigured, except for evidence she saw of two nearly seamless additions. She recognized Carmen and Michael's decorating sensibility, although they'd used deeper colors and heavier fabrics, which gave the rooms a warm intimacy lacking in their open, sunny beach house.

As she studied her surroundings, she caught Gabe's unvoiced opinions on the cottage, including how happy he was to be here. *This is where I'm most relaxed and free.*

"The library is like that for me."

Gabe led them down a hallway to a corridor sitting room stretching along the back of the house and overlooking the water, and then into a small but opulent bedroom. The walls were wood-paneled, interrupted on one side by a stone fireplace and on the other by a doorway to a bathroom. Windows lined the back of the room, she presumed to take advantage of the ocean view. An enormous bed, covered in plush, inviting linens, anchored the remaining wall.

Kate leaned her head on Gabe's shoulder. "This is so perfect," she sighed.

No, Gabe thought, *what's perfect is being here, alone with Kate, everything out in the open between us.* He pulled her by her hands backward to the bed, and then caught her to his chest as he fell on the covers. He shifted them both on their sides. "Now, about that trick I wanted to try." He brought one of her hands to his chest and wrapped his other hand around her wrist.

He watched her and tried to reflect what he sensed back to her. He noticed the subtle increase in blood pressure from the last time he'd checked, each pulse echoing dimly throughout his own body with a dull thud causing a small shiver of desire to course through him.

Kate inhaled sharply. "What is that?"

"I can tell when you're about to ovulate. The closer you are, the more intensely we'll want, um, well, to be together," he stammered. They both laughed and blushed.

"You know, that's practically obscene."

Gabe grinned. "You wanted to know. And truthfully, it's a relief to tell you. It's like this force of nature very few of us can ignore. When we commit to someone, this is how it starts."

Kate became pensive. "So, if I'm about to ovulate, I might get pregnant."

"Chances are about a hundred percent," he told her flatly.

Kate arched a brow. "Sirens don't use contraceptives?"

He winced with self-reproach. "Not at first. It's part of how we bond."

He felt her dismay and caught her thoughts, over her job, her apartment, her parents, and the consequences a pregnancy would have. Maybe she could expand her blog into something to generate income, and she could create a few more choices for herself than what she might have with her office job. The idea kind of appealed to her, which thrilled him.

"We'll figure everything out, Kate. I promise." His confidence fed hers as he'd hoped, and he felt her apprehension drain away.

"Okay. We'll figure it out."

Gabe rolled them into the covers. Then, warm and dry and completely fatigued, Kate's eyelids drooped. "I'm so tired," she apologized, yawning.

"That's going to get a lot worse." He grinned wickedly but he helped her fall asleep. When her eyes had closed and she breathed evenly, he let his own exhaustion overtake him. He drifted off into a sound, anticipatory sleep.

Several hours later, he woke her.

Her pulse crashed through him now with deafening urgency, every beat gripping him in a flood of craving he could barely control. "Kate," he called quietly, willing her eyes to open. They did, briefly registering his desire before his mouth hungrily overtook hers. His yearning surged through both of them like a tidal wave, inexorable and elemental, jettisoning all that was not their union. He felt her immediate response, registered how his taste and warmth filled her senses, saw their intent as a shimmering, pervasive presence around them.

Their supple bodies twisted and strained together, their hands moving fervently over each other. With effort, Gabe held himself motionless when Kate tensed in initial pain. He kissed her tenderly for several long seconds, until she moved against him again. "Gabe," she whispered in his ear, her voice bruised with longing as she pressed herself more tightly to him.

His joy overflowed then, his heart releasing a torrent of warmth and love that coursed through them both in an unbroken current, permeating every cell and traveling the length of every nerve. The rest of the world floated away as they immersed themselves, at long last, in each other and nothing else, every kiss a prayer answered, every touch urgent with desire too long withheld.

CHAPTER SIXTEEN

Anna was in her sea cave tending a bed of mussels when her daughter, Penny, found her and shared her bizarre story. Something about a man named Will planning to jump to his death, and how he'd drawn dozens of their women to witness him. Everyone was floating at the base of Carey Rock, according to Penny. Her description of the man tugged at Anna's memory, and she swam with her daughter back to the waiting throng of mermaids to investigate.

The waves would have carried Will into the face of the cliff, not out to sea as he speculated, an erroneous belief intuited by all of them watching him from underwater, Anna included. They all knew his body would have been smashed to bits in a matter of seconds without their intervention, which they were eager to provide after an entire afternoon spent watching him and drinking in his delicious, rich sentiments. As it was, he fainted well before he hit the water. He never saw the creatures who softened his fall and kept his body from annihilation, not that they would have allowed him to remember them.

One of the women had noticed him standing at his perch near the time he arrived there, and, as the day wore on, others gathered under the water's surface to watch too. His feelings radiated forcefully off him, creating a yearning they were not supposed to indulge in but by the time Anna joined the fray, she was too late to interrupt. His allure had intensified during his all-day stand at the edge of his rock. The women now sang to him, to ease his anxiousness, and to invite him to join them in the water.

I will love him, Lydia announced.

No, I'll be the one, Bridget argued, and then others spoke up, each vying for primary custody. They squabbled playfully as they waited.

Perhaps we could share him, one of them suggested, their prolonged attendance urging them into a frenzy Anna believed was dangerous. Their interest had progressed far beyond simple caprice, and none of them had any real experience keeping humans alive in the water.

I came to see about all the commotion, Penny told her. *I saw your face in his memory and came to get you.*

As Anna gazed at the figure above, she felt his scattered thoughts and became convinced she had met this man before. When he jumped, she heard his wife's name, Dana, and then she remembered.

Sisters, she apologized to the siren women around her, *this is the husband of the sister of John Blake's wife. We cannot have him for ourselves.*

They emitted a collective sigh of disappointment. They pleaded, *just for a while, Anna. We'll keep him safe. Go to Cara and John but in the meantime, we will keep him alive. And warm.*

Anna hesitated as she thought through the logistics of her new responsibility, which was to find the sirens connected to Will. He really was better off here while she went to Griffins Bay. *Keep him unaware too, please,* she requested. They all nodded, too enthusiastically for her taste, but then she thought of the human saying, *Beggars can't be choosers.* Indeed. She swam off toward Griffins Bay.

Carmen worked at her desk when Anna arrived, with Michael seated across from her reading a scientific journal. She got right to the point. "A group of us caught Will Fletcher, Dana's husband, making a suicide jump off Carey Rock this afternoon. He's unharmed, and they're keeping him at sea while I'm here."

Carmen and Michael leapt to their feet. "Who has him?" Michael asked.

"The Seward clan. Well, the women in the clan." Michael bolted toward the door.

"Wait!" Carmen pleaded. "Anna, you told them to keep him safe, right? To take extra care?"

"I did." She was uncertain though, which, she saw undermined her credibility.

"Michael, someone has to go to John and Cara, and someone should probably collect Dana . . ." Carmen trailed off.

"And someone needs to make sure Lydia and Bridget don't literally drown Will with their affection," Michael asserted, still poised to leave.

"You're right, of course. Go get him, if you can wrestle him free, and take him to Shaddox. I'll fetch Cara and John, and at least one of us will chase Dana down. I'm thinking we'll probably all bring her back." She stared over everyone's head a few more seconds. "Yes. We'll bring Dana to the island, you bring Will, and we'll figure out... *something*... together."

"I can go with Michael to spring Will from the Sewards," Anna offered.

Michael's smile was full of gratitude. "Thanks. I'll take all the help I can get."

CHAPTER SEVENTEEN

Cara called Dana to find out where she was, and Dana was immediately suspicious of her. "What's the matter?" Cara wished she'd taken care to sound less freaked out.

"Before I answer, where are you? Have you heard from Will?"

"I'm at my hotel in Dallas. And no, I haven't talked with him today. Why?"

"When do you get back to Philly?"

Dana consulted her itinerary. "Noon tomorrow. What's going on?"

She struggled to think of a plausible lie. "I need your advice on something." She knew she sounded lame.

"So, go ahead and tell me what's up." Cara remained silent for too long. "Cara, you're worrying me."

"I'd prefer to talk in person," Cara hedged until inspiration finally struck. "Can I meet you at your house?"

"That's it. Tell me what's going on right now."

"You don't need to worry about anything. Anything at all. I just, sort of, have some ideas for a new business, and I… have an immediate opportunity. And I want to go over it with you. And Will.

I already talked to Will this afternoon a little bit." She thought this last lie might help rope Dana in. It did.

"Oh." Dana sounded mollified. "Well that'll be fine. I'll call my office and tell them I won't be in until Friday and we can have the afternoon. I'll be glad to help you out."

"Great!" Cara gushed, which Dana apparently disliked.

"You really don't sound right, Cara. Do you have to buy a building by the end of the week or something?"

"Something like that. I'll let myself in and wait for you tomorrow. I'll see you then." She hung up.

John had his assistant clear his calendar for the rest of the week. Cara called Alicia, and, citing a family emergency, requested she keep Everett overnight, which she agreed to do. The plan was first to intercept any suicide message from Will, and then intercept Dana, herself. They could have flown and avoided the time commitment involved with a road trip but they expected to keep Dana as mentally compromised as possible when they brought her back and didn't want an audience for that effort. Cara offered to drive.

"We'll know more when we get to the house," Carmen opined once they were down the road. "I mean, if he left a note, we can maybe figure something out by reading it. And then we can have Dana make any necessary arrangements for them both to be gone, ideally without too much fuss."

"What's happening with Will?" John inquired.

"Anna and Michael — and Lydia and Bridget, who insisted on, oh, let's call it *helping* — are taking him to Shaddox. He's going through delirium tremens, more easily than most, since the Seward women have him pretty well sedated. He has absolutely no idea what's going on, which I suppose is a good thing."

Cara couldn't contain her curiosity any longer. "What are we going to do with them both?"

"Don't tell any of Sewards," Carmen replied, "but my sense is their marriage could and should be fixed. I think we're going to try some standard, old-fashioned hazing to get Dana and Will back together."

John's gaze was thoughtful. "We could take them to see Xanthe."

Cara was confused. "Who's Xanthe?"

"She's a kind of diplomatic counselor for our people," John informed her. "She judges in matters requiring stronger resolution than we can achieve on our own. She's dangerous, occasionally terrifying, and she resolves conflict like nobody's business."

"He's right," Carmen agreed. "Xanthe has ended wars, divided oceans, thwarted despots, and mended economic crises, all simultaneously."

John's expression became dry. "I don't know if she's ever engaged in marital counseling but she might be willing to do it for Carmen."

Carmen winced. "Yeah, I hate to call in a favor for this. Let's see what we can figure out, first."

John agreed. "We'll know more tomorrow."

The sun was high above the cottage when Kate asked how long he meant for them to stay in bed. "Aren't you hungry? Dehydrated?"

"Nope." Gabe buried his face in her neck.

He felt her astonishment as she responded to his fresh attempts at seduction. "Good lord. Are all the men in your world like this?"

"I don't know." He frowned. "I've never slept with any men from my world."

"Ha. You're funny. But really, how long does this go on?"

"Three days." He tasted his way up her neck and behind her ear. "That's how long a woman is fertile."

He leaned away to extricate himself from the twisted covers, and Kate took advantage of his distraction to roll off the bed. She scooped her robe off the floor as she headed for the door, hurrying from the room before he could stop her. "I'm getting us some water," she stated. "And some crackers or something."

Gabe rose reluctantly and stretched before following her to the kitchen. He was dead tired but felt fantastic. As Kate filled two glasses with water, he stood behind her, held her hair to one side, and placed a series of kisses along her neck and shoulders. Chills coursed through her but she defended her quest for sustenance by stepping away, drinking her glass of water and firmly handing him his. She avoided looking him in the eye, which he intended to talk her into. Although maybe he should let her eat before bothering her again.

After gulping down all of her water, she rummaged through the cupboards, retrieving a bag of potato chips and opening it. To his surprise, she dropped it on the floor. He was officially fascinated. She went to the fridge.

"This is really entertaining," he commented, leaning back against the counter. Kate didn't answer him.

She fetched a tub of yogurt from the refrigerator door, grabbed a spoon from one of the drawers, and ducked down to sit on the floor, scooting her seat until she was next to the bag of chips. She opened her yogurt and spooned some into her mouth, closing her eyes with pleasure as she did. She ate a potato chip, sighed, and ate another.

Gabe sat on the floor too, grinning impishly as he grabbed Kate's foot and dragged her, the bag of chips, and yogurt clutched possessively against her chest, toward him. She continued to eat, still keeping her gaze anywhere but on him. She slapped his hand away when he tried to undo her robe. "Oh, but this is fun," he told her as he retrieved a potato chip from her stash.

"Kate, honey? Can I please have a bite of your yogurt?"

Slumping and reluctant, Kate finally caved and scooped a spoonful of yogurt into his mouth. As expected, her focus on lunch was undermined seconds after their eyes met. And despite her initial disapproval, he made sure she felt his devotion in the hopes she would forgive him. She smiled and looped her arms around his neck, and he wrapped her legs snugly around his waist. They abandoned lunch in favor of more lovemaking. They did not decamp back to the bedroom.

Cara struggled with guilt over the deceit she'd perpetrated with her call to her sister. Consequently – and also because they arrived after midnight and she was tired – she fumbled with her keys to the front door of the Dana and Will's home. She eventually got it open and ushered her makeshift rescue team inside.

John found Will's note in the kitchen and pumped his fist after reading it. "There's hope," he announced triumphantly.

Carmen was more relieved than excited. "Which is good, since it means we didn't come for nothing. But we need to snoop too." Over the next few hours, Cara led an investigation through desk drawers and computer files for insight into the Fletchers' life together.

After a thorough ransacking, the threesome convened in the living room to plot next steps. "Looks like all we have to do is kidnap Dana and brainwash her and her husband," Carmen suggested, and Cara laughed.

"Such a bright pronouncement to do evil," she chided. "But I'm all for it, of course." John chuckled, yawned, and then stretched.

"I'm beat. We should turn in."

Cara wound her arms around his waist. "Let's go upstairs, and I'll make sure everyone gets a bed."

Dana was surprised to see all three of them, bleary-eyed and drinking coffee in her kitchen when she arrived the following afternoon. Cara was grateful she wasn't mad at her for presuming to bring unapproved guests but she supposed her siren escorts had something to do with her lack of concern. Carmen went to Dana before she'd spoken a word, clasped her upper arm, and led her to a stool by the center island. John took Dana's other hand, and Cara suppressed a laugh as she watched her sister relax and smile beatifically at her attendants. She knew first-hand what Dana was feeling.

"How wonderful of you all to come!" Dana exclaimed. "Cara, thank you ever so much for bringing them along!"

"Yeah. Well. About that –" Cara started to respond, but John cut her off.

"We've actually made plans for a surprise vacation for you and Will. And we'll need you to call your offices to arrange for the time off."

Dana's smile faded. "But we didn't fill out vacation request forms."

Carmen removed one of her hands from Dana so she could punch a number on the phone, which she held to Dana's ear. She positioned herself before her. "Repeat after me."

"Will Fletcher's office," a voice answered on the other end of the line. Dana parroted Carmen's exact words. "Hi, it's Dana. I'm calling with some bad news, I'm afraid; Will's been in an accident. He's stable but I'm flying to Maine to be by him. I'm not sure when he'll be back in the office."

Cara heard a flurry of anxious questions from the other end of the line, and then John took the receiver. "Yes, this is Dr. Blake, and I'm sorry, but Dana isn't able to talk. Would you please convey her information to Will's superiors? I'm sure the Fletchers will be in touch as soon as possible."

"You didn't feel the need to mention you're an *eye* doctor?" Cara teased after he'd hung up.

John's glance was disparaging as he dialed Dana's office for a repeat performance, after which Dana became upset. "Will didn't really have an accident, did he?"

"Will's just fine," Cara assured her. "Let's get going so you can see for yourself."

In the car, Cara drove while John and Carmen sat with Dana between them in the back seat. John started questioning her. "How has Will been doing, Dana?"

"Oh, you know. He's such an achiever. He works too much, but I don't know how to get him to ease up." Her voice dropped to a conspiratorial whisper. "I think his masculinity depends on him doing well in his job." She smiled widely at John. "And, of course, I worry about him." She stared at her lap. "Really, it's funny you bring it up, because I've never told this to another living soul but I think he might have a drinking problem." Again, she smiled widely, this time to no one in particular. Cara rolled her eyes. John disguised his laughter as choking.

"Why do you think that is?" Carmen pressed.

Dana eyed her speculatively, still grinning. "You people!" she protested. "These are private matters! Oh well, you've always been so good to my poor, dear sister." Cara harrumphed. "I feel just like telling you everything!"

"Tell us everything," and "share everything," John and Carmen said in unison.

"You know, we both were so ambitious when we were dating," Dana confided. "I'm a little embarrassed, but Will reminded me of my dad, always talking about my goals and things I did at work. You guys won't approve but success was everything to us.

"And I guess it still is," she continued less certainly, "but it sure hasn't been any fun the past few years. Can I tell you a secret?" Her question was sudden enough to make everyone in the car jump.

Carmen recovered first. "Go on."

"Don't tell anyone," Dana checked over each shoulder, "but I've kind of had it with my job. It's the same old thing day after day. The only reason I stay with it is so Will feels secure. Like maybe if he knows he can count on me, he won't have to worry. Or drink so much."

John was kind in his approach to what Cara knew was a difficult topic for her sister. "Did you and Will ever talk about having children?"

"Oh, that's something we decided before we got married. We didn't want to have kids in the way, you know." Her bravado faded into sadness. "I sometimes regret that decision. I actually thought about *forgetting* to take my pill a couple of times, but that wouldn't have been fair to Will. Plus, I'm in my forties now. I don't know if it's possible." Both Carmen and John wrapped a hand around each of her wrists, and after a few seconds, Carmen used her free hand to unzip Dana's overnight bag. She found the flat, round box of birth control pills, which she flicked out the car window. John chuckled quietly while Cara grinned hard into the rearview mirror.

Although she was tired from driving the entire way, Cara was pleased with the progress Carmen and John had made with her sister. And she'd been able to listen to all of it: the dissection of what had gone on in Dana's house, the reasons behind Will's despair... and she felt confident in a happier outcome. Also, Dana was exhausted from her inquisition, which left her out cold so the rest of them could discuss what to do when they got to Griffins Bay without inquiry from her.

"Unfortunately, Xanthe really would be the quickest means to our end," Carmen lamented. "I don't want to call her for this. But I will."

Once in Griffins Bay, John and Cara dropped Carmen and Dana off at the Blakes'. "We're going to pick up Everett, and then we'll all swim out and meet you," John told Carmen before he drove away. "Where's the rendezvous?"

"Let's meet Michael and Anna by the pier so we can pick up Will together. Then we'll all make our way to Shaddox."

In Childress, Cara went to collect Everett while John stayed home to pack. As he was finishing, he heard a knock at the door. He opened it to find Hank Gifford, the town sheriff, there in full uniform.

"Hi, John, sorry to bother you."

"No problem, Hank." He was a little alarmed. "What's up?"

"Well, I'm wondering if you guys have heard from Kate in the past couple of days." John reached with his senses to ascertain Hank's specific worry and immediately felt sick. Was Kate in trouble?

"I haven't but I can check with Cara when she gets back. Why?"

"A guy from the police department over in Griffins Bay called because they towed a car from the lot by the public beach. It's Kate's car."

He almost laughed with relief. Kate's car would be at the beach by the Blake house for one reason alone. He suppressed a grin.

"Ah. That makes sense. I forgot about this because she's out on her own, now. But I believe she'd planned a boating trip with the Blakes. She must have left her car in the lot where she shouldn't have. I'm sorry. She should have known better."

Hank sagged against the doorframe as the tension ran out of him. "That's the best news I could have hoped for. I was worried about a possible drowning." He jerked his head as if to negate the thought.

"I don't think so," John assured him. "And I'm so sorry for the trouble. I'll send someone over to the impound lot for the car, okay?"

"Good idea. But just so we know for sure, could you get a hold of Kate and let me know you've reached her?"

"No problem, Hank. I'm almost certain there's no need to worry. But thanks for coming by."

Cara squealed when he called and gave her the news. "Omigosh, I've got to call Carmen immediately. This is so great!"

When she reported back, she relayed Carmen's suggestion they pay a mass visit to Shaddox, which she supported. John didn't believe Gabe and Kate would welcome their company but Cara's enthusiasm was infectious, and he agreed. "I'll see if we can use the Mattegins place. Because something tells me the kids won't want to share the cottage." He and Cara giggled.

John knew how anxious Cara became when Everett swam these days, so he made sure she understood he had their son in hand on their way to Shaddox. "If he swims away, I'll catch him. We'll have an easier time since we're going at night too, with no humans around to see him." Everett, of course, loved the *fish game* more than any other and transformed well for his age. As expected, he changed from unstable toddler to agile swimmer in seconds. John had almost as much fun chasing his son as his son did running away.

CHAPTER EIGHTEEN

The harsh light of the setting sun through the windows woke Kate from her nap. She peeked at Gabe, who was not so disturbed, and began inching out of the covers with the idea she might get in a shower. Gabe's eyes opened a second later, however, and his unspoken request to stay by him had her crawling back in to snuggle. They stared quietly at each other for a while, the beat of Kate's pulse failing, for once, to pierce their fatigue.

"We're taking a break?"

"Yep. I'm shot."

"At last!" She collapsed onto her pillow. "Don't get me wrong — this has been the best time of my life — but I was beginning to think we'd never get out of bed again."

"I like that idea better than exhausting ourselves with babies and medical school at Chapel Hill. That's what we're signed up for, by the way."

"Let's just keep it to one baby for a while, please. And you're already enrolled?"

"I'm accepted at UNC Medical, which is where *we're* going. I'm thinking family practice at the moment. We're short family practice docs in our community – everywhere, really – and I like the opportunities that go with preventive care, before people get really sick." He shifted to his side. "You might have twins, you know, so it could still be babies. There's a pretty high incidence among couples like us."

"You'd better go into psychiatry, then. Because I will want antidepressants. I remember when Everett was born, and even with a three-to-one ratio of adults-to-kid, we had all we could say grace over."

Gabe tucked her hair behind her ear. "We'd get help, preferably of the non-pharmaceutical variety, from our mothers." He stroked her cheek with his thumb, and she once again felt blissful and relaxed. "And I can provide my own form of antidepressant, right?"

"Ah. Yes. It's wonderful. But how come I'm less swept away than I was when you first did that? I mean, I still feel heavenly, but I also feel more aware. Like I'm actually awake."

Gabe affected a leer. "You wouldn't if I really put my back into it." She shoved him away playfully. "No, actually it's a matter of concentration on my part," he explained. "I'm not worried about you feeling anxious, so I'm not trying to influence you. And we're on land, not in water, where you're more susceptible. And your system builds a sort of immunity. So I can't just make you jump off a bridge or something. But if I concentrated, or if there were a couple of us working on you at the same time, you'd be oblivious."

She propped her head up on her arm. "So. Let's talk more about life since we were seventeen."

Gabe grabbed her free hand. "Okay. Should we start with the evil intervention of our parents, or talk about our respective lives of academic slavery?"

"Let's start with the evil intervention part. What was the big idea there?"

"The big idea was to preclude us from bonding too early."

"And how did they know we would?"

"My mother has basically been scheming against us since I lured you off that boat when we were five, after you and your mother moved here. I think she showed you an astrological chart she started for you?"

She nodded.

"Yeah, well, between our astral compatibility and my initial addiction to you, she and Dad both figured we'd make a good match."

"And we couldn't have maybe seen each other in high school? Maybe gone to prom, or something normal?"

Gabe shook his head. "Not a good idea. It's hard for someone who's not one of us to understand but we don't date." He seemed to reconsider this response. "Well, we do participate in group social activities in school. Not many, though. And we never do anything like one-to-one dancing."

"Tell me more."

"I always feel like our society is too structured and restrictive when I talk about this but we don't do months of emotional exploration prior to coupling up. There's a kind of emotional inquiry we make when we first meet someone, but we don't have to go to plays or dinner to know if we can bond. We just kind of know."

She considered how she would have felt if Gabe had not been drawn to her. "It would have killed me if you'd found someone else. I really don't think I could have watched."

"Trust me; I felt the same way about you. And I was so sure we were right for each other, I could hardly wait to get this deal done. Our parents had their hands full distracting me away. And keeping you otherwise occupied too."

"Is that what all the heavy academic lifting was for? The massive over-scheduling of schoolwork?"

"Absolutely," he confirmed. "But our parents had more practical reasons."

Kate lifted her eyebrows. "Just making sure we don't start having babies at sixteen?"

"Exactly. The thing with sirens is we have pretty high standards of personal responsibility. Everyone has to be able to support themselves before it's considered okay to marry."

"That's not such a bad idea," she countered.

"Maybe not, but that's not the whole story. We all work a certain amount for the community, pay into a common fund used for our educations and basic housing when we start out in life, or for medical expenses if any of us have a problem. We pay based on ability, so the obligation isn't onerous for anyone. But we have to be able to both pull our weight and contribute. Pride is as big a motivator as the legal mandate, although we do have a mandate."

She pretended horror. "Omigosh. I've married a communist."

"Not really," he disagreed lightly. "We're also free-market-based – we're only about ten degrees off from the tax system you guys have on land. It just works better for us because we have a much smaller population and less economic – and cultural – disparity in general."

"Well, what I remember about my sprint through high school and college is how all that pressure made me feel self-destructive after a while. Seriously, I understand why people pick up smoking, or a fast food habit."

Gabe's expression was rueful. "I know. Maybe there's a better way to skin that cat. But you have to admit you're ready to support yourself if you had to, and you have the self-discipline to do lots of things you otherwise wouldn't. As much as it sucked, we're more ready for adult life than most other people our age."

She frowned, unconvinced. "I suppose. I don't really care now that it's over and we're together. So, tell me more about you, about being a siren."

Gabe stretched. "What do you want to know?"

She thought through her growing list of questions. "Are there a lot of you out there? I can't believe you haven't been discovered."

"No, not many. Maybe a couple hundred thousand or so worldwide. That's one reason we haven't been found out. And we're really, really good at appearing to be something else. That's another reason.

"My mother would have an exact population count for you. Remember how she told you and your mother about her genetics background?" Kate nodded. "Well, she's the person responsible for keeping our genetic and census records, including who's related and how. And she evaluates non-sirens as potential mates for some of us." He poked Kate in the ribs. "Her research on people's families is so she can learn if the person might fit in, where they came from and what their astrological chart holds. She uses this information to make calculated suggestions concerning marriage, like a matchmaker."

"Does this happen often, where one of you marries one of us?"

"Sometimes, if it can be done safely –which is to say, without exposure –we marry land people, non-swimmers such as yourself. We have issues with genetic diversity, and intermarriage helps. The party at my parent's house, the one you and Maya called the Blake orgy?" Kate smiled at the memories this question evoked. "It was a matchmaking event. My mom sets them up according to what's going on with our population and some lunar schedule she uses for predicting good outcomes. I don't pretend to understand it. She'll have one for the ladies here at some point. I'm told it's pretty funny to see."

"And do you have a say at all in who you end up marrying? I don't like that something so personal could be so prescribed."

"Everyone has a say. It's actually very much like what you saw at my parent's house the night John got together with your mother . . ."

"Holy cats!" she interrupted. "John's a siren, isn't he? And what about Everett?" She was stunned, mostly because John's siren status hadn't occurred to her until now.

"It's not for me to tell you about John, but you can figure it out. As for Everett, the siren gene is dominant, and offspring are always sirens."

"Can people become sirens?"

"No. However, humans in our company make some pretty significant adaptations."

"Such as?"

"Such as the ability to hold your breath longer. Right now, with my help, you can hold your breath for about ten minutes. Just like a baby whale." He brushed her nose with his forefinger. "If we swim together regularly, you'll be able to hold your breath on your own for up to twenty minutes. Forty minutes if one of us is holding onto you."

"For how long can you hold your breath, Gabe?"

"About four hours. Longer if we're in really cold water and not moving around too much."

"Wow. What else can you do?"

His face lit up with excitement. "You wouldn't believe how fast we can swim. It's exhilarating. We're all really agile, and much stronger than you land lubbers. And we can sort of blur the concept of time."

She thought of their first foray into the water as children, and how all the people on the boat were sure only minutes had passed while she and Gabe swam, when in fact, hours had gone by. She regarded him thoughtfully. "Go on."

"You live longer." His expression clouded. "We live three hundred years typically, although a few of us are older. If you live with a siren, your lifespan grows to about one hundred and fifty years." His eyes watered. "And it's very hard to lose your mate."

"What other adaptations do people make?" She wanted to discuss something less painful, although she resolved to go over longevity questions with him another time.

"You know how we can communicate under water?" Kate nodded. "It's really an advanced form of intuition. You think we're mind reading even though we're not. It's more a sensitivity you gain to people's thoughts and feelings, which we apprehend because we're particularly attuned. We're best in the water, although we can kinda pull it off on land, if we're touching the person and concentrating pretty hard. You process what comes to you as words but you're actually interpreting what you sense. Which is kind of cool, because no matter what language someone speaks, you can always understand what they're saying.

"Humans can do this too," he continued, "but their sensitivity becomes more developed after prolonged cohabitation with us. The ability to suggest false images comes from the same skill, and some people pick that up too."

"Ooo! This has puzzled me, like, my whole life – what's the deal with the Clark Kent glasses? All the people who wear them are sirens, right?"

"Yep. Our eyes are a little different from yours, and we need to keep them trained so we can see well underwater. If we don't wear the glasses, we lose the ability to focus when we're hunting. Or just plain see where we're swimming."

"So, back to how you choose who you end up with. You were telling me how individual choice is involved."

"Yes. And some of our choice is dictated by timing. As in, we start looking when we're biologically ready. During that time, we meet in groups my mother has defined, where any of the people there could marry and it would be good for them and for the community."

"Which doesn't quite sound the same as having free choice."

"It's not so different in your society, Kate. I mean, you tend to marry people you're exposed to. You don't choose some hypothetical person in another country. Usually."

Kate considered his explanation. "I guess I see your point. I remember my mother saying something similar to me once when I was little, when I asked how it worked, finding your husband, and if each person has to find the one other person on earth they can marry." She smiled at her former naiveté. "I was worried about her, whether she'd be alone the rest of her life after losing my father.

"Anyway, she told me the miracle is in the bond you form as you live with someone, not in how perfectly suited – or wildly attracted – you are to each other at the beginning. I was encouraged."

"It's similar. We can successfully bond with a number of people, but once we do, the commitment is absolute and final."

"And you never wonder if you made the right decision later on?" she teased.

"Never."

"Good thing. 'Cause I'm not willing to let you go." She squeezed him when he drew her close. Then she cast him a sideways glance. "So. Does your mother know you're here?"

Gabe laughed into her hair. "Not precisely, although I do have first-hand knowledge of what her opinion would be." His expression deepened as she placed a series of weightless kisses across his face, and the lightness of their exchange darkened. She lay by him and searched his hungry expression.

"If I had said, *No, thank you,* what would you have done?"

"I would have convinced you otherwise." She knew he tried to sound cavalier. "No, that's not right," he admitted. "You're forgetting when we touched all those times, I knew your feelings." His gaze rested tenderly on hers as he placed her hand over his heart so his devotion flowed through them both, enveloping them in its warmth. "I felt exactly the same way, of course." She felt tears begin to form, stinging her nose, and she pressed a kiss to the palm of his hand. He emitted a small, frustrated laugh. "It was so easy to know what could be, and so hard to wait."

Kate felt a succession of strong emotions that changed swiftly from relief to humility to gratitude to joy, sensations she felt altering as Gabe intuited them and sent them back to her, which she apprehended and mirrored yet again. They shared thoughts and emotions in a reflective cycle, accustoming themselves to their particular habits of feeling and response.

Gabe broke their concentration. "Someday, this sharing will tell on us, you know. It'll be like our personal signature when we're around others." She raised an eyebrow in question. "It means we'll be able to feel each other's presence without the aid of any other senses.

And others will know we're together because of what we throw off."

"I love it."

They lay quietly then, limbs entwined, each contributing feelings and promises toward a bond they believed would forever be uniquely theirs.

Later in the evening, Gabe froze, and then, with a long, regretful sigh, rolled away from Kate to sit on the edge of the bed. He inclined his head toward the door.

He waited to announce what he sensed, wanting to confirm their impending disruption before he alarmed Kate. But yes, both sets of parents had just entered the cottage.

He was attuned enough to his dad and mom to intuit their actions even from a distance, which meant he felt his dad's amusement after he switched on the kitchen light. He was reviewing the detritus from their lunch on the kitchen floor. Gabe even caught a picture of what he saw: the bathrobe, the open bag of potato chips, the empty yogurt cup, and then glasses trailing down the hallway.

Then he heard John's muttered comment. "Sex camp." Carmen and Cara, he noted, both smothered laughter, albeit poorly.

"What's the matter?" Kate asked.

"Remember your question about what my mother would think of this?"

"Yes?" She braced herself.

"We can question her in person. She's here."

Kate hissed, pulling the sheets up to her neck.

"Mm-hmm," Gabe confirmed. "So's Dad, and so are your folks."

"What!" Kate shrieked, this time rolling off the bed to search frantically for her clothes. Gabe huffed and donned a shirt and pair of shorts. He held his hand out to Kate, glowering in the direction of the kitchen. "Let's get this over with."

Kate would have rather died than leave their room to greet everyone but agreed they should get the meeting behind them. As they entered the kitchen, she glanced at the items on the floor, blushed scarlet and tried to run away. Gabe's hand on hers was all that kept her from bolting. She closed her eyes, vacillating between humiliation and seething anger, and, somehow, stayed put. She glared daggers at each of the newcomers.

Gabe radiated his own irritation as he visually excoriated all four people in the room. "What the hell are you doing here?"

John's coughing was no disguise. All of them were trying not to laugh. Cara and Carmen couldn't even face them, instead clutching each other doubling over. Michael stepped forward to take the heat, managing to contain his amusement to just a smile. "Hi, kids! It appears congratulations are in order!"

Carmen and Cara came to them then, clucking apologies as they approached. The couple stood stonily while their mothers petted them, Kate feeling nothing but annoyance now. She wondered if there was any chance they did not look like they'd been having sex for two straight days, but a glance at Gabe, especially at his tousled hair and swollen mouth, destroyed all hope along those lines.

"Seriously, Mother, I could so cheerfully kill you right now."

"Indeed," Gabe intoned.

"Don't be mad, honey," Cara begged, laughing as she rocked Kate in her embrace. "This is exactly what we've all wanted for you both, from the time you were children." Her words softened Kate up a little.

"But did you *have* to physically show up here? Didn't we get you a cell phone a while back?"

"We maybe could have called," Carmen soothed. "But, we're all really happy for you two and wanted to tell you in person, and we kind of came for another reason too." She explained what they knew of the situation with Will and Dana.

"Wow." Kate forgot her embarrassment for the moment. "A suicide attempt. Is he okay?"

"Some of our watery friends saved Will — he's unharmed — and we just got here with Dana an hour ago. They're both, um, sedated, or whatever the right word is for being kept under siren influence." Kate's gaze darted to John then, considering him as if for the first time. He smiled back sheepishly. Gabe cleared his throat.

At which point she remembered why she so very much didn't want her parents — or his — around. As Gabe stood behind her broadcasting his over-ripe intensity, she once again flushed with mortification.

Michael locked onto Gabe's expression then, comprehension seeming to dawn on him. "How long have you two been here?"

"Not quite two days," Gabe answered, an unarticulated *scram* hanging from the end of his statement heard by everyone there. He wrapped his arms around Kate so she was plastered against him. She tried to hide her face in his neck.

Their parents all started moving and talking at once. "We'll be pretty much unavailable for the next couple days," Michael said as he retrieved spare blankets from a chest. John excused himself to go get Everett, and Cara and Carmen's comments overlapped one another as one went to a closet for pillows and another fished some fruit from the fridge.

"We're staying at the Mattegins' if you need us," and, "We'll be in the water all day tomorrow, so we'll catch up later in the week," they babbled. Within a minute, the entire crew had vacated the cottage.

Kate started to complain, but Gabe's kiss stopped her. As the front door *clicked* behind their parents, he lifted her to him, her feet dangling over his as he walked back to the bedroom. "If they come back, we're ignoring them," he threatened against her lips, kicking the door shut behind him. Kate sighed in resignation. At the very least, they would not be interrupted again.

CHAPTER NINETEEN

Dana couldn't remember ever feeling better. She was completely rested – a delicious novelty – and despite a small effort on her part to remember urgent duties she knew waited for her at work and home, she couldn't muster the tiniest amount of concern.

Unprecedented. Bizarre. Delightful.

She floated through the light-filled water not noticing how she was propelled, lazily contemplating her many smiling female companions. They twisted gracefully around her, their agile bodies and swirling hair moving in a fluid, joyful ballet that seemed choreographed in its complexity. Dana luxuriated in the caress of the warm water against her skin and in the constant backdrop of her friends' singing, their voices echoing around and within her, soothing and evocative.

As if in a dream, Dana watched her beautiful escorts and was awed by their individual and collective loveliness. She marveled at their figures, both curvaceous and lean, and at the rich variations in color they presented. From the iridescent but discernibly human top halves of their bodies, each woman's waist faded into large, colorful scales running from gently flaring hips down the impressively long and fish-like lower half of her body, and terminating in a tremendous, diaphanous end fin that rippled and floated in the most mesmerizing way. Most tails were entirely one shade, with a lighter, contrasting color saturating the pelvic and caudal fins, although some sported stripes. Dana saw every conceivable hue represented, from brilliant turquoise to crimson red to lemon yellow.

Eventually, the swirling dance and singing subsided, and quietness settled in and around her. Dana found herself and her entourage stopped in what appeared to be an enormous underwater cathedral. Its massive, ancient walls vaulted to the surface in an awesome display of majesty, inviting the eyes upward, while powerful shafts of sunlight cast rippling columns of light on the floor and reflected sunshine everywhere else. Dana felt the effect within her very soul; the soft, holy illumination washing through her with a cleansing calm she felt was the very essence of grace.

A striking and bizarre fish-woman ghosted into her field of vision, her appearance distracting Dana from her trance. Her slender form was topped with wildly long tendrils of green-tinged, white-blond hair framing her entire body, each section curling and extending as if riding a current of its own. Her emerald green eyes stared out from a delicately chiseled face saved from severity by softly arching brows and a full, generous mouth. Dana was fascinated by the play of sunlight on the woman's iridescent skin, and awed by her savage, haunting beauty. The woman smiled at her as she guided them slowly toward the top of the cathedral.

I am Xanthe, the woman told her without speaking. *You are Dana, sister of Cara Blake and wife of William Fletcher.*

Yes.

They drifted, and Xanthe's hypnotic stare faded from Dana's view as, by slow degrees, her own thoughts absorbed her awareness. Eventually, she no longer saw or heard the world around her, only images and sensations within herself, where a myriad of sharply defined memories began to dance like a cinema reel through her mind. She sifted through them with forensic concentration to find... something.

Something to refresh her life and marriage, she decided. In a strange voice a little like her own but not, Dana was instructed to examine the hardest things carefully, without judgment or disapproval. She began to think of work, home, and her husband.

Will had reminded her of her father when they met. Not physically, but in his ambition and recognition of her accomplishments. He'd showed her the same kind of appreciation her father had showered her with during childhood, shaping her desire to be a good student, to excel in school, to get a high-paying job. It dawned on her the approval she'd received for her efforts was synonymous with something more important, and this thought tugged at her attention.

Synonymous but not the same, her voice cautioned.

She thought back on several interactions with her parents, remembering her father's fervent pride when she'd received an award in elementary school for reading the most books. Melissa, her mother, had smiled at her kindly and ruffled her hair as Norman, her father, boasted about her to the parents of a classmate. She'd wondered why her mother wasn't as openly proud of her, and she remembered how this doubt was obliterated when her father picked her up and whirled her around. She'd found his encouragement intoxicating and much preferable to her mother's quiet support. She realized she believed her father loved her more.

She recalled her angst during a lesson in advanced math in high school, when the reserved, skinny boy next to her wrote the answer to a problem in his notebook in one try as he usually did. He'd studied the equation on the blackboard and then confidently written out three lines of proofs, so sure of his answer he didn't need the instructor to check it. Dana, meanwhile, struggled to identify any pattern that might lead toward a solution. In her frustration, the boy's facility had offended her.

She'd loosely kept track of him after high school and knew he'd excelled in college, and had gone on to obtain a graduate degree in aerospace engineering. At the last reunion, he was a department head at a highly respected aeronautics company but had mostly wanted to talk about his family and hobbies. His brilliant career was genuinely *not* all-important to him, which Dana did not understand.

She'd come across these cases before, of course, people at the top of their professions who cared more — or even just equally — about other areas of their lives, and she wondered what glitch in their perspectives allowed them to demote accomplishments which had surely required tremendous focus and effort. Her own belief that perseverance could overcome all obstacles, and glory and honor ensued ad infinitum in this context was challenged in these encounters, and she'd never quite known how to think about these people. They seemed relatively happy, perhaps even more so than she and Will. Were they?

As she pondered this situation, not for the first time, she was eventually able to acknowledge two truths to herself. Firstly, some people had natural talents for which hard work by people without them did not compensate. She did not need to feel defensive or regretful as she had talents too. Secondly, she needed to rethink her definition of accomplishment and success. The formula she'd followed since childhood was no longer compelling to her, and she admitted she wanted to think differently, act on something new. She suspected a change would help and allow their lives to expand.

What I want, she thought, *is a life that feels good, not just one that looks good.*

Excellent, her voice agreed. *You should seek a broader definition of yourself, reach beyond the realm of work and career. By searching deeper, you will find opportunities for fulfillment and foster true joy.*

Dana thought of her husband. Will was unhappy, she suspected for the same reasons she was. She remembered the many times she'd seen their unhappiness, and because she didn't know what to do about it, ignored her misgivings. As she continued this contemplation, she saw how they no longer found pleasure in what delighted them once upon a time, their home and their lifestyle specifically. And with growing certainty, she knew neither of them would ever again be enchanted with the life they'd given everything to build.

How could this be? She thought extensively on this question. After a while, she realized how hard they'd both tried to overcome their waning belief in a life they'd outgrown, how they had stubbornly enforced definitions of happiness that had only briefly applied to them. After all, they'd formed their ideas about life and marriage as emotional infants. This approach was doing them no good, she decided.

Yes, her voice encouraged. *You should not fight against your disbelief.*

So, what if they did something different? How much harder could new choices be versus pretending to want only what they had? The question caused a thrill of hope to blossom in her chest. Usually, she rejected the idea of significant change out of hand. Now, she was able to consider alternatives, such as a new job in her field – *not a meaningful change*, her voice advised – or moving, or switching careers – *better, but keep thinking.*

Coming to the same dead-end she typically did when she considered small, work-related adjustments, Dana ventured outside her usual, comfortable thoughts, to contemplate something entirely new. And with the firm, loving presence of her voice, she felt okay.

She thought of her niece, Kate. Her love of cooking was not market-driven, although her passion was also reflected in her choice of careers. Dana thought of her sister's love of gardening, and of colleagues who played in community orchestras or studied painting or piano, almost always with the focus and intent she herself reserved only for her work. Cara, she recalled, had chosen her vocation based on flexible hours and only adequate pay so she could garden and cook and be with her daughter. She'd disparaged her sister for that choice.

Life's value is not transactional, her voice instructed. *Personal interests and their development are the richness of our time here.*

She could help herself and Will by ferreting out something different to do, something different to care about, she conceded. Which to be honest, they'd discussed many times in a roundabout way and even made a few half-hearted efforts to fix. They'd been mildly involved in several different activities at one time or another, including European travel, wine appreciation, investment clubs and various book clubs. None of these pursuits withstood the test of time, however, and none had been compelling enough to inspire either of them to put in the time necessary for anything like mastery of them.

Their jobs eventually provided their predictable, pat excuse to disengage. *I'm simply too busy at the office right now to participate,* was the epitaph of virtually all of their extracurricular activities. After a time, Dana acknowledged the hunt for hobbies had been little more than a search for distractions they didn't really want, or ones they knew, somehow, wouldn't fulfill them. Perhaps nothing could fulfill them, she'd come to believe. But she'd been unable to suppress a consistent, nagging suspicion there *was* something else they could do. She knew Will felt the same way, knew they both wanted change but felt they shouldn't retreat from the solid decisions they'd made.

Her voice confirmed what she had never before acknowledged;

they wanted a family-centered life and a child. This line of inquiry was the most threatening of all, because it begged a series of questions challenging all of the values they'd sometimes evangelically espoused. And yet, despite Will's oft-stated satisfaction with their childlessness, Dana doubted their commitment to forego having children herself, and she was confident Will would reconsider if he felt he could. She'd seen his face fall when he heard news of other couples adopting or having a baby, seen him stare longingly at a playground filled with little ones. She'd also seen his boredom and disappointment, sentiments she shared, in their perfected home and neat routines.

Darling, she thought sadly, *we no longer have the capacity to care only for ourselves.*

You want to give yourselves to something you find meaningful, her voice deduced. *You believe having a child would be meaningful, despite the personal and professional sacrifice it would require.* Dana felt proud of herself when her voice told her that this desire was good and right. *Follow this avenue of thought,* she was counseled.

How silly, she mused, as her self-judgment bled away. When she examined her decisions objectively, she saw no reason for resistance. But how had she come to this point, she wondered? How could a lifetime of believing and behaving one way transform from something so absolutely right to something utterly wrong? Their ambition had yielded them the American dream, shiny, whole and unassailable. Why did they no longer want to live this way?

Dana considered herself from what she guessed was her sister's perspective. Inexplicably, Cara had never seemed impressed with her professional accomplishments or trappings of success. Dana had always assumed she was jealous at some level and just hid her envy to avoid confronting any feelings of inadequacy she harbored. But what if she didn't value the same things? Even when Cara had an opportunity to train for a job with higher earning potential, she didn't. What if she hadn't bought into Dana's formula for happiness in the first place? Their mother certainly fell into this category but she was from a different generation, one comfortable with backing down. How could Cara come to any conclusion other than the one she had drawn?

The idea she might achieve in a new way would have held no credibility for her up until this moment. As she questioned her own assumptive premise now, however, deliberating a true shift away from it, she reconsidered. Maybe her sister had never believed happiness had but one clear definition, achievement only one path.

Happiness must be bigger, her voice agreed. *Think of all the evidence you've seen.*

Dana did. She thought of family, friends, and coworkers over the years who had helped her and others or performed acts of kindness without a thought to what they might receive back. She recalled classes coworkers had taken, in music or art or writing or spirituality, none of them pursued with the intention of boosting anyone's career, but all of them studied seriously. She remembered work opportunities passed up in favor of volunteer efforts, extended vacations taken without pay. In her relaxed state, hundreds of examples came to mind, and she allowed herself to feel a new appreciation for their importance.

Such a simple thing to consider these activities in a fresh light and yet such a profound switch in my perspective, Dana thought.

This brings us to the heart of the matter, her voice urged.

Dana asked herself deliberately, pointedly about what she would change based on all she had just reviewed. She directed herself in the most loving way to identify a specific course of action to create a more satisfying life for her and her husband. She already knew the answer; she just had to think the words.

I want a child, she thought. *I want to be a mother.* She wanted to be unanchored from their former wants and material desires. She was certain Will wanted what she did, to invest himself in a more enriching home life, to distance himself from the yoke of professional advancement.

Go in this direction, her voice commanded.

A sense of peace pervaded her. The changes she would make, the love she would seek, would not come from her ambition. She would court happiness by opening herself up to possibilities with outcomes she could not know or control. She would talk to Will, and she knew things would be all right without knowing how they would be. Tears of relief mingled with the water around her and floated away. She had never felt so grateful.

Slowly, she began to perceive the world outside again, light in the underwater cathedral penetrating her awareness and bringing the space around her into focus again. *All that you are is good, and all that you've done is good,* her voice promised as she came into consciousness. *Your strong mind and open heart have instructed you, and you will have love and joy from what you undertake.*

When she became fully aware, Xanthe was gone. Her aquatic friends were in a circle around her, attentive and watchful. She did not hesitate to tell them what she needed.

I want to see Will.

"I had fun," Xanthe told Carmen as she handed her a cup of tea.

Carmen cringed self-consciously as she thanked her. She offered cream and sugar. "I hate to think of what I took you away from to help out my family."

"No, really. If we'd all do what Dana just did – choose to be more loving and accepting of ourselves and others – I wouldn't have any other conflicts to solve. I'm glad I was able to help, Carmen."

"Yes, well, if you ever want to set up a marriage counseling practice, I'm sure you'll be a smashing success."

Xanthe laughed. "Let's see how this one goes, first."

"From your lips to God's ears." Carmen toasted Xanthe with her teacup.

CHAPTER TWENTY

"I think I want a wedding," Kate mused, lying on her back.

"Mmm-hmm," Gabe agreed sleepily.

"I definitely do." She faced her *husband*, and the label gave her a thrill. He was barely awake. She scooted closer to him. "A small wedding," she insisted. "Just our families and the Wilkes as guests."

He opened his eyes and shifted to his side as well. "I guess this is pretty important." His smile was indulgent. "Where? On the beach?"

"How about the library?"

"Reception on the beach?"

"Deal."

"In that case, I suppose I should have given this to you a few days ago." Gabe rolled off the bed and complained, "My body feels like it's filled with cement." He trudged to the bureau, opened the top drawer, and came back carrying a black velvet box.

She noted the anticipation on his face and felt like dancing. "You are completely adorable. I mean, the gift is for me, and you're the one squirming with excitement."

"I know! I know! Hurry up and open it! I'm dyin' over here!"

She lifted the lid of the box to see an elegant diamond solitaire engagement ring wedged in the center. The stone was a brilliant cut set in white gold with a delicate filigree engraving circling the band. "My mom designed it. Fresh and modern, yet classically beautiful, just like you." He darted in to kiss her cheek. "Do you like it?"

"Honey... It's perfect. You're perfect." She put the ring on and they both admired it on her hand. "I didn't realize until this very second that I would care about a rock, but this is gorgeous. How long have you had it?"

"Mom's had the idea in her head for a while," he hedged. "But it was part of my backup bribery plan if you were on the fence about committing yourself to me body and soul.

"Actually," he confessed in an eager rush, "my parents gave it to me when you graduated from high school, as an incentive to stay away from you until you got through college. I've been plotting your demise since adolescence." He hid his smile in her neck.

"So, let me clarify: you were given a ring to give to me, and that was bribery to keep *you* away?" Gabe wrinkled his nose and nodded.

She flopped backwards on the bed. "This can't be happening to me. I feel like I'm going to wake up in my apartment any minute now, realize this is all a dream, I'm late for work, all my clothes are dirty, and I'm out of mascara. At which point I'll kill myself."

"No-no. No dying allowed from here on out. All possibly fatal activities will henceforth require joint approval."

"Does that include a near-fatal amount of sex?" Kate teased.

Gabe kept a straight face. "No. Death by sex is okay. Speaking of which, I'm exhausted." He rolled back on his pillow. "Let's take a nap first and plan the wedding later." He held his arms out to her.

She smoothed his hair out of his eyes and then snuggled next to him. "All right." She gave him a quick kiss, and they relaxed into the covers until sleep pulled them under.

After several hours of rest and a hot shower, Kate was prepared to face the day, which she fervently hoped would commence with a big breakfast. After taking inventory of the sparsely stocked kitchen, she questioned Gabe on the availability of eggs and milk on the island.

"I'm really hungry, and I want pancakes. So bad I'll swim back to North Carolina to get them. But if I can get my hands on eggs and milk, I'll make them here."

"We have a market down the road. But I think I'll raid the Mattegins' cottage first, 'cause that'll be easier."

"Is that where my mother and John are staying?" Her desire for breakfast was rivaled only by her desire to see Cara and discuss her recent adventures.

"Yes. Do you want to go?"

"Definitely. I want to catch up with my mother. And maybe grill John a little about lying to me the past five years."

"He didn't have any choice, Kate. The penalty for betrayal is pretty severe."

"Yeah but everyone was in on the plan except me," she complained lightly. "And what is the penalty for 'betrayal,' as you put it?" She thought about this question another few seconds before adding, "In fact, what constitutes betrayal?"

They closed the front door behind them. "Sirens who reveal themselves intentionally, or if they're deemed a risk to the community because they can't keep themselves under wraps, are either jailed or exiled. It depends on what the problem is, if it's a matter of intent or inability." He grabbed Kate's hand and swung it between them.

"But if a person is intent on sabotage, why would shunning them stop it?"

"Our bonds with each other are essential to our survival, Kate. It's not like it is with you people on land, where everyone can more or less keep to themselves. That craving you feel from me when we're touching?" She gave him a withering glance. "No, not just the physical desire part, but that emotional reaching you feel, especially in the water?"

Kate reflected not just on how she was with Gabe but also with John and Carmen and Michael. Then, she thought of the severe hazing she'd experienced at the hands of Peter Loughlin at Solange's wedding as well. The constant in all these interactions was the peculiar sensation of being drunk in, either close to them or when these people touched her.

"I see what you mean."

"That's not something we choose to do, it's something we literally *have* to do," Gabe continued. "We need those connections with each other, the communion. That's why our society is so peaceful and stable — relative to yours, anyway — because getting sent away is unbearable."

"And so, when someone is exiled, what happens?"

Gabe closed his eyes. "It's painful to even consider it. Usually, we die. I'm told it's something like starving to death."

She shuddered. "Why the need for secrecy in the first place? Why not just come forth and announce yourselves? You could be like the Chinese or Atlantians and demand your equal rights."

Gabe's regard was condescending. "Humans are pure, unadulterated crap when it comes to race assimilation. I mean, look at how long it's taken Americans to make any real progress, and they're the most open society on the planet." He huffed. "Moreover, sirens have a biological need for community the way we define it. We've actually tried opening our world to humans in isolated cases, and, without fail, they try to colonize us and capitalize on us. The effect of this oppression is we die. We don't just take our beleaguered selves off somewhere, we actually die."

Kate knew he was right and was filled with remorse for what her people were capable of. She couldn't mount a single defensive argument. Gabe became contrite. "Not with you, honey. Not with your mom or Solange or any of the people you know who've married with us. But when it gets to a larger scale, when governments become involved, it doesn't work. We won't take the risk."

She offered the only words she could. "I'm sorry, Gabe." She was silent the rest of the way.

The aroma of coffee and the sound of Everett giggling greeted them at the Mattegins' door. "Hey guys!" Gabe called as they stepped in.

"We're back here!" Cara yelled from the kitchen. She was drying her hands on a dish towel when Kate came to her and hugged her tightly. Her mother held her at arm's length to inspect her. "And how's the happy couple this morning? How's life outside the cocoon?"

"We're good, Mom." Kate hugged and greeted everyone in turn, her earlier embarrassment forgotten. She poured herself a cup of coffee and stood behind John's chair to place a hand on his shoulder. "You're a sneak," she chided him but without any real anger. He patted her hand and flashed her a disarming smile.

He winked at Gabe. "You must be hungry."

"Ravenous," she complained. "I could eat a horse, but what I really want are pancakes."

"Gotch-ya covered," her mother responded, opening the cupboard to take out a mixing bowl. John rose to ready the griddle.

"The Loughlins are on the island," Carmen announced from behind her newspaper. She set it down and addressed Michael. "We should see if we can catch them while we're here. I owe them a report, and we could avoid the circus involved in having them come to Griffins Bay if we see them here. What do you think?"

"Makes sense. I'll call Kenna's assistant and see if they can squeeze us in." He exited the room dialing a number on his cell phone.

"How much time do you two have left here?" John inquired.

Kate was gleeful. "I have three more weeks off!" She sat on Gabe's lap and craned her neck to address him. "And I have no idea what you had planned before I so rudely changed the course of your life last week but I should tell you I don't really care." She picked an apple out of the bowl on the table in front of her and bit into it.

Gabe nuzzled her neck and laughed. "Not that it bothers me but you've got everything backward, Kate. If you recall, *I* asked *you* to meet *me,* and then hauled you into the water to make sure you wouldn't get away." He faced John. "I'm enrolled at UNC Medical next fall, and I thought I'd lurk around and try to fast-talk Kate into hanging with me for the rest of her life. I overestimated how much time it would take." He smirked at Kate. "I had no idea you'd be so easy . . ." Kate shoved him playfully and tried to rise from his lap but he held her fast.

"Really, I have some studying to do though I expect I'll be playing house-husband and helping Kate with the baby for a little while." Cara stilled

"Kate's going to be pregnant." She seemed more shocked than happy; although Kate was gratified she looked generally pleased. She herself had forgotten about this particular consequence of their tryst and felt a sensation like stage fright settle just north of her stomach. She smiled nervously at everyone around her. Gabe squeezed her.

Michael reentered the room with the announcement Kenna would see them on Friday afternoon. "I told her about Gabe and Kate, and she insisted they come along so she can offer her congratulations in person."

Kate grimaced at the prospect of giving up an entire afternoon away, and Gabe didn't appear any more pleased than she was. She had the feeling once the outside world was allowed to enter, it would intrude too much, maybe compromise their happy intimacy. She acquiesced, however, knowing the meeting was important to their parents. Gabe accepted for them.

"I know Kenna's invitation in an honor, Dad. Of course we'll go." He sounded polite if not actually happy.

Michael clapped his hand on his son's shoulder. "Responsibilities, Gabe." Then, softening a little, he added, "It'll just be for a few hours, and then you kids can be back on your own."

CHAPTER TWENTY-ONE

Peter Loughlin could acknowledge his strange childhood without self-pity. Heavens, so many people came from impossible circumstances and made good, he had no business lamenting how he'd missed his mother, who was, in any case, always around. The fault wasn't even hers; she was a queen, and her time – her very body – was not hers to manage.

He'd been given the privileged upbringing of all royal children, which included the requisite nursemaid, dedicated governess and a host of tutors pre-eminent in their fields to school him. What he'd been denied was what he'd longed for most, and that was time with Kenna.

When he was little, his mother was primarily a shining, ephemeral idea to him, her company only achieved with diligent effort or good behavior. Then, when he'd received good marks in school or dominated in some sporting event, his mother visited his quarters to congratulate him. He would never forget his feelings of anticipation and fear prior to her visits, or the fuss and ado from his attendants who groomed and chided him during their anxious preparations.

When he was very small, he remembered being sent out onto a

ballroom floor to wish his mother goodnight during some formal reception she hosted. The gesture was political, encouraged so the guests could see first-hand the endearing bond between their queen and her son. His reluctance became terror, however, when he realized he didn't know which one she was; after considering the expectant smiles of a dozen or so women around him, he ran into the arms of one he thought might be her. She was so kind and soothing as she carried him, and he buried his face in her neck with gratitude.

"I don't want you to fret even a little bit about this, darling boy," she'd whispered in his ear. "I'm taking you right to your mother, and I think you're very brave to come out here all by yourself." By the time she finished talking to him, they'd arrived before his mother, who graciously accepted him onto her lap to the indulgent, charmed titters of the guests. The next day, his caregivers placed a photograph of his mother in the nursery so such a mishap could be avoided in the future.

As he got older, Peter gained insight into his mother's structured life by watching other royals, and he came to understand why he so rarely saw her. When he was thirteen, his mother's sister, who was close in line to the throne and heavily involved in matters of state, gave birth to a daughter. Following a few short hours after the delivery, where mother and baby were sequestered in his aunt's private chambers, a wet nurse came and took the little princess away. Thereafter, his aunt visited her daughter daily for brief periods of time during her first six months of life, and less frequently afterward. Peter surmised his own birth and infancy had been much the same.

He never knew his father, or even had any idea as to who he was. This was by design; in order not to show favoritism, Kenna had chosen an anonymous mate, thereby denying the conference of power or lineage to any faction over another outside the castle. Peter also learned his parents had never bonded in the traditional way, again, in order to protect the balance of power. Even when he was young, he knew this to be nearly impossible among his kind.

He never learned exactly how his parents accomplished their union, but by the time he was an adult, he'd developed a plausible theory. His best guess was his mother and father were drugged, albeit consensually. He came to this conclusion by observing Kenna in various public situations over the years, and while he would never know definitively the circumstances of his conception, he became confident in his eventual hypothesis.

His primary rationale came from what he saw of his mother in emotionally provocative circumstances. Before a meeting involving contentious issues, Kenna and her doctor retired to her chambers for fifteen minutes, after which, Kenna emerged with the serene, vague expression that characterized, as far as Peter could tell, only active rulers in the aristocracy. Calm detachment in the face of emotional stimulation was antithetical to siren nature, although the royal class unilaterally adhered to this difficult standard. He knew, from his own experience and by comparing sirens with humans, his race was passionate and over-sensitive; and he knew of no means by which this nature could be sublimated other than sedation. As no other viable explanation existed, Peter accepted it as truth.

Over the years, Peter persisted in the habits he'd formed when he was too young to judge them, which meant trying to meet the high expectations of him by his caregivers and the court. He surpassed everyone's hopes for him, and, at each triumph, was rewarded by a brief visit from his mother, who lavished praise on him and encouraged him to continue his efforts. He didn't understand his disappointment after she left until he was much older, when he realized he felt cheated by this reward system; the visits were a weak consolation for what he really wanted, which was to be taken into his mother's arms, to be petted and held by her. He wanted her to ask him about his day, about what he'd had for lunch, or about his friends at school.

He wanted her to take an interest in him.

His only access to her, however, remained formal visits following some accomplishment, and as unfulfilling as these visits were, they were all he had. He continued to excel.

The constant emotional deprivation he felt growing up fostered another side effect, one he appreciated above all others: his cloaking ability. He'd shown natural signs he could cloak, even as an infant, when caregivers remarked on his charming propensity to appear briefly as whichever sea creature he dreamt of during his sleep. As a child, he used it as a coping mechanism against the constant pressures from his governess and tutors to reflect perfect behavior and academic discipline. As he learned to project new outward images, he also learned to hide any internal thoughts and feelings suggesting softness or failure.

By the time he reached his mid-teens, his intuitive abilities had become the only retreat he had where he was truly free to relax and govern himself. With no other emotional avenues available to him, he focused his prodigious powers of concentration ever inward, resulting in an intense and constant exploration of ways to both be and appear worthy of love. His need drove his abilities until he far surpassed the understanding of those around him and their knowledge of what it meant to cloak. He began to hide himself from time to time with such skill no one, not even those in the castle with the world's most vaunted intuitive skills, could find him. He could even do better than this but he saved such knowledge for himself, unwilling to have it exposed to the clinical dissection of his overseers. His beauty, strength, and superior social and academic skills protected him from over-scrutiny.

Much, much later, when he was a statesman himself and assisting his mother in her day-to-day governmental duties, he was finally granted the time with her he'd craved as a little boy. He came to understand then the tremendous toll her duties had taken on her, and while this understanding did not eliminate his sense of loss, he was able to forgive her for abandoning him as an infant. The sad irony of this revelation was it didn't really alleviate either of their suffering, Peter's at having been denied his mother's attention, and Kenna's at inflicting the separation and denying her own need to mother him. His forgiveness did nothing to help her, as he knew Kenna would never, never forgive herself, despite her belief she had done the right thing. Avoidance of this constant knowledge, via her medications, was Kenna's sole escape from this particular grief, he believed.

Peter's cloaking skills protected him on this front, as well. As tortured as he felt at times, he did not devolve into the idiosyncrasies – or pathologies, in some cases – afflicting many in the aristocracy, because his intuition let him know in the clearest of terms emotional fulfillment was out there to be had. He never doubted the prevalence of nurturing love among his people, believing he had only to reach the right age or achieve a specific cadre of accomplishments before the opportunity would be his. He could see and feel it all around him, had been given it in small doses, and, as with every other endeavor, he had only to apply himself to find the path that would lead him to it.

CHAPTER TWENTY-TWO

Everyone enjoyed the stroll to the Loughlin estate despite it being nearly an hour away on foot. Kate didn't mind, though; the island was beautiful, the weather ideal, and they were relatively unencumbered, since they'd left John, Cara and Everett at the beach. Here on Shaddox, Everett had siren playmates, which she knew was a rare treat for him and a particular relief for his parents. John and Cara usually had to be careful due to Everett's low capacity for subterfuge, but not here.

The palace was at the exact center of the island, and it resembled a stereotypical stone castle with a couple of significant exceptions, which Michael described to them as they advanced. The structure surrounded an inland, salt-water lake, which circulated to and from the ocean via underground tunnels. The tunnels themselves formed half of the palace, widening into rooms containing offices, entertaining spaces and recreation areas for inhabitants and guests to indulge in their alternative natures during visits. The rooms also contained exit tunnels to the ocean surrounding the island; so theoretically, anyone could enter or leave the palace at will underwater.

"That sounds like a security problem to me," Kate commented.

Michael went on to explain security wasn't the issue for sirens it was for humans, as she would see; because of their ability to sense thoughts and feelings, the palace staff didn't need complicated systems in place to catch deviants, and anyone with ill motives knew better than to try and enter, because their intentions would be immediately known. The most serious security measure the royal family undertook was to hire sirens who were particularly gifted at reading others, and they reputedly had the best staff on earth for this purpose. They arrived on the palace grounds just as Michael completed his overview.

They approached via an expansive courtyard formally landscaped with low boxwood hedges defining clean, geometric spaces filled with tropical flowers of every color.

"I wish my mother could see this," she reflected aloud. They saw the palace ahead. "I'm a little nervous," she confessed so Gabe alone could hear her.

He squeezed her hand as they entered the atrium leading to the palace offices. Michael and Carmen led while she and Gabe trailed behind, looking around them with caution as they advanced. Kate silently begged Gabe for his calming influence.

"No problem," Gabe replied in a low voice. "I'm nervous too. I've never been this far inside the compound, only out in the main hall."

She was surprised enough to stop walking. "You've never met the Loughlins?"

"I've been in their private company before, but we've never conversed. And I've never been to their offices on Shaddox. My parents have been advisors to their family since my mother began managing birth and marriage records, and I've only been on the island when she's reported or made recommendations." Gabe leaned down so only she could hear him. "But I can tell you, I'm pretty sure they're nuts."

"Why do you think so?" she whispered.

Gabe shrugged. "It's just a feeling I get. Peter's got some amazing talents, making him difficult to read. I'll tell you about him later. But see if you don't feel the same way after you've met them."

They stopped in a foyer outside a set of ornate double doors and waited while an aide went in to announce them. Kate thought everyone seemed on edge, which made her feel like less of a rube. No one spoke.

When the double doors opened, the couple Kate thought had so rudely intruded at Luke and Solange's wedding appeared before them, and they were just as regal and austere as she remembered. Able to watch while they greeted the elder Blakes, she examined their faces for signs of Gabe's diagnosis. Kenna, she saw, wore the withdrawn, unfocused expression of someone who was not fully paying attention. Her manner also suggested she was deeply distracted.

She paid attention to Peter then and was jolted by the force of his penetrating stare, the same one that had unnerved her at the wedding when she was seventeen. Gabe, who was still holding her hand, stiffened. Kate was peripherally aware of Kenna greeting Carmen and Michael.

In the brief moment Peter's gaze locked on hers, she saw him glance at her hand in Gabe's, felt Gabe's hostility, and she intuited from Peter a staggering emotional hunger, a loneliness big enough to devour her and everything in the room. Almost as soon as she had this impression, it disappeared as Peter pivoted to address his mother. All further sense of him vanished.

"Mother, why don't I take Gabriel and Catherine on a tour and leave you to talk privately with Michael and Carmen." Kenna inclined her head, giving her son a vague smile as she exited through the double doors. Michael and Carmen trailed behind her.

Peter once again targeted Kate with the full force of his attention, giving her a smile that did not reach his eyes while he tucked her hand into his arm. He walked forward then, effectively removing her from Gabe's grasp, while he commented on how good it was to see her again.

"You've grown into a beautiful woman, Catherine." His influence made her foggy, although even the sensation of being sedated was not enough to alleviate all her distrust.

"Kate," she corrected him automatically, feeling as if she addressed him from behind a wall of gelatin. Gabe bristled at Peter's compliment and she felt his urge to retrieve her. Peter stopped, recaptured Kate's gaze in his, and placed a hand on Gabe's shoulder. Kate briefly registered the diffusion of Gabe's concern and felt a dull lethargy descend over both of them.

The rest of her time with Peter passed like she was dreaming it. She had an insubstantial memory of an attendant taking charge of Gabe and squiring him off, leaving her alone with Peter. He talked hypnotically about different items they passed, all the while examining her face, holding his hand over hers to keep it in the crook of his arm. She knew he used his siren influence on her and she did not understand why. She did not feel afraid. She could discern none of his thoughts or feelings.

He interspersed historical information on various items of consequence in the palace with incongruent comments and questions she should have found out of place in their mostly one-sided conversation.

"Sixteenth century tapestries made by the monks at... and how long have you been bonded with Gabriel Blake?" She didn't know if she answered him out loud or if he intuited her responses but he carried on as if he had the answers he sought.

"...chalice was given to my great grandfather by the Duke of... so sorry to hear you lost your father at such an early age, and how did you and Gabe meet? ...palace was first built in thirteen twenty-two... do tell me more about your courtship... charcoal sketches made of my mother when she was six... Ah, yes, I see your feelings for each other were confusingly intense for you... winter home in Spain... my own arranged marriage once... a baby, won't that be wonderful... never could find the right situation... survived more hurricanes than anyone remembers, so we keep it even if it is hideous... ability for love and intimacy in the aristocracy is a joke, I don't mind telling you... ridiculous crowns are actually still worn on occasion... can't help but want my own, real family... a rose, especially developed to commemorate the first century of reign... tell me more about your mother..."

She felt relaxed and mostly drugged during their exchange, although she maintained a small sense of herself. This pleased her as it was something she had been unable to do when she'd encountered Peter at the wedding. She answered his questions patiently, feeling a tiny, indomitable vitality despite the stupor threatening to completely suppress her. She thought of Gabe most of the time, and her happiness for their newly declared commitment kept her calm and confident even if she wasn't altogether aware.

Finally, they arrived back at the doors where they'd left Michael and Carmen with Kenna. The weight of Peter's hypnotic efforts lifted as she saw Gabe approach from down the hallway with another attendant. At a nod from Peter, the attendant offered the Loughlins' official congratulations and hoped Gabriel would accept their wedding gift, which he'd been instructed to present at this time. While Gabe's attention was engaged in accepting a small, flat, rectangular box, Peter bowed to place a kiss on the back of Kate's hand. He lingered longer than custom required.

"It was a true pleasure to see you again, Kate."

By the time Gabe faced them again, Peter stood erect and at a respectful distance from her. Gabe gave him a curt nod Kate thought was barely civil. "Gabriel." Peter nodded back, and he left. The double doors opened and Carmen and Michael emerged.

"I'll lead you out," the attendant told them, indicating they should follow.

Peter fled to the ocean to hide. As he raced through the tunnels to attain his release from the castle, he felt every cell in his body explode with longing and regret, longing for the fantasies flooding his mind unbidden, unstoppable, for a life with Catherine Blake. Regret, because there was no going back now. His heart, tenuously balanced between his royal commitments and his emotionally lost mother, shattered in his chest, never to be put back to how it was.

He was stunned from the moment he saw her this time, his intuition reaching into her of its own volition to apprehend every part of her beautiful mind and heart. In an instant, he knew her, clever, loyal, kind, and emotionally capable and whole. He had never been gifted with prescience but he saw too clearly the life he would have had with her if only she'd bonded with him instead of Gabriel. He observed her condition, how she was newly attached, her guileless joy and devotion, and thought he might dissolve with grief.

Before, when he'd seen her at the wedding, he'd toyed fleetingly with the idea of taking her, guessing at the woman she would become, although the urge to seize her seemed an errant compulsion, one he'd dismissed as fatigue-induced nonsense. He thought of her occasionally thereafter but generally did not, foolishly rejecting her as someone inconsequential to him.

He was devoured with longing for her.

He thought of her home life with Gabriel Blake, practically tasting the nurturing warmth she would create, knowing, without a doubt, the restorative sanctuary her husband would enjoy every day. She would be a wonderful wife and mother, the kind every man dreamt of. He could not bear to think of it, and yet he could think of nothing else.

He burst from the castle tunnel with blinding speed, disappearing into himself to become invisible to anyone and anything around him. He swam as fast and as far as he could and tried, unsuccessfully, to outrun what had been unleashed inside him.

Gabe waited until they were safely away from the castle to relate the story of their exchange with Peter to his parents. "I've never experienced anything like it," he finished. "I thought we couldn't influence each other like that, just land people."

Michael's expression was grave. "I've heard stories about Peter but I've never seen him in action. He's famous at Coral – his athletic records from a hundred years ago still haven't been broken. I was told he has the most acute intuition of any siren ever born, and that's how he finds his opponents' weaknesses, how he knows to dominate them."

"He's a cloaker," Carmen announced.

Michael's eyes widened. "Of course. I remember now."

Kate spoke up. "What's Coral, and what's a cloaker?"

"Coral Academy is the boys' school all our young men go to, our high school for male sirens," Carmen explained.

"What a pretty name for a school," Kate commented. "Is that the one you went to, Gabe? It sounds kind of sweet."

"Yes. So did John and my dad and all the cousins you met at the house. And they make you study 'til you fall over, and they beat you with rocks on the sports field, so don't let the name fool you. In fact, students have their own, very non-sweet titles for the place – "

"And you can save that information for the locker room, Gabe," his mother interjected. She addressed Kate. "A cloaker is someone who cannot be read, someone who can hide his or her thoughts and feelings and go about undetected. They broadcast nothing, only intuit what others think and feel."

"They're pretty hard to beat in a sporting competition," Michael added, "especially someone like Peter Loughlin, because he can read everyone around him really well and almost simultaneously but no one can get a sense of what he's thinking, or how he'll act. And really good cloakers can basically disappear, I've heard. You can't get any sense of them or find them in the water at all."

"They're pretty much unstoppable in sports," Gabe agreed. "You always hope, if there's a cloaker on the field he's on your team."

"Are there a lot of them?" Kate inquired.

"No. They're rare," Carmen responded. "And someone who can completely cloak him or herself, that's almost unheard of."

"I knew one at school," Gabe chimed in. "He wasn't especially good at it but he could still mess with you."

"I've met three in my lifetime," Michael told them.

"But what would he want with Kate?" Gabe wondered. "He separated us – again, I've never felt anything like it – and then basically hypnotized her to get her life's story from her. Why would he do that?"

"I don't like it," his dad agreed. "That's not something we do, incapacitate another siren. I didn't even know it was possible." He nudged Gabe with his shoulder. "At least now you know what it feels like."

Carmen's next words were at odds with her expression. "We shouldn't have to worry. It's against our laws to separate a husband and wife, and you and Gabe are bonded. So he'll have to be happy with whatever he got from you at the palace. Unless you have any ideas, Kate. What do you think he wanted?"

Kate shrugged. "I don't know. At the very beginning, I got the tiniest, briefest sense he was pretty curious about me. And he seemed – and again, we're talking a fraction of a second here – like he's lonely. As in claw-your-own-heart-out lonely. But I can't be sure. And he wasn't threatening. He was basically gracious and charming. I just don't understand why he influenced us the way he did. That's what makes me uneasy."

"Me too," Carmen agreed. "It shouldn't be a problem, though," she concluded, her expression hopeful. "There's no reason for you two to see him much, if ever."

Gabe approved. "I like that approach. The guy's got problems, and I don't want him alone with my wife."

Or our baby, Kate thought. Gabe scowled.

Back at the cottage, Kate wanted to see the wedding present Peter had given them, and Gabe retrieved it for her from the table where he'd left it. "Go ahead and open it."

She lifted the cover to find a multi-colored gemstone bracelet set in silver. Smooth stones of various sizes studded a wide chain of silver forming the base. Gabe snorted. "That's a gift for you, not us."

"Do you not want me to wear it?" She tried unsuccessfully to hide her admiration of the piece.

Gabe softened and smiled at her indulgently. "No, go ahead. It's perfect for you."

She hesitated. "You're sure you don't mind?"

He reached for the piece and put it on her, kissing the underside of her wrist. "I don't mind, I promise. But I'm curious. Didn't you think he was nuts?"

Her answer was confident. "I didn't get that sense, which is not to say you're wrong. The only thing I got, like I said, was he's lonesome."

"Let's forget about him. How'd you like to go for a swim? We need to build your stamina."

Kate flashed him a smile and nodded. "Okay. Let's go play." She went to get her swimsuit.

Convincing Will and Dana to go back to Griffins Bay proved a harder sell than bringing them to Shaddox had been. They didn't want to leave. Carmen and Michael, along with other sirens who had convened to divert them initially discovered they'd done too good a job; they had to work a lot harder to remind them of the responsibilities they'd trivialized on the front end of their visit.

They succumbed after Carmen, Michael, and John worked on them together for an hour, which Kate found humorous to watch. She contacted the couple's employers, who knew to expect them in two days' time and was pleased they hadn't hired replacements, since she wanted her aunt and uncle to leave on their own terms.

John was feeling the pressure of tasks undone too, Kate knew. Four days away from his practice meant he was almost constantly on the phone at this point. And while she was now happy over everyone's impromptu visit to them, part of her was ready to be left alone again with Gabe. She listened while her siren family planned their trip back to the mainland with humans in tow, and she tried not to encourage them to leave earlier.

The afternoon before everyone's departure, the family, minus Will and Dana, gathered at the Blake cottage. Kate and Cara's offer to cook dinner met with enthusiastic support, which made Kate proud. But she questioned the timing of their mass exodus.

"Why at night, after dinner? Don't you worry about predators? Like sharks?"

"This is so cool, Kate!" Cara responded excitedly. "Get this: *sharks don't like sirens.*"

"You mean, they chew them up and spit them out?"

"No," Carmen replied. "We smell bad to them. They won't even try to hunt us or anyone swimming with us either."

"Even if you're bleeding?" Kate pressed.

"Especially then," Gabe told her. "Our blood is the problem. Sharks swim away screaming."

"That's terrific!" she exclaimed. "I mean, I've always had this fear of swimming in the ocean because I'm afraid of sharks." She cast Gabe an adoring look. "My hero! I'll never be freaked out again!"

"The only thing we fear in the ocean is human beings," John cut in harshly, and her smile faded. "They're all that can hurt us, with their nets and commercial fishing."

Carmen regarded Kate kindly. "We don't have a huge problem but sometimes we get caught in fishing nets and get crushed or drown. Especially our little ones. But it doesn't happen often."

"Often enough," Michael countered. Carmen placed her hand on his arm.

Kate was subdued but couldn't hold back her questions. "Aren't you exposed, when one of you is brought up crushed or drowned in a net?"

All sirens at the table seemed to consult each other before John answered her. "We dissolve. Haven't you read *The Little Mermaid?*"

She had. The tale had left her heart-broken each of the many times she'd read it, and it bore little resemblance to the Disney video she'd watched over and over when she was little. In the Hans Christian Andersen version, the little mermaid behaved like her animated counterpart up to a point by falling in love with a human and selling her voice to be by him.

But in Andersen's story, the man the little mermaid loved did not love her back, choosing a human woman to marry instead. On the eve of his wedding, the little mermaid's sisters came to her with a poison dagger, which they had procured for her by selling their beautiful, long hair. She had until the first rays of the sun hit the sea to plunge the dagger into her lover's heart or she would die herself, and they pleaded with her to save her own life. She refused to kill the man she loved, despite his rejection of her, and as the sun rose, she died, dissolving into sea foam.

"I thought Hans made that up," she reflected sadly. "Actually, I thought he made up the whole idea of mermaids, but now I know better."

"As far as he knew, he did make everything up," Carmen told her. "He guessed accurately when it came to how we die, though."

Cara raised her hand. "I've got a question. If there's no evidence after one of you dies, how do you know for sure they died? I mean, if someone just disappears, how do you know what happened?"

"There's evidence," John answered. "If the siren is older and nearing the end of his or her life, they start to show physical signs they're about to die. They kind of fade, and shimmer around the edges, and they can't tolerate being in deep water any longer. Also, when one of us is ready to die and showing these signs, the death is usually witnessed by the community."

"You mean people lurk around so they can watch?" Kate didn't quite hide her distaste.

"I mean there's a public event so we can all see the person off," John replied. "It's a spiritual rite of passage for all of us to witness death, to join with the person leaving us. We sort of send out our spirits to let the person feel our support, and help him or her release the energy keeping them tied to their failing body. It's very beautiful, a privilege to see."

"It sounds amazing," Cara murmured.

Kate was confused. "So what if someone is killed accidentally and no one sees? How do you know that person died?"

"It doesn't happen often," Carmen assured her. "If one of us is caught in a net, we can usually cut ourselves away." She gestured toward the knives they all wore around their waists. "But with an accident, the people — or sometimes the person if it's a mate — closest to the deceased can feel it. Family members, usually. There's a . . ." Carmen paused to find the right words. "There's a void you feel. A part of you dies, too, and you just *know* that person is gone."

John cleared his throat, and his voice when he spoke was thick with emotion. "It's like having your heart ripped, bleeding and pulsing, from your chest. You're told you can survive, but you don't feel very enthusiastic about living." Cara went to stand behind her husband's chair, looped her arms around John, and rested her chin on his shoulder. He pressed his cheek against her hair and placed a hand on her forearm.

Michael stood up. "No more gloom and doom, my friends. This is supposed to be a honeymoon, for crying out loud."

Carmen joined him. "You're right, of course." She faced Gabe and Kate. "We're leaving at sunset. We should spend these last few hours doing something fun."

"You could leave early, if you want. Like now, even," Gabe suggested, not quite innocently. The men laughed, and Michael clapped a hand on his son's back.

"Wouldn't dream of it, Gabe. This is our celebration too, you know."

John rose. "Let's get in the water. Maybe we could hunt for the kids, so Gabe doesn't have to choose sea bass over his bride for the next few days."

As she strode to the cottage with Gabe to retrieve her swimsuit, Kate revisited their conversation about siren intuition and the need for talking. "I mean, I could kind of — *kind of* — sense the thoughts back there, but we all talked to explain ourselves. Why didn't we just sit around and stare at each other until we had it all figured out?"

Gabe was amused by the idea. "We communicate better in a group by talking. And we weren't in the water, so our intuitive abilities are more sluggish. Mostly it's easier, though. Everyone takes turns, we don't have to work to know what people want to say, or try feeling them out in a less conductive environment. And listening to too many people at once can give you a headache. The concentration is hard to maintain with more than one person."

"Huh."

"You're dealing with all of this really well, Kate," Gabe remarked. "Are you sure you aren't secretly freaked?"

She nudged him with her shoulder. "Wouldn't you be able to tell if I were?"

He laughed. "Yeah, I suppose I would. I'm just trying to put myself in your shoes. I don't know if I'd be able to roll with it like you do."

She pressed herself against his side. "It's because I'm with you. You could breathe fire – "

"Become a frog?"

"Breathe fire, turn into a frog, and dance the Watusi for all I care. Sign me up."

"Oh, you're signed up," he threatened. "Good luck getting out of this one, Blake." His eyes grew wide. "Say! You're already a Blake! Guess we don't have to decide whether or not you're keeping your maiden name."

Kate flipped her hair over her shoulder. "Yeah, I've decided to keep it. It's already on my lease."

Gabe seemed amazed. "This is terrific. I wonder if they'll think we're related when we file at the courthouse."

"Ooo!" Kate giggled. "Let's tell them we're cousins." They reached the cottage pretending they were inbred relatives talking to some horrified clerk.

CHAPTER TWENTY-THREE

Sirens, when not in human society, didn't wear anything to go swimming, which made sense to Kate, but she wasn't exactly comfortable with a family party on the beach where the family was nude. She and her mother arrived by the bay in swimsuits and kept their attention on the water until everyone waded in.

Once there, Kate's reservations disappeared, since the sirens seemed less exposed in their fish forms. Carmen, John, and Michael chastised her for being prudish, truly unable to understand why anyone would care. She understood maybe she shouldn't care. But she did.

Deal with it, she told them.

If she were to do nothing for the rest of her life but watch sirens swim, Kate knew she would always be in awe of their strength and grace. And, goodness, they were fast. With one small flick of their tails, they could move ten yards. She'd never seen a siren's true potential when it came to speed; she wondered if perhaps today, when they were hunting, she'd get a glimpse of their storied quickness.

The sirens needed no adornment but each wore some small

decoration nonetheless, a coral ring or leather wristband or mother-of-pearl necklace or comb. They also wore thin leather ropes at their waists, which secured small pouches, a knife and sometimes a few beads. The only accessory Kate and Cara wore, other than their swimsuits, was a facemask so they could see. Everything was so beautiful and neither wanted to miss anything, although they lamented the horsey-ness of their goggles.

We'll never look as good as they do in the water, anyway, Cara said ruefully.

Kate was too distracted by the scenery around her to care much, anyway. She was enchanted by all of the colors, and riveted by her husband's handsome form. She also noticed how each siren's knife was unique, the hilts individually carved and decorated with various inlays and gemstones.

I'll make one for you, Gabe promised. She squeezed his hand by way of thanks, and they all continued swimming away from the beach.

Let's hunt the reef, John suggested.

They'd entered the water from a natural beach that curved all the way around the bay in which it sat. An extensive reef stretched across the mouth of the bay, protecting it, Gabe informed her, from the more violent forces of nature raging farther out at sea. She and Gabe had practiced her swimming thus far in this warmer, protected expanse. And in the week and a half they'd been on Shaddox, her stamina had already improved; she was able to stay submerged fifteen minutes at a time, now. Her mother, she saw, was comfortable for a full half hour – with a little help – before needing air.

Carmen attracted Kate's attention as a slow color change crept over her skin the farther they progressed. At first, she thought it was some trick of the light in the water, but as none of the others exhibited the same phenomenon, she sent a silent question to Gabe.

She's turning blue.

Not as blue as some, but yes. Carmen was adopted. Apparently, she's part Illyrian, because Illyrians are blue underwater but the color fades on land.

I thought Anna and Lydia were her sisters, and they aren't changing color. Were they adopted too?

No. All of us refer to each other as sisters and brothers, especially to humans, to explain our similarities. Kate nodded and forced her gaze away from Carmen to avoid appearing rude.

Everett was going to be a separate problem, Kate saw, requiring constant siren oversight. Watching him dart off toward whatever interested him, she knew her mother wouldn't be able to keep up.

I've got Everett during the hunt, Carmen promised, and Cara thanked her.

With this nagging worry dispatched, Kate gave her attention to the dazzling tableau before her. Sunlight played across the varied surfaces of the reef, highlighting the already brilliant colors in a mesmerizing display. On the side facing the ocean, the range of wildlife expanded to include larger fish, and, as the reef sloped downward, it encompassed topical indentations and sheer drops that seemed to disappear into the sea beyond.

John, Michael, and Gabe broke off from the group to descend down the slope in search of prey. Kate watched them, fascinated.

Working together, the three men positioned themselves around a school of Blackfin tuna in a wide triangle. At some unseen signal, the two hovering above the school drove inward and down, splitting the fish into two schools as they fled the reef. Michael, who had been positioned below the swarm, quickly seized a fish, and even more quickly, the other two joined him to secure the catch. Then, Michael clenched one arm around the head of the fish and the other near the tail, and in one fluid motion, twisted each section in the opposite direction, breaking the fish's spine.

Kate checked on Cara to see if she was enthralled too. She was.

Now we know how fast our boys can go.

That's got to be difficult to do with bigger fish, Kate remarked.

Yeah. I expected them to use their knives.

Carmen brought Everett to them. *With a bigger fish, two of them break it. One would twist from the head and one from the tail. And they only cut the fish as a last resort, because they don't want to attract other predators.*

Gabe tucked the newly dead fish under one arm and dragged it back toward Cara and Kate to show it to them. The women's minds were a cacophony of recipe ideas. *Fry it in butter? Olive oil? Wrap it in bacon? Grill it?*

Whatever sounds good to me, Gabe chimed in. *Of course, we'd eat it raw, too.*

Ugh. The recipe ideas halted briefly while the women considered this strange and unattractive option. Kate decided for them. *Let's bake it in salt.*

Yum, Cara replied.

Kate was especially pleased by how much the professional fish eaters enjoyed her preparation that night.

"This is almost as good as raw," Carmen complimented her. "And I never say that."

John agreed. "It's not salty at all. I would have thought a salt crust would have ruined it."

Gabe helped himself to thirds. "It's amazing. Better than cake."

Kate leaned back in her chair, too full to sit up straight. "Where are Dana and Will? We have enough to share. And shouldn't someone be watching them?"

Michael's answer was so brazen it startled her. "They're having sex at the Mattegins. The Seward women are checking in from time to time."

She took a second to compose herself. "Is everyone all better?"

"Better and probably pregnant," John answered, smirking.

"That's kind of funny," Kate mused. "Dana and I will have babies at the same time."

"It'll be great," Cara promised. "Hopefully she'll be close enough for you to help each other out. Another pair of arms can mean the difference between making it through the day and going completely nuts sometimes."

Kate elbowed her husband. "I'm trying to get Gabe to go into psychiatry so he can prescribe help."

Everyone at the table chuckled, and then Carmen, John, Cara, and Michael all rose to leave. "I'll get Everett ready," Cara called as she left the room. She reappeared with her napping son, who she handed to John. She hugged Gabe and then Kate. "Are you coming back home before you head back to work, Kate?"

She glanced at Gabe. "We haven't talked about it, yet."

"We'll stop in," Gabe decided.

Kate felt a guilty pang as she thought of Maya. "Don't say anything to the Wilkes, will you? We need to call Maya first."

Cara stroked her hair. "I understand. Mum's the word."

"We'll have the guest house ready for you," Carmen offered. "Just let us know your plans when you have them."

"We'll make them, and then we'll tell you," Kate assured her.

Everyone congratulated them again, made their goodbyes, and wished them a happy – and private honeymoon – from here on out.

CHAPTER TWENTY-FOUR

For the third time this week, Peter observed them, making sure he, himself, went unobserved. He'd tracked them in the water, which was not difficult; he knew where the Blake cottage was of course, and the bond between them was so fresh and strong, it was like a cyclone, sucking him in. He limited his spying to the water, when they were swimming, and where he could most easily hide himself. If he needed to, he could get away in a fraction of a second.

He knew he shouldn't be doing this, just as surely as he knew he would.

So, here he was, posing as a ray, or more often, a sea turtle, perfectly reflecting his subterfuge and masking all mental and emotional signals so no one was alerted to his real presence. At least he could laugh at himself, a decorated prince stooping to voyeurism, not that they were having sex in the water, thank goodness. Such evidence of their closeness would have been difficult for him to see. But their bond, so vital and vibrant, was sweetly romantic, so intensely intimate. And it was not something they were intentionally sharing with him. That was what made him a voyeur.

They were irresistible. No Kate, in particular, was irresistible to

174

him, and it was getting worse, seeing her devotion to Gabe. If only she were at his side.

He knew Gabe helped Kate become a stronger swimmer, was building her stamina for longer swims they would take together and preparing her for motherhood to a siren who would want to play in the water. Peter used his prodigious intuitive abilities to detect the life she grew within her, but there was as yet no signal. Whatever child, or children, she carried were masses of still-independent cells, which made now an ideal time for her to train, since oxygen deprivation was not the issue it would become later.

He stayed as close as he could, unable to withdraw from the heady emanation of their attachment, their feelings surrounding him like a balm whose restorative effects he craved all the more strongly as he felt them. He watched and lurked and drank them in like an addict. They seemed unaware – in fact, Peter knew for certain they were – although Gabe had given him a piercing look on two occasions. But he'd eluded true scrutiny and apparently convinced him he was what he appeared to be. He was an extremely capable cloaker.

He smiled at the irony of his situation; he was able to be near her, to intuit her goodness and beauty because he was invisible to her, and perhaps more importantly, her siren mate. Were he not such a flawless cloaker, unmatched really, he would not be able to be by her, which made him crave her all the more. He could almost laugh. He had to tear himself away when they left the water for the afternoon.

He could not fully consider the obvious outcome of his current activities. What *would* he do after all this? The answer was floating just beneath his consciousness, and still he refused to think of it directly. If he left now, discontinued this insanity, he could return to his life of regal inconsequence without hurting anyone. If he kept stalking them, if he continued to follow her and make her feelings his own, he would destroy someone, either her or Gabriel or himself, possibly all three of them. He understood these risks, and yet, each day, he found them and watched, becoming progressively more enthralled with his own fantasy.

He would not think of the natural conclusion to the steps he was taking, but neither could he stop himself from taking them. For now, he committed himself to studying them, their bond, the signature character of their communications, and Gabe's personality in particular. His voracious intuition supplied him with the information he would need for a very detailed, profoundly complex deception, one he told himself he did not intend to undertake. But he prepared for it nonetheless.

Soon, he would need to watch Gabe on land to fully apprehend his mannerisms and persona. He puzzled over logistics as he swam back to his castle, his preparations the only diversion strong enough to seduce him away from his newfound obsession.

Despite their unwillingness to share their honeymoon with anyone, Kate admitted she felt better – as did Gabe – freer to relax and enjoy their time, now their families knew they were together.

"I actually feel more married after our mothers fussed over us," she told him.

Gabe's eyes widened. "Meaning you no longer want a ceremony at the library?"

Kate laughed and conceded, "I don't need a human ceremony. We should file legally, though." Gabe agreed, and just like that, she considered them wed.

During their third week on Shaddox, they arrived back at the cottage after a day of leisure to find a courier from the palace waiting for them.

"Roger Dimmick," Gabe acknowledged, extending his hand to the man seated on the front steps. He rose to shake it. "This is my wife, Kate." After greeting her as well, Roger revealed the reason for his visit.

"We're witnessing a death at the castle tomorrow for an elderly count. The event will be in the inland lake, and the Loughlins have sent me to invite you to attend."

"What time are we gathering?"

"Sunrise. May I report your intent to participate?"

Gabe checked with Kate for her approval, and she nodded. "Yes, of course. Please thank Kenna, Peter, and the count's family for their invitation. They are generous to include us. We'll be there an hour before dawn."

After Roger left, Gabe briefed her on the ceremony they'd be attending. "It's called a sending. The people closest to the one dying will form a circle around him, and the rest will gather around the core group. We'll probably hang out on the periphery, so we can take you to breathe without disturbing anyone."

"What will we do? You and Roger used the word, *participate*. What does that mean?"

"I could explain it to you but I know you'll understand as soon as we're there. Basically, we all connect with each other to help the dying person let go." She regarded him quizzically. "You'll get it right away, I promise," Gabe assured her.

Early the next morning, they proceeded in the dark to the palace. The cool morning air and surrounding gloom heightened Kate's senses, breaking through the dreamy lethargy she associated with the sunny, lazy days she'd passed so far on Shaddox. Despite her solemnity, she was excited to experience the rite Gabe and his family had described.

Gabe was also happy for the excursion. "I think you'll find the event meaningful. It is, as John said, a privilege to witness. But we'll be emotionally drained afterwards."

The palace was abnormally busy at that hour, already filled with dozens of people advancing with reverent purpose through the corridors, running errands or exchanging hushed communications in preparation for the upcoming death. The air was electric with import.

One of Kenna's assistants met them and led them to the offices they'd visited two weeks earlier. There, Kenna herself, along with a small entourage of companions, greeted them.

"We're so glad you could come. Welcome." She focused on Kate. "Will this be your first sending?"

"Yes. And thank you for your invitation." The sirens, in a way she found sneaky, migrated toward her. She smiled at them nervously, and then they *really* drifted too close and gazed at her like she was the main course at Thanksgiving dinner. She clung to Gabe.

They're unable to resist your good feelings. They want to feel more of them. He kissed her temple then and smiled smugly. *And I should get the credit, here since I'm the one making you so happy.* Kate relaxed and laughed, deciding she was more flattered than afraid.

Kenna interrupted their reverie. "We won't be in the family's inner circle but you'll have an excellent vantage point by us, if you'd like."

"Yes, please be our guests," Peter said from behind them, startling everyone except his mother. Kate whipped her head around in his direction, wondering how long he'd been there. Gabe stiffened with irritation.

Peter smiled graciously at him. "My apologies. It's a habit of mine, nothing more."

Gabe stared hard in front of him. "I cannot read this guy," he bit out.

Kenna smiled fondly at her son. "You'll get used to that. Trust me when I tell you it's not personal."

Kate noticed the intent with which Peter watched her and did not even remotely believe his mother. But she was fascinated in spite of her distrust. She recognized his typical siren beauty – the faintly glowing skin and eyes, his lean, strong frame – with frank if unwilling appreciation. Peter seemed encouraged by her attention and immediately engaged her in conversation. Kate registered Gabe's disapproval, which Peter ignored. As he had during their earlier visit to the palace, he gave Gabe his back and tucked Kate's hand into his elbow while strolling forward.

"Kate, my dear, you look lovely. Marriage must agree with you." She did not think Gabe was mollified by this compliment... but she couldn't withhold her attention from Peter. Her gaze caught on the jeweled hilt of the knife tethered to his waist, which he offered for her examination.

"Every siren has a personalized knife, as you probably know. It's beautiful, don't you think?" He brushed the metalwork surrounding a mass of semi-precious jewels with his thumb. "This was forged in Ireland in fifteen-seventy for Queen Elizabeth. I'm told she wore it in her garter." He imparted this information as if it was scandalous gossip. "Catholic sympathizers opposed to Pope Gregory's edict to kill her gave it to her in the hopes it would protect her."

Kate traced one of the serpents coiling around the center ruby with her finger. Kidnapping plots, secret agents, romantic intrigue – this knife had seen it all. Peter explained how his family had come into its possession, a conversation that kept her separate from Gabe. She tried to hide her concern for her husband, who she knew was distressed by Peter's appropriation of her.

"Shall we find our places?" Kenna suggested, and Kate seized on the opportunity to excuse herself and return to Gabe's side.

Once near the central lake, the sirens disrobed and entered the water without an ounce of self-consciousness. Kate undressed discreetly to the swimsuit she'd worn under her clothes, which she folded and placed on a bench. No one paid her any attention, even Gabe, who stood by her side but remained absorbed in the emotional center of the morning's activities. Perhaps because she'd become more sensitive to how sirens perceive the world around them, she also felt the draw of something profound and compelling underway. She studied the elderly Count and his family gathering in the middle of the pool.

Earlier in the week, she'd learned about the history of the central pool from Gabe, so she knew it was larger than the palace itself and extensive enough to hold hundreds of people without becoming crowded. During its construction, workers had excavated the basin to be uniformly fifty feet deep, after which they drilled the entrance and exit tunnels, which provided a continuous flow and filtration of seawater. Over the course of time, all of the ocean life populating the shallow shelves around the island established colonies in the interior bay as well, to the point it was no longer discernible as a manufactured entity. Aside from the presence of several sculptures and the arena, the space appeared identical to the ocean with which it shared water.

Gabe and Kate accompanied the Loughlin group to an elevated tier on the periphery of the gathering. For the first time since they'd been together, Gabe's attention was not fully on her, and his distraction felt strange to her. As the morning progressed, however, she came to understand it. The sending riveted her, was easily the most fascinating event she'd ever attended or even could have imagined. Knowing as she did how drawn sirens were to emotional intensity, she could only guess at what her husband was experiencing, because she herself could not look away.

At the very center of the sirens gathered, an elderly siren floated and shimmered within the circle of his family, all with joined hands and bowed heads, each inclined toward the count in an attitude of prayer. At some undefined point in time, Kate heard a low chant begin, starting in the inner circle, and growing to include everyone present. As each tier of sirens joined in, they also clasped hands and inclined toward the dying man, just as the family was doing. Kate remained behind Gabe, keeping a hand on him to help her stay submerged and also to better apprehend what was happening. Eventually, she swam alone to the surface and back for air so as not to break Gabe's concentration.

Gabe was aware of her, but only just. Because of her hand on him, Kate knew how completely absorbed he was in the death, and she understood his and the others' role in facilitating it. And while she saw how the community helped the dying man, her husband's intuition gave her a much richer interpretation than her own senses provided. At some point, she closed her eyes to more fully participate.

It was hard work to die, she realized. She was most reminded of Everett's birth, seeing the effort required to come into and leave this world as commensurate and exactly parallel. Even with the end result intended and supported by everyone present, the process was no easy thing but the community was helping. The dozens and dozens of sirens gathered each projected their individual life force toward him, creating an extraordinary collective energy that flowed to and encompassed all present. For his part, the old siren swam suspended, with his arms open and face upheld toward the surface, a smile breaking through as the chanting strength of those around him filled him and carried him in a forceful eddy of pure love.

After four hours in the pool, with an ebb and flow of nearly unbearable tension emanating from the dying man, his shimmering outline convulsed once, then twice, and then, in a moment of perfect stillness, he exploded into a million particles of white light releasing not only him, but also the will and effort of those around him. The particles of light reminded her of a brilliant burst of fireworks, briefly dancing up and out until their glow faded and then disappeared.

Something between a sigh and a moan, a sound of victory and hope, burst forth from every siren present. The great collective energy dissipated as each came into him or herself again, and mutual accomplishment bound them all with a sense of camaraderie. She felt euphoric. She and Gabe left the pool in silence, both overwrought, and both too tired to think.

"Come," Peter Loughlin invited. "Let us feed you. You can refresh yourselves and rest a bit before leaving." Kate – and she strongly suspected Gabe too –wanted nothing more than to hurry to bed but she didn't have the will to enforce her wish. Neither did Gabe, apparently.

Kenna agreed to join them, although Kate thought she appeared too tired. They proceeded to the palace kitchen.

The meal was a welcome one, and while it did not alleviate their fatigue, Kate did feel fortified for the journey home. After a brief conversation between dinner and dessert, they finished their coffees, thanked their hosts again for their hospitality, and made their departure. They arrived at the cottage in silence and fell into an exhausted sleep.

Peter sighed with satisfaction after he waved Kate and Gabe out the door. The interaction had provided him with precisely what he needed. Tired and relaxed, they didn't bother to edit themselves, and he'd been able to study their expressions and private interactions freely. They had no idea how much information they'd just given him.

He'd never studied another siren with the intention of mimicking him, and the process gave him insight into some of his own characteristics he'd never given much thought. He and Gabe were alike in many ways, which would be helpful. They were both about the same size and height, for example, although Gabe's figure was slighter. And Gabe was dark while Peter was fair, which didn't much matter. They were both intellectually serious, both ambitious and intense, and were, each in his respective area, academically accomplished.

When it came to personality traits, however, he noted several wide differences, and he found himself wanting by comparison. For one, although he'd always thought himself to be energetic and positive, Gabe's natural optimism showed him what a positive outlook really meant, and he admittedly did not share it. By contrast, Peter saw himself as merely diligent, and he thought he probably appeared duller than he'd believed.

The biggest difference he noted was in their respective appetites for life. Gabe approached a new idea with open curiosity and a willingness to go out on an emotional limb. Perhaps this was due to the difference in their ages, but Peter believed he had always been more introspective and careful. While Gabe seemed eager to explore new experiences, even hypothetically, Peter's initial response to real or potential change was to protect himself, to withdraw and observe first, and then select engagement later on a peripheral level, where he could evaluate before participating.

One quality he worried about replicating was Gabe's boyish exuberance, because he didn't know if he'd ever been as guilelessly open as Gabriel Blake. He expected this component of his act to provide him with the most difficulty. The analogy of a former beauty queen struggling and failing to appear just as she did in her youth flashed in his mind, and he shuddered with distaste.

Hopefully, it wouldn't be a problem. Kate would be the only one to notice, anyway. He would think of a plausible excuse to give her if necessary, and he would simply divert her if she remained unconvinced.

CHAPTER TWENTY FIVE

After three blissful weeks on Shaddox Island, Gabe and Kate made the swim back to Griffins Bay, sadly saying goodbye to the place she had spent, Kate believed, the very best time of her life.

They returned to the beach house first as promised, calling from Carmen and Michael's to let her parents know they were back and would stop in to see them that evening. They intended to spend four days at the guest cottage before making the trip to her apartment to set up house together. Kate couldn't wait.

After unpacking their few belongings and greeting their families, she left Maya a message to call them because they had some good news to share. "We need talk to you in person. Can you come home this weekend?"

As tempted as they were to visit Jeremy and Alicia, neither felt right about seeing them before they talked to Maya. Kate fretted over the situation. "I know she'll be happy for us but I feel just rotten we've been together a month and haven't called her. It's pretty selfish of us."

"I know," Gabe agreed. "And we're not having a big to-do, so it's not like she can play bridesmaid for us."

Kate was glum. "Don't forget about the half of our lives we can in no way explain, either. I mean, it's not like we can say, *we didn't call sooner because we went to an island for mermaids*, and, *we're not having a wedding because, according to siren law, we're already married.* She flopped onto the couch.

Gabe was silent for several seconds. "I've got no ideas."

"Maybe she could be our witness when we file at the courthouse," Kate proposed.

"Good idea. Remember the courthouse is only open until four on weekdays, though."

"So let's leave a day earlier, go through Philadelphia and register there," she suggested. "I'll call and see what we'll need, make an appointment if necessary, and then Maya can witness for us, if she's up for it."

"Plan."

Maya knew instantly what was going on when she heard Kate's message. And she was happy for them, mostly. The only surprise she felt was over their timing; she'd sensed a connection between them almost from the beginning, and Kate's circumspect avoidance of Gabe as a topic of conversation in high school had clued her in on just how important a matter he was to her. She'd been a good friend though, never once forcing Kate into a conversation she didn't want.

Back then, Maya had tried on the idea of her own romance with Gabe, just as she'd considered the possibility with several boys at school, but she'd conducted her early romantic explorations with guys she ran with in her broader social circle. At any rate, she'd always suspected she would hurt Kate's feelings if she tested those waters, and so she hadn't. She picked up the phone to call Kate back, prepared to be happy and supportive.

"Maya?" Kate answered. She sounded worried, and Maya's heart completely softened; she knew the worry was for her. She dispensed with the formalities.

"When's the wedding?" she asked brightly.

"Oh, thank God you're not mad at me," Kate breathed. "How on earth did you know? We haven't told *anyone* aside from our parents!"

"Kate, you suck at keeping secrets." Kate snorted. "And you

forget, I've known you since forever. I always knew there was something between you and Gabe. Everyone did."

"Wha — we never, never talked about it. Even to each other."

Maya rushed to reassure her. "I'm not saying our classmates knew, I just think your parents — and mine for that matter — aren't surprised you two are together."

"Well, about that, we're a little more than *together* now." She launched into an overview of their reunion three weeks earlier, their decision to get married without clergy, and their desire to file their status legally with Maya as their witness.

"I know this is probably all too sudden, and we're complete jerks for waiting this long to call you but we want you to be part of this. Will you do it? I'll even get you a corsage," she wheedled.

Maya shuddered. "Hell, no. If I ever wondered if you love me, I don't now. Trust me, the kindest thing you can do for me is *not* have some big affair, where I have to wear a bad dress with bad shoes that would make me twist an ankle. Just ruin my athletic career. Plus, I'm already, like, almost six feet tall.

"Come to Philadelphia, with my blessing," she concluded. "It'll be great to see you guys, and I'll be more than happy to haul your butts down to the courthouse."

Kate laughed. "Ahhhh. Such sweet words, Maya. Lighten up on the gooey romance of it all, will you?"

Maya sniffed. "You want gooey romance, call your other friends."

They chatted a while longer, Kate promising to come through town with Gabe and stay with her Friday night. Maya hung up feeling as if their easy friendship was affirmed. She also felt like some clog in the universe had been cleared, and she exhaled with relief. She didn't hold Gabe and Kate's need for privacy against them, not even a little bit. She figured that was why they'd always gotten along so well; even in the throes of adolescent neediness, each had valued introversion over the less tasteful options offered them by the world around them.

Friends to keep, she thought with satisfaction.

Peter climbed the steps to the Blake home hiding in his invisibility and steeling himself for what he was about to do. He mentally reviewed the layout of the interior as he knew it, took a deep breath and allowed the image he'd practiced more than any other in his life flood through him. He let himself in and entered the foyer.

"Hi, honey," Carmen called from her chair in the living room. "Where's Kate?"

The man appearing to be Gabriel Blake picked an apple out of a bowl near the door and sauntered into the living room to peer over Carmen's shoulder. He bit into his apple. "She's down at the guesthouse going through e-mails. Whatchya reading?"

"Just an article on climate change and the Great Barrier Reef. It's pretty depressing, and I'm about to put it down."

Michael strolled by on his way to the kitchen. "Hi, Gabe. I'm going to make myself a sandwich. Anyone else want one?"

"I'll take a sandwich," the false Gabe said. "Whatever you're having. Thanks, Dad." He shifted his attention to Carmen. "I wanted to peek at Kate's and my charts at some point if you wouldn't mind, Mom."

"Again?" She gazed at him quizzically. "I just had them out yesterday for you. But, yes, of course you can see them. Now?"

"Yes, please, if we could." Peter revealed none of his chagrin over his slip.

"Fine with me. I can't bear to read any more of this." She rose and tossed her magazine onto the coffee table. "It's not very responsible of me but I can only stand to think about how evil and wasteful we've been for so long each day before I start resenting the problem. Not very helpful, I know." She smiled at him. "Let's go get you taken care of." He followed her down the hallway. "We'll be in my office, honey," she called to Michael.

She laid the charts on her oversized drafting table, and Peter examined them, starting with Kate's, recalling the details of his own, which Carmen had done for him long ago. So many of the interpretations had tantalized his pride during that first reading, which indicated unmatched strength and athleticism, high intelligence, and a talent for governing and leadership. All were attractive qualities for a monarch and exciting affirmations for an ambitious young man.

The most terrible depiction for him, the fate he was determined to change, had to do with his solitary walk through life, which was, according to his astrological map, likely to persist. Carmen had, perhaps out of kindness, suggested alternative interpretations, namely how he was a protected prince without the context of a wide population of friends and family. The solitude indicated might merely be relative to people with siblings, children, neighbors, and professional colleagues; and the suggestion could well be he'd have only a few close companions, which was preferable, didn't he think?

Unfortunately, companionship and genuine intimacy eluded him, and emotional distance proved, time and again, the overriding characterization to all of his associations. Early on, in his optimism and conviction he could overcome any insufficiency, he'd entered into a disastrous marriage in an attempt to force a different life for himself. She was a full-blooded siren, a minor princess to whom he was very distantly related. Despite concerted effort, however, she'd been too emotionally stunted for anything to come of their relationship. After months of trying to draw her out, he found himself wrestling with the same loneliness – made all the more crippling because he expected its alleviation – that had compelled him to make such a rash union. For her part, she could not tolerate being continually asked to give something she could not. Within a year, she ran off. He declined to follow her.

He hadn't hoped for much from a relationship with a woman in a very long time.

He and Kate would have been well matched, he was satisfied to note. When he perused Gabe's chart next, however, his good humor faded. Gabe and Kate were perfectly suited, not that this would matter now. He pored over the details to glean any information he might use.

Carmen noticed his irritation, which Peter perceived quickly. "You're upset. Why?" He realized she felt something unusual from him and was starting to reach with her intuition to discover what was off.

Abruptly, his ire disappeared as he hurried to distract her from further scrutiny; she would not be able to discern who he was but he could not effect the emotional flow Gabe could with his mother without causing suspicion.

Time to sidetrack her. "Not upset, just a little concerned, Mom." He indicated three identical points on Kate and Gabe's charts. "These suggest death, or something equally upsetting in the current timeframe."

Carmen clapped her hands. "I'm impressed! You've never shown an interest in our astrology mapping. You must have picked some of this up from being around it so much." She focused on the points Peter had indicated. "Yes, I've studied this alignment and had the same worry. It doesn't necessarily mean death or division, although that's the usual conclusion. But it can also mean a breaking off from your former life, and with Kate being human, maybe your marriage – and the new baby too – maybe the pattern indicates a profound event. Because, especially for her, marriage and a life with you is a pretty big departure from reality as she knew it. More of a metaphorical death."

Michael entered with plates and coffee. "I gave up on having you join me in the kitchen. I'm bringing the mountain to you." He placed a sandwich by Peter. Carmen caught him up on their conversation while Peter ate.

"Okay, I'm gonna get back to Kate," he told them, and drained his coffee cup. "Thanks for going over these with me again, Mom, and thanks for the sandwich, Dad." He made his goodbyes while ducking out of the room.

"Hmm," Carmen commented after he'd left. "No hugs. I can't remember the last time he left without hugging us." She pouted.

"He's just going down to the guest house, honey."

Carmen inclined her head. "I suppose he's thinking about the division he saw on their charts." Then she brightened. "But there'll be a new baby to make a chart for soon."

"Or babies." Michael grinned at her.

Carmen chuckled. "Kate wouldn't like that. But I would."

Kate sat with Gabe on the couch in the living room of the guest house, where she'd just finished describing her childhood. "What I really like about both of our parents is they put us first. And by *us* I mean the family itself, not child worship. Even though everyone worked – and my mother raised me alone – the job was secondary, more of a means to an end."

"I'm with you. My mom could certainly have had a bigger-deal job but she wanted to be around. She was no martyr, either, making some big sacrifice. She chose her work and the time it gave her with Dad and me."

"I love that you always had a mom and dad around."

Her smile faded as she considered how to start the next part of this conversation. "I have a question for you about what you want to do when the baby comes, and it's got more to it than just *how should we schedule primary care responsibilities.*"

"Let's hear it." Gabe caressed the back of the hand he held with his thumb.

She squirmed. "I feel ridiculous even bringing this up, like I shouldn't have to. But I do." Gabe's regard was open, his manner patient, and she felt encouraged to continue. "It has to do with gender roles." She watched his face closely for a reaction. "I mean, I feel like I should take primary responsibility for our children's care — whether or not I want to seems irrelevant — and that strikes me as a pretty unenlightened idea, and possibly not fair to you. Would you ever want to stay home with the kids? I also want to know how you feel about hiring the job out to someone else."

Gabe nodded slowly. "I have the same dirty little secret you do, except unlike you, I'm pretty judgmental about people who don't agree with me." His smile was wry. "No, I don't want to stay home with the kids. I will of course, but I want to go to medical school and become a doctor. I feel even more excited about this choice now we're together and about to start a family, though I suppose I could see these events as mutually exclusive.

"But I don't see us that way," he asserted. "What I'm about to say is not a mandate, okay? I'm not insisting anything."

"Go ahead."

"I want one of us to be mostly home while the kids are little — we can handle it in shifts or together or however you want — and later, for me to work close by — I'd love it if I could walk to work. And then... I don't know, we'd have each other and our children and our jobs, but our lives can be about us. What we do, what we want to do, will revolve around our life together. That aside, if you want to pursue a journalism career, I'll do whatever it takes to help you, including hiring out or shouldering child care."

Kate closed her eyes and sighed, pleased to have this issue finally aired. "I think what I most want is flexibility, to work at something professionally on my own terms somehow, and do it around being home with our kids. I've got this blog I could play with, maybe make something of... but you know, I'm so hung up on what I *should* want,

I can't say what I *do* want. I kind of feel like it would be morally wrong to abandon my job. I mean, all I've done for the past several years is work like mad to get this exact position, which is dang hard to get. I feel like I'm betraying... something. Like I shouldn't even consider leaving it."

"You know we'll be okay financially, right?" Gabe offered. "I mean, we won't be wealthy, and until I'm through medical school it'll be lean, but we'll have a house and a small monthly allowance from the community."

Kate's smile twisted. "In a way, I'd have an easier time if I knew I had to work, because then the decision would be made for me. My mother assures me it's better to choose, and she thinks I won't care much about my career after I hold our son or daughter in my arms." She paused to let this wonderful, terrifying thought settle between them. "I don't want you to think whatever we do is my decision, though. This is your family too." She smiled at him. "And I know we won't just think about our own personal fulfillment – a ludicrous modern habit in my opinion. A child, a family, should take priority."

"Ah, my wonderful little wife, this is exactly why you are going to make a spectacular mother." He squeezed her hand. "I feel the same way but I get pretty irritated by what I see in human families where there's no center, no stable base to fall back on. In the end, I want you to be happy, and I want us to be happy. And I know we'll figure it all out, Kate."

Gabe's familiar optimism had its usual effect, diffusing her concern. She calmed with the knowledge they both wanted the same thing and began to think instead on their plans for that evening. "Okay. I'm done having deep conversations for now, and I want to do something mindless, like make popcorn and watch a bad romantic comedy."

Gabe stood and stretched. "Sounds good, although we're going to argue over genres. I think it should be a bad action movie." Kate waved her hand to indicate apathy. "Whatever, as long it's stupid." Gabe pulled her off the couch and led them toward the kitchen. "I probably should have known this before I hauled you to Shaddox, because it could've been, you know, a deal breaker, but do you know how to make popcorn?"

Kate crossed her arms and pretended offense. "Can *I* make popcorn? Are you joking?"

Gabe laughed and was reaching for her when he saw a motion at the kitchen window. He pulled away and focused his attention outside. He couldn't tell what it was but he heard someone scuttle off, he assumed in an effort to avoid detection. "Someone's watching us," he hissed, and before Kate could respond, he launched himself out the door. "Call my dad!" he yelled over his shoulder as he left.

He leapt over the railing to land like a cat by the scaffolding supporting the deck and stairs, scanning the approaches with his eyes and reaching with his mind to ascertain the presence of another. He intuited nothing but saw a shadow between the wall sections protecting the walkway to the water. So fast he almost flew, he traversed the hill under the stairwell to reach the side of the path, where he hugged one of the sections of wall hiding it. At the same time, he felt his father skim down the slope from the house. Good. Kate had gotten to him. They mentally identified each other and oriented themselves for maximum surveillance of the stairs and passageway, with him creeping low and silent along the partitions, his dad moving to the unprotected side of the path for a clear view to the water. He knew they both reached with all of their senses for the trespasser… and they felt nothing. In the next instant, they heard footfalls racing toward the ocean.

They sprang in unison, sprinting toward the water. In seconds, they heard a splash off the end of the dock and immediately dove after it. They identified a trail but lost it four hundred yards out.

It had to have been one of us, Gabe remarked.

Someone who didn't want to be seen, Michael agreed, gazing toward the open water.

A cloaker, they both thought. At the same moment, Gabe also thought of Peter Loughlin.

Michael closed his eyes, and Gabe knew he prayed his Peter hypothesis was inaccurate. *It was someone strong and fast enough to out-swim both of us*, Gabe reminded him. *And neither of us could detect who it was.*

Which is unbelievable.

They broke the surface of the water. "What was he doing when you saw him?" Michael asked.

"Watching us. I don't know how long he was there. Kate and I were pretty involved in our conversation."

"He couldn't have been there long, Gabe. I mean, you just left the house, what, fifteen minutes ago?"

He stared at his father in confusion. "I haven't left the guest cottage tonight. What are you talking about?"

His dad appeared very concerned now. "Gabe, you reviewed your charts again, yours and Kate's. I made you a sandwich. You were with us for over an hour."

Neither had an answer but both acknowledged something very strange had just occurred. "I'm taking Kate back to her apartment tomorrow. We have to get away from here."

Michael reluctantly agreed. *We'll figure out what we can on this end and call you,* he told his son silently.

Peter easily escaped Michael and Gabriel Blake, perhaps due to the adrenaline rush he felt upon being noticed. Fear and exhilaration occupied his psyche in equal measure as he reviewed the events of the past hour. He'd been stupid at the end. If he hadn't stopped to spy on her, he would have gone undetected.

He had succeeded though, and done so with Gabe's own mother and father. They might suspect something now, however; at least, they would guess another siren was watching them.

He would have to act tonight.

Gabe slid into bed beside Kate, hoping to not disturb her, although she was awake. She spooned into him.

"Who was it?"

"We don't know. Dad and I chased whoever it was into the water and then lost the trail. We couldn't read him, and we couldn't catch him, so it was definitely one of us." He carefully concealed his thoughts concerning Peter Loughlin.

He felt her concerns, which revolved around the impossibility of anyone eluding both her husband and her father-in-law, not just on land but in the water, and she was worried. "What would motivate someone to come here in secret? Why…" she began. Her questions hung heavily between them.

"Neither of us could think of a reason. I told Dad we'd leave for the city tomorrow. Maybe it's unnecessary, but I feel like we have to get away from here, go inland."

Her alarm pricked his insides like a cactus. "You feel like running?"

"Yes, but again, it's just a precaution. I don't want you to be worried."

He wrapped his arms tightly around her. Fat chance of her not worrying, he knew, because he was worried and doing a poor job of hiding it. But he reasoned nothing could be too awful if they were together, and he started to relax, which helped Kate do the same. They drifted off.

His slumber was unusually heavy that night, an eerie, atonal hum serving as the backdrop to his dreams. In one of them, he felt Kate roll away from him and rise to leave the room. His body was as leaden as his thoughts, however, and though he wished to follow her – rebelled, in fact, against this particular separation – he slept on, unable to conquer his torpor.

Near dawn, he sat up groggily in the bed, slow to orient himself. What an odd sleep. He noticed Kate was not beside him, and he reached with his intuition to feel where she was in the house.

She wasn't there.

Almost completely sublimated by the wind, he heard her calling his name. She was out on the water. The sound electrified him, and he flew to the deck, searching the waves for her. He saw her nearly three hundred yards off shore, much too far out for safety, her cheerfulness at odds with her perilous distance from him. He started to run.

"I'm out swim... furthest I've ever gone... be so proud... come..." She dove down, her head disappearing just as Gabe hit the water. He raced like a bullet, frantic with a sense of impending, unstoppable tragedy. His heartbeat thundered in his ears as he pushed himself faster and faster.

But he was not fast enough. From too far away, he saw her start to swim toward him, an ecstatic smile on her face. Oddly, perhaps because of the overwhelming fear he felt, he could not sense her, only see her. As he swam desperately to reach her, he saw the shadow of an immense bull shark hover behind her, and he knew he was too late. In one, rapid strike, the shark clamped its teeth around her torso, killing her instantly. With a vicious shake of its head and a tremendous gulp, Kate was gone.

He drifted to a stop, stunned. His wife, their baby, gone. This wasn't possible. He stared at the space where she'd been only moments before, unable to process what had just happened.

For some undefined amount of time, he floated, feeling a disembodied sense of calm. His initial horror faded first to numbness, then to nothingness. Soon, he could not think of one thing, feel one thing, and with no impulse to compel him, he remained where he was, motionless, suspended. Eventually he closed his eyes, withdrawing into himself more profoundly than he ever had in his life. With this insulation, he stayed where he was, and, by the thinnest of margins, continued to exist.

Carmen felt uneasy when she woke and roused Michael beside her. "We need to find Gabe." They dressed wordlessly and made their way to the guest house. No one answered their knock. They let themselves in to find the place empty.

Carmen frowned. *They were leaving today, but their things are still here.*

They didn't leave, Michael asserted. *Gabe would have said goodbye.*

I can't feel where he is. Something's wrong, Carmen thought. She felt her husband reach with his own intuition but he couldn't locate Gabe, either. They drifted onto the deck and began to scan the waves.

Carmen moved first, more on a whim than certainty. *Let's check the water.* Michael followed as she descended toward the dock. They dispensed with their clothing along the way and dove into the sea feeling an urgency they did not understand.

Carmen found him and knew something was terribly wrong but she couldn't intuit what. She and Michael swam to their son's side, Carmen placing a hand on his arm. *What is it? Where's Kate?*

Her heart lurched as Gabe's awareness seeped back to the present from far away, his eyes blank. He shimmered around the edges as only someone dying or grief-stricken did, and her whole body keened with a terrible, foreboding ache.

Gabe's gaze was vacant, his emotions disconnected. *She's gone. She came out here alone to practice swimming. I followed her but I was too late.* He shared the image of the bull shark sinking its teeth into Kate, which caused both Michael and Carmen to flinch.

Oh, no. No, they thought. Carmen clasped her son's arm and placed her forehead on his shoulder. She silently encouraged Michael to do the same, to help share his grief and keep him whole.

She was only vaguely aware of the other sirens who straggled into their periphery, drawn, she knew, by the intensity of their sadness. Those closest to their family formed a circle around them, as they would have in a sending, and Carmen was grateful for the energy and support they offered.

We will not let him release himself, they promised. *We will help him heal.*

It was the kindest way, Peter rationalized again as he watched Kate sleep in their suite at the palace. Exhausted from her long swim, the emotional manipulations she'd endured, and her pregnancy, she was resting without his influence while he sat in a chair near the bed, reflecting on how well he'd maneuvered everyone that evening.

His plan was the best he could make it. Killing Gabriel was the only alternative, which would have left Kate free for Peter to court, but also would have necessitated Michael and Carmen's demise. They would have tried, perhaps successfully, to investigate their son's death, and their abilities and resources made that option too risky. Killing Gabe would have been difficult at best anyway; he was quick, strong and intelligent, perhaps as talented as he himself had been at his age.

No, if everyone thought Kate was dead, he was free of scrutiny from his community. This way, he could more easily achieve the fantasy enslaving him, one of a home and family full of love and genuine intimacy he did not have to question.

Perversely, he was glad she was pregnant; sooner than otherwise, he would have the family life he craved, delivered to him whole, anchoring Kate at his side. Kate, he believed, would disregard any inconsistencies she felt with him and blame it on her pregnancy, or the fact they were in hiding. And she would certainly put aside any of her own concerns for the good of her son or daughter.

Their son or daughter, he corrected himself. He reached again with his senses to confirm the single heartbeat he'd identified during their swim here.

He was amazed his scheme had worked so well, despite his meticulous preparations so it would. Before the test to project himself as Gabe to Carmen and Michael, he'd considered a variety of options for staging Kate's death, including drowning or even just disappearing, but with a drowning, a family of talented sirens would know to save her, or at least find her body; and a disappearance would involve the same talented crew searching for her.

The impending death of his housekeeper's aged mother, Maureen, inspired him. He took personal interest in her decline, his solicitousness seen as an honor. "Your family has been with us for so long," he explained when they protested he was far too busy to concern himself. "It's the least I can do." Maureen was over three hundred years old. Her eyesight and hearing were poor.

He visited to support his plan for abduction, of course, not to comfort the dying woman or her family. He questioned her and her caregivers closely during each visit, using all of his knowledge and skills to gauge precisely how much time Maureen had left. He knew he had a window of several days, give or take, where he could personally achieve her death. When he pinpointed an exact timeframe, he set a later date for Maureen's public ceremony. No one questioned him.

He prepared a cave by Griffins Bay.

Extricating Kate from the guesthouse was no trouble since he'd been honing his performance so feverishly during the previous month. Gabe, already asleep, was easily influenced; and Kate, being human, was a piece of cake. He called her semi-aware from her bed and met her as her husband in the kitchen. He folded her in his arms.

"How'd you get in here so fast?" she inquired sleepily.

He ignored her question. "There's been trouble in the community," he whispered. "Some humans, a large group, have found one of us, and they're launching a search. We have to go into hiding."

She'd scanned his face and then nodded trustingly. "Now? What about my parents?"

"There's no time to contact them, darling. John will take care of your mother and Everett." And just like that, he'd led her away. A lie to one person was easier to support than lies to many, he reasoned.

He escorted her to a hotel and told her to wait, saying he'd be back for her in a couple of hours.

"Where are we going?"

"Back to Shaddox. The whole island is shielded, but we'll be staying at the palace just to be safe."

Kate was incredulous. "At Peter's?"

He instantly saw Gabe's warnings against him in her tone, and his jealousy flared. "This is a challenging time for our community, Kate," he responded too harshly. "The Loughlins are offering their protection." He'd left abruptly then, unwilling to defend himself to her.

He'd had only two hours to prepare Maureen. He brought her from the cave to the coast near the Blake house and began to effect the most complicated projection he'd ever executed. For Maureen, he told her she was surrounded by love and family, her time had come, and the community was present to help her let go. She smiled with gratitude. She was ready, she told him. Peter's intuition flowed into the old woman, sensing acutely her hold on life and his ability to time her release.

Near the end, he brought her to the surface and in her delirium, had her call to Gabe. In what he hoped was an effective projection, he fashioned her image and voice to match Kate's. He dragged Maureen down with him when Gabe hit the water.

At the moment of her release, he himself holding the final threads of inner vitality tying Maureen to her life, he became the bull shark and set her free. His apparent bite coincided with Maureen's dissolution perfectly.

He didn't need extraordinary intuition to feel Gabe's response. His performance had worked. He swam away to collect his new wife.

Now, his dilemma was over what to do next, how long to keep Kate hidden, or how to change her appearance so he could take her out in public without jeopardizing his claim. How to appear to her as Gabriel Blake, and to his mother and the court as himself. Also, Kate could never again be in the company of anyone who had known her well, certainly none of the Blakes. Even if he changed her appearance, her emotional signature was too distinctive.

He wasn't entirely sure how to tell her she could never see her family again. He smiled bitterly at the irony of his new predicament; his own emotional deprivation had been strong enough for him to risk everything, including his life and hers, to have her. And yet, his first act in taking her was to deprive her of all the people who loved her. He hoped, fervently, she would love him and the baby, and that this would be enough.

He stood and went to her sleeping form. A thrill of accomplishment ran through him. A wife. A baby. A family. He lay down next to her, carefully so as not to wake her, and stared hungrily at her profile. He rested a hand on her stomach and watched her breathe and sleep.

Welcome home, darling.

"And yet so deep had the mistake taken hold in my temper that I could not satisfy myself in my station, but was continually poring upon the means and possibility of my escape from this place."
– Daniel Defoe, *Robinson Crusoe*

PART THREE

CHAPTER TWENTY-SIX

A scruffy dog bounded up the stairs to Michael and Carmen on their back porch. It sat beside Michael's chair and yelped once for attention.

"Well look who we have here," Michael remarked, patting his head.

Carmen rose to scratch the mutt behind its ears. "Whoever he is, he's too well cared for to be a stray." The dog placed a paw on her arm, which allowed her to reach for the identity tag. "Soley, property of Gabriel Blake, and there's a phone number." Michael detached the tube attached to Soley's collar and opened it. "It's a letter."

Mom and Dad,

I think Kate's alive. I can't explain or give you any details but I've gone to try and find her. I'm sending Soley to you to care for until I — we — get back. I love you both. Please do not follow me.

Gabe

Carmen's eyes instantly filled with tears, her sadness penetrating both of them, pricking them with a thousand needles. She regarded her husband, sharing her belief Gabe was suffering and in denial. "Should we ignore his request for privacy?"

Michael equivocated. "Let's give him a little more time, honey." She knew if she argued the issue, he would relent.

She did not though, and they both gazed at the sea, raw pain flaring within both of their hearts, holding them in agonized silence. Three months had passed since Kate's death, and her grief – their grief – was still tender, too easily brought to the surface. If one of them spiraled into it, the other soon followed.

After a while, Carmen rose from the table, her entire body throbbing with the sharp ache of her misery. She advanced toward the stairs, needing an escape from herself. *I'll be in the water*, she thought, and Michael inclined his head. She descended to the dock, anticipating the small freedom she would have from her pain as her wilder, faster siren form twisted, swam, and dove, her only company other sea creatures who did not grieve and would not hurt her.

Gabe knew his disappearance worried people, although he called from time to time to let his parents know he was still among the living. Those first two weeks had been the strangest in his life; he could barely remember them and certainly could not place the events of that time in proper order. He continued then as he did now to replay Kate's death in his mind, horrified by it again and again but unable to shut the images off. He was searching for something, his concentration dedicated to the task like a continuous-loop software program, where the review would only stop when the information it sought was found. He knew this was draining him but he did nothing to divert himself.

He could not believe she was gone. He couldn't think of an alternative but he felt with certainty it could not be so. He examined the sequence of events that morning again and again, and then examined them harder, seeking some small illumination, anything to resolve the feeling of incompletion he carried.

He'd accompanied Carmen and Michael to see John and Cara, all of them a walking, breathing morass of anguish and despair. That exchange had been every bit as terrible for him as watching the shark devour his wife. John felt them coming and met them at the door, tense and already shocked from what he sensed in their approaching broadcast. Cara's intuitive reach was slower but also engaged, because their bereavement was so profound. She stood behind her husband, bracing a hand against his back in an unconscious attempt to stay the bad news she felt was coming.

Gabe wished she'd kept her hands to herself, because he knew she felt too much through this contact. John had grasped Gabe's forearm, his face fierce and terrifying as he saw what Gabe had seen, his own response intense enough to send every nuance of horror related to Kate's demise into the ether. He was sure Cara had seen everything too; because she withdrew her hand as if she'd been scalded. It was too late, however. She fell to the ground and retched. The sirens all stood motionless with closed eyes, unwilling to absorb her terrible feelings, but unable by their natures to withdraw. Gabe felt her horror most keenly, dropping to his knees as well, heaving convulsively with her.

Later, John had found him, swimming in an aimless pattern around the place he'd last seen her. This was when Gabe first had the suspicion Kate was still alive, and John unwittingly introduced the idea. Having lost his first wife, John knew exactly what the death of a spouse felt like. He communicated nothing specific along these lines; he simply stayed by Gabe to provide his company, and, if necessary, protect him from dissolution. As a matter of course, Gabe evaluated his cousin's experience as only a siren could, and he saw a crucial, fundamental difference between them.

And the more he reflected, the more convinced he became John's loss was not the same as his own. When Alice died, John had felt, as he once explained, as though one of his own organs had been extracted. Gabe could still literally locate the excision, the hole Alice's death left.

He did not have this out-and-out disappearance of part of him. He felt the pain of separation from Kate — If she was out there somewhere, she was certainly far away — and he felt the horrifying loss accompanying the belief he'd never see her again. But he did not feel her actual death.

Maybe that's a gift, Gabe, John thought. *I wish I'd felt as you do, and I could have somehow escaped the overwhelming burden of Alice's leaving.*

My observation is not a coping mechanism, Gabe insisted, growing more and more certain. John unsuccessfully withheld his disbelief.

Gabe then committed all of his concentration to reviewing the attack of the bull shark, and also to the events leading up to it. He started with his last memories first, and methodically worked his way backward. As he had after the event, he retreated completely into himself, feeling within him a dense center of gravity, which kept his thoughts and feelings on an ever-inward pull, like a black hole attracting light. It was the only way he could stand to remember.

Gabe, John called in alarm, dimly breaking through his thoughts. He slowly resurfaced to meet John's questioning stare.

You were cloaking, John told him, surprise coloring his expression.

Gabe was surprised too. *I didn't mean to. What did you see?*

You faded from sight. You disappeared for nearly three seconds.

Gabe retreated into himself again, but only a little, and watched John's reaction.

What are you thinking? Now I can see you, but I have no sense of you.

Interesting, Gabe thought. *Let's go back.* They swam toward the house. Gabe felt a dim spark of hope and was inspired to explore this ability further, but in private.

Over the next several days, he experimented with cloaking and diligently practiced all he could in terms of projection and withdrawal. Counter-intuitively for a siren, he found the exercise a tremendous relief, since every interaction for him during that time was a nearly unbearable mixture of raw pain – both his and everyone else's. And had others detected his disbelief, he would have attracted even more attention and concern. Cloaking allowed him to escape this overbearing scrutiny and consider his thoughts without censure. More than the support of his community, this insulation helped him avoid dissolution, he knew.

He could not accept Kate was dead, because evidence of her death simply wasn't in him as it should be. Which meant his senses were on constant alert now, always searching outward for evidence of her, even in sleep, which he never fully achieved any longer. Her disappearance was torturing him, he knew, not the death he could not truly feel. It was her distance from him that he could not tolerate. He could not, did not, shut off his ranging, raging effort to locate her.

John questioned Carmen and Michael when they got back to the house on a possible link between cloaking and grief. They didn't know of one. "Cloaking is so rare for us," Carmen explained. "There haven't been enough sirens who know how to do it... we just don't know much about it." Gabe knew they all assumed his disappearance was grief-related, a way to cope. They believed the ability would disappear as he came to accept Kate was gone.

He couldn't stand to be around Kate's mother, couldn't even think about the grief she carried. Cara, in her own way, also disappeared according to John. Everett, John suspected, kept her from being catatonic, since the day-to-day responsibility of caring for their son engaged her at least minimally in life. John was holding Everett when he made this report, and Gabe thought the boy summed up their dilemma perfectly.

"Mama sad," Everett said gravely. John hugged him close. "Yes, Everett. Mama sad."

Gabe had to get away. He couldn't think straight in this swamp of agony, and he didn't have the strength to overcome his own hurt, much less the hurt everyone around him also vomited on him. He packed a shoulder bag with basic articles and some cash, and he left not exactly sure of his course.

"I don't want you to worry about me," he told his parents. "I won't do anything foolish. I just need to get away and think. I'll call in."

As tormented as he felt in the middle of his family's overwhelming bereavement, he knew he was only trading that torment for loneliness, which would be almost equally unbearable. He rented a duplex in a small town on the coast well north of Griffins Bay and set out to find a dog.

He'd seen a sign for free puppies posted on a telephone pole, written in marker on a piece of cardboard. He strolled down the small main street to the hardware store where the sign directed him. He wasn't interested in a puppy, but the sign for free dogs when he needed a pet pretty badly seemed fortuitous, and he wasn't about to spit in the face of providence.

The puppies, three months old and very cute, were corralled in a makeshift pen under an eave at the back of the store. Three adults and several kids relaxed around the dogs, often picking one up to kiss or scratch or cradle it. Gabe admired the pups, with their round tummies and big, clumsy feet but he felt drawn to an older mutt resting dejectedly on the open end of a tailgate to a pickup. He felt everyone's gaze on him as he approached.

"These are these the free dogs advertised on the sign?" he asked no one in particular.

The oldest boy stood up from by the pen and dusted off his knees. "Yep, and they're real good dogs," he said earnestly. Gabe could tell none of the children wanted to give them away.

He smiled at the fledgling salesman and reconsidered the animal on the tailgate. It was medium-sized and of indiscernible origins, although a terrier appeared to have stormed his genealogy somewhere along the line. The dog was in pain, and while he didn't seem neglected, neither was he exactly well cared for. Gabe scanned the few adults surrounding him as best he could; they were tired, and, as far as he could tell, anxious to be divested of the responsibility of all these animals.

The older dog caught on to his interest and perked up to watch Gabe. Its warm black eyes made a direct appeal, and Gabe felt an immediate affinity for him. "What about this one here?" The dog's tail thumped tentatively.

A little girl cast a dismissive glance his way before resuming her play with one of the puppies. "He's lame. Broke his leg a while back, and it just won't heal."

"Who's his owner?" Gabe inquired, at which point one of the adults came forth to talk to him.

The man extended his hand. "Jim Grafton. Missy's right, this one's lame. His name is Soley, because all he did as a pup was eat the soles out of all of our shoes." Jim laughed. "He's a good dog but his leg really won't heal." Gabe guessed the dog had not been taken to a veterinarian. Jim lowered his voice so the kids wouldn't hear him. "The kindest thing to do would be to put him out of his misery. You might be better off with one of the pups."

"I'm studying medicine – not veterinary medicine – but I could maybe take a look at Soley's leg. I need a dog and would prefer one that's house trained. I don't suppose Soley is for sale, is he?"

"Well, no, he isn't. But we have too many animals, as you can see . . ." Jim trailed off, his silence negating his initial no. "Maybe, if you think you could fix his leg, I wouldn't charge you for him."

Gabe rubbed Soley's neck and gingerly checked his leg, using siren influence to dull any pain. Soley's tail continued to thump against the truck bed, and he gave Gabe a soulful, trusting regard that put Gabe in good stead with everyone there. Soley was well liked, at least.

He stroked Soley's head. "What do you think, old boy? Wanna travel with me for a while?" He'd already decided this was the dog for him, and he concentrated to silently entice the dog and the humans in that direction. Soley's tail thumped more forcefully against the truck and he hoisted himself up to lean against Gabe, straining his face upward for attention.

Jim slapped his thigh. "Well. Would you look at that? He hasn't been that spry since he broke his leg."

"Can he walk?"

Soley answered by jumping down stiffly from the truck to trot three-legged around Gabe. He sat obediently at his feet.

Jim conceded Soley to Gabe with a bemused smile. "Appears you've got yourself a dog, mister." Gabe thanked the group before striding away. He called to Soley once, and the dog limped briskly to catch up.

Back at his apartment, he examined Soley's leg. It hadn't set properly, and as far as he could tell, the break was causing soft tissue irritation whenever the dog put weight on it. He hunted around the house for something he could use as a splint, finding a wooden paint stirrer. He rummaged through his pack for his first-aid kit and retrieved the gauze and a roll of tape. Then he placed a book for himself on the coffee table by the couch and sat down on one side of it, patting the cushion next to him. Soley jumped up and sank down onto his side.

He stroked the dog to soothe him. "This won't hurt a bit, I promise." He smiled at his new companion and then sedated him as only he could. When he was sure the dog was out, he carefully re-broke and set the leg, using the splint, gauze and tape he'd prepared. Keeping his hand on Soley, Gabe lifted his book from the coffee table and settled into the couch to enjoy a good read.

He stayed with him all night, sleeping with his head against the back of the couch and an arm around the dog, who awoke only twice to whimper. In the morning, Gabe carried Soley outside to relieve himself, and then set him back on the couch while he made them each a plate of eggs.

He toasted Soley with his cup of coffee. "You were a good idea." He sat on the couch again and considered his next course of action, stroking his recovering pet absentmindedly. Today, he would call Xanthe.

Kate felt as if she'd stepped into someone else's body. Everything was about twenty degrees off, from her husband to the people in the castle to the weird, new seclusion of her days. At first, she'd hoped Gabe would explain all the strangeness to her, but when his answers yielded no satisfaction, she chose to examine herself as the likely culprit. It wasn't anything else she concluded, so it had to be her. Gabe suggested she was compromised because of the pregnancy and because they were in hiding, and that made sense.

Her new appearance also fueled the surreal character of her existence; Gabe had insisted she disguise herself, although why she'd had to do it while no one else did was unclear to her. "Humans are hunting us, Kate, not sirens," Gabe had told her several times. "We don't have to hide from each other." Huh? Her mind was so slow and confused, which didn't help. Even when she tried, she couldn't organize her thoughts to express herself as she wanted.

She wasn't drastically different, Gabe assured her, but the change felt drastic enough. Her golden brown hair was now a deep brunette, and rather than wearing it down or casually back from her face as she was used to, someone came each morning to pin it into a tailored, formal style. The same person applied her make-up, although she'd begged to do this for herself.

"Honestly, I'd feel better if I could do my own grooming, Gabe," she'd explained as she made her bid for this one, small freedom. "I've been doing my own hair since I was eight, and my own make-up since I was fifteen. I'm qualified." She'd intended this last statement as a joke, but it fell flat.

"It's just for a while, darling," Gabe assured her, using what was a new endearment since they'd resumed residency on Shaddox. "Is it such a big thing to do to protect ourselves, protect our baby?"

"Of course, when you put it that way . . ." she'd conceded.

Not that she didn't like what she saw. Her eyes, perfectly outlined and shadowed, seemed enormous, and the darker brows gave her a soulful, dramatic affect she wouldn't have guessed she could pull off. She just wasn't used to wearing this much make-up.

"You're not used to wearing *any*," Gabe teased lightly. Then he'd brushed his mouth against her cheek and whispered huskily in her ear, "You're gorgeous."

The gesture confused her, and she regarded him with eyes full of questions she didn't feel she could ask. Unlike the very willing Gabe who had been so lost in love with her he couldn't keep away, this new Gabe hadn't touched her since they'd come back to Shaddox despite several affectionate advances on her part. This made her tentative and unsure he would pursue intimacy with her even if she offered it, and she now shied away from offering.

Peter knew things weren't ideal but he believed they would be. He too had no alternative but to hope for the best, because he couldn't undo what he'd done, and he didn't want to. His feelings remained unchanged; he was certain of Kate, certain of the life they could have, would have, if only she would let go of her old ideals, twist just a little bit the understanding she'd gained of married life in her few short weeks with Gabe.

Their initial days at Shaddox were, intentionally on his part, hazy for Kate, just so he could buy himself a little time to think of what to tell her. She knew her old life had been ripped away from her, but, as yet, she thought their situation was temporary, and she still clung to the belief everything would one day be as it was. Peter stalled, hoping whatever he told her would be easier to accept after she settled in.

During this time, he'd remained mostly euphoric over his success at getting her here, although he found himself not fully prepared to face the reality of his new situation. The day-to-day burden of upholding his pretense wasn't something he'd considered as he had the preparatory details surrounding Kate's capture, and the energy involved in keeping up appearances wore on him more than he could have known. His progress thus far, however, combined with his rabid desire for the nurturing he craved overcame any doubts he might have had about the abduction. Rather, he felt doubly anxious to do whatever he could to support his ultimate goal, for their bonding to be complete and whole. He would do nothing to jeopardize this outcome.

Following their first few days at the palace, during which time he essentially kept her sedated, she woke one morning brimming with her natural fire and energy, so buoyant he didn't have the heart to inhibit her. She'd bounded to the window and thrown back the curtains. She faced him with the light streaming behind her and shed her cotton nightgown. Her skin was pink from sleep, her face sweet and pretty and framed by a halo of golden hair. She smiled at him playfully as she pressed herself against him. "If we're going to be prisoners here, we may as well enjoy ourselves," she suggested huskily. Of their own accord, his arms wrapped around her to mold her tightly to him. Her mouth sought his.

Her taste, her emotions, were an elixir more powerful than he could have possibly anticipated, her desire coursing through him with a jolt of raw energy that completely overtook and commanded him for several long seconds. Had her eyes been open, she would have seen him shimmer and appear briefly as someone other than her husband, as his previously impenetrable cloaking abilities slipped in response to her. It was the single most intoxicating experience he'd had in his long life.

Had he been a younger man, he knew, his conscience would have played no part in his subsequent decisions. At first, he kissed her thoroughly, passionately, lost in the heady emanation of her feelings.

"Kate," he whispered against her lips, humbled by the realization he'd been right, that they were so good together.

"Gabe, I love you," she whispered back, and ice ran through his veins, dousing his ardor. He was not who she thought he was. He paused to rest his forehead on her shoulder, struggling silently with himself and the feelings her words invoked. The trust in her eyes, and the fluttering of the tiny heartbeat inside her sealed his fate. He needed to wait. He thought of a way to distract her, distract them both.

"I'm worried about the baby." Kate checked her flat stomach and laughed. "What baby?" He placed his hand on her midriff and reflected what he felt and heard, the tiny life growing, the small, rapid heartbeat.

Kate was ecstatic. "Oh! Gabe!" she'd cried. "It's our baby!"

Her joy sharpened his resolve. He wanted this, exactly this, but he wanted it to be for him, Peter. He would find a way to achieve it.

He let them talk for a while as soon-to-be parents do, how they hoped the baby had his mother's hair, his eyes, how they would do everything to ensure he or she would be smart, and healthy and happy. Eventually, Peter stood up and moved away from her, pleading hunger. "I'll go get us some breakfast." She should stay in the suite, he warned, stay hidden from the palace staff.

She smiled uncertainly at him. "But what about you? What if the staff sees you?"

"They'll just think I'm here on some errand for my mother. People are used to seeing Blakes around here, Kate."

She looked perplexed... and he couldn't worry about that too much. He felt her startle when he locked the door behind him.

CHAPTER TWENTY-SEVEN

Xanthe came the day after he called. Gabe watched her approach, her exotic, otherworldly appearance drawing stares as she made her way down the street toward his address.

He greeted her at the door. "Thank you for coming. I know how busy you are."

"It's my pleasure," she replied, with the strange combination of warmth and distance he associated with her. "I'm so very sorry for your loss."

He led her to the living room. "Yes. That's why I contacted you, actually. I'm not sure I have a loss." He invited her to sit. "It's not something I feel safe discussing with anyone else. Can I get you some tea before I tell my story?"

He felt her reach with her intuition anyway, an automatic response he knew she couldn't help. In seconds, she found his doubt, ascertained he did not, in fact, contain within him evidence of his wife's death. "Hmm," she mused. "That does bear some discussion." Gabe nodded and left her to make friends with Soley while he brewed their tea.

When he came back with a tray, Xanthe was on the couch petting Soley. "You've found yourself quite the little companion, here."

He smiled. "Yes, he's all part of my evil plan. Usually, our intuition is a strength but in this situation, I need to keep some secrets. I just barely made it away from my family without alerting them to my thoughts."

"You adopted Soley to sustain you?"

He heard the pity in her voice. "I know. Not the same as human or siren company. But isolation isn't viable, as you know. I had to get him."

He sat next to her on the couch and faced her, offering his hands. "May I?"

"Of course." They grasped each other's forearms, using contact to communicate Gabe's memories and conclusions about Kate. Xanthe flinched when she saw the bull shark attack, and her heart raced sympathetically as Gabe recalled his visit to Kate's mother. He then reviewed the strange visit they'd received the night before, including his—and his father's—blind chase after another siren into the water.

"You're right," Xanthe acknowledged. "It had to have been a cloaker, and he had to have been a very good one to evade both you and Michael." She sensed Gabe's accusation against Peter Loughlin.

"Not yet," she warned him. "I want more information first."

He told her everything, including what he could about his own nascent cloaking skills, and Xanthe released him. Her eyes became unfocused as she ruminated.

He gave her a minute to digest his tale. "Are you aware of a correlation between grief and cloaking?"

"No, but it makes some sense. From what I know, the ability comes from retreating into yourself, from a desire to hide. That isn't an option for most of us. In fact, I don't think many of us *could* withdraw. Our nature is to reach out, and if we're hurting we reach out harder."

She sipped her tea thoughtfully before continuing. "I understand humans withdraw, though, so perhaps sirens such as you and your family, ones who have spent a lot of time in the human world… maybe retreat feels reasonable."

"Peter has spent very little time among humans," Gabe reminded her. "And he's reputed to be the best cloaker of all time. Why would he think to retreat into himself?"

"Don't rush to conclusions, please. I'm not sure we're talking about Peter here, but, since you ask, being a child of a monarch is barely tolerable, in my opinion." She offered an overview of the familial deprivation accompanying a royal title, and how she attributed the high divorce rate and general emotional instability of the royal class to parental division from their children.

"As for Peter, he's the most stable example of royalty I've seen. He's intelligent and capable – he did really well in law school – and he's done a very good job running our affairs. Also, he's close to his mother, which doesn't happen often in the aristocracy. I've always seen their closeness as a sign of his mental health."

For Gabe, several things clicked into place at once: Peter's near constant presence at his mother's side, his lack of a mate despite a number of interested parties, and the visceral loneliness Kate had sensed on two occasions. Weighed in conjunction with the intense attention Peter had paid Kate, particularly when he appropriated her during their visits to the palace, Gabe was sure Peter had played a role in Kate's disappearance.

Now attuned to Gabe's thoughts and their context, Xanthe reluctantly agreed with his deliberations. "You've experienced too many coincidences," she conceded. "It's a shocking possibility, but one we unfortunately should consider."

Gabe spread his hands before him. "So you can see why I left Griffins Bay. My idea sounds nuts, and anyone who intuited it from me would, by implication, be involved in whatever problems I create now. I'd be putting everyone at risk." He waited for Xanthe's response.

"Peter is a powerful man but my job is to maintain our community's stability. I need to hear more about your cloaking practice. Show me. Then we'll discuss what steps we should take."

Gabe would not be diverted. "I'll need your help to get information on the Loughlins," he insisted.

"I understand your conviction, Gabe. We'll find out what's going on, and I promise I'll help."

Kate tried to keep up a positive front although her bravery caved as soon as she was left alone each morning. She had spent far too much time by herself and exhausted the distractions at hand, namely reading through the works of various authors she'd always intended to study in greater depth. During the past several weeks, she'd given up on Shakespeare because he was too tedious and his language distractingly archaic. If that made her an intellectual cretin, so be it. She found she wasn't much into other revered writers, either, namely Faulkner and Styron, because they were just too depressing. She wondered if their style of exposition was common to Southern authors in general, as the works of Flannery O'Connor and Carson McCullers soon joined her list of literature she could no longer tolerate.

In trying to decide what her problem was, she concluded she had no enthusiasm at present for exploring all the ways in which human beings could feel miserable and alone. In her darkest moments, she believed this was because the stories she read itched too closely beneath her skin, felt too synonymous with the circumstances of her own life. She chided herself for indulging in melodrama when she thought this way.

When she started to believe comic books might be her only option, she was saved briefly by Austen and Dickens, although they too, quickly lost their appeal. Fundamentally, she was tired of reading, tired of being sequestered. She remembered how often she'd fantasized about just this situation: her time was all hers to spend, no one demanded anything of her, and every work of literature she could want was at her fingertips. Only a few weeks into the effort, however, she was restless and bored, something she never, never thought could happen. She longed for the busy schedule of her former job.

Gabe didn't understand. "Just relax and enjoy yourself, Kate. Everything's taken care of, everything's easy here. Don't you feel, maybe, a little fortunate?"

Okay, that was alarming, and a perspective she wouldn't have attributed to Gabe. It made her feel more caged in, so she responded more sharply than she meant to. "I'm used to having a lot to do, Gabe, and I really need a stronger creative outlet, even for the short-term. Could I get my hands on a computer? Then, I could at least work on my blog . . ."

"You can't get internet service here," Gabe interjected quickly.

She leveled an incredulous stare at him. "You mean to tell me no one in the palace is able to connect with anyone off the island? I can't believe that's true. All of our parents were able to use their cell phones when they ambushed us last month."

Gabe's expression became harsh in a way she hadn't seen before.

"As you might expect, access has become restricted since the need for protection has escalated. I'll get you a laptop but you won't be able to use it to communicate with anyone."

Kate was astonished. Who was this person she was arguing with? "Gabe, are you mad at me? For wanting something to do?"

"Yes. I mean, no." He seemed to force himself to relax. As if each change in his expression was premeditated, Kate saw his face soften into something more familiar, saw him place his hands in his pockets and stand back on his heels as he often did… and she couldn't shake the feeling he was doing it to manipulate her. He gazed over her head and drew a breath.

"Look. I know things are tense, and I'm sorry you're bored. I'll find a computer for you, and I'll see what I can do about getting you internet access, okay?"

Kate was too weirded out to say much. Where had this mutual distrust come from? How could they have gone, so quickly, from being open and easy with each other to bickering like rivals? She resolved to try and fix it, at least as far as her own behavior was concerned. Still, she didn't quite manage to keep the sarcasm from her voice when she told him, "That'll be great. Thanks."

Peter was exhausted. He had, not surprisingly given his recent preoccupations, fallen behind in his work, and his efforts to both maintain his deception with Kate and run his government left him more and more depleted at the end of each day. He rose earlier and earlier to give himself more time at the office, which he knew left Kate feeling alone and wondering what had happened to her honeymoon. But it was a compromise he'd had to make, and, truthfully, the familiarity and control of governing was a welcome respite.

After her first month in captivity – for he knew that was how she was thinking of her time now – he abandoned his pretty plan to keep her contained to their suite but he hadn't had a viable alternative to offer her at first. The laptop he'd procured helped for a while, although she wasn't buying his argument concerning the palace-wide interdiction on internet access. She was technically savvy enough to figure out how to enable her wireless once – he'd just intercepted a missive to her mother – and he had no doubt she'd eventually figure a way around this control, especially given how solicitous she was of the few members of the staff he sent to her. They loved her, of course, and he knew her human pull might well sway one of them on any given afternoon, putting him in a jam sooner rather than later if she succeeded in getting an e-mail out.

Thanks to his excellent memory, he was able to identify all servants who had seen Kate when she'd visited with the real Gabe, and he made arrangements to transfer them in an effort to cover his tracks. This exodus left a gap in professional coverage at the castle, so he also put out a call for new replacement guards, people who had never heard of Catherine Blake. Meanwhile, he struggled to find a way to allow her to roam the castle and grounds more freely.

That was when he hatched the plan to change her appearance, and, after that, introduce her as someone other than who she was. For his part, he remained Gabriel Blake when he was with her, visiting on family business if he had to explain, which he never did in Kate's presence. His mother knew nothing of Gabe's – or Kate's, for that matter – guest status in her home. Kenna's medication and preoccupation with her work kept her safely in the dark, thank God.

Kate chose her alias. Peter, posing as Gabe of course, suggested she take one as an extra layer of protection and as a condition for her to leave their suite. Elizabeth Hughes had been Kate's paternal grandmother, and her family believed Kate resembled her. If he could not be with her when she was roaming, he prepared her with a bit of hypnosis to help her be more convincing in her projection.

If anyone stopped her, she was to report she was staying as Peter Loughlin's guest.

Her first request was to visit the kitchen. "It's one of my interests, and I can't stand to sit still and read another minute," she complained. "Is there a garden on the property I can dig in?"

"Sure." He smiled at her indulgently. "Vegetable or flower?"

"Um, vegetable, of course . . ." Kate trailed off, giving him an odd look.

Ah. Something Gabe would have known. He hurried to recover from his misstep. "I mean, I know vegetables are your first love, but you could try your hand at flowers too, if you want?"

"Oh." She seemed mollified. "No. Show me to the cabbages, please. And then where the white wine and bacon are so I can cook them for us." She poked him playfully in the ribs and grabbed his hand to swing it between them. He found her burst of enthusiasm encouraging, and he wanted badly to sustain her good mood.

And, for a while, this seemed to be the formula for success, letting her pass her days in the garden or cooking, which, he had to admit, she was good at. He, meanwhile, was free to attend to his work, which was suffering from his inattention. Even during the slowest times, he was used to putting in ten-hour days, and his time spent trailing and then keeping Kate amused had put him precariously behind.

"What do you do all day while I'm out living solely for my own entertainment?" she inquired one night. "You're gone for hours at a time now, and you come back spent. I have to say, I'm a little jealous." He felt her shame after she told him this, how she also felt freer, less oppressed without him hovering over her all the time. "I don't mean to be petty," she apologized. "You probably need the work, the diversion from being holed up, as much as I do."

He gave her an answer as close to the truth as he could manage. "Peter and Kenna have put me to work in their office," he revealed. Then he told her dryly, "You wouldn't believe how demanding it is to run a government."

Kate was surprised. "I would have thought you'd try to work at the local clinic, or a medical facility of some sort."

"Oh. Well, yes," he stammered to buy a few seconds of time. "See, there isn't much in terms of a viable medical facility here, and the Loughlins *need* help. So I've offered to dig in where I can. I'm getting quite the legal education."

She hugged him tightly. "I'm so sorry, Gabe. You're having to put your medical career on hold, after how hard you worked to make it happen. I've been so selfish. I haven't even thought of all you're giving up to be here."

"My darling." Peter stroked her hair, touched by her attempt to comfort him. "Don't worry. I've been thinking medicine might not be for me after all."

Kate froze. Gabe had never even hinted at an alternative career, and to hear him dismiss his former passion so casually shocked her. In fact, she felt something close to devastation.

"I mean, if this is what we have to do for the rest of our lives, I'm happy to do it," he quickly added. His expression became tender. "As long as we're together."

She felt her expression crumble and tried to hide her distress with a smile, which she saw he did not understand. But his mention of doing this *for the rest of our lives* hit her like an anvil to the stomach, the implications of this possibility too painful for her to consider. The life they'd so recently envisioned, her parents, their friends… all of it disappeared. She grasped at the first thought running through her head to quell the onrush of despair enveloping her.

"Help me feel the baby again," she begged, forcing back tears. Gabe, for once, did not cajole or cross-examine her. He did help her feel better, however, spanning her stomach with his hand. As he concentrated on the life within her and brought it prominently to her own perceptions, she relaxed and eventually smiled. Hope and calm flowed through her.

"We're both tired, darling," he soothed. "Let's go back."

Peter held her until she dreamed and then carefully climbed out of bed. He was so drained, he was afraid he'd sleep through if she woke in the night, which she'd started to do. He couldn't afford to risk appearing as Peter to her. He went to his office to crash on the couch, giving himself over, for the first time in months, to the sweet oblivion of deep slumber.

He sneaked back early the next morning, moving lightly and invisibly through the corridors toward his chambers. He stopped before entering to let the projection of Gabe flood through him, his cloaking efforts in this regard second nature to him now.

He sat in a chair by the window, watched her while she slept, and assessed their situation. Rested for once, he was able to take fresh stock of his progress, buoyed again by the success he'd had so far. He acknowledged his story had become, by necessity, dangerously convoluted, and he worried over all the ways his growing number of deceits could sabotage him should the details of his life escape beyond Kate.

He needed to draw her more transparently into the fold of his public life, to further his vision of bonding with her, but also to explain her ongoing presence in the palace. He thought as the sun came up, until a solution came to him. A slow, self-congratulatory smile spread across his face as he went through possible pitfalls and what-ifs.

It could work. In fact, if he acted wisely, Kate could be legally, physically and emotionally his within the month. He rose to set his plans in motion, leaving Kate a note he would be gone most of the day. Gabe's messy, nearly unreadable writing was distasteful compared to his own beautiful script, but he was glad this part of his act, at least, was easy to fake. He sauntered to his offices with a confidence he hadn't felt in weeks.

Gabe was used to studying but he put his concentration to the test with the rigorous effort he made to practice cloaking. He didn't yet understand how Peter could have staged Kate's death as he had, and so convincingly. He knew the man must be a far better cloaker than anyone in the community knew, and he continued his review of Kate's disappearance in his search for clues as to how he'd done it.

Cloaking, he was surprised, did come naturally to him, and he wondered why he hadn't seen evidence of this talent earlier in life. Granted, the impetus he felt from his overwhelming grief put him in a unique frame of mind; but he'd experienced high levels of stress before, and, to his knowledge, had never once disappeared.

He played with his skill now in an effort to expand and control it, drifting between conscious awareness of his surroundings, and the state of semi-conscious withdrawal he came to know as his place of hiding. As he drilled, he grew to respect the truly awesome ability Peter must have to execute the cloak he'd tried – succeeded in creating – with him and his family.

For the next few days, he mulled over every occurrence from the evening before Kate's disappearance, and then reviewed the events from the morning of the pseudo shark attack. He thought and meditated on these variables as he materialized and withdrew, sitting on his couch or floor, forming theories as his mind ebbed and flowed through this sea of wild possibilities and artful subterfuge. He focused all of him, the whole of his life's experience and interests, within these two planes of existence: one, where he focused on Kate; and another, where he concentrated on learning to cloak.

Xanthe's unexpected visit threw Peter's plans for the day out the window. He acted as though nothing could have delighted him more, of course, and he quietly cleared his calendar to accommodate her. His more urgent aim was to hide all evidence of Kate's presence and appear as though nothing had changed since the last time they'd met. He didn't think Kate and Xanthe had ever been introduced, but he knew Xanthe and Carmen were friends and he felt – unnecessarily, he hoped – the need for caution.

He discreetly penned a note to Kate, telling her Peter and Kenna had an important assignment for him.

I'll be kept late tonight, so don't wait up. We also have visitors at the palace today, darling, so you'll need to keep to the suite today. Love.

He knew having to stay in would depress her, so he arranged for a huge bouquet of flowers to be delivered as well.

Xanthe had fabricated a plausible excuse for dropping by – she owed the Loughlins information from a summit – but her primary purpose was to investigate Gabe's suspicions regarding Peter. She hoped they were baseless, because if they weren't, the whole community would suffer the consequences. She would have to consider very seriously what kind of conflict would ensue if Gabe's hypotheses proved accurate.

But she believed the truth would eventually come out, and maintained it was always better to address difficult situations directly and as soon as possible. She notified the staff she'd need a spare office for a half hour or so, and was directed to one across the hall from where she'd met with Peter. On her way, she passed someone carrying an enormous bouquet of flowers, and, without meaning to, heard the delivery man's thoughts: they were for Peter's girlfriend, Elizabeth.

Peter hadn't mentioned anyone was staying with him, which wasn't significant. But he was hiding this information – she'd used her intuition to query him specifically about a female guest and was stonewalled, which *was* significant. She'd also sensed nothing from him as he'd been ordering flowers, and she'd monitored him closely since her arrival. After a brief hesitation, she followed the courier with the bouquet.

Gabe's cloaking demonstration had been instructive, and while she herself did not have the facility, she did understand how she might, with great effort, edit her emotional broadcast. She tried to edit it now, and also kept her distance in an attempt to dilute her presence, which she could not do very well. But she did appear benign and unthreatening, and, consequently, no one paid her any particular attention as she watched the unfolding of events at the door of Peter's personal suite. Others' distractions, thankfully, also gave her cover.

After a knock on the door to what she knew to be Peter's private rooms, a woman she'd never seen before opened it. From Gabe's memory of her, she knew Kate had lighter hair, but this woman was definitely human and about the same age Kate would be.

And she was pregnant.

The door was open long enough for Xanthe to catch three more vital pieces of information: the woman named Elizabeth understood she was in hiding, and she was homesick for her human family in Childress. Most damning of all, she believed someone named Gabe had sent her those flowers.

She hurried back to the administrative area, her heart racing with the implications of what she'd just seen. She stopped a page outside of the Loughlins' main offices and relayed her apologies to Kenna and Peter but she had an emergency to attend to and had to leave immediately. She hoped the assistant, highly intuitive – because that was the only kind of staff the Loughlins employed – could attribute her agitation to the emergency she cited, a credible, even probable possibility. As the assistant left, Xanthe added another message as an afterthought. "Please tell Peter I've met someone for one of his guard positions. Very talented young man named Charles Gavin. I'll send him by."

She fled the palace, desperate to escape the scrutiny she would draw if she ran into anyone paying any real attention to her. She had no talent for lying, and no idea how someone who'd behaved as recklessly as Peter Loughlin had would react if her thoughts were discovered. No one stopped her, and she raced back to the mainland to see Gabe.

Anxious to relay her findings, she left the water leading to Gabe's distracted and agitated, unwittingly retaining more of her siren self than she should have on land. She realized too late what she'd done, or more aptly, what she hadn't. She'd done nothing to mask faint iridescence in her skin and hair. Her eyes probably had a thin film of mercury over them, and she was sure her affect was wild. She felt wild.

A true siren, she began to collect people during her brief stroll from the shore to Gabe's apartment, her strange beauty and need for emotional equilibrium compulsively broadcasting and attracting. She couldn't help it. Children drifted toward her first, followed by their mothers. A few otherwise respectable men on their way to work also became caught in her song, and trailed after her with the frantic pleas of lovesick suitors.

Within minutes she was trapped in the center of approximately twenty hypnotized, adoring fans, unable to advance another step. "Beautiful lady… my sister… my lover," she heard them whisper. She regretted the spectacle she'd caused even as she luxuriated in the swell of devotion surrounding her. She projected a silent plea toward Gabe, who was already drifting out onto his porch, pulled by the concentration of human emotion he felt outside his home. He comprehended Xanthe's predicament after one, sweeping glance, and seemed delighted with her debacle.

He cloaked to break into the crowd, which also protected him from getting drawn into the frenzy of human feeling surrounding her, she saw. He was jovial when he put his arm across her shoulders. "C'mon, Aunt Charlotte. Time for your cholesterol pill."

Xanthe guffawed. The absurdity of his words distracted the crowd just enough for she and Gabe to extricate themselves. They brushed against each person as they left, silently working to edit memories and feelings so they would forget her.

Once in the house, she laughed hysterically with him, which relieved her excess energy and stress. When they were calm enough to talk, they clasped arms so Xanthe could share her experience at the palace.

Gabe's expression progressed from despair to wild hope, to grim triumph, and by the end of her story, she watched as the knowledge Kate was alive flooded the desolate space in his heart with relief. He choked with emotion. He silently vowed to hunt down and kill Peter Loughlin for taking Kate away from him.

Xanthe registered this response with a sharp intake of breath and put her hand on Gabe's chest to stop him. He was justified, she knew, but these kinds of angry impulses were antithetical to their militantly civilized siren nature; and she was not comfortable with Gabe's quick assumption violence was the best course. She also wanted time to consider the least destructive option for resolving this situation in light of her community's stability.

Gabe shrugged her off with an angry, impatient gesture. "What Peter has done is not civilized. In fact, it's a grotesque violation, not just of our ethics, but of our – please forgive the term – humanity."

"I cannot give you permission to go after Kate with the intent of killing our prince," she told him harshly. "We need to address this through the right channels, Gabe."

Gabe would not say he would not attack Peter but he did promise to refrain from acting on his vengeance until they knew more.

"I need you to verify the woman he's keeping named Elizabeth is, in fact, your Kate. It's fortunate you can cloak, because you'll have to if you want to get within two hundred yards of the palace.

"I've also arranged for you to interview for a guard position," she continued. "Give me two days to set up your back story with papers and references. I'll send a courier with everything you'll need. I don't need to warn you to be extraordinarily careful?"

"You do not," Gabe promised, and his understanding of the potential repercussions of his assignment – she felt him out carefully on this front – assuaged her concern, if only a little.

Still, she reinforced her command with a quelling stare. "I want you to verify what I saw before we take further action, Gabe. The palace employs the most intuitive sirens on earth, and some of them can sense when another is cloaking. You'll have to be very, very good, and very, very, very careful."

"I'll await your courier."

She left through the back door to escape her former admirers. She all but flew to the water and sped to her office to put her plans with Gabe in motion.

Apparently, Kate was to participate in a mock wedding to Peter Loughlin. Yet one more bizarre decision in a long line of them lately proposed to her, even though it made no sense. Gabe's explanation had sounded reasonable; this final action would protect them forever by associating her with Peter, and no one would take interest in her past once she appeared to have married him. But in her heart, she could not, no matter how hard she tried, make this particular lie feel right. And how would marrying not just any siren, but *the* siren, dissociate her from that world?

"Gabe," she tried, her mind lethargic and confused as usual, frustrating her better attempts at argument. "You can't mean to do this."

"Do what?" Gabe responded sharply. "Try to protect us?"

"No. You can't mean to put us even more at the mercy of Peter Loughlin."

Gabe reddened with anger, something she had never seen before. "Peter Loughlin," he began, his voice escalating, "has sheltered us, hidden us, and done nothing but help us." He was shouting by the end of his sentence, and Kate turned away in disgust. What had happened to him? She rubbed her temples with her fingertips, knowing she was fighting a losing battle, but she decided to petition him one more time.

"Yes but we're giving Peter a claim on me, on our child. Even if it's a sham wedding, we'll have to maintain the appearance of a marriage. I'll be going to dinners with him and state functions, and he'll have family photos taken of him with me and *our* son or daughter." She could not bear to see his response when she whispered, "Doesn't our bond mean anything to you anymore?"

A formidable anger pervaded the room and his silence felt menacing. "Our bond is *everything* to me," he grated. She lost all sense of him and had to check to make sure he was still there. He was. His face was composed, and his sweet, loving gaze nearly made her weep, because it was perfectly reminiscent of the Gabe she'd married, and because she knew it was a front, not real. She shut her eyes, sure he did not intend to listen to her. And she felt actual loathing for him; for once, she did not care if she was wrong to feel it.

He approached her as if she was an unreasonable child then. "Kate. Is it such a big thing to do? Peter will owe us as much as we owe him."

"I don't see how that's possible." She sidled to the other side of the room, hoping a little distance from him would help her think.

"We're giving him a comfortable alibi," he cajoled, and Kate felt the disingenuous change to his argument. "He's constantly offered marriage proposals from power-hungry families, and this will make his public life much, much easier."

"I will do this if you really think we should. But I want you to know I don't like it. It's not good for us."

She was startled to hear his response from millimeters away. "This is going to be spectacular for us." His tone was laced with triumph, although his next words sounded like a threat. "This *is* us now, Kate." He placed his hands on her face and stared hungrily in her eyes. She lost her sense of time and place as a heavy veil of calm pervaded her, and her misgivings dissipated. He bent to her, brushed his lips against hers. "I'll even prove it to you." He kissed her. She was so hypnotized she wasn't sure of the words he murmured against her mouth, but they might have been, "We'll make love the night of the wedding."

He kissed her again, severing her self-possession and focusing her entirely on their embrace, on him alone. She released herself to him, her limbs and body mellowing, melting as he pressed her close, whispering incoherent encouragements in her ear. She was enjoying him although her thoughts and feelings were oddly disengaged. She wondered if this was what it felt like to dissolve in the water, because she felt like she was dissolving, with Gabe absorbing all the microscopic pieces of her.

"If we were doing this in the water, you'd drown," he teased. She felt him drinking her in, and his odd exultation.

"We're so close to being just right, Kate," he told her softly. "Your response to me now, your compliance... it's so delicious." And he kissed her again.

With regret, he set her away from him, anticipating a more complete fulfillment after she'd pledged herself in a bonding ceremony. He'd no longer be stealing another man's wife at that point, because she would be his wife. "After the wedding," he promised, and she nodded listlessly.

Almost there, he thought feverishly. Next Saturday, as she thought she was play-acting, they would gaze in each other's eyes and vow their devotion. She would feel it, he would make sure, and the rite would deal a final blow to her old understanding of what her life was supposed to be. After that, Gabe would be no more than a burden to her. He could have an unfortunate accident, and the last thread would be cut.

"Won't that be fun," she murmured. She stared out the window.

"I won't need your help falling asleep tonight. Didn't you want to sneak in another couple of hours at the office? Just be quiet when you come back, okay?"

The dismissal, which Peter found rude, exhilarated him further. Here, at last, was his Kate, disenchanted with *Gabe* and wanting him gone. Perfect. "Of course, darling." He grinned and sauntered out.

Several fortuitous events conspired to help Gabe attain a guard position at the palace. For one, he was able to perfect his identity, having explored and expanded and practiced his cloaking abilities to their fullest extent. He experimented first with the people in the town where he'd taken up residence, with mixed, sometimes comical results; and then dozens of times with Soley, who could not be fooled but let him fail without repercussion. Xanthe helped by sending a few stray sirens his way, instructing them to check up on the "newcomer" and welcome him to the area. These guests proved to be his most difficult tests but finally, he convinced anyone who didn't know him of his new persona, Charles Gavin from San Diego.

Xanthe's papers provided him with a history, background check, and impeccable credentials; and her personal introduction made his success nearly a foregone conclusion. The final obstacle, the interview itself, would offer the greatest risk, because he would be required to maintain his cloak in front of the most perceptive sirens in existence.

Good luck was with him that day. He was led into a waiting room by a distracted royal assistant rushing him along so she could run errands for Peter's human guest, Elizabeth. This guest was apparently troubled, and Peter had them constantly devising new distractions and entertainments to keep her occupied.

She was also helping plan Peter's wedding.

The news brought Gabe a dark sense of satisfaction. He knew Kate would never agree to a real marriage with Peter, so something desperate was underway. From the assistant's harried complaints, he also guessed at his wife's captivity, how she'd likely been restricted, and he knew she would be restless and miserable with her circumstances by now.

In the week between Xanthe's visit confirming Kate was alive and the time he was to interview at the palace, he'd deduced a few pieces of information he hoped would help his effort. Specifically, he believed Peter was cloaking to appear as him, Gabe, in front of Kate. He recalled his conversation with his father the night they'd chased their spy, who Gabe was now certain was Peter, into the ocean. The visit his parents remembered earlier that night had surely been from Peter cloaking as Gabe, a test he conducted to see if he could pull it off.

And he'd succeeded, which meant he was very, very good, indeed. This was an important clue; the siren community wouldn't suspect a crime of this magnitude because no one had ever attempted – or was, indeed, even capable of attempting – the level of sophistication needed to make such a ploy work. Gabe would have to expose Peter's effort, but if he could, he believed justice would be on his side.

He didn't know what story Peter had told Kate to take her from him, but it had to have been something distressing, perhaps as distressing as Peter's lie to him had been. Kate had not attempted to contact her parents or friends, or his family, which meant she'd been told something sinister. He seethed at the thought, which he could not afford to do before his upcoming meeting. He disciplined himself to focus only on his cloak as Charles Gavin, forcing scenes from San Diego and other details related to his sham identity to the forefront of his mind.

Mercifully, his interviewer was not one of the Loughlins. As hard as he'd worked on projecting his character, he knew Peter would have suspected foul play and, more likely, seen straight through his cloak had he been the one to evaluate him. He attributed this bit of luck again to Xanthe, as someone coming in without her support would have been put through a more rigorous review.

The man Gabe spoke with was from Great Britain, had not heard of the Blakes – a rarity – and he had never been to San Diego. This was unbelievably lucky. Not only did the interviewer have no reason to question him should his real name cross his mind, he also lacked subtle cultural knowledge which would have drawn suspicion.

Thus, without much difficulty, he was approved for work as a palace guard. He was to start in four days.

The private supper with Kenna and Peter occurred in the same dream-like sequence Kate experienced during her first visit to the palace with Carmen and Michael. Kenna, always vague in her attention to those around her, added to the evening's eerie progression with her distracted presence and oddly delayed responses. She seemed as if she was constantly on the phone, half listening to another conversation while trying to keep up with the one at the table.

Peter had met her outside her suite to escort her to his mother, his gentle smile and warmth immediately putting her at ease. Gabe had been nowhere in sight to see her off, something she chose not to think about. In Kenna's chambers over salad, she smiled at Peter without guile, was even grateful for his company. He was charming and solicitous, taking every care to make her comfortable.

Kenna's welcome was distant, her attempt at warmth strange to Kate. "We're so happy you could join us this evening, Elizabeth. You must tell me how you and Peter became acquainted."

Kate maintained only the dimmest sense of herself thereafter, the majority of her consciousness committed to the idea she was Elizabeth Hughes, engaged to Peter Loughlin, pregnant with their child. She couldn't have answered Kenna if she'd wanted to due to the happy fog hanging over her senses. Peter begged his mother's forgiveness for Elizabeth's tiredness; the baby was taxing her, he explained. He covered her hand on the table with his own as he wove a story for her of how they'd met. His eyes never left hers, although his address was to his mother.

Such a pretty story, Kate thought. She'd fallen off a boat full of other humans on a snorkeling tour, and he'd found her swimming aimlessly, lost and nearly exhausted. He smiled at her adoringly while he told Kenna he'd fallen in love at first sight.

She was an only child and her parents were no longer living. There was no one in her family for Kenna or anyone else to meet. They hoped to be married immediately.

Say something, darling, Peter urged her silently, and her consciousness hitched on the endearment for a second, which flowed from him with odd familiarity. As if in slow motion, she smiled at Kenna, surfacing enough to muster the requested comment.

"This must seem so sudden to you, Your Majesty." She felt as if she apologized, and like her voice was small, as if she spoke from the far end of a long hallway.

Kenna seemed pleased with the presentation she and Peter made. "You have my blessing, both of you," she confirmed, and then to Elizabeth, "Please, call me Mother." Her attempt at affection made Kate violently miss her own mother for a few thorny seconds. She quickly shut off these thoughts, knowing no good would come from thinking of Cara now. Peter readily gave her cover.

The rest of the meal passed in pleasant conversation Kate could in no way remember. She played her part effortlessly, thanks to Peter, so anyone watching them would have seen their comfortable intimacy and believed they were in love. They took coffee by the fireplace, where Peter rested his arm casually behind her back, and she, just as casually, nestled into his side. He played with the fingers of her left hand. Her warm smiles came more easily than she would have thought possible.

The wedding would be a relatively small affair, just a few dozen friends and members of the court, Kenna announced. They could hold it in one of the gardens but the weather was so unreliable this time of year, they'd be better off indoors. Would a week from this Saturday work for them? She'd have the staff arrange everything.

Eventually, even Peter couldn't hold off her exhaustion. She tugged on his sleeve. "Peter, honey . . ." She felt him thrill to her words. "I'm so tired."

"Of course, darling," He rose and offered her his hand. They thanked Kenna for the pleasant evening and left her suite.

Kate let fatigue overtake her, and feeling a sense of familiarity she could not explain, she continued their subterfuge as they went. She leaned willingly into him, and Peter put his arm around her, just as comfortable in their act as she was. He kissed the top of her head.

She hesitated outside their room, stretching to kiss him on the cheek. "Thank you for dinner," she said with polite, sleepy warmth, then put her key in the door. Peter bowed before leaving.

Gabe was not in their chambers, she was sad, but unsurprised to see. This non-interaction was just another in a long line of them illustrating the change in their relationship, one she was unable to explain and could not understand no matter how intensely she thought about it. She only knew something indefinable and solid between them had shifted, and with this shift, her faith and conviction in their capacity for happiness had leaked away.

Gabe appeared at her side, seemingly out of nowhere, which startled her. "I didn't hear you come in."

Gabe was as optimistic and relaxed as she'd seen him in months, and she was surprised by his tenderness when he wrapped her in an embrace. He buried his face in her neck, whispered an apology for being gone, and told her she was beautiful.

Before she could respond, he backed away, and the futility of her yearning — for their intimacy, for their marriage, for the husband she thought she knew — overcame her. The fullness of her frustration over what they'd lost nearly choked her. She regarded him with her eyes full, her silent, pained question swirling around them like accusations.

Don't you want me?

He did not answer her but she felt his emotional retreat into himself, which left her with nothing more than his carefully composed expression, a two-dimensional picture. He rested his forehead against hers and closed his eyes before moving away from her. "I'm sorry."

"Gabe."

He stopped but did not face her. "Yes?" His voice was barely audible.

Hurt, anger, and apology emanated from her to fill the entire room. "I'm sorry. For whatever I've done to cause... *this*. I'm so sorry."

He came to her and gazed at her intently. "You aren't doing anything, Kate. It's everything else, I promise." He drew her head to his shoulder. She remained stiff and resistant. "It's not us," he insisted.

She started to cry. "I know, but it feels like us, and I hate it." She pulled back to plead with him. "I want to go back. I don't care if they're looking for us. Let's go home. We'll be careful."

She felt his attempt at influence but this time he was only partially successful. Her bitter feelings were replaced, but with resolution, not hope. He kissed her forehead and told her he'd be back later. The door clicked softly behind him as he left.

She was used to him leaving at odd hours by now, and she no longer questioned where he went or what time he planned to be back. But without him by her, her thoughts cleared, cycling as always to their marriage and her gnawing dissatisfaction over it. Her trust in her husband, she feared, was irrevocably destroyed.

When she tried define exactly why Gabe had changed, she concluded he was, understandably, distracted. And while she still felt his craving for her, his devotion was different, their affinity for each other heavier and too strained. Given the futility of her efforts to date to change this dynamic, she resigned herself to the possibility of never again sharing the emotional connection she'd initially taken for granted. And if she didn't know why those feelings were gone, she also couldn't see how it mattered. The end result was the same.

But she wasn't going to be able to tolerate how they were, not for the rest of her life. She decided she would suffer no more melodrama from herself with this acknowledgement. Perhaps Gabe was right, and she would feel differently after the baby was born... but she couldn't hope she'd change.

She went to the window and leaned on her elbows to feel the wind on her face. Her mind was racing in spite of her exhaustion. She caressed her rounded belly, wondering for the thousandth time where she and Gabe had gotten off course, and she thought of her mother. After George's death, Cara had shouldered her responsibilities alone as parent and provider, in addition to and in spite of her diminished emotional resources. In doing so, Cara had set an example Kate viewed as a moral standard for parental behavior, and she would never forget how her mother soldiered on for her sake. She thought about some undefined point in the future, how once the threat hovering over siren society was resolved, she could go home... and she realized she wanted to do this alone, without Gabe. How sad such a prospect held the appeal it did, how freeing the idea of separation felt. But she was absolutely sure she would not stay by him with things as they were, not just for her sake, but also for her child's.

"I will make a happier life for us than this, little baby," she vowed.

CHAPTER TWENTY-EIGHT

Gabe avoided interaction with the Loughlins his first days at the palace. His new colleagues told him Peter had been exhibiting strange behavior, and until he knew more, he didn't want to risk exposure by being too forward or inquisitive. Especially with a psychologically unstable siren running the show.

He maintained his cloak without attracting attention, and he observed everyone carefully. He also studied the layout of the castle, including the locations of the private royal chambers. After two days on the job, he knew the castle in its entirety and had memorized Peter's and Kenna's routines. He watched patiently for his chance to search out Kate.

Waiting was the hardest. Much of his acceptance by the rest of the staff, his cover story included, depended on a calm, capable representation of himself, attributes he could not feel if he thought too much on the real reason he was there. If he were to become agitated or let the ferocity of his anger show, the other guards would evict him from the premises. Fortunately, he was just good enough at cloaking – and just lucky enough to avoid scrutiny – to maintain his front.

On the Thursday afternoon before Peter's wedding, he found his chance. A harried staff member, charged with too many assignments and not enough time stopped him on her way down the hall. "Charles!" she called, eyeing him exactly as a predator does its prey. "I need your help." She grabbed his lapel and pulled him along with her as she hurried toward the reception hall. She handed him an envelope. "This is for Peter's fiancée. She's in his suite. Do you know where that is?"

Gabe successfully represented himself as he should, with adequate but not precise knowledge of the castle layout, and as someone only blandly interested in helping. He accepted the note and progressed toward Peter's chambers at a measured pace in spite of the rush of adrenaline he felt.

He knew Peter was not likely to be there but he could not knock on his door in case he was; Peter would find him out in mere seconds. He approached the rooms cautiously, reaching with his senses to verify Peter's – and Kate's – presence. He could not tell if Peter was within.

But Gabe froze where he stood as an icy clarity stunned him into immobility. Kate *was* here. He extended himself to scan for the presence of other guards, and again for Peter himself, careful to protect himself as he did so. His immediate area was clear of everyone who was not cloaking. He refocused his attention to the spot where he knew her to be.

His misery of the past few months evaporated, euphoria taking its place as the distinct life force that was his and Kate's flooded him. His relief was so exquisite, he wept. He let the sensation pull him forward until he was sure of its source, until he reached the door he knew divided them. With tremendous effort, he held himself back to conduct another scan. Barging in could jeopardize her, him, their child, so he made a thorough evaluation of the room she was in from where he stood.

She was either alone or with Peter, and as he would not be able to sense Peter, he concentrated on Kate, hoping her thoughts would confirm her solitude.

Gabe. She felt him, and she yearned for him. She was confused and angry and lonesome, and ashamed of her desire to be free of this place but resolved to leave it. She didn't understand why, didn't know she'd been kidnapped. He felt her moving physically closer to the door and risked a question. *Are you alone?*

Yes. Something's different. You're different. She started crying. *I haven't felt this since before we came here. God, what is wrong with me, with us?*

He burst through the door and folded her in his arms. "I'm right here. It's going to be okay." He buried his face in her hair, her neck, inhaling her scent, her touch, everything. "God. Dear God. I thought I'd lost you." In the next moments as he held her, he apprehended what she knew of her situation: how Peter had tried to blame her feelings on the pregnancy; her frustration over the unfilled space in their union Peter couldn't replicate; and her despair over a loss she couldn't define, one that made her feel dead inside. She missed everyone and longed more than anything to be out of her isolation. She missed him, although this made no sense to her.

She also planned to leave him.

He was right; Peter was cloaking as him when he was with her.

He could tell her nothing. Even this visit, if she thought of it in front of Peter, would put her in danger. He frantically searched for something reassuring he could say, wrestled with his preoccupation to get away before he could be discovered, and he wished desperately he could stay by her.

"I have to go," he iterated, more for himself than her. He was more sorry than he'd ever been in his life these words were true. "You're doing nothing wrong, Kate . . ." He grit his teeth in frustration as he tried to think of anything he could do to help them both feel better, until he had an idea. He held her face in his hands and let their bond pervade them both, filling the drought of their separation to overflowing, eradicating any question what they had together was real. He heard how her doubts had been fed, how she focused on herself and did not dwell on Peter.

Kate closed her eyes and begged him stay with her. But he couldn't, and so instead, with all of his being, he told her a beautiful lie.

It's just this situation. You're fine, we're fine, and we will have the life we want.

Yes, she thought, so trusting, so desperate.

The next thought he planted required all of his influence. *You're dreaming this. I'm not really here, but you can believe everything I've said.*

Then kiss me, make love to me. If I'm dreaming, it won't matter.

He kissed her, shuddering at the pleasure coursing through both of them. His heart thrilled at the knowledge he intuited during this exchange; Peter had stayed out of her bed. If, miraculously, they found their way out of this situation alive, she would not be preyed upon, hopefully, by remorse. He didn't care if she'd been part of a harem, but he suspected she would be bothered if she thought she'd been unfaithful. Gabe sighed, grateful for this one, small mercy.

He sensed a guard coming, and although the mere idea of leaving was torture, he pulled back and smiled at her. *You are dreaming me. Everything is going to be all right, Kate.* With supreme effort, he stumbled backward several feet. She did not budge from her spot, her eyes closed, a small smile on her lips.

If he had spoken the words, if he had just whispered *I love you* to her in parting, the truth of it would have obliterated his carefully constructed illusion and thundered like a cannon around them. The presence of their bond would have reverberated to fill the palace, shattering the lie he'd created to protect her. Painfully, he helped her distance herself from him as he ran. Her *I love you* drifted from her in gentle echoes, and the effect was physical, causing his knees to buckle. He recovered and ran faster to escape her pull, ran because he couldn't stand to be so close and not be by her. And he fled to protect his cloak, which he desperately needed to maintain now if he and Kate meant to escape.

Peter found Kate by the window. She stared dreamily at the landscape, hugging herself and emanating a strange joy he did not understand. He moved closer to her to examine this perplexing phenomenon. He was pleased with her contentment but confused as to its provenance.

Kate's eyes shone as she clasped his hand in hers. "I just had a daydream about us." She pressed her lips to his palm. "It felt like it used to, and you told me we're going to be okay, and I believed you. I still believe you."

He became deathly still, sensing something odd. Not from her words, but in what she felt. The void, the nagging space he'd been unable to fill with his deception, was missing. She felt whole, the dull, pleasant veneer she'd constructed, which they'd both relaxed into accepting, was gone. He forced himself to remain calm and smiled carefully so as not to interfere with the accuracy of her response. "Where were we?" He made his voice controlled, polite.

"Here, in this room. You came through that door." She pointed. "You said you thought you'd lost me." She emitted a small, sad laugh. "Until a few minutes ago, I felt lost."

He pivoted toward the door, his mind racing through possible explanations that did not include Gabriel Blake's physical presence in his castle. "What's the matter? It was just a dream, Gabe." Kate placed her hand on his arm.

At her touch, his lie fell completely, irreparably apart. Gabe was here, somewhere, somehow, he was sure of it. He either knew Peter had taken her or he would very shortly. And he would have told others.

For Kate's sake, he kept up his pretense, at least in terms of how he appeared to her. She was already hurting and sad despite his hope he could one day make her happy. Perversely, appearing as the man who had come to destroy him was the only reassurance he could offer her.

Gabe had to have picked up some cloaking ability, he concluded. He couldn't be very good at it yet, because he couldn't cloak at all a few months ago. But he had to have achieved enough proficiency to get into the palace. Peter would find him and know how he'd gotten in, and he would do so this very minute. He would end this nightmare proactively. He would call him out, and he would do it now.

The decision gave him instant relief. Methodically and with calm purpose, he removed his shirt and tossed it on a chair. Kate tilted her head uncertainly, and he smiled bitterly in response. He grabbed the tether containing his dagger and tied it around his waist.

She frowned. "That knife was Peter's. Why do you have it?"

"It was a gift." Not quite the truth, but close enough.

"You're taking it swimming?"

He didn't answer her. He was so tired of this pretense. He briefly considered telling her everything, and the idea appealed so much he drew a breath to speak. But the trust on her face decided him against the impulse; she struggled already, and depending on the outcome of his next interaction with Gabe, he might need his disguise to win her. He could almost laugh his predicament, how he was off to fight – and probably kill – the man to whom she was truly bonded and he had to mimic his victim. The man who had come to take Kate away from him.

Raw jealousy burst inside him in a white-hot explosion, leaving no trace of the rationalism for which he was so well known. Why? Why was this simplest of life's experiences, a wife and a family, continually denied to him? The usual arguments no longer held any merit: privilege carried responsibility, his higher call to office – he disparaged these excuses quickly, decisively. He'd rather live in a hut with a woman who loved him, would eke out a living in remote seclusion instead of shouldering these beliefs any longer.

He went to her. "Kiss me goodbye, Kate." She hesitated but stretched up to comply, and in a gesture he found heartbreaking, attempted to send him her empathy and goodwill. He kissed her with all the passion and frustration he'd hid from her, holding her uncomfortably tight until she squirmed and shoved him away.

"Gabe, what is *wrong* with you?"

His laugh was humorless. "My darling, you are about to find out. I'll be in the central pool," he called over his shoulder as he left.

In the corridor outside the royal offices, Gabe heard Peter's challenge from the central pool.

Gabe, Peter called silently, his invitation a dark taunt. *I'm waiting for you.* He felt Peter's anger and almost laughed.

Defiance rushed through him, electrifying his senses and focusing him on the physical conflict he now knew was imminent. He wanted nothing more than a straight-up fight to bring this trial to a close. He hesitated for one second as he remembered Xanthe's request to address this issue legally, discounting the thought the instant it occurred to him. He wanted to get out of there with Kate *now*. The vision of them safely away and Peter's invitation beckoned irresistibly. He made one forceful projection to warn those around him.

Peter Loughlin kidnapped another's bonded mate; he lied and broke a sacred law. His assertion carried not one atom of dishonesty, and those around him who heard it were stunned. They hastened to tell others.

His accusation stated, Gabe growled in anticipation as he retreated inward, cloaking to be able to run unheeded and face the man who'd stolen his wife and baby.

Kenna burst through the office door behind him, her usually bland expression contorted with anguish and disbelief at the influx of aggression she felt leaking in. The call from Peter to fight, the suggestion of violence and perhaps even death, floated through the hallways like a thick, suffocating smoke. She immediately identified the source, focusing keenly on the new guard they'd hired. She watched in horror as his eyes shone silver and his shape shimmered briefly, revealing him to be someone else, someone she knew but could not in that instant name. Impossibly, someone had infiltrated their defenses. A threatening smile, directed at some distant point down the hallway, stretched across the man's face as he literally disappeared from her sight.

Her son's foe. She reached forward ineffectually to stop him, losing all sense of him even as she raised her hand.

No. Please. She wasn't sure what, or to whom, she was begging. A cloaker was here, had been here for who knew how long, someone accomplished enough to make himself invisible to her, Peter, everyone who worked there. Someone who meant to fight with her son, perhaps do him mortal harm. She could in no way summon her typically dispassionate approach to conflict, and she stood rooted in place, paralyzed. Others rushed past her.

Fight. There's a fight coming. The thought, heavy with worry and excitement, bled through every corner of the edifice. It reached Kate in her room and drew her out into the hallway, where she stared in confusion at all the sirens making their way toward the central pool. Despite the frenzy of distress building around her, a strange hope blossomed forcefully in her chest as she caught snippets of thoughts rushing past her.

Peter Loughlin... a kidnapping... someone named Gabriel Blake. Expectation spread like warmth throughout her body, filling her with a confidence she hadn't felt in months.

Gabe. He was really here, just as she'd dreamed him. She would find him and they would be together as they first were, whole again.

Gabe, I'm coming, she thought, and her hope was a terrible fire within her.

From all the way to the inner courtyard, Gabe received her feelings, their intensity fortifying his resolve to find and defeat Peter Loughlin – today, now. He no longer thought of the rashness of his response as he entered the water, retreating inside himself with perfect self-control so Peter would not know where he was. He sliced stealthily through the water toward the emotional black hole radiating from its center.

Peter was cloaking, masking his presence with prodigious strength and all the finesse his gift afforded. He allowed his highly refined perceptions to range around him while taking care to remain invisible, knowing well the emotional signature that was Gabriel Blake and intent on finding it. His confidence faltered briefly when he realized he'd never fought in a contest against another cloaker.

But he knew he was the most powerful cloaker ever to have lived, and Gabe, no matter how accomplished he'd become in the past several weeks, would certainly be less capable. Peter's self-assurance returned to him.

He focused with lethal intention on Gabe entering the water, and how he might attack. He doubted his opponent had anyone's permission to engage him in mortal combat... but then, he was also willing to ignore any potential consequences that might ensue from a confrontation. His only desire was to remove the impediment in his life standing between him and fulfillment, and he let the desire ride him hard. He smiled severely, sure with the knowledge Gabe would end this very afternoon. By nightfall, Kate would be his and his alone.

Dozens of others had gathered to bear witness by this time, although they all gave the combatants wide berth. They were sworn to protect the queen and her prince, but they had intuited enough of the story by now to allow this public redress. The law protecting the bond between mates was so deeply revered, so sacred in the siren community; if the prince had stolen another's wife, all present believed he should face his accuser. If foul play was perceived from the prince's opponent – and they would collectively and individually know this – they would step in. The fervor brewing at the castle's center had everyone on edge; they, too, were anxious for the fight to begin, and for resolution.

Gabe darted randomly, blindingly, from one point to another, cloaking as effectively as he ever had as he worked to ascertain Peter's position in the pool. Peter was unfamiliar with Gabe's new abilities, which he hoped would give him an advantage. He needed one. He searched the pool without success, and thought how, no matter how much he had practiced in these past weeks, Peter had cloaked a lot longer. The man was ridiculously, astonishingly powerful.

But Gabe had nothing to lose and months of built-up determination driving him to end all this suffering. The adrenaline rush he experienced now sharpened him, his already honed senses further heightened until his intuition caught, not the lack of emotional output from Peter himself, but the seeking feelers he radiated around him. Sensing them, he tracked their emanation back to their source.

He *saw* Peter before he was noticed, and he frantically scanned for points of entry, for the chinks in Peter's armor where he could attack. Peter appeared as a ghost to him, not to his eyes, which could not see him, but to another sense almost like sight. He perceived Peter's form as if it was outlined in smoke, with a faint light glowing where his torso would be. Gabe closed his eyes, knowing they would deceive him now. Something in the downward tilt of Peter's head gave him an idea, and he moved in to strike.

Peter sensed Gabe's presence less than a second before he was behind him, his knife poised to run across Peter's throat. With lightening quickness, Peter twisted down and away, reaching behind him with his own knife to slash at Gabe's retreating form, catching his fluke to rend it its entire length.

Gabe ignored the cut in his tail, knowing the wound was superficial. He would only suffer a small loss in agility. Both he and Peter disappeared into themselves again, circling each other and making several, semi-successful attempts to maneuver or engage the other to individual advantage.

To the onlookers, they appeared only briefly in blurred flashes, the roaring movement of the water around them and small clouds of blood giving evidence of their location and the intensity of their battle.

Even if they had wanted to intervene, the guards would have had a difficult time finding and restraining them, but they believed the fight was ethically warranted and they did not interrupt. They communicated openly with each other about what they saw and heard, all of which only served to support their decision to let this struggle play out. As Kate and then Kenna joined the onlookers, the guards barred them from proceeding past a point where they could interrupt the fight, which they told the women they must not do.

Kate watched what she could see with desperate, rapt focus. More than anything she'd ever wanted in her life, she wanted Gabe to prevail, but the thought of Peter getting hurt also gave her a hollow pain. As angry as she was to think she might have been living a lie all these weeks, her heart broke for the siren prince, for the terrible burden of loneliness he'd carried and was now defending. She understood from the thoughts of others around her Peter had kidnapped her, although she didn't see how. She hoped Gabe had somehow been dulled and redirected around her these past months and would return to being the companion she first knew, the one she'd seen not three hours ago in a dream.

Peter had never sparred with another cloaker and did not know how to sense his opponent beyond reliance on sight and intuition, which initially compromised him. But he began to follow the dark shadow of energy he perceived, knowing it must be Gabe. When he next pinpointed it, he charged, grabbing the ghost across the chest with one arm while he brought his other around to pierce a kidney. Gabe broke the hold with surprising strength just before he was stabbed, flexing out and away in a corkscrew twist. Without pause, Gabe charged back with unexpected speed to make his own offensive strike.

It worked. Gabe's knife plunged into Peter's abdomen, which he clutched in surprise as Gabe twisted. The two men glared at each other, chest to chest, while Gabe grabbed Peter's other wrist to bring it and the hand holding his knife behind his back, incapacitating his opponent's arm from the shoulder.

Even wounded, Peter struggled mightily, and Gabe was only just strong enough to maintain his hold. He desperately searched for something else he could do, another weapon he might use to sway the struggle in his favor. He thought of Kate, and then he thought of a way to weaken Peter.

Gabe stopped cloaking completely, releasing fully all of the anger and anguish within him, a tremendous emotional burden for any siren, and he felt Peter's strength slacken. He replayed Kate's death in his mind, engaging Peter in the painful memory of her abduction. As Gabe recalled the false dissolution, he was able to intuit Peter's method of effecting it and learned the details of his plan leading up to the moment he took his wife, including the taking of the dying old woman he projected as Kate.

Kate was not your first kidnapping, I see, Gabe accused with another twist of his knife, and he felt Peter's fear, knew the man understood for the first time he might die. He struggled less, his will to fight softening more with Gabe's emotional foray than his knife could ever achieve.

Gabe continued, using Peter's attachment to Kate against him, just as he'd used her attachment to him, Gabe, against her. He needled his way into the weakening man's mind, searching out his motivations and revealing them for the sickness they masked. He recalled finding Kate earlier that day, reflected to Peter the oppression she felt, the strength of her attachment to her real husband despite his efforts to sublimate it; and reflected the final resolution she'd made, how she would prefer to raise her child alone rather than pretend the life Peter envisioned was enough.

For all your efforts, she would have left you, just like your first wife, Gabe assured him. *Here, let me show you the difference.*

Drawing on the devotion emanating from Kate herself on the sideline, Gabe combined what was between them and projected the feeling that was uniquely his and Kate's, sharing with Peter the full depth of their union. He felt Peter's surrender.

Without this stark comparison, Peter might have continued to deceive himself that he could replace the bond Kate had with Gabe, but with the evidence Gabe offered, he knew he could not. Gabe's merciless emotional attack hit him with the force of high-speed train, and Peter capitulated.

The fight bled out of him. He couldn't win, he saw now, and he didn't mean the fight with Gabe; he meant the fight for the life he'd tried to force with Kate. He'd thought of it all wrong. Gabe was right; Kate would not love him as she'd loved Gabe, because their bond was already made, and because, he, Peter was too compromised. He'd tried to engineer a life filled with love in the same way he negotiated professionally, and the effort was ineffective. Worse, it was pathetic, which he really could not tolerate.

Peter had not thought of consequences when he entered the pool to confront Gabe, but he thought of them now. If he survived, which at this point he thought he still could, he would lose all hope of constructing a normal life, even for him. In fact, chances were pretty good he'd be outcast, and he'd be denied even the insubstantial love he was used to. Of course, he would lose his crown, not that this mattered much, his mother be damned.

He looked in Gabe's eyes now, a new resolve forming as he took in the young man's fervency and dedication. Of course he would fight for his wife and child. Of course he should ignore legal and social conventions to challenge a powerful prince. There was nothing more precious than the future Gabe had within his reach, which made Gabe's willingness to risk his life not just understandable, but commendable.

Peter thought such a treasure might be worth his own life, as well. He regarded Gabe levelly. *I concede*, he told him. To his community, he said, *I want to confess*. As neither statement contained any deceit, Gabe released him.

Peter knew he could not atone for what he'd done. In fact, he couldn't even feel sorry for wanting something so wholesome and good in his life. But he could acknowledge defeat gracefully, and he could try to make things easier for Kate after today. He held no love in his heart for Gabe because his jealousy left no room, but he dropped his cloak now, so everyone present could know the truth about what had happened, what he'd done. He'd been cloaking for so long at some level or another, he struggled to stop.

Kate met his gaze fearlessly, and her expression was full of questions and accusation. He assumed the image of her husband and then dropped it to appear as himself again.

I wanted what you had with Gabe and I took you. I've been pretending to be Gabe, projecting myself as your husband this entire time. There is no need to hide. There has been no discovery. Your family is safe.

He faced the rest of the gathering, avoiding eye contact with his mother, whose face was a mask of horror, her hand half raised toward him. *I have felt an appalling, unbearable lack*, he began, saturating everyone there with the feelings of loneliness that had defined him since before he could walk. The poignancy of his emotions pierced each individual, and the community convulsed as they experienced first-hand their prince's hurt. Peter continued for some time to feel and remember his deprivation until all present understood his motivations for going down the path he did.

They understood but they could not condone his actions, he acknowledged, and he felt their confusion, knew they were at a loss as to how to proceed. His suffering, his feelings of abandonment, were unconscionable; unbearable even sensed as distant memories, and no one relished the prospect of inflicting more punishment on him. *You have been horribly hurt,* they apologized, *and so we have all been horribly hurt, because your wounds are ours.*

Peter's offered them a sickly smile, little enjoying this attribute of his community, so adept at sharing his pain and seeking to comfort him while placing him in a position he had never been able to tolerate, a position that had caused his misery in the first place. He saw no way out, graceful or otherwise. In fact, he had no desire to recover from his self-orchestrated tragedy, something they all felt and saw. He was tired of it all. Tired of fighting, tired of trying, tired of wanting what he never could have.

Kate knew what Peter was thinking before the rest of the community did. She was upset enough to hope for the worst but not before she'd had her own chance at redress. He owed her that, she believed. She placed a hand on her nearest guard to gain his attention. *Let me go to them,* she demanded. The guards all studied her intentions before accompanying her to where Peter and Gabe were floating.

Kate clasped hands with Gabe, reveling in the sense of homecoming and unity despite her hurt and outrage. Her confidence, her belief in a happy future, were restored, showing her how far from the truth Peter had tried to take her. Peter observed their clasped hands, her defiant expression, and he seemed to shrivel. She almost didn't care. Every lie he'd told her for every hour of every day during the past several weeks, every part of her he'd tried to undo, had meant nothing, and she wanted him to see her resilience.

She'd intended to state her accusations, but his expression showed her she already had. And she didn't relish hurting someone in pain, even someone who had behaved as monstrously as Peter. Worst of all, he bled awareness, of how each and every part of this disaster was his fault, the result of shortcomings he had no hope of fixing. He was without the comfort of even a single rationalization, had no sense of denial over what had happened to him. She glanced at the hungry, gaping crowd waiting for him to act, and she pitied him.

You don't have to give up, she told him.

She didn't know what she was saying, Peter believed, but she was sincere, and he felt some small relief from her effort. And here she was, vital and aware in a way she had never been in his company. He wondered if he would feel so steady if their roles were reversed and decided he wouldn't. Which meant her undeserved encouragement touched his very center, released a knot in his chest, and freed him to do what he knew he must.

Thank you, Kate.

Peter gestured to his guards, ostensibly to remand himself to them. He paused halfway to them, causing some small confusion as he lifted his face toward the surface and spread his arms. His shape shimmered, the edges of him blurring into the water around him. Instantly, everyone understood what was happening, that he wished to let go of his life and had the strength to do so on his own. Rather than stop him, everyone sang a song expressing their sorrow and love for him. They told him they forgave him and wanted him to be happy. In almost no time, Peter released himself, his dissolution a beautiful burst of light. All the angst and grief he'd imparted with his confession disappeared with him.

Kenna's moan came from the other side of the pool, where her guards freed her. *"Nooooo!"* she cried, and all attention focused on her as she shot through the water to where her son had just been. Several sirens reached toward her but she withdrew, hissing, *"You are not to touch me. You have taken everything from me now. My son, my little boy . . ."*

She reached to catch the last of the particles of light that had been Peter, and she convulsed with grief. She saw with merciless clarity how the choices she'd made in her life, both for herself and her son, had brought everyone present to this juncture. Her well-worn rationalizations, which had served at every other time, felt empty and meaningless now. When she'd chosen to serve her state and forego bonding with a husband, as she'd procreated anyway for the good of her office and then handed her infant off to the nursery, as she'd chosen in every single instance to put the emotional needs of herself and her family last — she'd experienced and caused nothing but hardship. And her cherished son was gone.

The rest of the community absorbed her sadness and circled her, whispering their support and encouragement. She shimmered before them, caring nothing for their needs, their losses, her responsibilities to them any longer. *"I love my son,"* she repeated over and over. *"My beautiful, gifted son. I caused this. My fault. He's gone."*

She gave herself over to her intent with no care for the distress she unleashed. She wanted nothing of this life any more, a thought which spread alarm all around her.

"Not in sadness, Kenna," they begged. *"Please don't leave us in sadness. Let us help you. Live, and then, in the fullness of time, you will leave in joy."*

But their pleas were too late. Kenna had committed to her course as soon as she'd seen her son's body shiver with the first signs of dissolution. Whereas Peter had left peace in his wake, however, Kenna filled the sea with anger and hurt. As she let go of herself, these feelings remained like a corrosive acid no one could wash off.

"My queen," they cried in anguish, as if she were still there, as if she could reverse the events that had led to this tragedy.

Gabe only had eyes for Kate. Had they not been separated for the past four months, his cultural responsibilities would have required him to stay and grieve and share the community's burden. But no one questioned Gabe's unwillingness to participate further in the drama underway now.

"Let's go home, Gabe," Kate pleaded, and her need to be away from this place compounded his own.

They held each other, and nothing, neither the compelling need of his people nor the death of his queen, could make him deny her. He touched her face, her arms, her hands, to reassure himself she was real, and his heart broke with happiness.

"Let's go." They left the confusion and grief surrounding them without a backward glance.

CHAPTER TWENTY-NINE

Kate didn't need her husband's superior intuition to see the toll her absence had taken on her mother. Cara's entire body declared the fight required to cope with what she thought had been her daughter's death, from her hunched shoulders to her overly thin, hollowed frame, to the shadows in and around her eyes. Her face radiated an agonized, shaky hope Kate could see from down the street as Gabe pulled their car to the front of the house. Her mother stood on the front lawn with John, who held Everett in his arms. Carmen and Michael watched behind them.

Despite her awkward condition, she bolted from the passenger seat and ran to her mother. The two women clung to each other, choking on tears as they voiced incomprehensible words of loss and recovery. The rest of the sirens present soon joined them.

On their way into the house, Cara and Kate kept their arms around each other's waists, unwilling to let any space separate them. "You look so beautiful, honey," her mother commented. "And you colored your hair? I mean, it's nice, but . . ."

"Gabe insisted," she interjected, tossing a teasing glance over her shoulder to her husband.

Gabe was defensive but laughing. "Now-now. Don't make me the bad guy." He explained what he knew of Kate's changed appearance, which she had reported when she shared the whole of her experience the previous evening.

Everyone was astonished at the lengths Peter had gone, but none were more stunned than the sirens present. "That is just… *spectacularly* outside normal behavior for us," Carmen marveled.

"I think it worked because no one would ever worry about that level of deceit," Gabe remarked. "There's not even a reasonable point of departure conceptually, nowhere to start from that would lead you even to the possibility."

"That's one for the record books," John commented. He addressed Gabe. "Seriously, you must be pretty good at cloaking to have pulled off what you did. And you never had any idea you could cloak before?"

"None," Gabe admitted. "I talked about it with Xanthe, and the only thing we could come up with was I had extraordinary motivation, and I was predisposed because of my family's regular association with humans. Because humans know how to withdraw."

"Yeah, well, that's great and all," Cara broke in sternly, although her voice shook, "but I'd like there to be no more disappearing for a while."

"And, I know you two are already an old married couple," Carmen ventured, "but I think we should celebrate your homecoming – and announce your marriage to those who don't know about it – with a reception."

"Um, Carmen?" Kate raised her hand. "I don't know if all our friends and family need to see me waddling around in a formal dress trying to play the blushing bride." John, Gabe, and Michael guffawed.

"Shush," Carmen told her, including the men in her reproving stare. "You don't waddle yet, and this actually has only a little to do with you." Kate looked plaintively at Gabe, mouthing the words, *Is she nuts?*

"Maybe." Carmen *tsk-ed*. "But I can see her point, honey. We should celebrate the end of the debacle with Peter. And bring closure for the community."

Kate balked. "What exactly do you mean by 'community?' I mean, how many people are we talking about, here?"

"Just a small crowd, I promise," Carmen replied, too innocently,

Kate thought. Gabe's smile was off, as well, bland and completely insincere. Which she understood to mean he would not oppose his mother on this issue. John barked out a dark laugh and retrieved his car keys from a hook by the door.

"I'm going to check in at the clinic. Just let me know how many hors d'oeuvres to order." He grinned at Gabe before leaving the room.

"It's not that bad, honey," Cara wheedled. Kate remained unconvinced.

She stared at the hundreds of people meandering the grounds outside the Blake home, knew she'd have to talk to each and every one of them, knew the questions, direct and indirect she'd be taking for hours on the subject of her recent abduction. She thought she might throw up.

Her voice quavered with hysteria. "I'm too fat and too tired to do this, Mom."

Cara stifled a laugh before composing herself. "No, you're not. You're pregnant, not fat. And you can help you and your family close the door on your experience at Shaddox by doing this."

Kate knew she was right but didn't feel any greater enthusiasm for the gauntlet she was about to run. Thankfully, Gabe arrived then. "You're gorgeous." He kissed her soundly, which eliminated the starch from her resistance. Maybe she was as puffy and tired as she feared, but her husband thought she was beautiful, so she decided she didn't give a rip.

They had held a small ceremony after all, at the library as Kate wanted, with only family and the Wilkes present. Kate latched onto the idea promptly after Gabe reminded her Peter had felt more comfortable planning to marry her because they hadn't had a human ceremony. "Not that I expect anything like that to ever, ever happen again," he joked, "but I will feel better if I'm holding a marriage license up the next time I take after one of your suitors." Kate waved him away and made immediate arrangements.

Will and Dana's relief over her safe return touched her more than she would have believed – they'd all cried together. At the Blake home after the ceremony, she marveled with Gabe over how relaxed and healthy they appeared; Dana was radiantly pregnant and unapologetically happy about it; and Will, too, was lighter, leaner, and bright-eyed from his sobriety. "We may be moving closer to you," Dana told them after Kate inquired about their plans. "We're thinking of opening a bakery, of all things."

"That sounds wonderful!" Kate told them. "I'd love it if our kids could know each other. And if you need help at the shop, I'll fill in." They promised to keep her apprised.

To the uninformed humans at the reception, Kate's story was she was abducted by a distant relative on Gabe's side. The man was more troubled than evil, and he'd killed himself when Kate got to a phone and called for help. The part where everyone thought Kate had died was addressed by Gabe and Michael, who explained how they'd found her jacket while out on their boat.

Not too far off the mark but far enough for their families to be careful about what they said and to whom.

Maya pretended disgust over having to wear a dress and new shoes after all but she was so relieved her friend was still alive, Kate knew she wasn't really mad. She confessed after the ceremony she'd play her entire next season in high heels if it meant she'd never have a scare like that again. Soley, as best man, was almost respectable in a canine tux, although he gave the maid of honor, Maya, no time at all; he only had eyes for Gabe.

"C'mon," Gabe encouraged her as they surveyed the people milling around the lawn. "Let's play offense, score some points, and blow this pop stand."

"This was your idea, don't forget," Kate grumbled, but she put her arms around Gabe's waist and approached the crowd with him.

Everyone was more kind and respectful than Kate anticipated, and she felt guilty about her earlier tantrum to her mother. While Cara and John entertained those who had no knowledge of their secret, siren life, she talked openly with the guests who knew better, Gabe sticking close by her, which helped her feel stable. The disrespectful questions she sensed – did she sleep with him, was the child Gabe's – were never voiced, and, she had to admit, she might have wondered those things too. She decided to be magnanimous, giving out more information than strictly necessary in the hopes of staving off future inquiries.

"You have to remember, I didn't know Peter was Peter," she

explained to one questioner who'd wondered her if her captivity was oppressive. "I did feel oppressed but I thought it was because we were in hiding, not because Peter was unkind." She hesitated as she thought back on his last tirades, knowing they were the result of his frustration, and, she believed now, his precarious mental health.

"He was good to you?" This person was doubtful, and Kate thought about her answer several seconds before giving it. "Aside from the fact that he kidnapped me and tried to cut me off from everyone I ever cared about . . ." Her face fell. She was least comfortable with this part of her experience, where she'd been duped. She couldn't hate Peter for his motivations—she could only feel terribly sorry for him—but she almost despised him for making a victim out of her. It was a role she wanted no part of, and she was anxious to forestall any offers of pity that would cast her as a martyr.

"He was just awfully lonely. I think it was something as simple as his mother not spending time with him when he was little, and him not ever knowing his father. He wanted to be loved, and when he saw what Gabe and I have, he tried to force a situation that would give him that love.

"But he never touched me." Kate saw the crowd was skeptical. "Really. He told me, as Gabe, he wanted to wait until after the wedding—which I was opposed to, by the way. In the meantime, he tried to cater to my interests and give me every comfort he could. In his way, he did try to make me happy."

"And the baby," someone else interjected. "Were you worried about your child?"

Gabe, who kept quiet throughout her questioning stepped in to reply. "This is the fascinating part. I sensed his thoughts on the matter when I was fighting him, and the thing is, he was *happy* Kate was pregnant. He wanted a wife and family as fast as possible, and he really was prepared to welcome the child as his own.

"Of course, his acceptance had a dark side," Gabe continued with considerably less charity in his voice. "He knew Kate would put her own misgivings aside to be a good mother, and he saw the baby as a way to further tie her to him." Gabe snorted in disgust as he recalled Peter's convoluted ideas. "Truthfully, I could kill him all over again when I think of that."

His listeners exchanged nervous smiles.

"I know the idea of murder sounds strange to you, but if you were in my shoes, you would feel as I do. I'm sure you'd all fight to get your families back." They nodded and edged away from him.

Feeling she'd explained all she cared to for one day, Kate escaped to hide behind her in-laws, leaving Gabe to answer further questions from people she barely knew. Carmen gave her cover while she and Michael met with Xanthe.

"What will happen to the monarchy?" Michael asked.

"We've never had this situation before," Xanthe confessed. "A double suicide . . ." She shook her head. "Every time I think about what Peter and Kenna did, the predicament they left us in, I just feel irritated." Her expression became bleak as she continued, "This was a pretty serious blow to our collective confidence. To be honest, most of us can't really consider what happened; between the abduction of someone's mate and the desire to engage in mortal battle... those motivations are so far outside our cultural lexicon. Most of us can't understand the premise, much less get to the conclusion." She huffed. "What a mess."

"So, who's governing now?" Carmen inquired. "And who's deciding what happens to the crown?"

"The Viceroy has formed a temporary government," Xanthe replied. "He's charged with keeping the status quo until more is decided. And, since you brought it up, we're forming a council to formulate a plan for government structure moving forward. I'm on it, and I was hoping we could talk you into serving as well, Michael." She addressed Carmen. "You have enough responsibility as it is, but you'd be welcome too, Carmen."

Carmen extended her palm. "Thank you for the invitation but I'd prefer to sit this one out, if you don't mind."

"I don't," Xanthe confirmed.

"I'd be honored," Michael told her.

On the back porch overlooking the ocean, Kate joined Gabe as he chatted with Luke and Solange. Alicia, Jeremy, Cara, and John rode herd on all the unruly toddlers. "I hope nobody makes a break for the water," Kate commented. "Do your parents know anything yet?"

"No. But only because we live so far away and they don't see us often," she replied. "They're no fools, though. They have to wonder why we never take the kids swimming." She grinned. "You can't reason with a two-year-old siren who wants to be a fish. And one who actually *can* become a fish."

"How do you manage?" Kate wondered, marveling at the amount of running around she saw their parents doing. She sensed, with dim prescience, the toll such constant vigilance would start to take.

"You'll find out," Solange smirked. "I won't go into it, since there's nothing you can do at this point." Her expression softened. "But you shouldn't worry. It really is the best thing ever."

Luke weighed in too. "Everything everyone says about it — you give up your life, the sleep deprivation part, it takes everything you have to make it —it's all true. But you wouldn't trade it for anything." He and Solange shared a knowing smile.

Gabe snaked his arms around Kate's waist and settled his chin on her shoulder. "You're not worrying, are you?"

"Maybe a little. We're going to have a lot to do in a few months, with a new baby, and school for you, and whatever's going to happen with my job. I hope we do everything right, and I hope we can keep up."

Gabe kissed her temple. "We'll figure it all out, you know," he whispered in her ear.

His optimism was so beautiful. She twisted around to see his face. A broad smile came unbidden to her lips, and she contemplated again the bright future ahead. "Yes, we will," she agreed.

EPILOGUE

Some parts I really don't remember. I recall my mother yelling for me and the sound of the boat's motor starting, and someone calling on the radio for help. Despite the terror in her voice and the frantic maneuvering of everyone on board, I was unconcerned. I ignored their request to grab my life vest, to stay put.

I did not see a dolphin in the water with me, either. When I fell overboard, I saw a little boy, wild and glistening and about the same age as me, pleading with me to please play with him. He told me his name was Gabe. His smile was infectious and easy, and I said, "Yes-let's-play-dolphin-and-I-can't-swim-without-my-vest-we-must-hurry-my-mother-will-come-for-me-I'm-Kate," all in one laughing breath. My life vest floated away. *It's too slow*, Gabe told me.

Tell them you'll be okay and we'll swim to shore, Gabe said, and I called this out to my mother. Then we were gone.

My mother remembers following me to shore, seeing me wave at her from the beach a few minutes after I disappeared with the dolphin. She found me on the beach with Gabe's family and took me home.

I remember more.

Gabe and I swam for hours, although I had never learned to swim. We talked incessantly but without sound, and differently than we did out of the water. We would both be six in a couple of weeks. We had no sisters or brothers, although he had a lot of cousins. We were going to the same school in the fall. I had just moved from Kansas. He had lived here all his life.

Contained as I was in the sea's embrace, I did not focus as I might have on the heavy pressure of the water; instead, I felt as if I were flying, and, contrarily, as if a light, fresh burst of air was circulating around me. For the first time in a long time, I felt anticipation for the life my mother and I were starting and this swim signaled a wonderful beginning. Back in Kansas, we had lived a life of emotional subsistence defined by duty and grief, unconsciously becoming as dry and shriveled as a windswept plain in August. As I knew nothing different, I didn't judge our diminished existence; but now I felt, by contrast, how beautifully hope colored and brightened the world, how it wakened my dulled senses, and inspired me to expand my old habits of thinking and feeling. From that point on, I yearned toward something more.

We regretted leaving the sea, unwilling to participate in the sunny universe outside that promised separation. As we built our sandcastle, we continued the conversation we'd held underwater, refusing to share ourselves with those around us. When my mother led me away, I waved at Gabe over my shoulder, sad I would not be in his company, but not truly concerned over our departure. I was sure I would be with him again.

What we saw that afternoon amazed me – the vibrant colors, the fantastic corals and fish; but what I left the water with, what I kept with me, was not the pretty images. It was a new understanding of the world on land, my world. Sometime during our swim, I let go, without knowing I was doing so, of an unconscious belief concerning love and loss, about how these attributes had characterized my days and how they would impact my reality moving forward. In the space of those brief hours, I came to reject that grief and loneliness were the very definition of life – mine, my mother's, and presumably everyone else's. By the time Gabe's mother lifted him out of the water and Anna led me by the hand, I'd reached outside myself for something new and unknown.

In the confusion of growing up, I rarely understood how my

decisions would play out even minutes after I made them, much less any long-term implications; and, especially since I'm a mother now, I know how hard my own mother worked to help and guide me. I believe now no one, not even the most loving, dedicated parents, can steer a child clear of emotional hardship – it simply comes – but I saw how the personal attention of my mom and the periodic intervention of well-meaning adults did, collectively, get me to some sort of platform, a stable base from which I could create independence and happiness. The better part of this effort, the part I really learned during that long-ago swim with Gabe, was that many of life's rich gifts come unbidden, not from what a person can manufacture and bring forth. All I had to do to receive these gifts was say yes; yes to a swim in the water, yes to the unsupported idea that there was something better out there, happiness to be had I couldn't see. And the amazing thing is, it's still out there, unknown and unpredictable, but it's coming.

The End.

Thank you for reading *Updrift*, the first installment of the Mer Chronicles by Errin Stevens. If you enjoyed it, please share your enthusiasm with others, especially in the form of a review on your favorite social media platform(s).

For now, please enjoy the following preview of the sequel, *Breakwater.*

Breakwater, The Mer Chronicles, Book II

PROLOGUE

She sensed his death, and then ignored the possibility for several days. She couldn't be sure, couldn't know after all this time, could she? More than forty years had passed since she'd last seen him, and they hadn't bonded, not truly... how could she know?

But she couldn't stop herself from thinking about him; she'd felt his dissolution, and it was not a feeling one could confuse. But... Peter? Why?

She experienced no real grief — she'd grieved over him, over their emotional catastrophe of a marriage, when she was still with him. But there was a distinct emptiness in her now, and a sadness that one of her kind was gone, someone she'd known as well as she knew anyone. Still, she felt unsure.

When she could no longer tolerate her uncertainty, she dove into the lake and transformed, a delicious freedom she craved especially when she was troubled. Lake Superior had taken some getting used to — she was less buoyant here than in the salt water back home — but her feelings were clearer when she swam. She came here when she needed to think.

What did she perceive? She sifted through her thoughts and sensations, examining each one carefully. No, she was not mistaken: Peter Loughlin was dead. And here, far under the water where hardly any light penetrated, she suffered for her clarity, felt her remorse more keenly. She cried, both for him and for herself.

The decision she had always put off would never be made now, the one to tell him, or at least get him word, that he had a daughter. Now he would never know he'd been a father, would never hear from her an apology for leaving him without telling him she was pregnant.

She liked to believe he would have forgiven her, for running away as she did and for protecting their baby from the environment that had crippled them both. Peter's inner distress, so like her own, would have schooled him, she hoped, would have helped him accept that, if there had been any other way, she would have stayed.

Her uncertainty dispatched, Seneca meandered to the surface, watching the play of light on the rippling waves above when she paused, and she contemplated doing the most thrilling, heartbreaking thing she'd done since running away four decades earlier. She could no longer do right by her husband, but she could find their daughter, could explain to her who she was, where she came from. Seneca wept with relief at the prospect; how many hours over how many years had she yearned for her child?

The orphanage and people who ran it were long gone, Seneca knew because she'd checked, but her little girl had stayed there until she'd graduated from high school. Surely by now her daughter was aware of what she was, although Seneca was pretty sure they had followed her directive, had kept her daughter from the ocean when she was small. She'd used all of her influence, not inconsiderable, to ensure they would.

Seneca broke through the surface of the lake, took a breath and re-entered the water, propelling herself face-up and parallel to the sky, so she could watch the clouds, which made her feel like she was flying. Her understanding felt clear now and the decision to go right. She headed for shore and thought about all it would mean for her to leave this place.

And the more she contemplated a return to North Carolina, the more eager she was to get on with it and go. Carmen. Her beautiful baby, her girl. She would find her and explain everything.

CHAPTER ONE

Xanthe floated thirty feet below the ocean's surface in the submerged cathedral where she typically meditated and held court. She was stationary except for her tail, which flicked periodically as she mused over the current political complications she was charged with resolving.

Things were a mess. With a committee formed to recommend government changes moving forward, Xanthe had retreated to her sanctuary to ruminate in seclusion. She still needed to find an overall direction to accommodate the cultural shifts happening under her watch.

She reflected on the recent actions of the monarchy—namely the double suicide of Queen Kenna and her son Peter, the crown prince. She needed to come up with a way to resolve the confusion their deaths had caused the siren community and normalize the power structure as quickly as possible. If she could gain some perspective, she could share it with the advisory committee and help her people heal and rebuild.

She marveled at the incongruity of it all, how a cherished member of their ranks—a prince no less—suffered such extreme loneliness he secretly kidnapped and isolated someone. And this in the context of a heretofore transparent society where bonds were protected and emotional connection revered. Unlike humans, who were given to periods of introversion that sometimes spanned years, intimacy was vital to siren survival, as necessary as food and water. What had changed so drastically in their community, implacable and stable for centuries, to produce such a situation?

Granted, Peter's cloaking ability—he could mask his identity even to his own kind—was unprecedented. If she hadn't witnessed the sequence of events leading up to Peter's suicide herself, she wouldn't have believed it could happen. Or that anyone could accomplish such a complicated deception. But he had.

If she was being objective, she'd seen other, less noticeable, signs their society was shifting, understood sirens everywhere had inaugurated an era of transition before Peter and his mother had voluntarily dissolved. Tempted as she was to dwell on the more dramatic behaviors of their former regents, she disciplined herself to focus on the larger issue at hand. Sirens everywhere had demonstrated individualistic tendencies evidencing a significant departure from tradition. Dozens of examples came to mind as she thought back, from increased assertion of individual will in matters of group governance to a new, pervasive curiosity for all things human. More and more sirens were hungry to explore the earth-bound world, and not just in groups as had been their habit.

The common thread, Xanthe realized, had to be human influence and interaction. With the advent of easy intercontinental mobility (and a human society eager for it), run-ins with their non-aquatic cousins had exploded over the past century. The relatively new practice of human/siren marriages also coincided with the arrival of these changed behaviors... but the marriages were a necessity Xanthe acknowledged; sirens needed the genetic diversity these unions offered. And she could not discount the raw, commanding pull humans held for her kind. Human emotional broadcasts, especially in the water, were an irresistible enticement to every siren within range, made them forget themselves as nothing else. Xanthe well knew how consorting with humans evoked a visceral, elemental response none of them would ever be able to suppress. Unlike some in her world, she knew they would be foolish to even try.

But something had to be done, and as wonderful as humans could be, her people had also experienced enough of their cruelty to explore the option of complete separation. All sirens understood the need to court human ignorance with sophisticated evasion and illusion because they knew the miracle of what humans offered—their stunning creativity, their dynamism, and their soul-drenching evocations—did not mean they could be trusted, unfortunately.

Sirens had successfully hidden from humans for centuries, but an increase in interactions threatened their secrecy and fed what many saw as a dangerous deterioration of their world. A year earlier, Xanthe and a few other officials had even hatched a plan to establish community outposts in places that would offer, if not complete seclusion, at least limited opportunity for human traffic. The idea was to create a refuge like Shaddox Island, where sirens could be at leisure and enjoy life without human interference.

In fairness the idea was also born of a need to address the problem presented by several of their young men who had developed what many felt were counter-cultural behaviors. These men had all voiced dissatisfaction with the choices available to them concerning their roles in siren society, a dissatisfaction no one had seen before. Rather than examine too closely the whys and wherefores of these sentiments, however, the decision had been made to send the group to form an outpost, one that could eventually serve as a safe congregating spot for all of them. Somewhere without a human population.

Xanthe laughed at the earnestness with which they'd chosen the location; Antarctica was as removed from siren society as it was from humans, and her government's avoidance of its people's problems struck her as comical in retrospect. The decision was a clear duck and run, with the most prominent malcontents assigned to the development task force and sent away to clear the territory. They thought such work would alleviate the men's lack of enthusiasm for pursuing an academic career or profession in one of the sciences, show them the error of their ways by committing them to manual labor. Xanthe saw the mission now as far more cowardly; rather than examine any systemic unhappiness, those who were unhappy were simply dispatched, their discontent hidden.

She thought how, in this way, sirens and humans were fundamentally alike, both races reacting cautiously or fearfully to the prospect of change even when it was too far underway to stop.

Still and all she was reluctant to believe her community's long-held stability was completely failing, still trusted things would improve if they could better avoid land dwellers and their world. She knew, given the size and prevalence of the human population, outright isolation wasn't practical and, in any case, couldn't be enforced. Sirens had always relied on human academic and financial institutions—to the betterment of both societies, Xanthe believed. They were currently too integrated to disengage.

The better approach might be to prescribe more careful interactions, although she couldn't think how this would be accomplished, either, since she could have no control over human travels.

Regardless of the changes she saw taking place, Xanthe had confidence in the order inherent in her society, knew it would not falter, and this comforted her. Even as more of them adopted individualistic habits, individual happiness was too closely tied to the overall community's well-being, and *that* wasn't going to change, not ever. So the new key to her people's stability could be working with this evolution rather than against it.

Yes. She felt the knot in her center loosen, the impossibile become possible. Her intuition told her resolution lay along the path of careful coexistence, even if she didn't yet see the specific course of action to achieve it. But she knew to trust herself, and trust she'd found the way they might all to continue to thrive.

Xanthe relaxed further and pondered the puzzle of accommodation, rightness and change. At least the problem had definition now, and a path to resolution. With consensus and help from whoever would become the new head of government, their world could find its balance.

CHAPTER TWO

Maya sat with Sylvia and Kate on the couch staring at the screen in front of them, her friends wearing the same rapt, dreamy expression she assumed she also wore. This was the fourth time in two weeks they'd convened at Sylvia's for movie night, the scope of which had narrowed to include superhero flicks only. Tonight's selection was *Superman*, which Kate declared was her new favorite.

"No argument from me," Maya pronounced. "In fact, I'm free tomorrow night, too. I could be here by seven."

Sylvia sighed. "I love this part, when she steps on his boots and he takes her flying."

"Yeeessss," Kate hissed.

They all strained forward as Superman and Lois drifted upwards from the top of the Daily Planet, the music swelling as they ascended into the night sky, and Kate slowly released the breath she held. "The first time I saw this scene… well, it was so sweetly erotic I couldn't sleep for three days."

"Did you ladies want popcorn?" Gabe grinned from the doorway, and all three of them jumped. Maya shot him a venomous look while her sister, Sylvia, scrambled for the remote and punched "pause."

Kate squealed and launched herself toward her husband, no small feat given her advanced pregnancy. Once plastered to Gabe's side, she buried her face in his neck and asked, "How long have you been here?" in a muffled voice.

Sylvia rose from the couch and headed for the kitchen. "I really don't need to see this."

Maya crossed her arms over her chest. "Yes. How long *have* you been standing there, Gabe?"

"Not very." Gabe smirked, pressing his nose into Kate's hair. "Long enough to hear a lot of sighing and something about 'sweetly erotic.'"

Kate groaned and kept her face hidden. Maya tented her eyes with one hand. "I'm going to get a gun so I can shoot you, Gabriel Blake."

Gabe ignored her. He craned his head away from Kate, pretending irritation at her. "I got back twenty minutes ago," he bussed her on the cheek, "to find you *not* waiting for me at home."

"Yeah. *Superman* with the girls is my new gig when you're gone. But now that you're here," she waved a hand dismissively toward the television, "I'm no longer interested in what's-his-name. Lois can have him. Let's go home."

Gabe's low laugh sounded suggestive to Maya, but maybe that's because she made a study of other people's habits of intimacy these days. The couple wasn't staying for her brood-over, however; she watched Gabe loop an arm around Kate's neck as they walked out. "I'll see you at the bakery tomorrow, Sylvia!" Kate called over her shoulder.

In the kitchen, Sylvia rifled through cupboards while Maya sat at the table, head braced on her hands. She hated feeling jealous of her friend's good romantic fortune but still felt bitter.

"I think they're gone," Sylvia commented tonelessly, and Maya was uncharitably pleased she wasn't the only one in low humor.

"Yeah," she replied. "So let's make popcorn and finish the show. I need the distraction."

Sylvia frowned as she poured oil in a pan. "So do I."

Back on the couch with a bowl between them, they paid only partial attention to the rest of the movie. Maya knew a little of Sylvia's romantic conundrums and certainly indulged in a few of her own, which had just been made all the more unsatisfying against the backdrop of Kate and Gabe's newlywed euphoria. Maya had been seeing someone on and off for a while—which mostly meant texting and talking on the phone since her guy lived out of state. She didn't feel particularly enamored, but as she had nothing else going on she continued to talk and flirt and hope their exchanges would launch a more compelling attraction.

Sylvia was in a faux relationship, in Maya's opinion, with a man she'd met at culinary school. Maya had met Ethan and understood his appeal—he was handsome, a talented cook… and had charmed all of his female classmates from what she could see. Which meant Sylvia was gone on a prospect who was much less gone on her. In fairness, the guy *had* solicited Sylvia's affection, a little more than with the other girls, perhaps, although he never invited Sylvia out on an exclusive date. Her sister's joke to Maya was, "Sometimes he seems really into me." Maya had no patience for him or for Sylvia's tolerance for such weak affection. "He's a tease," she retorted.

Lately Maya knew Ethan's quirky, all-inclusive approach to romance had led to kicking, cussing—albeit private—tantrums on Sylvia's part, after which she vowed to Maya she would save her love for someone who wanted it. "I will not be a pathetic hanger-on," she insisted once after Maya made the observation she essentially served in a harem. But Maya would inevitably catch her venturing out again with the same crowd, pretending she found whatever attention Ethan tossed her way acceptable.

In rare moments of clarity Sylvia confessed her exact motivation, saying she knew she simply wanted someone to love who would love her back. And she thought Ethan could honestly be that person, although she also conceded evidence in support of this hope was thin.

Sylvia stared gloomily at the screen in front of them now and mused, "I'm an idiot."

Maya appraised her with a sideways glance. "Because you keep going out with Ethan?"

"Mm-hmm."

"Yeah. You are," Maya agreed. Her smirk faded. "But I'm no one to criticize."

"You could channel our mother for me. Help me get off this train maybe." Their mother, Alicia, always argued hard when Sylvia mooned and took the blame for Ethan's disinterest. "What you want, someone to love who will love you back, is good and worth wanting," she'd insist. "Even if Ethan's not the right one for you - and I certainly have my own opinion on that score - do not think you're in the wrong." Maya agreed with her.

On this occasion she decided to rely on Kate's example rather than her mother's standard lecture, however. "Think of the demonstration we just had from Kate and Gabe. The one that just pissed us both off."

"I feel like too much of a jerk," Sylvia intoned. "I mean, who suffers because a friend is happy?"

Maya understood this reaction too well, since her own shaky rationalizations crashed just as hard when Kate and Gabe were around.

Kate went so far as to decimate her carefully constructed excuses out loud, although she didn't realize what she did. But she was just so dang happy, as well as annoyingly open—evangelistic even—on the wonderfulness of love and marriage.

"Feeling blue? Out of sorts?" Kate would say to introduce what had become her new life's mantra. "Get married! Have a baby!"

Maya had been Kate's best friend from the time the two were in grade school, but even she couldn't talk Kate down from her 'love-conquers-all' perch. "Can it, Blake," she told Kate irritably during their last movie fest at Sylvia's. "It's like you think you've found the cure for cancer."

Kate leaned in more closely to tease, "Maya, what's bothering you. Can't sleep? Got a hang nail?" She paused and breathed in her ear, "You know what to do."

Sylvia grit her teeth. "God. Someone please kill me." Maya swatted them both away.

At least Sylvia had the bakery now, which was a lot more than Maya had going on. SeaCakes was her sister's big bite outta life and she was rightfully proud of herself for it. Maya envied her the satisfaction of realizing a professional goal so young, not to mention the thrill of exercising skills honed since childhood. She wondered how it would feel to be competent and have a career plan. Maybe it made up for a directionless personal life, although the accomplishment didn't seem to help Sylvia figure out her troubles with Ethan.

"How's Steven these days?" Sylvia asked.

"Stuart," Maya corrected without enthusiasm. "Fine, I guess." She kept her eyes on the screen. "But he's no Superman."

Gabe hung the car keys on a hook by the door and followed Kate into the kitchen. "Did you eat already?"

"Pound cake and peanut butter. And a banana," Kate replied. Gabe grimaced and surveyed the contents of the fridge.

Kate sat down at the table and rested her chin on her palms. "How was school this week?"

Gabe had missed the fall semester of medical school while he searched for her after she'd gone missing. The university had been unwilling initially to re-admit him in the spring, but he'd spent summers in college—and some of his college career as well— engaged in studies that covered the program's first-year subject matter, something he was able to do with his father's help and because he had the disciplined, voracious intellect of all sirens. Despite his several-month absence, he first asked and then coerced those in power to let him enter the year late. He was allowed in only after serially hazing nine administrators and instructors, which he did without hesitation or compunction.

"Dry," Gabe responded, and then laughed at his own humor. "And by that I mean both the lectures and the fact that Chapel Hill is inland. I'm having a sandwich. Do you want one?"

Kate shook her head. "Have you been able to keep up? Do you wish you'd waited?"

"Nope," he said. "I mean, yes, I'm getting something out of it; and no, I don't wish I'd waited." He devoured a slice of cheese while he assembled his plate. "I have a hard time being away from you all week, and I have a hard time away from the ocean, but I'm glad I'm back on track with my evil life's plan." He looked at her adoringly. "I've got it all, you know. You, a career, our baby…"

"Which is taking its own sweet time coming out," Kate complained. "How long, do you think?" Gabe's sensitivities gave him a special bead on the greater happenings in life, such as when someone was going to be born or die. And since Kate's pregnancy was uncomfortable to her now she tended to ask this question often in the hopes his answer would change. "If I get a say, tonight would be ideal."

Gabe laughed sympathetically and straddled her chair to wedge himself behind her. He reached his hands around her abdomen, rested his chin on her shoulder and guessed, "Two weeks, give or take."

"Please let it be 'take.'" She let her head fall back against his shoulder.

"You're doing great," he said in her ear, "and it's almost over."

"Easy for you to say," she retorted, but she groused without rancor. Gabe cradled her stomach, running his nose along her neck and into her hair until she yawned. "Can we go to bed yet?"

Gabe moved his hands to her hips and nibbled at her neck, signaling his desire for a different kind of activity. She smiled and dropped her head forward to better accept his attention, and then frowned as her eyes lit on her pregnant middle. "I'm not actually in, ah, good form for anything too… well, *gratifying*." Gabe refrained from comment, but continued nuzzling her until she reconsidered her initial refusal. "I suppose we could work something out, though. You could just, you know, lie back and think of Africa." Her frown deepened.

Gabe's muffled laughter tickled her neck. "They say sex can bring on labor, you know," he suggested, and she swiveled her head around to see if he was kidding.

"They do? If that's true, then have at me."

"Oh yeah," Gabe confirmed, continuing his seduction efforts. "We could even run over to my folks' if you want." Kate stiffened since the idea of intimacy at her in-laws' doused her enthusiasm like water over coals. Gabe's low laugh echoed down her spine.

"No, not in the house," he said huskily. "Off the pier. We could leave our clothes on the dock."

She brightened instantly. "But… but I *love* sex in the water!"

"Yes," Gabe replied with a lazy smile. "I know this about you." He drew his hands up the insides of her thighs. "How about it? Care for a midnight swim with your husband?"

She stood up quickly and pulled Gabe with her to the door. She stopped before they stepped out and peered at him. "Brings on labor? You're sure?"

Gabe's eyes glittered. "Absolutely." He propelled her forward until they were outside, then shut the door behind them and led her toward the ocean.

When they returned to the pier after their swim, they found towels anchoring a note from Carmen and Michael. "An invitation to stay the night," Gabe announced. Kate sighed in defeat. She should have known there was no sneaking around when it came to her mother-

and father-law—even at one in the morning—but she could never completely get past her unease over the level of awareness they had of them, especially in matters of intimacy. She tried to shrug off her discomfort, knowing discretion at this point was a lost cause. "Oh, why not."

Once in bed, they lay silent for several minutes, Kate lost in her thoughts, Gabe playing with one of her hands. She stroked her stomach absently with her free hand.

"Gabe?"

"Mmm?"

"I've been wondering." She shifted to face him. "Why are you an only child? I mean did your parents ever talk about having more kids?"

"Sure they did. For a few years anyway. But Mom felt like we had a better quality of life as we were. You know, with a smaller family. And then siren women only ovulate once a year so there's less opportunity than with you people, so in general it's just not a sure thing. Something like three in ten couples don't conceive, and those who do have one, occasionally two, very rarely three children."

Kate thought back to one of their first conversations at Shaddox, when Gabe had explained siren marriage to her for the first time and how conception, at least with her kind, was part of it all. "Doesn't that interfere with their bonding?"

"Not exactly. My parents say children divert the focus of a marriage, although they think it's a worthy diversion. They say having a child gives a centering weight to the relationship. But no. Couples who give themselves to each other bond regardless of whether or not the woman conceives.

"We take child rearing pretty seriously, though," Gabe continued, "and bringing up baby is more exhausting than living without such a responsibility. I'm sure you remember when your mom and John had Everett. That's why my mom was ultimately glad to just have me to chase after." He flashed her a wicked grin. "She says I wore her out."

She sniffed. "You were an ideal kid. You were smart and well-mannered, an all-around 'good' boy."

Gabe's grimace was playful. "My folks might argue with you. But in that I didn't end up a disaffected criminal, it was because Carmen and Michael and I were pretty close." Kate smiled fondly, wondering how anyone could *not* want to be by him all the time. "Mom assures me it was trying enough with just one of me," he concluded.

"Well. I don't know what I think about that," Kate said, "about having only one, I mean. I always assumed I'd have a couple, and now I wonder."

"Which is not a decision we need to make tonight," Gabe finished with a yawn.

"I suppose not." Kate shifted deeper into the covers.

They talked quietly for a few more minutes, about how they hoped to be attentive, involved parents, and then they discussed home improvement projects they wanted to start that weekend. Finally Kate relinquished her hold on consciousness and drifted away.

BOOKS IN THIS SERIES

Updrift (Book 1)
Breakwater (Book 2)
Outrush (Book 3)
Crosstide (Book 4, out 2020)

Made in the USA
Middletown, DE
13 May 2022